A Journey of Two Ends

**This book is dedicated to all the storytellers:
past, present, and future**

If the path be beautiful, let us not ask where it leads
~ Anatole France

Myths which are believed in tend to come true
~ George Orwell

A Journey of Two Ends

Deborah Rowland

First published in Great Britain by Deborah Rowland, 2023

Copyright © Deborah Rowland

Deborah Rowland has asserted her right under the Copyright, Design and Patents Act, 1988 to be identified as the author of this work.

A CIP catalogue record for this book is available from the British Library.

ISBN 978-1-9163788-4-1

Ardraig

Florence Hobbes: author; co-founder of the Artless Press Collective (APC)

Rae: Florence's daughter; artist; co-founder of the APC

Levon Tyler: Rae's partner; campsite manager

Briar: Rae and Levon's daughter

Cavell: Rae and Levon's Irish terrier

Gabriel Darby: Florence's nephew; APC and campsite staff

Neville Hobbes: Florence's father; retired librarian

Kathleen Dalgety: Neville's partner; proprietor, Kath's Van

Danny and Ros: campsite owners

Kinsley

Theo Coppersmith: Sheelagh's partner; Viola's father; former book seller

Tulip: Theo's Labrador

Erica and Hughie Briggs: Theo's friends; Leaf and Loaf café staff / builder

Margery Crisp: Sheelagh's school friend; Leaf and Loaf café manager

Sean Nesbitt: owns The Village Stores

London

Dr. Phillipa Darby: Florence's sister; Gabriel's mother; medieval scholar

Alec Darby: Phillipa's husband; Gabriel's father; taxi driver

Sheelagh Spicer: Theo's partner; Spicer Kennedy Publishing board member

Viola C. Spicer: Theo and Sheelagh's daughter; literary agent at Quirk

Jono: Alec's school friend; publican, The Tuppeny

Gary Moncrieff: Alec's school friend; printer

1
The Call

Florence Hobbes scanned the length and breadth of the beach. She and Cavell were alone, which wasn't so unusual given that the holiday season hadn't yet started, and the easterly wind was sharper than a razor's edge. According to the dog years calculator, Cavell was an octogenarian, but this grand age hadn't dampened his enthusiasm for paddle. As an honorary local accustomed to keeping a low profile, Florence took care not to trespass on her neighbours' morning-tide rituals. Yoga Joe was the last of these early risers. The trail of fresh footprints snaking the length of the bay were evidence of his daily beach clean.

At the water's edge lay another innocent casualty of avian flu. Without needing a reminder, the rangers would soon safely dispose of the guillemot. This grisly task had kept them extra busy for months. Florence shivered. Any sensible person would wear the thermal balaclava, but as it was officially the first day of Spring, she was determined to face down what was hopefully the last of the long winter squalls. If you chose to live on the Scottish Highland's most northerly coast in an increasingly unpredictable climate, being unprepared was not an option.

Cavell had scooted back to the campsite for breakfast. Florence would follow on soon enough, but for now, the sedative sea-swell had rooted her to the spot, and besides, what was the rush? That was her previous life, her London life, where the only way to stay afloat was to swim with the latest tide. From the depths of her jacket pocket, Florence felt the comforting presence of pencil and notebook. Along with her head gear and binoculars, these, too, were constant companions. Writing novels was neither pressure nor burden. On the contrary, there was scarcely a time when she wasn't pondering a potential storyline, character, or location. The combination of Ardraig's stunning backdrop and unending flow of fascinating holidaymakers afforded oodles of inspiration for her modest readership's entertainment. In return, their loyalty financed three no-frills livelihoods, and benefitted a number of charities.

With a last lungful of ozone inflating her reserves, Florence crossed the dunes towards the static caravans, one of which served as her 'temporary' home. Rae had arranged a meeting at their office in the old brewhouse, at eight-thirty or thereabouts, to discuss the forthcoming book launch. What began as an experimental mother-daughter project, the Artless Press Collective had grown into a full-on creative hub. Florence had anticipated a lull in Rae's energetic output, particularly when she had Briar, but six years on, her daughter's ability to get things done, and often ahead of schedule, was nothing short of remarkable.

*

In a former life, the brewhouse lived up to its name as a building whose sole purpose was to brew beer and ale. When the wind blew in a certain direction, the air was scented with an ancient tang of hops and barley. The single storey whitewashed stone building, separated from the adjoining campsite by a row of static caravans, was one of several dotted around the croft. Its deceptively spacious interior functioned as publishing house, art studio, and general meeting place, and was where the magic happened.

To the right of the main door, and behind an extended folding screen were racks of art materials and books, a kitchenette and cloakroom; opposite, an assortment of generic office furniture and large art desk indicated the work area. At the far end of the space were two rooms, one of which served as a chill out zone. The stylish 1950s teak sideboard had been liberated from Florence's parents' London maisonette. The record player was in fine fettle, as was the frequently aired vinyl collection. Loitering around the well-worn sofa like extras on a film set were a number of guitars and fiddles on stands, while on the pale walls hung the complete series of eye-popping book cover originals, designed and painted by Rae.

By contrast, the other room resembled a grand medieval interior: twelve cross back chairs with scarlet velvet cushions graced a rosewood table, *the* 'Round Table,' whose inlaid marquetry depicted a blazing sun; suspended above was a pewter hoop chandelier with eight alter candles, and on the wall hung a single vivid painting of a Celtic Cross, entwined in rose briar.

Florence closed the door behind her and was enveloped by the log burner's woody warmth. She unzipped her coat, unwound her scarf and in a well-rehearsed ritual, kissed her daughter's raven hair. 'Coffee?' Without waiting for a reply she went directly into the kitchenette, leaving Rae to scrutinise the computer screen.

'Morning, Mum. Tea's in the pot. Hey, d'you remember that sweet little thatched holiday cottage I found for you and Aunt Phillipa, but it wasn't available?'

'Bookbinders, in Kinsley, the birthplace of our maternal ancestors: *A perfect example of an historic dwelling on Herefordshire's* 'black and white' *trail.*'

'That's the one. This email came through last night, from the owner.' She read it out.

'If you are still interested in hiring Bookbinders and can accommodate a little disturbance due to the finishing up of out-building work, we'd like to offer you the cottage at reduction of fifty percent on the entire three-week period. Your generous suggestion to bring a compost bin and secateurs won't be necessary as our housekeeper deals with these matters, but our village historian will be happy to assist with your mother's genealogical research, should that still be a requirement.'

Florence set down two steaming mugs and a biscuit tin before casting her eye over the email. 'A housekeeper, eh? And a ninety word paragraph with only two full stops.'

'Formal, but not unfriendly, Mum.'

'Hm. Pip will be pleased.'

'Aunt Phillipa's never liked roughing it. A night under the stars would loosen her bodice.'

'Maybe, but a cosy cottage is the next best thing.'

'When your pernickety sister discovers that Kinsley has three pubs and a cider press, don't be surprised if her intended four night stay eats into your three weeks.'

Florence noted the warning. Through a process of trial and error she had worked out that a maximum of five days in the company of her increasingly erratic sister was enough to sustain their relationship. Inevitably, regardless of pub or restaurant, Dr Phillipa Darby, career medievalist, regular BBC Expert Woman, *and* film industry consultant would announce her credentials to anyone within earshot. To be fair, she was entitled to crow – hadn't Florence's novels benefitted from Pip's expertise? But it was her wine-soaked outburst at the previous year's event in Norfolk that had kept the family from offering support this time around. Maybe Pip had forgotten? She had insisted on coming to Kinsley, and Florence hadn't the heart to refuse. 'Have you confirmed the booking?'

Rae nodded. 'It's a great offer. Bookbinders officially sleeps four and is fully equipped. The garden and adjoining meadows are perfect for Cavell. I can't imagine the old boy will be fit for many more trips around the British Isles.'

'Don't write him off yet, Rae. Your dog gets more attention than me.'

'But that's exactly how you like it, Mum – shine the spotlight on anyone but you. By the way, all the tickets for the Ludlow event have been sold. It's Ellis Eckley's biggest event yet.'

Rae held her breath. Every year, her mother stepped into character as her alias, *Ellis Eckley*, ready to travel across the country to meet readers and research book projects before returning to the campsite to write, during the long winter months. To begin with, these gatherings were held in intimate, offbeat venues, but as the readership expanded, Rae had persuaded her mother to host a 'special event'.

What could be more rewarding than to share a stage with the poets, artists, and musicians she'd met along the way and who'd made cameo appearances in her novels? The first *Ellis Eckley with Friends* evening was held in a converted Derbyshire stable in which the enthusiastic audience were treated to a memorable night. This tradition had continued unchallenged, and relatively unchanged, ever since.

Despite her self-effacing mother's reluctance to promote a social media profile, (which, ironically, had played in her favour) Rae had triumphed in cultivating a sizeable network of devoted readers through a membership only book-club and exclusive website blog. It had been fun to create a mystery around Ellis Eckley, and there was no shortage of willing volunteers to help at the events, especially as they were gifted a first edition hardback, dedicated and presented in person by their elusive storyteller. An ebullient fan had coined the term 'folk writer' and this had caught on: Ellis Eckley was one of the people who wrote for the people.

The subsequent mushrooming of these unique gatherings was no surprise to Rae, but there was a risk. If they got too big, or too demanding, her mother would put away her pencil, pack up the campervan and disappear. To feel either tied down or out of her depth were Florence Hobbes' worst nightmares. It had always been a fine line to tread, and as this year's venue was the most notable so far, Rae had no idea how her mother would react.

She finished the oat cake and smiled hopefully. 'Your schedule is confirmed. Shall we have a run through?'

'Ready when you are, Rae.'

'You arrive in Kinsley on Sunday. That gives you four

days to settle in before the first signing at Hopton's Gallery, in nearby Presteigne. After another break, the second session is at Leominster, on Tuesday. Aunt Phillipa arrives the following day, in time for Thursday night's Ludlow gig. That leaves a week for R&R.'

Florence scanned the comprehensive schedule. 'That looks do-able. Pip will have time for her ancestry research, and a good snout around the area before she breezes off home. I may need those extra days to recover. How will it work at Ludlow?'

'Joanne Quinlan will meet you in the Assembly Rooms lobby at three o'clock. She's set up rehearsal time, an early meal with your guest performers, and Cavell's care for the evening. During the usual market place 'meet and greet', Joanne will announce the raffle prizes for the chosen charity, Friends of Giltspur Forest. Performance-wise, Henbane will play three songs and Ebony Farrell's poetry reading is somewhere in the middle, but I've left it for you to fine tune.'

'How many are we expecting?'

A pause. 'Two hundred and ninety eight … and before you say anything Mum, it'll be fine. Henbane have swelled the numbers, that's all. They're a popular folk rock band, even more so since you bigged them up in your last novel. Remember, it's only for ninety minutes, which will fly by. You should be pleased so many people want to come. It's a massive compliment.'

Florence went into the kitchenette to refill her mug. Yes, she should be pleased, and Henbane's vignette in *Marcy McBride* had enhanced the plotline, but there was no disguising that sinking feeling. It wasn't particularly that she was nervous. Performing before any crowd, however small, usually created a flutter and was a perfectly natural response, but this was something else. After all these years, she was still plagued by the dreaded imposter syndrome.

The Ellis Eckley disguise was a gateway through which Florence had been able to explore the hidden aspects of her personality, when she got to play interesting, spirited roles alongside more talented folk, but these were only ever meant to be walk on parts. Mostly she liked to move about unnoticed, observing life from the side lines, making no waves – well, maybe just a ripple here and there – and it was a fair exchange: a good story for a handful of coin. But there were always those who wanted more, expected more, and this event proved it.

Maybe this was a sign to call it a day? For a decade, the solitary nature of writing had suited her; she liked to be alone, to draw upon her own resources. But as stimulating as it had been to travel to unknown spots across the country, Florence encountered the same hopes, fears, and regrets, no matter what direction the weather vane was pointing. Giving it up would be easy enough. The accumulated royalties from her previous book sales would cover her slimline living expenses, (even Cavell was Rae and Levon's dog), and the site's campervan was freely available for ad hoc holiday jaunts. With her family and a handful of good friends nearby, there was plenty to sustain her.

But she had responsibilities. Rae's involvement was incalculable. Without her daughter, the Artless Press Collective wouldn't – couldn't have existed. Rae had created the perfect role in which to grow her artistic and marketing skills whilst earning a reasonable wage and without being tied to a company. In addition to raising their six-year-old daughter, she supported her partner Levon, on the croft. By contrast, the only commitments Florence had were the occasional promotional trip and replying to the clutch of fan letters, most of which arrived after a new publication. If she stopped writing, the financial and emotional impact on Rae would be considerable. And there was her nephew, Gabriel.

Florence walked back to the desk where her beautiful, expectant daughter waited for a reply. 'Rae, you're right. It is a compliment, and I'm grateful. So, tell me more about Cavell's date for the night.'

2
Grumblings at Cleavers

The ancient oak door groaned. From his comfortable position beside the fire, Theo raised his eyes to the mantlepiece clock: 8.17. Sheelagh was early. He dashed into the kitchen, poured a generous slug of Tanqueray gin into the frosted glass, dropped in a half slice of lemon, and topped it with room temperature tonic water. As he re-entered the living room, a haze of huffs and puffs floated in the air like mystical dragon's breath. Sheelagh had thrown herself onto the sofa and was in the process of unbuttoning her waistband.

Theo waited until she was organised before passing over the glass. 'I didn't expect you back so soon.'

'Erica's announcement cut the evening short. This was her last session with The Book Worms. She's returning to her original group. Without needing to spell it out, it's obvious our choices are beyond her.'

'You knew this would happen, Sheelagh. I'm surprised Erica has lasted this long. You didn't embarrass her, did you?'

Sheelagh ignored the question, as if it were too idiotic to warrant an answer and gulped the liquid. 'But Erica has promised to help out at the festival. Incredibly generous, eh?'

'Don't be mean.'

'Well, it's like pulling bloody teeth. I've done my utmost to inject a dose of culture into the people of Kinsley and this is the reward. The Worms are reduced to four, and that's on a good night.'

'Sheelagh, you're a whirling dervish while the villagers meander like a warm summer breeze. It's a clash of temperaments, nothing more.'

'But they haven't objected to the money, Theo. My literary festival has put Kinsley on the map. They've had a new village hall and a bloody good café out of me, not to mention the pubs and the B&Bs who cash in throughout the year.'

Theo dropped another log on the fire and poked it about. A chorus of hisses and spits echoed the sentiment. He'd heard it a thousand times. Sheelagh Spicer *had* put Kinsley on the map, but many would have preferred to remain off-piste. Despite the festival's overall popularity, several villagers were openly critical of the disruption, the parking problems, the over-expectation. It wasn't personal. These Doubting Thomas's generally objected to the slightest whiff of progress.

Theo changed tack. 'I popped into The Sexton earlier. Had a chat with Hughie.'

'Please don't tell me he's stalling *again*. We've lost thousands in rental revenue due to his spectacular inability to manage a rural, two-man building business.'

'The delays aren't his fault. Sourcing materials is an ongoing worldwide issue. Anyway, I have a solution.'

Theo was of slim build, and yet the ancient armchair protested when he sat on it. The maroon leather wingback had belonged to his late father. Its seams released more tufts of horsehair with every passing week.

'Do you remember the enquiry which came from the north of Scotland, from the daughter of a certain Florence Hobbes? She wanted to hire Bookbinders for three weeks. At the time, Hughie was considerably behind schedule, but as he's confident of completing the job before the festival, I wrote back with an offer to reduce the rental fee by half if Ms Hobbes is willing to accommodate the minor disruption. Hughie will start at half past nine and finish at four.'

Sheelagh pulled herself upright. 'They've agreed terms?'

'Our guest was prepared to bring a compost bin, of all things. She has a small, well-behaved dog, and has enquired if her sister might stay for a few days, and perhaps a nephew. Believe it or not there was a reference attached.'

'This is too good to be true. The old girl must be deaf if she's unconcerned about the noise. What's the reason for the visit?'

'Ancestral research, and possible relocation.'

'What did you say the surname was?'

'Hobbes.'

'No Hobbes here.' Sheelagh finished her drink. 'Wait, what about Erica? She's already out of pocket from the building delays, and we can't risk losing her housekeeping skills before the holiday season starts.'

'Erica has agreed to call in weekly to mop and change the linen. We'll pay her the usual fee.'

Sheelagh held out the empty glass to Theo's outstretched arm. 'Finally, some good news. We could do with fresh blood in the village, even if the newcomer is on the crusty side. Go easy on the tonic will you, else I'll be up all night.'

At least I'll be spared that. Theo returned to the kitchen to prepare another drink. Long after Viola was weaned, Sheelagh had kept to separate bedrooms. Maintaining her mountain of working commitments without a decent night's sleep would have been impossible, she had insisted, and so the arrangement had remained. Raising their daughter had been the single most important role Theo had ever undertaken, and he had loved every minute of it. Viola's arrival couldn't have come at a better time, both professionally and personally. Disillusioned with the industry in which his own family had lost everything, Theo wore the title of 'stay-at-home-parent' with pride.

Although the Farringdon house more than met the family of three's needs, weekends and school holidays spent in Kinsley were a boon. Some years later, when Sheelagh inherited Cleavers from her mother, Theo had waltzed through the front door without a backward glance, leaving her to continue her frenetic London life as before, but with occasional breaks whenever the need arose. Feeling lonely rarely occurred to him. Viola was tremendously affectionate. She messaged him regularly and visited as often as her work allowed. With a number of good friends and Tulip for company, village life suited him very well.

It was a pity the same couldn't be said for Sheelagh. Kinsley was her ancestral home, but her presence was regarded as lukewarm at best. Even the house seemed to be excessively disgruntled when she was in it. Cleavers was a classic example of a seventeenth century 'black and white' timber-framed house, the type of which perfectly fitted the Victorians' entrepreneurial plan to link several of Herefordshire's historic villages in an effort to promote the area. From a distance, in its prime position at the top of the high street, adjacent to the church and village stores, it caught a distant eye.

Alice Spicer's generous bequest to her only child came with a coda: Cleavers was a money-pit. But Sheelagh's reluctance to sell it had provided Theo with an interesting project. He'd grown accustomed to the draughts and creaks, and in resolute Pavlovian manner had trained himself to avoid crashing into the old oak beams. And as the leaks and fractures were gradually put to rights, at the risk of sounding frivolous, he and Cleavers had come to an understanding.

Theo returned to the living room to find Sheelagh fast asleep. He lifted her legs gently onto the sofa and covered her with a rug. Tulip was curled up beside the fireguard and already deep in slumber. One by one, he turned out the lamps, extinguished the fire, and with the untouched drink in one hand and Malory's precious *Le Morte d'Arthur* in the other, Theo ascended the narrow winding staircase to his room.

3
Something's up

'Phew, it's warm out there, Rae.' Gabriel wedged open the office door, shucked off his windcheater and took two bottles of craft beer from the fridge. 'I thought you were picking Briar up from school?'

'Mum and Grandad have taken her into Lochinvar for ice-cream, to celebrate the new season. I wanted to get these paintings finished. What d'you think?'

Gabriel passed Rae a bottle and studied the mesmerizing jellyfish. 'Lion's mane, and a blue. These will look terrific on the page.'

'Thanks. How did you and Levon get on?'

'Your fella's a dynamo. We finished insulating the ceilings and walls, ready for Yoga Joe to plaster. Won't be long before the old hay barn is finished. Levon can't wait to get cracking on the recording studio, but that'll mean extra labour and …'

'Money we don't have. He's convinced that bands will flock here.'

'He's right, Rae. Ardraig isn't an impossible dream. It'll be the next Big Pink, or Rockfield, just wait and see.'

'If *Marcy McBride* does as well as predicted, we'll be a step closer.'

'Talking of launches, did Aunt Flo pick up the gauntlet?'

'Well, she didn't scarper for the split rock when I mentioned the Assembly Rooms' seating capacity.'

'I should have been here to back you up.'

Rae swigged the beer, her eyes crinkling.

'Flo went for it?'

'Yeah, but she's definitely weighing things up. I may be her one and only, Gabriel, but even I can't be sure what the outcome will be. There's a lot of change coming Mum's way. When Levon and I suggested she move into the hay barn, she just nodded in that enigmatic way of hers. Mum's never had her own place. It's too permanent.'

'Another winter like the last one won't be much fun. Flo knows you need to replace the old static caravan in time for your autumn programme. She's the last person to stand in your way. Maybe she thinks Yoga Joe will make a move. Levon reckons his joss stick is still burning.'

'Mum and Yoga Joe? I think not, cousin. All that 'free spirit' waffle is camouflage. He mistook my mother's listening ear for someone who was interested. Besides, she's been on her own for ever. It's great to be with people, but then she has to shake us all off.'

'She must get lonely.'

'Do you get lonely?'

'Point taken.' Gabriel yawned. 'Sorry. It's an early night for me.'

'At the rate you're going, the hay barn will be finished before the campsite opens. By the way, the Kinsley cottage booking is confirmed. It may be a bit tight, but as you don't intend on staying long, the sofa bed should do okay. Have you spoken to Aunt Phillipa yet?'

'I promised Levon we'd get the job done.'

'It's me you're talking to, Gabriel Darby.'

'I don't want to risk another blow up like last year. That's why I've decided not to go, as much as I want to support Flo.'

'Does Mum know?'

'Yeah, and she's cool about it. I think she was relieved. Anyway, I messaged my mum – said we'd catch up at Dad's sixtieth party, in July. He's having it in The Tuppeny. As it's their local pub, Mum shouldn't find it too stressful.'

Rae bit back a comment. Her cousin was upbeat, and that was all that mattered.

'Levon reckons we should sprinkle our Celtic sparkle over the Londoners: him and me on guitar, you on the melodeon, Flo's fiddle and Grandad Neville's penny whistle.'

'Sounds fun.' Rae put down her beer. 'Look, Gabriel, don't be surprised if being back at Eastgate Road feels strange. Our grandparents' flat may be long gone, but the house you were raised in is still your home.'

'Ardraig is my home, Rae, unless you're thinking of kicking me out.' For a split second, Gabriel wondered if that were a possibility, but then he remembered there was no need to panic. Rae was just checking he was okay, that was all. He'd made a great life for himself, surrounded by lovely people with no expectations. The only time he felt remotely anxious was when his parents called, although the recent chat with his dad went well. With luck, his mother would be in a better frame of mind, and a reconciliation might be possible.

'Gabriel, even if we wanted you to take the high road, Briar would cling to your spurs. You're her shining knight.'

'Briar's got taste.'

'My daughter's been brainwashed, you mean. Anyway, let's check out the feedback. *Marcy McBride* is going down a storm with the fanbase:

> Stayed up till dawn to finish MM. The sledgehammer strikes again! Can't believe Ellis killed off her number one darling – don't you just love to hate to love her!
> Peg Franklin

> We didn't see it coming either, Peg, but it was sooo the right thing to do. Jake's death had me sobbing so much that Craig threatened to call the paramedics!
> Larry xxx

> We've booked an Airbnb in Dorset. If the coastline is half as wonderful as Ellis describes it, we'll be super thrilled. BTW, if anyone's got spare tickets to the Ludlow gig, let me know. Have you guys checked out the Grail? Henbane on YouTube are a-maz-ing! Kimxx (kim.t.danko@browbeat.co.uk)'

Gabriel laughed. 'Ellis Eckley strikes again! Readers can't wait to follow up on the bands and the poets. Flo's idea to put a family tree and map at the front of her novels, and a Grail at the back makes for the perfect bookends.'

'That's Grandad's influence. His penchant for a chivalric story is alive and kicking. He and Briar are reading *The Knight Princess*.'

'Cornelia Funke. Yeah, I remember those. On the subject of children's books, these paintings will look a treat in the next *Betsy Pugh* adventure series.'

'Thanks. Six is a good age to introduce sea creatures and wildlife. Kids love rock pooling.'

'They sure do. Does Briar know the *Betsy Pugh* books are based on her growing up in Ardraig?'

'Gabriel, with our bite-sized sales, there's no danger of Briar sharing the same fate as Christopher Robin. What better way of capturing her fabulous childhood than illustrating it in a picture book? She'll have something to show her friends when she's older. Anyway, I've decided to call a Round Table. We need to discuss the details with everyone before Ellis Eckley hits the road.'

At the sound of a car door slam, Rae glanced out of the window. 'Ah, my baby's back. Before I shoot off, would you mind double-checking the list for Mum's trip. I've boxed up my artwork but haven't started on the hardbacks.'

'No worries, Rae.'

'And don't forget, Levon's making chowder for tea.'

Gabriel watched his cousin hurtle across the yard, pick up her daughter, and swing her like a Maypole. Their rambunctious reunion filled him with joy. Reflecting on the mythical adventure stories that had bound three generations of Hobbes, the irony hadn't escaped him that it was the women who saved the men. Grandad Neville had always maintained that without Nanny Lally, his working life in the dockyard would have ended as it had begun. She had urged him to apply for the library position, the outcome of which had changed the direction of all their lives. Levon had said more or less the same about Rae. Even though the campsite was in business before she arrived, her innovative ideas (free wetsuit, boat, and board hire; 'help-yourself' herb beds;) had pitched in to make Ardraig a repeat destination. In fact, Gabriel's own rescue had been nothing short of a miracle, thanks to Rae, and his aunt Flo.

Over at the sideboard, he flicked through the stack of vinyl and pulled out Lindisfarne's debut album, the record that had transformed him from boy to man. Gabriel placed the disc reverentially on the deck before beginning the satisfying task of boxing up the *Marcy McBride* hardbacks. It was an exciting time of year. When Flo emerged from her winter hibernation with a final draft to mark the start of another literary journey, everyone stepped up a gear.

Just a few weeks before, the clan had gathered around the table, and with a wicked soundtrack and cold beers on the go, Flo kicked off the session by signing the newly minted novels in her customary purple ink. Then, with Rae's hand-painted bookmarks tucked inside each copy, Gabriel and the team packaged them up, ready to go. The local printing company, Ullaprint, were perfectly capable of posting out the hardbacks in conjunction with the main print-on-demand run, but this was an important ritual, one of a number that made the Artless Press Collective the fantastic venture it had come to be. And according to Aunt Flo, he was an essential part of the team.

Those three years had flown. Rae had set him to work from the get-go, and it wasn't long before Gabriel knew every step in the super-sleek self-publishing process: from converting the final draft manuscript into a print-ready text, to advising the British Library of publication, to monitoring feedback. To begin with, he wondered why Flo didn't make use of the various media platforms to promote her books, but as they grew closer, he saw his aunt in a different light. She was a lone artist-adventurer who used the stuff of life as a canvas for self-expression rather than self-promotion. It was through the invention of Ellis Eckley that Flo met new people, visited new places, and wrote stories that celebrated the joy in small things.

In addition to the various Artless Press Collective projects, Gabriel worked on the campsite and on the croft. No two days were the same, and there was always fun to be had. Island hopping was a particular favourite. Like a Persian caravanserai, they'd nip across to Lewis, Harris or beyond, and sleep under the stars outside of midge season. It was during these escapades that Gabriel discovered the nuts and bolts of storytelling. Flo described it as a full-on sensory experience in which her 'camera' constantly recorded the world around her: changes of wind direction; sky hues; facial expressions; moods; snippets of conversation. Adding colour and flavour to scenes was essential, as was getting the feel of a place (taking its pulse, as she described it). Then she'd sit awhile before attempting to write it. Flo had a knack for encouraging strangers to share their biographies. *What was the first record you bought?* or *where was your most memorable holiday?* were the sorts of questions guaranteed to reveal treasure.

But there was another reason to admire his aunt. Of all the family members, she had consistently remained the most sympathetic towards his mother, whose eruption after the Norfolk launch still reverberated. When Gabriel made his excuses for this year, Flo totally understood, but had counselled him to be patient. *Whatever your reasons for leaving home, Gabriel, you will always be Phillipa's son. Don't be too hard on her.'*

Few of Gabriel's happiest childhood memories had ever taken place at his parents' house. 96 Eastgate Road was located at the gentrified end of the long East London street, whilst at the other was his grandparents' ground floor maisonette, in a block called The Barbers, (named after the barber's shop that had stood on the site for two hundred years). The uninspiring two-storey concrete edifice was incongruous by comparison to the row of smart Georgian houses, but that was the only place to be, not least because Flo and Rae lived there with his grandparents.

It was more than a second home. When they weren't making or baking, his nan would put together a picnic to share at Clissold Park, and on Sundays at the local swimming pool, Grandad Neville would throw him up and over when the lifeguard wasn't looking. And after, in the café, they'd dunk chunky biscuits into mugs of hot chocolate before trooping back to The Barbers for tea, and sometimes he was allowed to sleep over.

The A-side had finished. Gabriel flipped the vinyl and finished taping the last box. In thick marker pen he wrote 'Hardbacks, Assembly Rooms' across the lid. With half an hour to chill before dinner, he wandered over to the window, silently acknowledging Lindisfarne's achingly soulful *Winter Song* as a perfect complement to Ardraig's brooding sky.

The folk rock band's golden DNA strands tied him to his grandad and Levon, but not so his dad. This type of music was far too sedate for the likes of Alec Darby, but then again, his old man had never listened to the powerful lyrics. His specialist subjects were punk rock, football, and the socio-political failings of government. To be fair, his dad used to drive him to after-school clubs and cricket practice while his mum worked late at the university. But when she was home, her one-track needle was stuck on homework and college choices, unless he brought up the subject of philosophy, and then she'd talk until the cows came home.

Thankfully, Esha had shared his passion for cricket. They'd known each other from primary school right through to university and continued to support the other's efforts, on and off the pitch. Her parents occasionally took him along to The Oval, to watch the women's teams in what was always a super friendly atmosphere. When Mrs Mehta (she insisted he call her Parminder) asked him for dinner, he was invited to give her a hand in the kitchen, which, according to Esha, was a minor miracle.

Gabriel pulled out his phone. Esha's last message was mostly about work, and how there wasn't much time for socialising. He longed to ask if she missed those Eastgate Road days, but what was the point? She was in Stockholm, working for an independent educational non-profit fighting global misconceptions, while he was in Ardraig, cleaning campsite loos and maintaining his aunt's website.

A shiver shot through him. There it was, the shadow, lurking in the recesses of his psyche, subtly intent on extinguishing his inner light. Gabriel went over to the sofa and sat down. He took the string of mala beads from his neck and began counting – from one, to one hundred and eight – his finger and thumb moving over the smooth sandalwood orbs while the gentle, reassuring *click, click* chimed with his breath until balance was restored. He was safe; he was well, and his flame burned brightly. Smiling now, Gabriel picked up a guitar and threw open the shutters to his febrile imagination.

The members of Lindisfarne have gathered at Charisma Studios and are about to record Nicely Out of Tune. *When the banter settles down, genius singer/songwriter Alan Hull and the guys saddle up, while Gabriel stands at the back, ready to strum along.*

4
All change

The wind had snuck its way into every chink and crevice of the ailing caravan. Florence *had* to move out. She'd known it after last January's storm, which had threatened to blow the static to the Isle of Lewis. As fond as she was of the unfixable dwelling, the cold weather affected her so much more these days, so further delay was out of the question. Rae and Levon's generous offer to rent the hay barn on a flexible basis was too good to refuse, but to commit to buying it at a later date was something else altogether.

Moving into the replacement caravan would have been ideal, particularly as it was due to be delivered any day now, but it was earmarked to accommodate Rae's artistic retreaters and Levon's future music makers, when his dream project was finally realised. Her daughter was genius at envisioning new ways to create income streams, and the off-season creative breaks would be another winner. She had suggested they co-host a weekend – what better way to inspire novice novelists than to witness the entire draft-to-print process in action? Self-publishing was gaining in popularity, and the Artless Press Collective had a useful role to play, except that Florence was reluctant to offer herself up as an expert. Commenting on other people's endeavours wasn't her style, but to collaborate with Rae was always worth considering.

Whilst attempting to secure the window, Florence spotted her father cutting across the campsite to join her for their regular walk. Sometimes the gusts tossed their helpless, giggling bodies about like marionettes while on other days they'd sit quietly, watching the wavelets ripple along the pale sand. It was a far cry from Eastgate Road, when the implosion that followed her mother's sudden death was so immense, Florence feared for her father's (and her own) sanity. No one had known what to do until Rae and Levon pulled them from the quicksand of grief by offering respite at Ardraig. Once here, neither she nor her dad had the inclination to return. The pace may have been slow, but events moved fast. Who would have predicted that within eighteen months, Neville Hobbes, devoted husband, loving father, and quietly influential librarian, would move in with another woman.

Kathleen Dalgety: childless, widowed, and retired midwife. For the Ardraigians, she was an openly acknowledged asset, and in no danger of slowing down any time soon. Her popular fish and chip van served the community, in season, three times a week. Out of season, when she wasn't knitting bonnets and cardigans for the hospital's premature ward, Kathleen kept the community's welfare robust. She was the first to befriend Rae when her whirlwind romance with Levon was made permanent. And when Rae's waters broke earlier than expected, Kathleen and the local paramedic acted swiftly to deliver the bonny bairn. This momentous act further cemented her standing within the Hobbes family, but not for Phillipa.

Florence sighed. Her sister's vocal objections to Rae's unscripted northern flit signified the beginning of her withdrawal from the family, and their father's 'inexplicable infatuation' was the last straw. But from Florence's perspective, Neville Hobbes had struck lucky – twice.

She opened the door and in he blew. 'Hi Dad. I'll be with you in a minute. Just been collecting up my things for the Herefordshire trip.'

Neville pulled up a kitchen chair. The lower half of his face was muffled by one of Kathleen's thick-knit scarves, while his wiry hair fought its way out of the matching hat. He yanked it off. 'Are you looking forward to it, Flo?'

'Yes and no. Have you heard about the Assembly Rooms?'

Neville nodded. He wasn't in the least surprised. Florence had the storyteller's flair, and those books of hers were page turners, and he knew a thing or two about books. Kathleen's friends couldn't wait to get their mitts on the latest novel. The Artless Press Collective, or the APC as it was known to insiders, was a well-guarded secret. It didn't matter whether Ellis Eckley's novels were on the *Sunday Times* Best Seller list or for sale in a charity shop, the villagers had their very own writer-in-residence. 'Three hundred people willing to pay to see you, Flo – I'd take that as a compliment.'

That's exactly what Rae said.' She grinned. 'I'm thinking of making an announcement.'

'*Greenaway Women!* That'll please the crowd.'

Florence sat opposite her father and was suddenly

nervous. 'Do you think so, Dad? Is it wise to revisit former themes, former plotlines? And my writing style has changed so much over the last decade.'

'Look at us, Flo. Could anyone have predicted we'd trade Eastgate Road for the wild Highlands? Life moves on. As for *Greenaway Women*, your readers have absorbed your stylistic growth without realising it. It's not as if they'll be asked to compare and contrast the books in an essay, is it? At every event someone asks about a follow up, so now's your chance to change the subject.'

'Yeah, I guess you're right.'

She zipped up her jacket and followed her father outside. The shapeshifting sky was typical for the coastline. You could never guess if a shower would soak you to the skin, or the sun would roast your bones. Though windy, the afternoon had a hint of mildness, and within minutes they had made their way across the dunes, climbed the steep path to the stile, and from this vantage point, paused to sweep the panorama through their binoculars. Then they continued on, traversing the undulated greens, towards the enormous Torridonian sandstone rocks – the split rock – which had been sculpted over aeons by the elements. These overlooked a smaller, hidden bay, affectionately known as Briar's Bay. From their position up on the headland, the views reached from Ardraig's white sand, across the aquamarine water to Lewis, Harris, and Suilven, and back again. Always tantalising; never dull.

Sheltered from the wind, Neville perched on a boulder. He trained his sights across the bay. 'Look, Flo – a *selkie*.'

Florence smiled at her father's use of the vernacular whilst zooming in on the sleek gunmetal seal as it flipped and twisted and rolled before disappearing under the water. After a while, she took out a flask and a picnic box from her father's back pack. 'The scones look scrummy. I wonder if Kathleen can spare any for my journey tomorrow.'

'She's made a batch for you.'

'That's good of her. Briar is allowed to stay up late tonight. I'll miss her.' Her father turned his gaze towards the shimmering Atlantic Sea. Florence couldn't tell if the mist in his eyes were weather or heart related. 'I'll miss you too, Dad, but you know that.'

'That I do. You'll give my love to Phillipa. Maybe this time she'll tell you what's really going on.'

'Pip is a riddle that even Alec hasn't been able to solve, and they've been together since secondary school. I've been thinking about Mum's middle-child theory. Pip felt side lined, so she poured all her frustrations into her studies.'

'I don't know about that, Flo, but it was you who gave us sleepless nights. Your mum and I rarely argued, but your education caused a right ruckus. Looking back, she was right to have shielded you. I was blinkered by books, couldn't see past the piles of them. They were the only way to a better life, or so I thought. Your mother left school at fourteen, but she knew every Latin name for her plants and flowers and could count longhand in her head. *Those books will break up the family, Neville.* Lavender Hobbes was wise in many ways.'

Florence had worked it out a long time ago. Within a month of graduating, her brother Jason had accepted a job overseas, and her parents, (more particularly her father), had taken it badly. Jason's obsession with bioecology wasn't supposed to take him away, and it was likely that

Phillipa was to embark on a similar journey. Naively, their father hadn't considered that a 'good education' might mean his children actually left the country. Under the circumstances, it wasn't surprising that her parents had kept her close by. Florence couldn't have been happier. The leap from primary into secondary school had been a struggle, and making herself invisible only went so far. Academia was, in her opinion, best left to her appreciative siblings. 'Even if Pip had felt left out, it doesn't excuse her behaviour towards Kathleen.'

'That's not such a worry. What concerns me more is that the longer this goes on, the greater the risk of a permanent rift between Pip and Gabriel.'

Florence finished her coffee, wiped the cup, and handed it back to her father. Although proud of Jason's achievements, he still missed his son, and was clearly heart-broken by Pip's self-imposed exile. If only she'd acknowledge Kathleen as his partner, they might build bridges. Was it any wonder he had refused to go to Alec's sixtieth birthday party without his partner. Surely Pip didn't expect their dad to devote the rest of his life to their mum's memory? And yet, Florence had her own rucksack of guilt to haul around. Since moving to Ardraig, Gabriel had come on leaps and bounds, due in no small part to his close bond with Rae and Levon, and the community. While Florence was blessed to spend so much time with her nephew, how could she ignore Pip's agony at their estrangement?

Confused and frustrated, she shoved her binoculars into her rucksack. 'We'd better get going, Dad. I've an early start tomorrow.'

They set off down the headland. At the gate, Neville paused. 'I asked Kathleen if she might make a rice pudding.'

'Mum was a marvel at so many things, but she couldn't get that one quite right.'

'But her jam roly poly was fit for royalty, wasn't it.' Neville wrapped his thickly padded arms around his daughter. 'I'm a lucky man, Flo: three healthy kids, two terrific grandchildren, Princess Briar, and a second shot at life with Kathleen, even if she doesn't iron my underfugs.'

'Too much information, Dad.'

They laughed and he said, 'Now, don't you go fretting about Phillipa. She'll come around in the end.'

Reassured, Florence walked through the gate and down to the beach.

5
Escape to the country

Alec Darby hung the shammy leather in his special cupboard beside the washing machine, satisfied with a job that didn't need doing in the first place, (although it had to be said, a grubby vehicle was as inexcusable as a surgeon with dirty fingernails.) It had been a long, but surprisingly good day. The American tourists he'd picked up at The Langham wanted a peek at the sights before their pre-show supper in Covent Garden. They were a nice old couple from Vermont – grateful, and seriously generous.

Contemplating the hallway stairs as if they were the Himalaya, Alec ascended with the ease of a man in dire need of a knee replacement. His wife was in their bedroom, pondering the contents of her semi-packed suitcase. 'Tea's on its way, Pip. D'you want a hand?'

'Now let me think, Alec ... four nights out in the sticks with my early-to-bed sister. No, I think I can manage.'

'Sorry. Didn't mean to sound patronizing.'

'No, I'm sorry,' Phillipa replied, and sat heavily on the bed. 'It's been a stressful week. The Pentacle Film contract still hasn't arrived. After months of schmoozing, we finally agree terms and now I'm getting the silent treatment. It almost makes me wish I were still on the college payroll.'

'You don't mean that, Pip. Resigning your research post was the first important step in our plan, remember?' He lowered himself on the bed and took her hand, his forefinger and thumb resting on her wedding band. 'Come next week, you'll have a good old rummage around for our new home. If you pick a winner, I'll drive up pronto for a second viewing.'

Phillipa shook his sweaty hand off and leant over to grab her mother's silk fan from the bedside table. It was weirdly effective at cooling the flushes. She must make that appointment with the doctor soon. Getting back on hormone replacement therapy was now a priority. Her fickle sleep patterns were causing havoc, but that may have been due to the circumstances. As the departure date for Kinsley approached, anxiety swelled in her gut like a half-baked baguette. Gabriel wasn't joining her after all. He was committed elsewhere, and where that was, she hadn't the slightest bloody interest. Wretched, that's how she felt: wretched, and wrung out. She'd waited an entire year to see him, but the memory of their last meeting was so utterly dreadful, she stamped it down only for it to bob to the surface, usually during the middle of the night.

'You don't have to go, Pip.'

'Of course I have to go, Alec. It's Flo's biggest event to date. She needs me there. And as no one else is going, there's little chance of my causing a scene.'

'I'll come with you.'

'No.'

'It's good of you to offer Alec,' she said, softening, 'but it'll be fine. This break will be good for us. Living with me hasn't been much fun of late, has it? You'll have the house to yourself, or you can invite your mates. Ask Gary to bring his Stranglers albums.'

It was common knowledge that Gary Moncrieff's precious record collection was kept under lock and key, but Alec was always in the market for a miracle. 'I might just do that. Look, why don't you have a shower while I make dinner. We'll have a quiet evening. You can choose the film.'

'Now there's an invitation you might regret.'

Alec kissed her cheek before manoeuvring himself off the bed, unsure if the moan came from his mouth, or from his cartilage-free knee joint. Clutching the banister rail like an inebriated tight-rope walker, he descended one step at a time. Thirty-eight years of driving, and a prolonged period of seven-a-side footie, why wouldn't it flare up. Moving to Kinsley had to be better for both of them. Fresh air, gentle walks, pub lunches, well, that's what those daytime telly programmes promised.

To be truthful, he didn't know anyone who lived beyond the M25. All his mates, and the remnants of his family lived within a five mile radius of Eastgate Road. There was talk over the allotment about escaping to the country, but that was mostly from Gary which was comical. He'd never been north of Watford, not even for Chelsea's away games – couldn't see the point when the footie was on BT Sport. When Alec insisted that their move to Herefordshire was imminent, the silly sod had laughed so much he had to use his asthma pump.

Alec pulled the curtains, plumped the cushions, and turned on the lamps. Then he slid Madeleine Peyroux into the CD player, confident that her dusky tones would sooth Phillipa's raw edges. Standing back, he admired his handiwork. With the scene nicely set, he hobbled from the living room into the stylish open-plan kitchen to scrub his spotless hands. That had been another smart decision. After years of procrastination, Phillipa had agreed to update the house. Gary's builder brother had done a fabulous makeover, and it had taken her mind off of things, for a while, at least. With their relocation on the horizon, 96 Eastgate Road was now an estate agent's dream. Top dollar was assured, or so matey from Sullivan Tuck had promised. If his old man were alive today he'd never believe that the run down Victorian terrace bought for peanuts after the war, was now worth a mint.

Alec selected a red onion, an orange pepper, and a garlic bulb from the bountiful vegetable rack. Wednesdays were pasta night. Claudio had recommended adding a dollop of harissa paste, to *zhuzh* it up, and to follow, the lemon *panna cotta torte*. Who was he to argue with the culinary maestro of Pepper Row? That grocer's shop would finish him off, so bloody convenient on the corner, and the food was literally to die for.

With the olive oil and garlic gently simmering, Alec began chopping the onion. His mates might not be taking their relocation seriously, but there seemed to be an inevitability about it. Not only was there the ongoing drama with Gabriel, which was bad enough, but Phillipa still hadn't made it up with her old man. You could have bet your last farthing that Neville Hobbes would have turned up his toes in Eastgate Road. Everyone respected him, and some of the kids had gone on to do good things as a result of his innovative library projects. Alec had lost count of the number of demonstrations Nev Hobbes had organised in an effort to stop the closures, for all the bloody good it had done. And then, just as he's about to retire, Lally dies!

Shockwaves engulfed the neighbourhood. She'd been as fit as a flea one minute – tending her garden, her family, and the flower stall – and the next she was taken off this earth by a massive brain haemorrhage, and only just sixty! He'd never seen a funeral like it. The residents of Eastgate Road had lined the streets, and Lally's customers, the old boys stood with their caps in hand as her coffin made its way past the station and on to the church. Couldn't fit another soul in St Barnaby's, and as for The Tuppeny – well, Jono had to open the beer garden to cater for the crowd.

The sky was lavender blue that afternoon, just like the song, the one that Neville used to sing when Lally pretended to be annoyed at him. The poor sod had collapsed like a pack of cards, and Flo … well, Alec had known her all her life, and he'd never seen her crumple like that. But with Rae's help they got through it, and his niece hadn't been with Levon five minutes, but she had stayed on for weeks, bless her heart.

Pip's hop-picking heritage plan was nothing more than a coping strategy. She couldn't do anything for her dad, so she threw herself into researching family trees and village houses. Lally's dream had been to retire to the countryside, to the place where her mother's family came from. Alec never really believed the idea had mileage, but Dr Phillipa Darby was the most determined woman he'd ever met. The truth was that the project acted as a safety jacket, something, anything, to keep her from drowning during that terrible time, so he let her get on with it. And just as she picks herself up, Neville and Flo bugger off to the Highlands!

To be fair, Rae and Levon had included all of them in the invitation, but that was never on the cards, not with Gabriel's exams looming, and Phillipa's PhD students relying on her, *and* there was his cab to consider. Under no circumstances was he about to drop everything to live literally in the middle of nowhere because the Hobbes were subsumed with grief. But if that weren't enough of a bombshell, before you could say *Roll Out The Barrel*, Neville moves in with the flippin' fish and chip lady!

Blood trickled onto the wooden board. Blaspheming his way to the cold tap, Alec held his thumb under the water until it was numb, dried it with a paper towel and wrapped it in a plaster. First aid complete, he scrubbed the board, sprayed and washed the counter top, and resumed chopping, determined not to relive that particular nightmare. Phillipa's evening *had* to be peaceful, he'd make sure of it. There would be no sons and fathers on tonight's menu – just a nice dinner, a bottle of Saint Émilion, and a chat about happier days ahead.

6
The Wart's favourite hound

Theo waved at the rear end of Sheelagh's Volvo until it disappeared over the bridge and out of view. It was a habit acquired from his mother, one that used to frustrate him, but she'd been right all along. How could you be certain if you'd ever see that person again? This had been the case with his mother. Helped outside by a kindly staff member and swaddled in a violet knitted jacket and silk scarf, Frances Coppersmith had stood by the nursing home's entrance with one limpid hand grasping the walking frame, while the other waved a shaky farewell. Those same hands that, as a young boy, he had helped to pick and slice fruit while *Fantasia on a Theme by Thomas Tallis* haunted the autumn air. Theo's throat tightened. He hadn't thought about her in a long while. Perhaps it was the appearance of the bluebells that very morning, under the old sycamore. His mother had always loved them.

A passing car tooted. It was Erica Briggs, on her way to the café, laden with extra supplies from the wholesalers to cater for the forthcoming festival. She had offered to collect them, and it was *no trouble at all*. This perfectly summed up the Briggs' can-do attitude. Theo waved. Erica and Hughie were his good friends, and were integral to Kinsley's wellbeing, regardless of Sheelagh's opinion to the contrary. Why should it matter if they didn't read the same broadsheet or listen to the same radio station? Theo had spent more memorable evenings with them than he'd ever enjoyed in London.

Dog walking with Erica's friends, of which he was usually the only human male, was a particular highlight. He didn't join them every morning, partly due to embarrassment, although why, he hadn't resolved to any satisfaction. Admittedly, the language could be a tad spicy, and the intimate revelations were occasionally eye-watering, but having raised a daughter, Theo wasn't totally in the dark when it came to certain matters. But it was the manner in which he was included, as though he'd always been part and parcel of Kinsley that was so flattering. How could he articulate that sentiment to Sheelagh?

Tulip ambled to the gate. He gave the stoutly Labrador a pat before following her into the house. With Sheelagh away until the following week, as soon as he'd ticked off the items on her list, and completed the regular tasks required to upkeep house, garden, and café, he was free to please himself. Earlier that morning Theo had darted over to Bookbinders to check that all was in order, in time for the new arrival. Erica had put out fresh flowers, aired the rooms, and had re-set the heating to an ambient temperature. Hughie was as good as his word. The adjoining out-building restoration was almost complete. Noise levels would be minimal, as would any mess, although his builder friend was assiduous when it came to his tools and workspace, so there was little danger of tripping over an angle grinder. Florence Hobbes would barely be aware of Hughie's presence, unless she was amenable to a chat which, within reason, might be nice for both.

Theo checked his watch. The previous evening's leftovers were perfect for a late lunch, after which he and Tulip would take a stroll, via the boardwalk to Bookbinders, and in good time to greet their guest.

*

When approaching the cottage from east or west, it was easy to miss the necessary turn, even with a comprehensive map. Bookbinders was situated at the end of an untarmacked 'no through' track, which deterred casual drivers and walkers alike. It was the perfect spot for a quiet country holiday. Like Cleavers, it had been built at the time of George 11 and had been sympathetically restored in the nineteen-seventies by its previous inhabitant, a friend of Sheelagh's mother.

Behind the cottage lay Pignut Meadow, one of three fields gifted to Kinsley by the owners of High Court Farm. These had subsequently been regenerated by the gardening committee and a healthy contingent of enthusiastic villagers, Theo being one. He was only too willing to roll up his sleeves, not simply due to the meadow's proximity to Bookbinders, but for the opportunity to do something creative after his illness. Kinsley was the first village in the area to commit to the county councils' sustainability pledge, which, alongside other initiatives, had won Herefordshire's 'greenest village' award for four consecutive years.

Before Bookbinders went up for sale, the owner offered it to Sheelagh who, without consultation or hesitation, snapped it up. Theo could scarcely protest about the manner in which her inheritance was spent, and the idea to use it as a holiday let made sound financial sense, but the necessary updating arrangements had been left to him. Thankfully he had Hughie's listed building expertise to call upon, and with the added eco-features and a charging point, Bookbinders began its reinvention as a desirable holiday cottage.

Sheelagh's propensity to act alone had been one of the few sticking points in their relationship. She was a commander in every sense. Her formidable reputation for results was drawn from the combination of strong will and self-belief (delegation was Sheelagh's forte) whereas cultivating a good relationship with local tradespeople and the café staff was Theo's task and, incidentally, matched his skill set very well. Though fairly effective at loosening Sheelagh's inflexibilities, his attempts to discuss her blind spots had proved futile, no matter that she occasionally remind him of his. But her honesty, generosity, and loyalty were healthy counterbalances and in a strangely discordant way, they had rolled along for a quarter of a century, helped enormously by their beloved daughter, Viola, and copious periods apart.

Tulip's throaty bark catapulted Theo from the kitchen and into the front garden. He hovered behind the hedge, a useful vantage point from where he could wait for his guest to get organised without giving her a start. Tulip, however, had other ideas. Intoxicated by the unfamiliar scent, she trotted off towards the stationary car and in the space of a minute, welcoming noises rose from the far side of the hedge. Theo walked around it to find his guest in a crouched position, rubbing his dog's generous belly.

She stood, and said, 'Hello. I'm Florence Hobbes.'

Theo unconsciously shook the hand of the freckled, pony-tailed woman wearing jeans and a hooded sweatshirt, while frantically reframing his previous image of a bow-backed, liver-spotted octogenarian. 'Yes, of course! Theo Coppersmith.'

'Not what you were expecting.'

Theo found himself laughing with her and was nudged by a jet black terrier whose collar was of grey and rose tartan. He stroked the wiry coat. 'Hello, Tulip's new chum.'

'This is Cavall.'

'The Wart's favourite hound!'

'My dad used to read the Arthurian classics to us. TH White's *The Once and Future King* was a favourite.'

'Mine is *The Acts of King Arthur and His Noble Knights.*'

'And Tulip's?'

'Not too sure, but the tulip is my daughter's favourite Spring flower,' he replied, smiling. 'May I help with your luggage?'

Inside the folded down boot were a collection of sizeable cardboard boxes, a violin case, a dog bed, and a potted maidenhair fern. Theo carried the suitcase into the cottage and was followed by Florence who had balanced the plant on the top of a cool box. 'The kitchen is through here', he said, expecting her to follow on, but she paused inside the front door.

'This is cosy. Your website doesn't do it justice. And you've a log burner. I promise not to set fire to the cottage.'

'We were about to remove it for that very reason, but

your daughter specifically asked if you might use it, and as you've been so accommodating, we could hardly refuse. By the way, the building work is all but finished.'

'That's good to know. My sister will be thrilled with Bookbinders. Caravanning or tenting isn't Pip's thing, so she usually stays in a hotel when we hook up on my road trips.'

'Road trips? How often do you embark on these adventures?'

'When the mood takes me.'

'How fortunate you are. My frequent hints at undertaking such a quest have become the family joke – *The Road Trip That Almost Was.*'

'Good book title, that.'

I'd much rather it not be a fiction.'

'*Journeys end in lovers meeting. Every wise man's son doth know,*' said Florence, and felt herself flush 'Tea?'

While Theo's mind rummaged for the source of the unexpected quote, Florence boiled the kettle, found the mugs, and made tea in her own pot, as if Bookbinders were her home and he the guest. Of the many people he had had the pleasure to greet, Florence Hobbes was the most singular.

'What are the pubs like?'

'The Sexton is good for beer and a light supper. Avoid Wednesday as it's pool night. The Apple Mill serves, as the name suggests, a fine local cider. They offer a more adventurous menu, except on Mondays. For a healthy lunchtime platter or a tasty treat, try the Leaf and Loaf Café, in the High Street.'

'Do the staff mind the customer's loafing?'

'On the contrary. The Kinsley Book Worms meet there, and as you might expect it's a great place to earwig on the village gossip, as is the hairdresser, and the village stores. You'll find a list of useful numbers and information in the living room, along with the local historian's details,' Theo announced, feeling increasingly gauche. 'You mentioned a family tree?'

'My sister is researching our mother's line.'

'Hobbes isn't a common name here, but that's not to say …'

'Eckley is my mother's maiden name. If there's anyone who can winkle out the family skeletons, Phillipa Darby's the one.'

'That wouldn't be Dr Phillipa Darby, of *Faces from the Past*?'

Florence nodded. 'Pip's joining me later this week. I apologise in advance if we shoot up the town.' She poured the tea. 'Let me guess: medium strength, with a wedge of lemon. How about walkies? Recommend places and times to avoid.'

'Before 7am or after 9am is best for a solo stroll. Pignut Meadow is at the back of the cottage and is delightful, even this early in the season.'

'Pignut is …'

'A small, delicate white flower, belonging to the carrot family.'

'One of the good ones.'

'The soldier beetles think so.' Theo sipped the tea. The flavour was strangely familiar, and yet his refined taste buds couldn't' quite capture the blend. Suddenly he was aware of a pair of eyes resting on him. 'From the back gate, follow the footpath which takes you to the River Arrow. We've listed the various trails on a local map. Erica Briggs is our housekeeper. She'll pop in next week to offer her services. Her husband Hughie, is our builder. The Briggs are a mine of information and will keep you entertained for as long as you've the time. A word of caution: I've warned Hughie about bothering you for tea.'

'Why would I be bothered?'

'Oh, alright then, as long as he finishes the job sometime this century. Kinsley's annual literary festival begins next month and every available room will be required.'

'Sounds impressive.'

Florence had leant against the counter top, and her gaze blazed through him as if he were gossamer. 'It's not quite Hay, or Cheltenham, but Sheelagh's speakers really are first rate.'

'Sorry, I didn't meant to be … is there anything else I should know about the cottage?'

Florence took the empty mug from his hand. He was once again an awkward teenager, loitering outside the local cinema while Bennett, his self-assured older brother, chatted up Daisy Foy on his behalf. Accompanying Florence upstairs felt too ridiculous to contemplate. 'Erica has set the heating. Adjust it as you require. Help yourself to the wood store in the old workshop, which is accessed through the kitchen door, as is the garden. There are bicycles, garden furniture, and a selection of Wellington boots at your disposal. Fresh linen is stored in the bathroom cupboard.' Speech finished, Theo made his way to the door with the speed of a thief dodging arrest.

'Thank you, Theo. Bookbinders will be a wonderful nest for the next three weeks. And thanks so much for the discount. I'll spend my savings at the Leaf and Loaf.'

'Good, yes – well then, I'd best be off.' He called for Tulip. 'Come on old girl, say good bye to Cavell, until the next time.'

And as Theo turned into the lane, instinctively he knew that Florence would watch him until he was out of sight.

7
The mint silk blouse with the Peter Pan collar

After a hot shower and dressed in cool pyjamas, Florence carried her cocoa wearily up the stairs and into the bedroom. The drive from Moffatt was easy enough, but the previous day's schedule had caught up. As her last visit to the dark sky border town was a number of years ago, arrangements had been made to meet the local reading group for afternoon tea. After that, she was entertained in the home of Gwennie Lyons, a spoken poet she had met along the way.

At the café, the usual volley of questions were fired: where did the inspiration for *Marcy McBride* come from; how did she set about capturing the sense of place; what was her writing schedule? And as usual, she was happy to answer to everyone's satisfaction (although she'd never met a person who truly believed that at a certain point, the story writes itself). That evening, she and Gwennie had talked until midnight, way past her usual bedtime, only to be miaowed awake at five o'clock by Pangloss the Ragamuffin.

Leaving the cocoa to cool, Florence pulled the heavy duvet under her chin, and was moments away from joining Cavell's contented snore, which drifted across the low-beamed bedroom like harvest dust. Theo hadn't specifically said she couldn't have the dog upstairs, and he wasn't *under* the duvet, so what was the harm? She was accustomed to being alone but when out on the road, it was reassuring to have company, human or canine, and Ardraig's dogs were fine companions. Bookbinders had already weaved a homely spell and now here, Florence was confident that these next three weeks would go well.

Aside from her notebook and pencil, the bedside table was a book-free zone. This was the season when reading was suspended in favour of researching a future story: far better to keep the mind clear, and senses on high alert to better absorb Kinsley's unique atmosphere. It had taken all of five minutes to become acquainted with Bookbinders. Bijou was the right term for it. The second bedroom contained a half-sized wardrobe and single bed which would do Phillipa nicely, although there was a sofa-bed in the living room should she want to spread out. If Gabriel had joined them, sharing a limited space would have increased the tension between them. The possibility of her sister's pot boiling over had an inevitability to it, and while Florence was fairly confident of keeping the lid on it for the duration, the prospect was unnerving.

During a brief pre-visit chat, she had felt like a needy student bothering a weary teacher and was relieved to have been passed over to speak to her brother-in-law, who had chirped on about house viewings, and how they were making strides towards a relocation. This *was* news. Pip hadn't said anything about house-hunting, but Alec was notoriously bad at keeping secrets. His 'excitement at pastures new' spiel wasn't in the least convincing, but they must have accepted that Gabriel had no intention of returning to Eastgate Road and were getting on with it. If this were the case, Alec might enjoy country life. Florence's father had dug up his inner city roots with very little effort, so why not him? Few people who had taken such a step ever regretted it.

Turning her thoughts to what lay ahead, Florence acknowledged the mix of apprehension and anticipation. If yesterday's session were an indicator, *Marcy McBride* had been well received. She hadn't planned to announce her intention to publish the sequel to *Greenaway Girls*, but in the convivial café atmosphere, and with earnest promises to keep it a secret, she had confided to the group that it was almost certain to be her next book. She hadn't said it might be her last, but there was something stirring. It was the same vague sense of needing to get lost, to be where no one else knew her, with no family or friends to be concerned about. It was that exact same feeling she'd felt at sixteen, when just the thought of untying herself from her mother was paralysing, but it had to be done, for both their sakes. Florence had set herself a quest, the grail being freedom from attachment, and she had almost achieved it.

But now, Rae and Levon wanted her to settle in Ardraig, in the newly renovated hay barn, with its own walled garden and guest bedroom. Her father had made it plain he was going nowhere. In fact, his and Lally's ashes were to be scattered at Briar's Cove when he passed. Apparently, Kathleen had raised no objections, and had encouraged him to do what was in his heart. Florence had no intention of letting this particular cat out of the bag.

Phillipa couldn't even bring herself to ask what their father or Gabriel had been doing, although she must have seen the WhatsApp posts.

Through the window (Florence generally left the curtains open), pale pink moon beams illuminated the various items of clothing hanging on the wardrobe door. The 'Ellis Eckley' costume had acted as an effective safety net between her and the author, and from that very first book signing in the local library, it had never let her down. Where had that decade gone? Florence cast her mind back to that fateful Friday evening. Phillipa had popped over to The Barbers, carrying a box containing every letter, postcard and photograph Florence had sent home during her teenage travelling years. *You're dying in that office, Flo. This is the call to adventure. I know you can write, so use these for inspiration.'*

Later that night, Florence trawled through the hundreds of pieces of correspondence encapsulating hers and Javier's European adventures. So many comical, emotional, and frankly terrifying scenes flashed past like slides through a projector, and by dawn of the following day, the germ of a story had sprouted. It was just as Tolkien had described it – every accumulated experience rotted like leaf mould in the compost of the mind, slowly feeding the imagination until, as in Florence's case, six months later she dropped an eighty thousand word document in her sister's lap. Those subsequent twenty-four hours had shredded her nerves, but when she returned from work to see Pip and her parents wearing grins the size of sombreros, Florence knew her life was about to take a U-turn.

It wasn't all plain sailing. As a published academic, Dr Phillipa Darby was accustomed to making extensive textual notes and comments and had a lot to say (irregular sentence flow; erratic punctuation; confusing dialogue; paragraphs too long, not long enough …), but as soon as her edit was complete, she promised to put together the all-important synopsis, along with a compelling covering letter. These would be sent, along with the first three chapters, to the appropriate agents for consideration. Of course, there was no guarantee that the story wouldn't end up on a slush pile or worse, but Phillipa was confident of getting her sister an advance, and perhaps even a multiple-book contract.

Far from feeling elated, Florence watched helplessly as the joy drained from her soul, and for weeks afterwards had set the entire project aside. But with her parents' assurances and the encouragement of her loved ones, she took on board some of Pip's recommendations, although when it came to polishing and refining her story, if *Greenaway Girls* couldn't be taken at face value, she'd rather not bother going down the agent's route. Surely there had to be another way?

Step forward Alec's best mate, Gary Moncrieff whose printing company had worked with a number of writers going it alone. This was when self-publishing was in its infancy and print on demand hadn't yet taken off. On paper it looked sound: as unit costs decreased with a bigger print run, why not order more? But as was often the case, over-optimistic authors were left with hundreds of unsold books on their hands. Gary's low risk plan made sense: they'd start with a short run and wait.

Phillipa accepted that it was this way or no way, so she set aside her frustration and pitched in. When the manuscript was fact and sensitivity checked, and Rae's artwork complete, the next step was to road test *Greenaway Girls* on a specially selected reading group. They were given no reviews, or synopsis, and neither was the novel available online or in bookshops. But if they enjoyed the coming-of-age story of schoolfriends, Gillian, Pauline, Tracy, and Anna, they'd be invited to join Ellis Eckley's exclusive mailing list which guaranteed hot-off-the-press publications, special offers, and event details.

The initial comments were encouraging (*captures inner city growing pains well; a good story that could be great with a smaller cast list; couldn't put it down*) and several asked if a sequel were in the pipeline. Florence's confidence was bolstered by these anonymous reviews. With the Ellis Eckley website up and running, it was time to tell the people of De Beauvoir and beyond that *Greenaway Girls* existed. But just as the low-key marketing campaign was about to begin, Florence panicked. The enormity of putting herself out there, sitting expectantly with pen in hand, even if it were the friendly library or café, had given her nightmares. When Pip stepped in with the idea of a disguise, it saved the project.

Florence finished her drink, turned off the lamp and slid under the duvet. She replayed the living room scene: Rae, Phillipa, Lally, and Aunt Maxine, visiting from Spain, were squashed together on the sofa, while Florence hopped in and out of various vintage clothes combinations, willing for a general consensus so she could her jeans back on.

Rae: Mum, for a casual style, wear the gabardine slacks with the tank top, and the low-heel Oxfords. Here, let me put this hairband over your lock. Hey, that's nice. I might even wear the outfit myself.

Phillipa: That's fine for afternoon tea, Rae, but in my opinion, the intellectual look is best. Florence, try this long-sleeved open-necked blouse and we'll tie the scarf loosely, so it looks casually formal. With the blue tortoiseshell specs, Ellis Eckley is a writer to be taken seriously.

Maxine: Go with the knickerbockers and polo shirt, Flo. It has 'un cierto estilo'.'

Lally: Trust Maxine to throw a Spanish spanner in the works. Look Flo, why don't you wear the long linen skirt with the front pleats, and the mint silk blouse with the Peter Pan collar? If it's cold, you can slip on the long-knit vest. It's a softer look, and it makes a nice change from those scruffy old jeans you live and die in.

To keep everyone happy, Florence combined their recommended items, and when her shoulder-length hair dried naturally, she actually looked like someone who wasn't Florence Hobbes. And so with everything in order, their campaign had turned into a fun family enterprise, and at the end of that first year, *Greenaway Girls* had sold five thousand copies, leaving a profit of sixteen thousand pounds. Florence calculated that if her second book attained similar sales, the office job could be consigned to history. By the time *Our Sunday Best* was published twelve months later, Ellis Eckley was on her way. And then, the entire world turned upside down.

The pain of her mother's death had faded to an occasional ache, and whenever Florence wore the mint-shade silk blouse, they were reunited. Yes, she'd wear it in Leominster. After all, this was the county where Lavender

Eckley's relations hailed from, and who knew what Pip would unearth when she arrived the following week. But for now, Florence planned to kick start this next adventure with a trip to the village stores, followed by brunch at the Leaf and Loaf Café. After that, she might pop into the hairdresser to make an appointment. There might even be a space for Pip.

8
Naked bungee jumping and other rumours

Situated on the corner of the high street, opposite the village stores, the Leaf and Loaf Café was unmissable. Everything about it shouted Step Inside! Pear green oak panelling; warm wooden floors; comfy chairs, the smell of roasted coffee beans, and row upon row of books, old and new, filled the shelves. Whoever designed it had clearly lost their heart to literature.

Florence left her umbrella in the wicker stand by the door and walked up to the counter. 'Morning. I'm looking for Erica Briggs. I'm told she works here.'

'You're Ms Hobbes?'

'The one and only.'

'I'm sorry, it's just that Theo said …'

'It's the pony tail. Knocks years off. Hi, I'm Flo.' Erica's smile reached all the way to her eyes – a good sign.

'I see you've spent your pennies at Sean-Village-Stores. He must have sold you at least two items you had no intention of buying.'

'The leeks were picked by his own fair hand, so it would have been rude to refuse. Talking of skills, Theo spoke very highly of yours, Erica.'

'That man has a lovely way with words. You've picked

the best morning to come in. We're bustling between eleven and three with tourists and locals. The groups tend to come in late afternoon, but my shift's over by then. But where's your dog?'

'Cavell's at the cottage, recovering from his early morning ramble. I'll introduce you.'

'Kiki will love that. You're welcome to join our daily morning walkies, usually around seven, on Pignut Meadow. Anyway, what can I get you?'

Florence examined the chalk board. 'The artichoke and cherry tomato *ciabatta* and an *Americano*, please.' She peered at the contents under the glass dome. 'And what might these beauties be?'

Erica's infectious laugh drew the attention of two stiff grey heads over by the window alcove. 'The beauties are apple and almond tarts: the beasts over there are the Gillespie sisters. They were expecting Margery to wait on them this morning, but they've got the woman with a dragon tattoo instead.' She pulled up her sleeve to reveal the mouth end of a fabulous serpentine creature. 'Margery Crisp's the café manager, but not the owner – that's Sheelagh Spicer, Theo's lesser half. Sorry, shouldn't bite the hand that literally feeds me. She and Marg get very crispy around this time of year. You'll have heard about the book festival, Kinsley's main attraction.'

Florence had hit the bullseye. So engrossing was Erica's stream of consciousness, she hadn't noticed the customer waiting behind her. 'Theo said you might pop over to Bookbinders. Why don't you come tomorrow for a cuppa, and one of Sean's irresistible buns?'

'That'll be lovely, Flo. I'll drop in after work. Grab a

seat, and I'll bring a tray over. Help yourself to the freebies on the left-hand racks. The books on the other side are for sale.'

Florence wandered towards the 'book club' sign. On the top shelf were six copies each of the latest Booker, Costa, and Guardian 'First Book Award' winners. Below that stood a selection of local authors' novels, four of which were *Marcy McBride*, tied, and with a note attached (*Jensen to collect Thursday am*). The discovery that her latest tale was about to be read by another group shouldn't have been a surprise, but it was. The only time Florence had seen anyone with an Ellis Eckley in public was in Dorset. She had just finished her pilgrimage to Max Gate when on a nearby bench, the unsuspecting reader had laughed out loud, (in a good way?) Whether it was Thomas Hardy's spirit that had discouraged Florence from approaching or her innate modesty who knew, but she was so glad to have resisted.

At the nearest table, Erica whisked the contents off the tray. Florence sat down.

'Apart from libraries, there aren't many places that offer book-clubs a free read. Do you belong to a group, Erica?'

'That's a question with an interesting answer.' Erica glanced in the direction of the curly perms. 'I'll tell you about it tomorrow, Flo. If you're a speed reader, I recommend the Ellis Eckley book. It'll get all your chakras in a spin, which is no easy feat, but you'll have to get it back by Thursday morning or I'm fired. Having said that, if the boss had her way, there wouldn't be any self-publishers on the shelf, but as the writer's family is from these parts and people ask for them, there's not much Old Spice can do about it. Enjoy your brunch.'

Florence stirred the coffee, quickly putting two and two together. 'Old Spice' was Sheelagh Spicer, of Spicer Kennedy, the publishing conglomerate! When Rae had suggested including a short biography to update the website,

(Ellis Eckley's descendants hail from London and Herefordshire. When not on the road, she lives with her two and four legged loved ones in the north west of Scotland)

as far as Florence was concerned, these two lines were more than sufficient personal information to make public. Who could have predicted that through such a tenuous link, her novels had found room on these illustrious shelves. Anyone remotely interested in literature or women's issues, would know the name 'Spicer'. Florence wondered if the famous woman regretted her infamous quote – *I'd rather bungee jump naked from The Eiffel Tower than read Romance fiction.* Maybe she hadn't said it at all, but these things had a way of generating their own vapour trail. No doubt Erica would fill in the gaps tomorrow. As was the case with many of the places Florence visited, the locals were willing to share knowledge and gossip. Sean-Village-Stores Nesbitt was another. He was also St Mark's church warden, and as keeper of the keys, he couldn't wait to give Dr Phillipa Darby from the Beeb a tour, *at her convenience.*

Brunch finished, Florence waved to Erica before stepping outside to find that the rain had eased into a drizzle. On an impulse, she headed for the churchyard where, according to Sean, the Eckley gravestones were located in the south-west corner, by the ancient yew. As she approached the church, a striking bell tower, the likes of which Florence had never seen, drew her towards it. She wandered around the perimeter, admiring the quality and skill of builder and building whilst making a mental note to ask her sister for a history lesson.

Further on were a number of impressive tombstones with the name Parry carved into the lichened marble, obviously to the manor born. And there by the yew, lay several generations of Eckley. Many of the inscriptions on the older stones were indecipherable, but one in particular caught her attention – a granite headstone, with the name Ruth 'Faerie' Eckley (1890-1949) carved into it. It was her great grandmother, buried with Joseph. Who could ever forget a name like that?

As a child, Florence used to imagine what Faerie was like. Did she hide her lacey wings under her dark cloak until nightfall, when she flew over the villages, wafting stardust? Now here, there was no disguising the thrill of meeting her ancestors, and there was no one better qualified than Pip to breathe life into these ghosts.

9
Flights of fancy

Viola bounced into the kitchen, flicked on the overhead light, and pulled up a chair. 'Good news, Ma. Harumi Kita has agreed to headline your festival.'

Sheelagh looked up from the newspaper. 'What fibs did you tell?'

'Didn't have to. It's a provincial affair with polite folk in tweeds, and we've a half hour slot that needs filling. Actually, I think it was the shepherd hut that swung it in your favour. I gave Harumi special dispensation to sleep in it – if she decides to stay, that is.'

'Thank you, Viola. You've saved Margery's sanity. Your writer's presence will rev up ticket sales.'

'Happy to be of service.' Viola picked an apple from the bowl, aware that her mother had clocked the remnants of black varnish clinging to what was left of her fingernails. This was the sort of thing that happened when Garvey was bored. 'What are your plans tonight?'

'No plans, darling. Thought I might put my feet up, order a takeaway, catch up on the news.'

'Let's have a girlie night in. We'll watch Love Island, and I'll paint your toenails,' said Viola cheekily, knowing that her mother had never experienced the delights of either pedicure or massage, although right now, either would do her the power of good. Self-care had never been a priority, and no one was less bothered to have been labelled a beauty, back in the day when such opinions were banded about. But at a recent event, when Viola overheard the editor of Scorpio Books comment on *La Spicer's unfortunate weight gain,* she decided to tackle her mother, only to be warned off with an ice-pick glance from those famously merciless indigo eyes.

In spite of her daughterly concerns, Viola acknowledged that hers was a privileged life. Even the agency signings were attributed to the Spicer/Coppersmith influence. There was no shaking it off, even if she changed her name – the publishing world's memory was elephantine. Quirk Literary Agency began life in the basement flat of her mother's town house. It was meant to be a post-university interim project while Viola contemplated her career choices but had subsequently taken on a life of its own. Finding a genuinely quirky story wasn't as easy she'd imagined. Quirk's rigid criteria excluded much of the new material out there, and with a once-a-year eight week acceptance period, anything posted before or after wasn't even opened. As Garvey liked to remind her, *given our super-fluid climate, it's eggshell city, baby.*

The impact of Garvey's departure, although expected, was immediate. Viola decided it was time for a review. If Quirk were to continue, she'd have to hire another assistant. Going it alone wasn't an option, but working alongside a group of committed colleagues in a new field was tempting. Her psychology degree would be a useful springboard into social or charity work, or she could go back to college, or move to Kinsley, and work locally. Gracie had dreamt of setting up a small holding in the shires. Keeping hens and growing purple sprouting broccoli were the only meaningful activities left in this impoverished world, or so she insisted, and to do it together would be awesome. That was until Gracie had fallen head over wellies for a mutual friend and six months on, Viola was still shattered by the betrayal.

She got up to fetch a glass of water. It wouldn't do for her mother to see her cry. Neither did Viola need reminding that the one-sided relationship was doomed from the start. Self-pity it may have been, but it still bloody hurt. Gracie's hostility towards her mother hadn't helped matters. That Kinsley had been transformed into a *déstination bibliophile* was totally irrelevant, and as for Fabula ...*that was nothing more than a rich bitch hobby, just as Quirk is for you, Vi*. So casual a dismissal of her mother's ground-breaking feminist publishing house should have red-flagged Gracie's deeply embedded narcissism, but her ex-girlfriend was right to point out the flipside to the famous Spicer drive. Was it any wonder her mother had ongoing health issues.

Unsurprisingly, Gracie and Theo got along. Her father was the epitome of *entente cordiale*. Even before the cancer, his generous spirit had engendered heaps of goodwill in Kinsley. The name 'Coppersmith' elicited genuine smiles from her peers unlike Spicer, which clearly still curled the occasional lip. It was unfortunate that after four hundred illustrious years, Coppersmith Press had met its demise in such a tragic way, but without it her parents may never have met. Erskine Coppersmith had second-mortgaged the family home to keep the ancient university press going, and it was Charles Spicer, Viola's other grandpa, who had stepped in to save the ailing imprint. Sadly, Charles' fearsome reputation outweighed many a good deed, but having never met either man, Viola's desire to unmask her grandfathers' lives had come to nought. Even if she were brave enough to attempt a double biography of these diverse publishing men, her mother would never agree to it, and her father would be reluctant to revisit such a traumatic period.

'Well, Viola, are you off on another flight of fancy, or are we discussing dinner?'

'Sorry, Ma. I was thinking about work. Now that Garvey's gone, I'm considering my options.'

Sheelagh put her newspaper to one side and rested her glasses on top. 'I thought you were happy at Quirk?'

'I am, but it's been forever since the last suitable manuscript came in.'

'Hardly surprising, with such an exacting criteria.'

'I know, but …' She sighed. 'Don't you sometimes wish for a totally new experience, Mum? Surely, deep down in your being there's a hidden quest, an unexplored expedition yearning for you to jump on board. What about Dad's road trip idea? Neither of you have commitments that can't be put aside for a few weeks. Why don't you let your hair down, roll a joint or two, get your motors running.'

'Your father will never do it. It so much easier to ride the crest of other people's fantastic waves. Theodore Coppersmith is as constant and as predictable as the waxing crescent, and as for me, I'm sorry to disappoint you daughter, but I'd rather paint my nails black.'

They laughed, and Viola set about making a lentil curry.

*

With her dressing gown belt secured, Sheelagh trundled downstairs. She should never have had that third gin and tonic so late in the evening. Theo usually made her a concoction, and without wanting to know either content or provenance, the distasteful gloop worked a treat. But of course she knew where it came from. Erica's friends had the hire of Birdy's back rooms, for their 'holistic centre'. The hair salon was no longer the business of old, and the extra rental money must have been useful. Sheelagh was no makeover expert, but it was obvious that a styling assistant was essential if Birdy were to survive. With the notable exception of the Gillespie sisters, there weren't many villagers still breathing who looked forward to a weekly shampoo and set under a rigid roof hairdryer.

Baking soda, that's what her mother used to take for heartburn. Sheelagh stirred a spoonful of the white powder into a cup of boiling water. While it cooled, she checked her phone. A mountain of messages filled every box, none of which were worthy of reading at two thirty in the morning. There had been nothing from Theo until the previous day when he called to update her. Apparently, Bookbinders' latest guest had her own teeth and hair, Hughie's renovations were on target, and Margery's festival nerves had settled. Theo had sounded cheery. He was off to Leominster for supplies and had promised to look out for that particular sauce she liked.

Sheelagh pulled back the heavy linen curtains. A beam of orange neon flooded the living room, casting a sickly glow. The necessity of carrying a torch when in Kinsley had made her aware of dark skies, and much more besides. Sleep was no easier there, though. Hearing the owls hoot recalled the nights when she and Margery scuttled over to the bell tower, armed with flash lights and flasks of sherry or gin, while Alice Spicer wallowed in yet another lonely booze snooze. When Sheelagh's father bought Cleavers as somewhere the couple might spend the occasional weekend together, little did he know it would effectively end the marriage. When her mother's wish to return to her ancestral village was granted, Farringdon was out, and as Charles couldn't abide what he considered the 'tediousness' of village life, there was nothing left to talk about.

On the shelf, his imposing image was just about visible in the murky light. That particular photograph was one of three rare snaps of father and daughter and was taken when Fabula had received the Billingshurst Prize. Working alongside him during her post-grad years was tough, but the experience equipped her to face everything. *Business and sentimentality should never mix, Sheelagh. You'll do well to remember that.*

Charles Spicer had foreseen the industry's challenges long before anyone else, unlike Erskine Coppersmith, whose blind romanticism and poor business acumen led to the long standing family affair's demise, and an early grave. Spicer Publishing's merger with the American multi-national Kennedy Inc., had upset more than the applecart. In addition to Coppersmith Press, the conglomerate hoovered up other precariously placed imprints to further swell its assets, and its value. Immune to the furore, and content that his daughter was to remain on the board of directors, Charles Spicer did the unthinkable and stepped down. Before jetting off first-class to Canberra with his second wife, he gave Sheelagh the Farringdon house, a substantial share portfolio, and suggested she keep in touch, only not too often.

The soda had settled Sheelagh's stomach sufficiently to return to bed. On the landing, she paused outside Viola's room. She ought to have moved out long ago, but with both professional and personal life in limbo, Farringdon was an easy option, and the arrangement suited them. Viola was good company and dealt efficiently with the domestic affairs, but clearly was ripe for change. Quirk had been a shoe-in. The contacts required for the venture were assured, and there was no financial risk, although that in itself posed a unique set of challenges. Chopping and changing career was all very well when money wasn't the motivation.

Theo was confident that Viola would undertake an aspect of social work once she'd scratched the publishing itch – after all, with both sides of the family in the industry, it was inevitable. Sheelagh tended to agree. Viola hadn't inherited the Spicer ambition gene and was much more like Theo in that respect. If he hadn't been so loyal to Erskine Coppersmith, his choices might also have veered towards the caring professions. Nevertheless, he was grateful for her life buoy when Coppersmith Press went under.

To begin with, Theo seemed to enjoy attending the various books fairs, and it was at the end of a lively week in Frankfurt that they spent an unexpectedly passionate night together, before embarking on what Sheelagh assumed to be a fling. A serious relationship at that critical stage of her career hadn't been factored in, and never, ever, a baby. But Theo's enthusiastic and practical response had changed her mind. While her father was relieved she intended to carry on as before, he was appalled that a university-educated and well-connected man such as Theo Coppersmith would jettison a successful career in favour of raising a child, but with no satisfactory answer forthcoming, the subject was dropped. Although the pregnancy and birth were a nuisance, Sheelagh was intensely relieved to have been endowed with a profound new-mother love, previously assumed to be impossible, and though perhaps not expressed as others might, that love for her daughter endured.

And now Viola was driving her parents' relationship forward. *Why don't you hit the tarmac, let your hair down?* Admittedly, there was little in Sheelagh's diary that couldn't be shifted, although Theo's workload was on the increase. Even if it were possible, where might they go? Consuming carafes of local wine whilst mulling over restaurant choices was not Theo's ideal vacation. Predictably, he'd bugger off in search of heraldic trails while she browsed the museums and galleries on her own. But Viola's suggestion wasn't without merit, only not now, as sleep had finally come to claim her.

Sheelagh slipped off her dressing gown and climbed into bed. If there were one lesson Theo had taught her, it was to expect the unexpected. Being in control couldn't always guarantee the right outcome. Viola would find her way, the festival would happen, with or without a sell-out crowd, and Cleavers would further diminish her treasure chest.

10
Settling in nicely

'Thanks for the tea and the munchie Flo. We don't usually get the five-star treatment. You seem to be settling into Kinsley very nicely.'

Florence took the empty mug and plate from Hughie Briggs' dusty hand. With the last of the ridge tiles cut, he might have emerged from a sand storm. 'You and Erica have made me feel so at home. She's constantly feeding me up with goodies, those hazelnut flapjacks being a fine example.'

'Thought I recognised her baking. It's a notch above Sean-Village-Stores packet jobs. Erica said your sister will be here tomorrow, to research the family tree. The Briggs have lived in these parts for centuries … hey, we could be related.'

Hughie was a rangy red head and towered over her mid-brown five feet two, but why not? Theo's description of this lovely couple was spot on. They were warm, playful, and were mines of information. In fact, Erica had been extremely generous with her knowledge, and it had to be said, gossip. That first 'pop in' had extended to tea, followed by a dog walk, and was an indicator of how the hours rolled placidly along. Cavell showed no signs of his vintage years with girlfriends like Tulip and Kiki in his slipstream. Kinsley's topography was a world away from Ardraig's sparse and often bleak coastline. This land, mostly agricultural, had remained largely unchanged since it was first farmed in the neolithic period, and the sheer number of trees, curving pastures, and ancient buildings were striking.

As a stranger in a new landscape, Florence was mindful of her father's advice to always expect the best from folk, and to a large extent, that was what she received. But no village or town were without its factions. Erica had been forthright with regards Sheelagh Spicer and Margery Crisp's controversial impact on Kinsley. Their friendship dated back to infant school and had been interrupted when Sheelagh was sent to board in Gloucestershire, returning only during the holidays. But when she took off for London, via St. Hilda's College, Margery thought she had lost her best friend forever, until Viola arrived. When Sheelagh inherited Cleavers, Margery thanked God and St. Mark for the second miracle.

To begin with, the changes were welcome. The renovation of the village hall and the new cafe had earned Sheelagh brownie points, and while the literary festival wasn't universally popular, Theo was on such good terms with everyone, the annual invasion passed off largely without protest. But when Sheelagh and Viola flew to Canberra, leaving him to navigate prostate cancer treatment alone, the goodwill evaporated. Even Margery had been stiff lipped during those six weeks. In addition to tending Cleavers' riverside garden, she had joined the rota to drive Theo to hospital for daily radiotherapy sessions when his brother and sister-in-law returned to Northumberland.

Interestingly, Hughie was the only one who knew how the patient felt about the 'abandonment'. Theo had encouraged Sheelagh and Viola to go. Who else could unravel the terrific mess that her father's estate had been left in following the death of his second wife? He hadn't felt unwell, and with friends queuing up to look after him, what was the point in delaying.

'Penny for your thoughts, Flo?'

'Sorry, Hughie, I was thinking about the tribulations of village life. I'm taking my sister to dinner tomorrow night. Theo said The Sexton was a good bet.'

'As a rule, yes, but it's pool and darts night. Might be rowdy.'

'Pip might like rowdy. Should I book a table?'

'No need. I'll be in there early and will keep one by. It's Erica's day to see her mother, so I've got a pass. Come over around seven. I'll tell the lads to be on their best behaviour.'

'It takes a lot to shock a cockney, Hughie.'

'Wow, a real, live East Ender! You'll have to teach us some of that rhyming slang.'

'Any time, me ol' mucker.'

Hughie's bellow drew Cavell into the garden.

'Here comes my sidekick. I'd best take him for a gander. Pip will enjoy meeting you, Hughie.'

'If she's half as much fun as you are, Flo, we're in for a treat. Erica said something about her being a doctor. Should I watch my alcohol intake?'

Florence laughed. 'No, but you might want to keep an eye on hers.'

*

At the riverbank, beside the enormous weeping willow was a bench, made from the limb of a fallen oak tree. This was now Florence's spot. Leaving Cavell to dip his white paws in the bubbling water, she relaxed back. Her lack of routine consisted of long sleeps, meadow meanderings, chit chat, fiddle practise, and lots of lovely food. Without Rae's programme to mark time, she'd be hard pressed to know what day it was. The river Arrow passed through many villages on its way to the Wye and was a real find. Flanked by fields of dandelions and Lady's smock, this was one of a number of beauty spots from where she and Cavell wallowed in bucolic bliss. *Lush, verdant, rolling –* these adjectives often read like clichés, but in Kinsley they were authentic descriptions of the Herefordshire countryside.

Several days passed before Florence saw Theo again. The first occasion was during a morning stroll around Pignut Meadow, with Erica and her friends. They were surprised to see each other. He responded to the women's banter with chuckles and nods, and in a quieter moment, asked if she were in need of anything. Short of a cook and bottle washer, Florence replied that she was as content as she'd ever been. Conversation that morning was dedicated to their mothers, and how several had been/were keen gardeners.

Lavender Hobbes was a member of the De Beauvoir Gardening Club. It was there that she met Jude Moraes, the landscape gardener and writer, and this meeting had transformed her approach. The Barber's L-shaped cottage garden, enclosed behind wide iron railings, was enjoyed by neighbours and passers-by alike, many of whom used to stop and ask Lally for advice, and often would take away cuttings or seedlings. Theo's mother adored Sweet William and Sweet Peas, and these filled every available space, inside and out. It occurred to Florence that Frances Coppersmith's benign ministrations had left an indelible impression on her youngest son.

That was on Thursday. The following Sunday, she and Cavell had taken the old soldiers' trail which led them past Cleavers where Theo was tending the picket-fenced back garden. He was only too pleased to accompany them along the cow parsley and pink campion-lined path. That day, they talked about their daughters. Theo's over-protectiveness with Viola was at odds with Florence's hands-off relationship with Rae, but they agreed that ultimately it was the parent's role to free the child, and always with the hope that they will choose to return. Unable to invite her for tea due to an appointment elsewhere, Theo promised a guided garden tour before she left Kinsley.

Leaving the river's contented gurgles behind, Florence made her way back to Bookbinders. In the delightful garden, the star jasmine's pinwheels dowsed her in heady scent whilst finishing the last of her 'thank you' letters. Birdsong mingled with the soft sighing of silver birch leaves, whose spidery branches formed a protective ring on the north side of the old stone wall. It was reminiscent of Pip and Alec's city garden, which had been the recipient of her mother's fabulous plant collection. With no guarantees that the new tenants would care for Lally's plants, Alec and his allotment pals liberated them. It was just as well as apparently, the garden was currently being used as a dumping ground for old mattresses and broken toys.

St. Mark's chimed one o'clock. Florence gathered together the sealed envelopes and ink pen and hoofed upstairs to change. There was no need to fiddle with her hair. Birdy had curled her curls very well. Hairdressing was more than just a job for the vigorous silver-haired salon owner – it kept her perky, she said. Birdy might so easily have become another friend. As a rule, Florence avoided getting close to the people she met whilst on the road, but occasionally friendships occurred, as was the case with Hughie and Erica Briggs, and potentially Theo Coppersmith, who appeared to be everyone's best mate.

With the mint blouse tucked neatly into her long linen skirt, Florence stood before the mirror. *This is how an actor must feel.* Was it subterfuge, to pretend to be someone else, to eavesdrop on others' lives and write about them without their knowing? Her family didn't agree. Wasn't that how most writers found inspiration? If dressing up allowed Florence to earn a living by doing what she enjoyed, where was the harm. Readers' feedback consistently confirmed that Ellis Eckley captured the essence of people and places very well. How could she do that from imagination or digging into personal archaeology alone?

Pep talk over, Florence skipped downstairs, leaving Cavell to snooze contentedly for the next couple of hours. With her mother's favourite blouse and brooch as talisman, she slipped on her gabardine jacket, picked up her satchel and car keys, and set off for the historic market town of Leominster.

11
Nan's Place: a token

The list was ticked: ironmonger, health shop, post office – and now a coffee, before driving back to Kinsley. Nan's Place was Theo's regular destination when in town. Not only were the pastries delicious, but the shop stocked a certain sauce that Sheelagh was fond of, which in itself was unusual as she had little interest in food. It was simply an engine-filler, a necessity that allowed her to power on through the day and often into the night. Theo was no gastronome but experimenting with flavours had become a pleasurable pastime. During Sheelagh's regular absences, he occasionally invited Caradoc Crisp for supper and a game of chess. Margery didn't mind in the least. As couples they entertained each other semi-regularly, and a boys' night out as she called it, was healthy.

On his approach to the cafe, Theo was halted by a 'closed' sign on the door. He checked his watch: 2.54pm. A crowd of people were gathered inside, possibly enjoying a private celebration. Disappointed, he was about to turn back when a cheerful looking man came out. He was wearing overalls and work boots and was holding a book.

''Fraid you're too late, mate. I only just made it to the signing. Drove like Lewis Hamilton from Shobdon to get this for my wife.' He passed the book to Theo. 'This'll put me in credit.'

Theo expertly scanned the front and back cover. 'Your wife's a fan?'

'We both are. The bad news is we'll miss the Ludlow gig this Thursday. It's been five years since Ellis Eckley visited these parts and there's a real buzz.'

Theo was intrigued. He'd come across the author from the Leaf and Loaf's 'local writers' collection. Self-published books were a conundrum for Sheelagh's quality control radar, and this was partly why Erica had left The Book Worms. She had confided to him that they were undemocratic and elitist. Theo had to agree. If Sheelagh and Margery (and if he were being honest, himself) took the trouble to read these novels, they might have a different point of view.

Just then, a woman walked to the door, turned the sign to 'open' and stepped outside. While she and the man exchanged a few words, Theo peered through the window. In the far corner he caught sight of a woman dressed rather formerly in a long skirt and blouse, and whose corkscrew hair bounced in time with the conversation. Although she was obscured from full view, the sound of her laugh turned a cog in his brain. Aware that the man was watching him, Theo turned back. 'Do you mind my asking why you can't attend the event?'

'A family thing, you know how it goes. Better to miss it and avoid an argument down the line.'

'There's wisdom in those words. How do I get a ticket?'

'Sold out. Shelly booked ours months ago. She's gutted, especially as Henbane are on the programme.' He noted his questioner's quizzical expression. 'They're a five piece ensemble – fiddle, banjo, that sort of thing, and have been making a rumpus, around and about.'

Theo was now thoroughly on the scent. 'So, what exactly is it about Ellis Eckley that grabs your attention?'

'Well, for starters, the stories rattle along, and before you know it you've arrived at the Grail.'

'The Grail?'

'Yeah, there's one at the back of every book. I s'pose you might call it an index, a record of the artists and other references mentioned in the stories.'

'And they rattle along, you say.'

'Hard to put down. I remember some years back when Shelly nagged at me to read *Our Sunday Best*. I couldn't believe Ellis was a 'she'. I was convinced it'd been written by a fella. Shelley reckons those books have saved us a fortune in marriage guidance,' he grinned. 'We also like the fact that the Artless Press Collective are independent. They keep it local, promote other people's talent.' The man checked the time on his phone. 'Look, why don't you have our tickets?'

'I couldn't possibly …'

'Don't see why not. You'll have a great night out and might even get home in time for the ten o'clock news.'

Theo took the tickets. 'This Thursday, you say?'

'Assembly Rooms, Ludlow. Doors open 6.45pm.'

'That's jolly good of you, Mr …'

'Clive Proctor, stone mason.'

'Theo Coppersmith, bits and bobs man.' They shook hands. Theo found the stone mason's callouses reassuring. He reached for his wallet. 'How much do I owe you, Clive?'

'Have them on us. If you'd like to contribute, buy a few raffle tickets. Ellis donates the profits to a local charity. Anyway, best get back to the job. These old churches might have patience, but not my boss.'

Theo waited for the generous benefactor to disappear along the narrow lane before sliding the precious tickets into his wallet. If his suspicions were correct, running the risk of meeting Florence, *aka* Ellis Eckley under these circumstances wouldn't be ideal for either of them. There must have been a good reason for the secrecy. He walked briskly back to the car, coffee and pastry forgotten.

12
Phillipa turns a corner

Phillipa felt her shoulders drop. Kinsley was now on the map. *So far, so good.* She had fought off the M25, vanquished the M42, and was now on a steady canter towards Kidderminster. Between London's transport network and Alec's taxi cab, keeping a second vehicle was considered unnecessary, but today she was driving the local car club's Vauxhall *Mokka*. It reminded her of the days when, as teenagers, she and Jason briefly shared a car and he'd play Queen as loud as the tape deck could muster before conking out.

There were benefits to driving alone, not least that she could choose the music. Phillipa opted for a Gregorian Chant, rather than catch up with a backlog of podcasts. As an over-enthusiastic undergraduate, she was eager to absorb every experience, so when her study buddy Dionne Fairleigh offered her a ticket to the choral society's performance of *Kyrie*, Phillipa grabbed it. It was a significant moment. The chants had become a refuge when the stresses and strains were overwhelming. Who would have predicted that she and Dionne would have taken such diverse roads, having worked just five miles apart for many years, she at Queen Mary and her friend at SOAS. In the early days of their respective careers, they used to meet for concerts, British Museum exhibitions, and for the occasional meal. Theology had been more than an academic subject for Dionne. Like blotting paper, she had absorbed enormous quantities of practical insight and common-sense perspectives which had the unexpected benefit of steering Phillipa through a number of tricky times.

With good friends thin on the ground, she had taken it for granted that Dionne would remain within arm's reach, but when she left teaching to live in Brittany, it took a long while to recover from the blow. One day soon, Phillipa would honour her promise to visit Dionne at *Le Jardin des hortensias*, just as Gabriel had done as a truculent teenager. Alec hadn't raised any objections to their son's declaration of independence – he was simply having a break with a family friend before going to Ardraig, for another 'working holiday'. At the time, Phillipa had been too distracted to unpack her husband's opinion. The controversial suspension of a respected colleague had plunged her department into chaos, and every last drop of her energy had atomised.

And then Gabriel announced his intention to quit university and move to Ardraig. In desperation she had called Dionne and was advised to take the long view. But of course Phillipa couldn't do that. She insisted Alec immediately drive them to the campsite where the situation rapidly deteriorated. After twenty four hellish hours (and one single night in Florence's shocking excuse for a home) they failed to understand why, with no word of warning, their son had abandoned his studies to live three hundred miles away, and all the while Kathleen's spectre-like figure had floated in the background. Driving back to Eastgate Road without Gabriel was by far, the worst day of her life.

The monster truck's headlights flashed in the rear view mirror, the effect of which was like that of an ice water bath. Phillipa spun the wheel into the inside lane whilst manically waving an apology to the furious driver. When the adrenalin surge calmed, she resolved to focus on the road. Florence's message said she'd be at the cottage, *with tea and tales at the ready*. Thank goodness Phillipa could rely on her sister for an easy ride, especially after the unexpected argument with Alec. Her father's refusal to attend his party wasn't in the least surprising – it was yet another in a long line of predictable actions from her unfathomable relations. But when she brushed off Alec's disappointment, he had turned on her. *You might not give a toss about your family, Pip, but if you don't pull yourself together, they'll cut you off forever.*

Phillipa was marooned. Her mother had been dead for eight years, and still it was impossible to reconcile herself to Gabriel's independence, and her father's love life. Neville and Lavender Hobbes' long and happy marriage was literally a 'death do us part' contract. To see him with Kathleen Dalgety was more than she could bear. At the previous year's event, her father had warned her not to make him choose. If she couldn't wish him well, or be civil to his partner, it was best they didn't see each other. In desperation, Phillipa had resorted to scrutinising What's App for crumbs of their lives. Gabriel's posts were few and far between. It was possible he didn't want his mother to know he was having a whale of a time and so kept his postings brief. Her father had no such sensitivity. Neville Hobbes' tourist booklets, the latest featuring the recently excavated iron age *broch*, and a history of the Lewis Chessmen, were regularly published by the APC and were selling well in the campsite shop, as were Kath's chick-pea patties.

There was nothing Phillipa wanted more than to be involved with her father's projects, but she was poleaxed by jealousy. Jason and Florence had accepted his revised relationship status easily enough, but this had only compounded her sense of isolation. Exchanging one-liners with Gabriel was demoralising, so Phillipa gave it up, and yet she was painfully aware that the longer he remained under the influence of Rae and Levon, the weaker their bond seemed to be.

A sudden and pressing need for the loo temporarily suspended Phillipa's mental anguish. She pulled off at the services, and hot-footed it inside. This recent habit was bloody annoying, especially as it didn't seem to relate to the quantity or type of liquid she consumed. Alec's nocturnal bathroom visits exacerbated her insomnia, which in turn increased her irritability. Maybe she'd talk to Florence. Not so long ago, her sister had mourned the loss of her menstrual cycle – it was the end of an era, she had said. Phillipa knew of a number of cultures in which the community honoured an event of this significance, but no such ritual existed in the west, although science had attributed an apt name for it: *climacteric*. It was exactly that – a turning point. How did western women accept the end of fertility and the potential decline in sexual desire without feeling bewildered? What was that if not bloody well climacteric.

Before setting off again, Phillipa checked her phone. The email from Pentacle Film had arrived – at last!

Dr Darby, we're so sorry for the delay. You'll find everything we agreed in the attached contract, and more besides. We are thrilled to have you onboard. If you decide to progress your secret project (which, btw, is still our secret), don't forget your promise. Best, Caleb

Relief swept over her. The consultancy contract carried the equivalent of a year's academic salary for the first series of *From the Embers* and was now confirmed. Independent film director Vanda Coltrane and producer Caleb Hegarty's courtship of her was a career high point. Vanda had studied Phillipa's texts whilst at college, and more recently had watched a number of medieval history documentaries on the subject of Celtic women that featured Dr Darby, whose observations matched her own. In between meetings at Pinewood Studios and scouting for prospective sites, the director had contacted her. Pentacle Film had earned a seismic reputation in the burgeoning fantasy film genre with their intelligent thematic vision combining myth with realism. Notwithstanding the violence of certain historical periods, Vanda was intent on making film without resorting to notoriety and shock-value. Phillipa had agreed to work with her for these reasons.

Whether she had drunk too much during that seminal evening, or had been flattered by the duo's unconcealed respect, it was impossible to recall what had prompted her confession. Even Alec was unaware of *Shadow Kin*, and she had been tinkering with the trilogy for decades.

Vanda was fascinated by Phillipa's female dominated epic fantasy whose central plotline was built around the clandestine separation of birth twins from the queen, one of whom, many years later, falls in love with the queen's beloved knight, with devastating consequences. Whilst being quizzed on character profiles, the pre-Plantagenet historical period and heraldic blood lines, Phillipa was suddenly aware of divulging the details of her precious project. When she attempted to change the subject, the canny filmmakers knew they had stumbled upon a sensation in the making.

Dr Darby, please be assured that Caleb and I aren't in the business of appropriating other folks' works of art for a quick buck. When you've completed that fabulous trilogy, we hope you'll consider collaborating with us on a screenplay.

Phillipa shivered at the memory. Caleb had given her the warmest hug and had kissed her on both cheeks before waving goodbye from the back of the taxi. His distinctive fragrance lingered for the rest of that night. Had she imagined a flicker of attraction between them? But even if he had made a pass, what would she have done? As unfashionable as it was, Phillipa was proud to uphold the sanctity of her marriage vows, despite her hormones having another agenda. Still, whether fantasy or reality, it was immensely pleasing to feel the rush of passion and more importantly, that it hadn't abandoned her altogether.

She set off, feeling brighter. This trip *had* to signify better times. In their last conversation, Dionne had reminded her that Gabriel and Neville were well and happy, and after all, no situation was irreparable, and she wasn't alone in her suffering. Florence must have felt guilty at having the pleasure of her nephew close by while his mother was left out in the cold. Maybe that was why Flo hadn't cancelled the Kinsley cottage, although there was every reason to do so. Until then, Phillipa hadn't considered her sister's feelings. As she recalled her family's pitiful looks when Alec had dragged her away from the venue after her rant, was it any wonder they chose to stay away this year. Everyone except for Florence, who was prepared to forgive her.

Phillipa was determined to ask Flo how *she* was. Yes, this trip to Kinsley would be a turning point, a springboard into a new beginning, and might even become the Darby's new home.

13
Unmasked

The Sexton Public House was the oldest hostelry in the area. For those who prioritised beer quality over stylish interior design, it was a must. Theo strode along the path towards the listed Tudor building. He was rarely late, but an unexpected turn of events had taken precedent. Upon his return from Leominster, Theo immediately began an online search for Ellis Eckley, and was directed to the Artless Press Collective website. Despite the biographical paucity, the site afforded a fascinating peek into Bookbinders' latest guest. Nine novels, and a collection of short stories had been published over the previous decade:

Greenaway Girls

Our Sunday Best

The Allium Graveyard: A Collection of Short Stories

Empty Silhouette

The Ghost Pond

Somebody Fine

Come Shine and Rain

Autumn, Mellow and Mild

Parting Shot

Marcy McBride

These were available in French, Spanish, Italian, Danish, and Japanese, and for sale through the website only, as were audio and e-book. In addition were a series of *Betsy Pugh* children's books, created by the Artless Press Collective, a selection of artwork made by Rae, and a free-to-download *Guide to Self-Publishing*. After tracing the company's back story through the blog pages, Theo noticed that the café had closed, so he crept over in search of an Ellis Eckley novel. He was in luck. Unfortunately, *Marcy McBride* had to be returned before ten o'clock on Thursday morning. Unlike Sheelagh, Theo preferred to savour his reading material, but he was confident of finishing the relatively slender novel before the deadline. Aside from whisking Tulip for her walks, everything else was postponed, and by the time Theo reached the last chapter, dusk was falling, and he was overdue at the pub.

It was with his thoughts somersaulting that Theo landed in The Sexton's congenial atmosphere where Florence and a flame-haired woman who he assumed to be her sister were encircled by a band of lively locals. Hughie bounded over, holding his pool cue like a trusted lance.

'Evenin' Theo. We just about gave you up.'

'My apologies, Hughie. I was unexpectedly entangled.'

'This is Flo's sister, Dr Phillipa Darby.'

Theo reached across the table to shake the long-fingered hand before turning to Florence, whose impenetrable expression threw him. Did she know what he'd been doing? He pulled himself together. 'Kerry has fed you well?'

'A fine innkeeper who keeps a fine wine. Nice to meet you, Theo. Bookbinders is delightful. Full of fascinating nooks and crannies.'

Florence edged her way around the table. 'I'll get a round of drinks in before rolling up my sleeves.'

'Hey, Theo, what d'you make of this? Flo's challenged me to a joust.' He grinned at his opponent. 'Let me get these, Flo. A pint of Whirly Bird for you, Theo, and for the doctor?'

'Funny *and* gallant,' said Phillipa, feeling very much at home in present company. 'Another glass of Malbec, please, Hughie. Oh, a word of warning – my sister may be slight of stature, but she'll topple you from your steed long before last orders.'

Hughie and Florence made their way through the banter to the bar while the merry band disbanded in order to resume their darts game. Theo sat beside Phillipa. If he wasn't mistaken she was 'in her cups' but hadn't yet passed the point of no return. If she had anything like Sheelagh's capabilities, at eight-thirty there was a way to go yet. 'I'm glad you've settled in. There are a number of villagers who can be of help with your research.'

'I've already had the pleasure of meeting Sean Nesbitt. I missed the turning for the cottage and popped into the village stores for directions. It was quite a welcome. We've arranged to meet at St. Mark's Church tomorrow.'

'That's impressive.'

'Ingrained work ethic, Theo. Will you excuse me for a moment. Nose needs a powder.'

Her smile instantly softened her sharp green eyes. Now he recognised the family resemblance. Often it wasn't a person's physical characteristics so much as their mannerisms that gave the game away, not that he was in any way an expert in these matters. Theo's interest lay in the interior life, the hidden aspects of a person's character, although he firmly believed that the majority of humans were kind-hearted and ought not to be written off as quickly as they often were.

Kerry arrived with a brie and cranberry baguette, a bottle of red wine, and a pint of ale. Hughie was a good lad, the best in fact, and appeared to be getting along famously with Florence over at the pool table. Hers was the same laugh he had heard whilst outside Nan's Place, and was confirmation that Ellis Eckley was none other than Florence Hobbes. To Theo's satisfaction, the first part of the mystery was solved.

Just as he was about to take a second bite of the delicious warm bread Phillipa re-appeared. His nose twitched at the freshly applied fragrance, but it wasn't in the least unpleasant. With lady luck smiling and a reputation for a listening ear, here was a marvellous opportunity to delve into the mystery of Ellis Eckley, provided Dr Darby was willing to divulge. 'Tell me, Phillipa, have you excavated any one-legged knights yet, or are you here simply to liberate your sister?'

'Ha! So, you're a quester.'

'I'm re-reading Malory, so that must be yes.'

'Cornflakes and courtly love were my staple teenage diet, and you may already know where that has led me. My brother Jason and I were the bookish ones. He's currently on a mission in Antarctica, attempting to discover how long we've got before the planet is subsumed by water. Florence is the youngest, and something of a conundrum: allergic to exams, authority, and institutions.'

'A noble set of siblings.'

'One way or another, we Hobbes are still answering the call.'

'Your parents must have been influential.'

'Dad was a librarian. What we lacked in coins, he made up for in books. Whenever a library closed, he'd bring them home by the box load. Neville Hobbes was an inspiration to a number of potential delinquents, including Florence. My mother sold flowers, made our clothes, and kept the home fires burning.'

Theo topped up her glass, aware of his motives, but strangely thrilled by his underhandedness. 'Is your career still as stimulating?'

'It was, until recently. Academia isn't immune to market and societal pressures, so I took the redundancy package while it was available. Now, my work is mostly consultancy. And you, Theo, what's your story?'

'Nowhere near as exciting, I'm afraid. Youngest son of a failed publisher, father of a beautiful daughter, never been much further than Frankfurt.'

Phillipa sat up. 'Would I know the publishing house?'

'Coppersmith Press.'

'Medieval literature – but that's where I source my texts from! Well, how about that for a coincidence.'

'Yes,' he said, and moved swiftly on. 'Have you travelled much?'

'Mostly around the British Isles, exhuming Celtic women's cultural contributions. Florence did my share of travelling.'

'How so?'

'She was sixteen and rudderless, so Dad suggested she stay with his sister. In the nineteen seventies, Aunt Maxine went to Spain to teach EFL and never came back.' Phillipa paused. 'Are you sure you want to hear the family folklore, Theo?'

'If you're willing to share it.'

'Dad thought that Maxine's influence might ignite Flo's interest in teaching as a career. What happened instead, was that she and Javier, Maxine's stepson, took off across Europe. I can count on one hand the amount of times I saw her over that period.'

'How did they finance it?'

'Teaching kids chat up lines and how to buy booze, I expect.'

Phillipa's mind whirled back to the events leading up to her sister's surprise exit from Eastgate Road. Florence was unassumingly bright at school, but as a teenager, began to invent all manner of symptoms and illnesses in order to stay at home with their mother. They were as thick as thieves. Not only was Florence encouraged to help out on the flower stall, but she also hung out at the library with their father, who was incapable of putting his foot down. His wits-end Spanish solution set off a chain reaction that no one predicted. Florence agreed to go to Blanes for one year. She returned five years later, unrecognisable and pregnant. Their mother was ecstatic – she had a daughter *and* a granddaughter to cherish. Even when Marcus Rafferty, the nicest guy on the planet came on the scene, Florence had remained at The Barbers, with their parents, rather than moving into his two up, two down in nearby Islington.

Feeling a raft of ancient frustrations rear up, Phillipa quaffed her wine and allowed Theo to refill her glass.

She'd drunk too much, but the attention from this perfectly charming man was a welcome distraction. This had to be her last, though, or Hughie would have to carry her to Bookbinders over his rather large shoulder. 'Do you miss publishing, Theo?'

'No, is the short answer. I'm much more content tending roses and attending parish council meetings – well, most of them. I was wondering about the Kinsley family connection.'

'Our mother's ancestors lived in this area, so I'm here to find out more, in addition to supporting Florence with her latest book launch … oops, not meant to mention that, although why it's still cloak and dagger is beyond me.'

Theo's hunch was right. There was no holding Dr Darby back once she had started to talk. 'I guess we all have our secrets, Phillipa.'

'But only if they're worth the effort of keeping, Theo. Florence will continue with the charade, although I must admit to having a hand in it,' she said, with some pride. 'When Rae came along, my sister needed a steady job, and to her credit, she kept the office job going for years, even though it shrivelled her spirit. I encouraged her to try writing. Florence has a gift for storytelling, you see. Anyway, some months later, she came up with *Greenaway Girls*.'

'Her first novel?'

'Yes, by Ellis Eckley, her *nom de plume*. It could have been a great story, but Florence wanted to know what was wrong with a good story. Typically, she wouldn't let me edit it. Said she didn't want it to be 'laundered' – much better to learn as she went along, or so she insisted. Being tied by a contract was an anathema to her.' Philippa threw up her hands. 'So, we put it out in local shops and libraries and arranged local press coverage, and it started to sell. My husband, Alec, was in his element. He loved the fact that his sister-in-law was prepared to do this on her own.'

'Ah, another family rebel.'

'Pseudo rebel. Alec is a classic example of Hardy's *Jude The Obscure:* contemptuous of institutions but super-proud of mine and Jason's academic credentials; critical of capitalism but happy to live in a gentrified house worth in excess of a million quid. Florence is the ultimate working-class hero. She owns nothing and makes a living without needing or wanting to conform. Alec has sold hundreds of her novels to his customers who are, in all likelihood, pinned in the back of his taxi cab by his blarney.'

'But it was you, Phillipa, who lit the touchpaper.'

Heat flooded Phillipa's face. She finished her wine, feeling warm and tingly, and all the while the room moved in and out of focus. It was slightly annoying that the conversation had revolved around her sister, but Theo had nailed it – she *had* lit the touchpaper, even though everyone else seemed to have conveniently forgotten that.

'Why the pseudonym?'

'Florence is really quite a private soul. That's why she wears the disguise. Oh, that was also my idea, the androgynous intellectual clothes, the specs. To this day, no one knows who Ellis Eckley is. You've never read her novels, have you?'

'No,' he lied, 'although there are copies of *Marcy McBride* in the café for book club use, despite the objections.'

'Why would anyone object ... oh, here comes Flo. Mum's the word.'

*

Theo let Tulip into the garden and stood at the door. What an incredible evening! He hadn't felt this animated in a long while. The Hobbes were a fascinating family. Jason Hobbes had featured on Radio 4's *Science Speaks*, and Dr Phillipa Darby was often on the airwaves in one guise or another. As for Florence Hobbes / Ellis Eckley, there was so much more he wanted to uncover, but first he had to finish *Marcy McBride* before returning the book to the café. Come tomorrow night, he'd witness, first-hand, 'Ellis Eckley and Friends' in action at the Assembly Rooms and could hardly wait.

Theo pulled the tickets from his wallet. Would Erica accompany him? As things stood, she was unaware of the reason behind Florence's visit, and her company would be nice. Sheelagh was the last person he'd invite. She might be curious to know about Phillipa, but Florence? In addition to career novelists, there were thousands of public eye people whose agents scrambled to get their clients' efforts under the public's nose, so what hope was there for the Ellis Eckleys of this world? This was entrepreneurialism at its best, and Sheelagh of all people ought to applaud the endeavour.

A single rain drop splattered on Theo's cheek. He waited for Tulip to amble in before locking the door. Then he carried a glass of water upstairs, ready to finish *Marcy McBride*. With Sheelagh away until Saturday, he had the freedom to go to Ludlow without being quizzed, the thought of which was immensely thrilling.

14
A frenetic calm before a super storm?

Phillipa lay prostrate on the bed, massaging her temples. 'Ooh, I've overdone the Malbec again.'

'You looked quite cosy, *tête-à-tête*-ing with Theo.'

'It's not often I'm paid that kind of attention, Florence.'

'Excluding your adoring husband, you mean.' She pulled the duvet over her sister. 'So, what were you and Theo talking about?'

'Family, history, your escapades … I think I mentioned *Greenaway Girls*.' She groaned. 'I might have blown your cover.'

'Oh, well, I'd better scarper before the press turn up.'

'Sorry, Flo.'

'Don't be. You're much more likely to be recognised than me. All this hush-hush malarkey is getting a bit stale. And besides, my knitted tank tops are straining under these inflated boobs.'

'At least you're filling out in the right places, whereas my weight has gathered around middle earth.'

'And Alec simply *lurves* to clamber all over it.'

'Not with those knees,' giggled Phillipa. 'I wish he'd have the bloody operation, but he loves to play the martyr. We can afford to pay for it, and free up a space for an NHS patient, but oh, no.'

'Maybe Alec's considering it.'

'A bit of 'how's your father' with Theo Coppersmith is worth considering.'

Florence hid her surprise. 'Mum would be pleased to hear you use her old expressions.'

'That's what happens when I'm with you, Flo. Ain't that the truth of it, me darlin'.'

Back and forth they batted their mother's favourite sayings, and when Phillipa threw off the duvet to attempt her version of *The Lambeth Walk* before collapsing in hysterics, Florence couldn't help but laugh. Her sister had never acted like this before. It was funny, *and* disturbing – a frenetic calm before the super storm? She wished her merry sister goodnight and turned out the light.

*

By the time Phillipa surfaced the following morning, Florence had walked Cavell, bought fresh croissants, prepared her outfit and the thank-you gifts, for the evening ahead. She never needed a script or notes with a memory such as hers, but as much as she tried to avoid thinking about the Assembly Rooms, the prospect of facing three hundred expectant people made her heart sink. This was not a good sign. Ebony Farrell and Henbane may have been revved up, but it was the lack of anticipation that concerned Florence. She wanted it to be over, to fast forward to her last morning in Kinsley because at that point, she would have made some decisions before returning to Ardraig.

At the sound of footsteps, Florence switched on the kettle. An apparition – sienna/white-streaked hair, emerald silk dressing gown and matching slippers – plonked itself at the kitchen table.

'Strong and black, please. What time is it?'

'And a very good morning to you, Dr Darby. It's half past nine.'

'I'm supposed to meet Sean at ten,' she grumbled, before scoffing a warm croissant. 'How do you feel about tonight?'

'I'm trying not to think about it, Pip. I'd much rather know about your research. Are you expecting to turn up a lord of the manor?'

Phillipa examined her sister's guileless face. 'To tell you the truth, Flo, I met with the agents. They've arranged another viewing.'

'What sort of viewing … a house, you mean?' Florence put the cafetiere on the table and sat down. 'Are you thinking of moving to Kinsley?'

'I meant to tell you, but with this Pentacle thing, and …'

'That's great! You'll fit in well here, especially if last night was anything to go by.'

'They were a good crowd. Alec wouldn't feel out of place in a pub like The Sexton. He says he's ready to leave Eastgate Road, but he's so used to humouring me, I can't tell what he really wants. Do you think it's a good idea?'

'Well, it's hardly a new idea. When Mum died, you were all set to decamp.'

'And look how that turned out.' Phillipa grabbed her sister's hand. 'Sorry, I didn't mean that. '

'It's okay, Pip. We should talk, but not today. I've got to keep it together. For what it's worth, Kinsley's a nice place. You could do a lot worse.' Florence finished her coffee.

'I've some things to do before we leave for Ludlow. There's plenty to eat in the fridge if you can manage it.' She put her hand on Phillipa's shoulder. 'Thanks for being here. Couldn't have done it without you, Doc.'

Phillipa hugged her little sister and watched her walk down the path, with the dog trotting behind. Florence had given her approval. Kinsley *was* a lovely village. It ticked all the boxes, and while the first viewing wasn't what she was looking for, the right house was there, waiting for them. In addition to the likes of Theo Coppersmith and Hughie Briggs, there was the literary festival, the historical society, and an enthusiastic gardening group, not to mention the myriad medieval towns and churches within touching distance. How could she possibly be bored?

With an apology message winging its way to Sean Nesbitt, Phillipa prepared for a shower. She thought about The Sexton, and her long chat with Theo. It would be wonderful to see him again, but the opportunity was unlikely to arise during so short a stay. When the Ludlow event was over, she *had* to focus on the family tree. Somehow it felt important, that she couldn't make a decision without knowing what was in store. There was also another property to look at, and the trip to Hereford Cathedral, although the Mappa Mundi had waited aeons for her, so another few months wouldn't hurt.

With the last of the soap rinsed, Phillipa turned the dial to 'cold' for twenty seconds before stepping out to dry off. She wrapped a towel around her dripping hair before darting across the landing into Florence's bedroom to fetch the hairdryer. Her Assembly Rooms outfit was carefully laid out across the bed: olive green palazzo pants, a short-sleeved ivory blouse, and on the rug, a pair of dark brown polished Oxford lace ups. Beside the pillow was a round-neck slipover, so soft it had to be cashmere. As Florence had pointed out earlier, it was necessary to update her collection from time to time, and there was no denying her impeccable taste. Phillipa lifted the slipover out of the tissue paper and ran her hand over the lilac and frosted pink pattern. A note, in place of a label, was a tucked inside: *Good luck, lassie*.

Kathleen Dalgety! Rae had worn something similar in Norfolk, and without being asked, had delighted in informing her aunt of the inspiration behind it. Pulverised by an unstoppable fury, Phillipa sank to her knees and sobbed.

15

Bright morning stars are rising
Day is a breaking in my soul
Oh, where are our dear fathers
They are down in the valley a-praying
Day is a breaking in my soul
Oh, where are our dear mothers
They are gone to heaven a-shouting
Day is a breaking in my soul

(Bright Morning Star abridged version
From the Archive of American Folk Song)

'Thank you *sooo* much for inviting me, Theo. Have I overdone it with my glad rags?'

Theo stepped out of the front gate. Erica's halter neck dress swished like cuttlefish fins as she did a twirl. 'Carnelian is most definitely your colour, but I'm not sure how you'll get on in those heels.'

Erica lifted a bag. 'Never fear, flip flops are here.' They laughed. 'You're looking good, Theo. Don't see you dressing down often.'

Theo blushed at the tongue-in-cheek compliment. The khaki jacket, a present from Viola, had endured one outing to date, while the touch of hair gel, (courtesy of her supplies) felt odd, but he liked the effect. He was grateful Sheelagh wasn't here to comment on the five o'clock shadow. Thinking of ways to disguise himself had taken the best part of the morning, but with the smooth sounds of *Flesh and Blood* releasing his inner Bryan Ferry, it was tremendous fun.

The feel-good factor pouring from *Marcy McBride's* pages had elevated Theo's mood. He found himself cheering Marcy as she settled into her new life, full of potential. Every character's arc was satisfactorily completed and even the deuteragonist's shocking exit was justified in the overall scheme. Theo was struck by the parallels between the young Marcy and Sheelagh's early life, and the manner in which Eckley had burrowed under the Jurassic coastline. Reading this had released a clutch of welcome memories of his first holiday romance and rekindled an urge to return.

'Hughie said I must buy you a pint, like I need reminding. How many can we guzzle with this?' Erica flashed a fifty pound note.

'Methinks serious inroads will be made into the Ludlow Brewery's cellar.'

'Ha! Need a pee. D'you mind?'

Erica clacked along the cracked terracotta path and into the cloakroom, humming a tune as she went. Theo smiled. He might had given her tickets to a Covent Garden opera such was her reaction, but it pleased him enormously. There was no valid reason *not* to invite her: she hadn't met Phillipa Darby; neither did she know about Florence's disguise, so why not enjoy an evening with a favourite author. Theo was confident of keeping out of sight. He mentioned having to return home directly, but that was fine with Erica.

As he waited in the glorious evening, a flash of pale apricot caught his eye. Theo ran his thumb gently over the rose bud's soft petals. It was reassuring to see Eustacia Vye reincarnate for another season. Margery had presented him with the rose bush when the radiotherapy sessions ended. It was to aide his recovery, she had said, with a shy smile. If the flowers were as fragrant and bountiful as the previous year's blooms, Theo had her to thank for it. Suddenly he thought of Florence, at The Assembly Rooms. Was she nervous or excited at what lie ahead? Contemplating her state of mind triggered a protectiveness in him, an urge to reassure her that it would be fine, just as he'd encouraged Viola before her numerous school plays and examinations.

'Okay, driver, let's rock and roll.'

Theo followed Erica's swish out of the gate and opened the passenger door to a delighted squeal.

'Hughie had better pull his socks up, or I might just take off with The Kinsley Crackerjack.'

*

The car alarm beeped and flashed. Under a canopy of glinting stars, Theo paused by the garden gate. Without fear of exaggeration, there was no question that the man who left Kinsley four hours before was not the same man to return. Erica was still on a high when she clambered out of the car just a few minutes before – a little worse for wear perhaps, but not too unsteady in her flip flops – and had thanked him for *the most wonderful night out, ever*. Theo unlocked the back door to find Tulip, as was her custom, waiting and wagging. After a fuss and a fresh bowl of water, he let her into the garden before making a camomile tea, which he took into the conservatory, in readiness to relive every memorable moment.

No sooner had they walked into the Assembly Rooms lobby when Erica had spotted a friend and was swallowed up by the crowd. And there was a crowd – the bar area throbbed, while exuberant fans queued for signed copies of Ellis Eckley's novels, jacket cover posters, and cards. Alongside a selection of Henbane CDs were the latest poetry collection by Ebony Farrell. Just as Theo paid for one of each, Erica squeezed through the throng clutching a pint of Ludlow Gold, which she thrust into his hands before taking off again, to spend the rest of Hughie's treat.

The first heart-stopping moment came when his raffle ticket number was called. Mercifully, it had been drawn before the show started, and neither Phillipa nor Florence were anywhere to be seen. Theo re-donated the *Marcy McBride* hardback to his generous benefactor, Clive Proctor, via the event organiser, Joanne Quinlan, who knew the stone mason personally, and had promised to send it on. Before Theo could finish his pint, he was swept along with the crowd to their seats.

In the next moment the lights dimmed, and without announcement or introduction, a fusion of spine tingling *a cappella* voices soared into the auditorium. It was a rendition of *Bright Morning Star*. Having just read the novel, the significance of the moment seized him, filling Theo's eyes at the memory of his mother's painful cry when his father's coffin was lowered into the cold, damp ground. When the song faded, Ellis Eckley stepped out of the darkness, and from under a spotlight she narrated a segment of the story against the single drone note of a shruti box. After the tumult of applause died down, Ebony Farrell drifted onto the stage to finish the opening sequence with a poem. To give the crowd time to catch their breath, the performers gathered together to share with Ellis their inspirational stories in a manner he'd never seen before. It was as if the audience were integral to this intimate circle as questions, comments, and compliments funnelled in a sort of feedback loop.

And then, the finale. Henbane performed a montage of mesmerising melodies, the last of which was a foot-stomper that pulled three hundred people to their feet, and with some even dancing in the aisles! To wrap up, Ellis thanked her generous readers for supporting the Artless Press Collective, and when someone shouted 'don't get famous, will you, Ellis', a roar rang out. But the biggest cheer came when she announced the long-awaited sequel to *Greenaway Girls*.

For ninety glorious minutes, Theo was immersed in an emotional riot. It wasn't until the rousing last song ended that he found himself hollering for more. As he was carried along to the lobby like driftwood on white water, there was a tap on his shoulder. It was Phillipa Darby, feverish and incoherent. Her attempt at a hug was cut short when she was led away to meet someone or other, but Theo was too discombobulated to be concerned about the outcome of their encounter. He was eager to absorb the rippling conversations from the thrill-seekers as they spilled out into the balmy Ludlow night.

Arm-in-arm, he and Erica wandered across the atmospheric medieval square towards the car park where overhead, glittering stars had turned out in tribute. Erica had fizzed throughout the homeward journey. She had shown him her purchases and said how pleased Hughie would be that she hadn't spent all his money. They agreed that it had been a unique evening and were extremely fortunate to have been gifted the tickets. Of the innumerable book launches, festivals and events Theo had attended, none had such a celebratory atmosphere. This was an extraordinary reunion. An unforgettable night.

And now he lay in bed listening to the river's harmonic tones underscoring St. Mark's worshipful chimes: two, three, four. If a clarion call were needed, the dawn chorus was proclamation enough. He'd been sleepwalking through his life, somnolent until tonight, and was now shocked into consciousness. Would she be on the meadow tomorrow? Should he confess? Would Phillipa have let on that he was at The Assembly Rooms? Florence was at Bookbinders for one more week. Theo was determined to know more of this amazing woman who shared her gifts and talents with a fortunate few, for, when Sheelagh returned, life would continue as before. But no, that was out of the question. In all likelihood, he was in the eye of a crisis – midlife, existential, spiritual – but whatever it was, the day had forever broken in his soul.

16
No news is bad news

Rae scuttled across the yard to the brewhouse, buttoning her cardigan over her pyjamas along the way. She had crept out of bed after desperately ticking off the minutes before calling her mother. This had to be done at the office, away from Levon, and Briar. For the first time since The Artless Press Collective began, Rae was anxious. At various times throughout the night and from under the duvet, she had watched the posts accumulate. By sun up, stacks of upbeat comments and reviews had flooded in. Too excited to wait, she tip-toed into Gabriel's room to find that he too was on tenterhooks, and as soon as he was dressed, they'd rendezvous at the office.

Once inside, Rae fired up the computer before filling the kettle for coffee. They would need it this morning. She wondered how long it would be before Gabriel asked about his mother: had she made a scene, or did she keep it together this time? Rae had endured many 'moments' with her aunt and was therefore no stranger to her idiosyncrasies. When Phillipa Darby was on your side, there was no better supporter, no one more committed to your cause, but if you didn't pull your weight or take on her ideas, her withdrawal was unmerciful. For the most part, Rae kept a healthy distance. She'd taken her mother's lead by choosing not to react to the silences and outbursts, although at the previous year's event in Norfolk, she'd come unnerving close to losing it.

Her mother was a saint by comparison. In Rae's view, she had no earthly reason to feel guilty that Gabriel had come to Ardraig. At nineteen, he was perfectly able to decide his future, and if he chose to leave college to live and work with his family, what was the big deal? Wasn't he following the family tradition? Hadn't Phillipa wanted to drag them all to Herefordshire when Nanny Lally died? All of this could be summed up by her aunt's loss of control. Phillipa had to stand by while her loved ones made their own way without her.

It was half past seven. Rae called the number.

'Morning, Rae. You took your time.'

Relief poured over her. 'How are you, Mum?'

'Cavell and I have had a nice walk over the meadow, and now we're having breakfast.'

'Mum.'

'Sorry. The evening went well. Have you read the comments?'

'Sounds as if you had a blast. I want to hear every detail.'

For the following fifteen minutes, Rae listened to her mother's unembellished version of the evening. There were no hitches, set-backs, or fluffs – in fact, no one dropped the ball. Every piece of artwork had sold, as had most of the books. Ebony Farrell and Henbane were inundated at the after-show party and expressed their gratitude for the APC (Ebony announced that Rae and

Flo were the *ultimate celestial mother-and-daughter-team)*. There were multiple requests for a return visit, but as predicted, her mother had remained non-committal. Then, after reading a selection of the reviews, Rae announced that the pre-order list for *Greenaway Women* was already on the rise, and in anticipation of this happening, she had designed a second edition cover while Ullaprint prepared for a run on the books. With nothing else forthcoming from her mother, and the conversation about to end, she had to ask the question, for Gabriel's sake. 'So, how's Aunt Phillipa?'

'Pip's having a great time. She's made a friend or two, which will be useful when she and Alec relocate here. The first viewing wasn't suitable but there's another one scheduled.'

'Oh! So they're actually moving to Kinsley. Does Gabriel know?'

'I've no idea, Rae. Pip only told me yesterday. She's also signed a consulting contract with a film company.'

'Well, we've all been waiting for her to move on, so I guess that's good news. Pity she hasn't told her son what she's up to.'

'Is Gabriel okay? We've messaged each other, but there was nothing out of the ordinary.'

'He's just like you, Mum, an expert at disguise. Shall I tell him that his parents are on the move?'

'I'll leave that in your capable hands, Rae. Right now, I'm too tired to deal with anything other than getting home in one piece. Gabriel has always trusted you. I know you'll do what's right.'

Rae's throat tightened. This wasn't the time for tears. 'Thanks, Mum. Anyway, let's not get maudlin and spoil your triumphant night. You've earned this next week off. Have a good rest, soak up the greenery, and book yourself a session at the holistic centre. Oh, and don't forget to call me when it all calms down.'

Just as Rae put down her phone, Gabriel rushed in.

'Coffee's in the pot.'

'Thanks, Rae. Sorry I've been so long. Briar didn't want her daddy to make breakfast, and then she asked for another slice of toast with her dippy egg, but without the crusts. So, how's the superstar this morning?'

'I'm not exactly sure. It went well, and the guests were terrific, but that's typical Florence Hobbes for you.'

'Did she say anything about the posts?'

Rae shook her head.

'I guess we'll have to wait until Flo gets home.' Gabriel put two mugs on the table. 'Erm, I don't s'pose she mentioned my mum?'

'Sit down a minute, Gabriel.' Rae saw his alarm. 'I promise there's nothing wrong. Phillipa didn't blow a fuse. Apparently she's having a fine old time, *and* she's buddied up.'

'That's a first. Apart from Dionne, Mum hasn't had much luck at keeping a friendship going. She must like it in Kinsley.'

'Your mum's been looking at houses. It seems that she and Uncle Alec are actually leaving Eastgate Road.'

Gabriel walked over to the window, his mind swirling. Something was wrong. There was no way his parents would leave Eastgate Road: not now, not ever. His dad wouldn't last five minutes away from his cronies, his football, and the streets of London. What on earth would he do in a

Herefordshire village, however beautiful it might be? This was yet another example of his mother's increasingly odd behaviour. Gabriel expected push back – she still hadn't got over his leaving London – but to have resigned her research and teaching posts after decades of hard graft had made no sense.

As for the contract to make a generic fantasy series, the type of which she had derided, was weirder still. His dad, unsurprisingly, had been chuffed with Pentacle Film's interest – *your mum has finally found something to get excited about* – but then again, when had he ever challenged her decisions? His mother must have reached the end of the line, just like she had when Nanny Lally died. There was nothing Dr Phillipa Darby wouldn't do to stop herself from going under.

'Gabriel. GABRIEL!'

Gabriel walked back to the desk. 'Sorry, Rae. I heard what you said, and no, I'm not surprised. It's positive, a fresh start. Let's scroll through the feedback. We've got a busy day ahead.' He gave his cousin a hug. 'Don't worry about me, Rae. It's all good'

It wasn't all good, but Rae mustered up a smile. With her fingers crossed behind her back, she prayed for her mother to come home soon.

17
A confession

When the call to her daughter ended, Florence felt in need of another burst of natural healing. She clipped on Cavell's lead for the second time that morning and headed for the old oak bench where shards of shimmering sunlight pierced the flowing water. As soon as he was unclipped, in went the dog, frolicking like a wolf reborn. Oh, to swap places with Cavell, with not a care in the world!

An image flashed up of Phillipa's long legs dangling from the top of a seesaw, having the best fun ever, while she was wedged on the bottom. Why wasn't she swimming in a pool of elation, riding the riptide of popularity, good will, admiration? She hadn't lied to Rae. The evening *was* a tremendous success for all concerned, and they'd raised three thousand pounds for the Friends of Giltspur Forest, but throughout Florence had felt dis-embodied, no longer Florence Hobbes, her authentic self, but had become forever trapped in the fantasy that was Ellis Eckley. She sighed. How ridiculous, and ungrateful. Ardraig and the APC more than met everyone's requirements. What other family unit enjoyed that level of freedom and creativity?

Feeling for her notebook, Florence pulled out instead

her phone. She really ought to delete Marcus from her contacts. His 'good luck' message was irritating. Obviously he'd been following her itinerary via the website. Although they no longer sent each other cards, she and Rae continued to receive birthday and Christmas text messages, but never from 'Marcus *and family*'. He couldn't bring himself to accept that they had moved on. Florence deleted the message. Maybe her low mood was the result of spending too much time on her own. Was it really three years since her last sexual partner? Living with her family brought many benefits, but a cuddle with someone who she wasn't genetically connected to would make a refreshing change. Exchanging phone for notebook, Florence scribbled down that last thought.

*

She was sitting on the fallen oak bench scribbling in her notebook, while Cavell pranced in the water. The scene was achingly lovely, like a watercolour, or an age-old ballad. Theo hesitated, his heart drumming under his shirt, and while he willed it to slow down Tulip lolloped over to play with her new chum. There was no choice but to step out of the shadows. 'Good morning, Florence. I hope I'm not disturbing you.'

Florence slid the notebook in her pocket. 'I've been listening to the water sing. It has a different pitch this morning.'

'The last substantial downpour is on its way through,' he said, and sat beside her. 'It often hurtles along at a formidable rate but today is …'

'Sedate.'

'Yes.'

'A sylvan symphony.' They laughed at her alliteration.

'Tulip and I have our own special seat.' Theo pointed to the opposite bank further upstream, to a zen-style bench which was positioned between two enormous lime trees.

'That's a fine lookout post. The scent must be heavenly.'

'Yes, and there's no melody quiet like it. In summer, the triad of bee buzz, lime flowers and river song is compensation for the toil.'

'You surprise me, Theo. I had the impression of a rural paradise.'

'Cleavers isn't the only demanding mistress in Kinsley.'

Florence tasted the hint of sour. 'Can you hear the river from inside the house?

'Yes, particularly from my bedroom. It's presence is reassuring.'

'Just like at Ardraig.'

She understands. 'I've often wondered why a curve is so pleasing.'

'It's supposed to signal health and fertility, Theo. My brother says that in addition to cleaning up our rivers, we need to re-wiggle them if we want to alleviate flooding and restore eco systems. Water doesn't naturally flow in a straight line. Talking of curves, I've been here for so long my bum's gone numb.' Florence stood and jigged about.

'Some years ago, I asked my brother why he had difficulty sustaining a long-term relationship. Jason said that his enduring love was called nature, and not everyone was happy to play second fiddle. It wasn't until I left London that I understood what he meant.'

'I was raised in rural Oxfordshire, with acres of space to get lost in. It took quite a while to adjust to London. Your brother must have possessed an acute sensitivity for an inner city child.'

'He was like Mum in that respect. They read Rachel Carson and Gilbert White together. Jason could name all those lovely wildflowers on Pignut Meadow, although I'm pleased to say that Ardraig has its own unique collection.' Florence called to Cavell. 'As reluctant as I am to leave this enchanting place, we're taking the long route to Bookbinders if you'd like to join us.'

The foursome set off towards the meadow. Theo felt a sudden urge to run wild, despite the awkwardness of his limbs, which had always felt as if they belonged to someone else. Physically, the only place he had ever felt at home was on a cricket green where his obligatory nickname was 'long arm'. Those days really were enchanting, and were forever fused in his synapses, even if the notion of a quintessential England was a literary fantasy. With two years elapsed and no cause to be concerned about his prostate, Theo was almost back to fitness, and eager to get back in the nets with Hughie and the lads.

'Where did you go?'

'Beg pardon?'

'You went off somewhere, Theo. Was it nice?'

'1978:Hepton Dray village cricket green.'

'First eleven, I'll bet. All-rounder?'

'Spin bowler. You know your cricket, Florence.' He slowed his pace. 'My apologies. I didn't mean to imply otherwise.'

'My nephew's keen to get something going in Ardraig. Gabriel's a wicket keeper – safe hands.'

'Phillipa must be proud'

'Dig deep enough and you'll find it.'

They walked on, and as was his custom, Theo hovered on the edge of silence. Florence appeared to be musing on some subject or other. She reminded him of a hand-held Xray machine, and it was impossible to hide anything from her. Had she spotted him at the Assembly Rooms? Should he own up? 'The forecast is kind for your last week. Erica and Hughie will be sorry to see you go.'

'When out on the road, you get used to leaving good people behind, but every now and then it's a wrench. If my sister makes Kinsley her home, I have an excuse to come back.'

'Do you need an excuse?'

'I guess not.'

Theo slowed his pace. 'Florence, I've a confession.'

'You're absolved.'

'You saw me!'

'Hard not to, with the Desperate Dan stubble,' she chuckled. 'Almost as effective as my disguise. What made you come along?'

'A chance encounter if you believe in that sort of thing. While you were inside Nan's Place meeting your readers, I was outside talking to a disappointed stone mason. He offered me his tickets. Erica and I had a marvellous night. Did you?'

Florence was thoughtful. It might be good to talk to Theo. He didn't know her, and in a week's time she'd be gone. What had she to lose? 'I'm still processing it. When Pip leaves on Sunday, I've decided to tell Erica the truth.'

'I'm glad to hear it, but you must know that it would

take more than a knitted pullover to alienate Erica Briggs. If you're amenable, may we discuss the evening?'

Florence smiled at his turn of phrase. It was as if he had stepped from the pages of an Evelyn Waugh novel. 'Sure.'

'Are all your events as enthusiastically received?'

'Yes. It's been a while since my last visit. Anticipation prompts all manner of emotions.'

'I agree, but having personally witnessed the evening, the response was justified. The song, *Bright Morning Star* – it was a magical rendition.'

'It's an Appalachian tune, Theo, over a hundred years old. Probably picked up by Cecil Sharp or Vaughan Williams. I can't listen to it without reliving the pain of losing my mum.'

'My sentiments exactly.' They walked on, each with their own thoughts and remembrances of times past. On approach to the meadow, Theo opened the gate. 'Are you familiar with John Clare?'

Florence rifled through her memory files, and there it was, under Poetry. '*Come we to the summer, to the summer we will come, For the woods are full of bluebells and the hedges full of bloom.*'

'*Summer.* A wonderful poem.'

'My brother gave me a book once. You'd get on well with Jason.'

'I believe I would. John Clare is a poet's poet. A prophet, in many ways, but a deeply troubled soul.'

'It goes with the territory, I guess. The written word is tremendously powerful. It's a pity we don't take more care with it.'

'Do you truly believe that Florence?'

'Yes, although responsibility isn't the same as motivation.'

'But I assumed you wrote because …'

'It was a love job?' She shook her head. 'John Steinbeck said he wrote best when he was under pressure – either from poverty, relationship breakdown, or death. When the motivation is gone, writing takes on a different meaning, but that's not to say I don't still enjoy it. As for responsibility, Ellis Eckley hasn't exactly set the world on fire for good, or for ill, so I guess I'm off the hook.'

They were within sight of Bookbinders. Theo wanted desperately to continue this conversation, particularly as anything remotely concerning the King Arthur was endlessly fascinating, but there were a mountain of things to organise before Sheelagh returned, and an invitation to issue. 'Have you plans for tomorrow evening?'

Florence felt her cheeks burn, or was it a hot flush? 'I don't think so unless Phillipa has rounded up the locals for a spot of wassailing.'

'I'm afraid Margery has divulged your sister's credentials to Sheelagh. You're both invited to dine at Cleavers.'

'Is this a summons, Theo?'

'Dungeon or dinner, Florence. The choice is yours.'

'For Phillipa's sake, I'll choose dinner. What time?'

'7.30 for 8 o'clock. Any dietary requirements?'

'Vegetarian for me. I'll bring a dish.'

'Viola is a vegan, so it's no bother.'

'We'll bring the wine, then. Anything in particular?'

'Sheelagh is partial to Saint Émilion. You'll find a bottle at the village store. Sean likes to keep certain customers satisfied.'

'She and Pip will get along famously.'

Theo couldn't disagree. Sheelagh had insisted *we must invite the sisters for dinner. I'd like to quiz Dr Darby before she leaves Kinsley.*

'May I bring Cavell? I might need to skedaddle, and a weary dog is a useful *get out of jail free* card.'

'By all means, Florence. An advanced warning: the conversation is likely to veer towards the polemical, so I shall seek shelter in the kitchen. You're welcome to join me.'

'I might hold you to that. On the subject of kitchens, would you like a cuppa?'

Theo checked his watch. 'Very much, but to dawdle any longer would be more than my life's worth.'

18
Bad taste

Florence walked through the back garden and into the utility room. She was pleased Theo had confessed, although it was Erica who had given the game away. Whilst passing through the Assembly Rooms lobby, she had heard her new friend's unmistakeable cackle. The duo weren't hard to spot in the sixth row from the front, but when she looked for them at the bar afterwards, she was disappointed (but not surprised) to find that they had left. Florence took out her notebook and in it scribbled 'John Clare'. It was the recommendations of others that often led her along roads less travelled. Artists such as Ebony Farrell and Henbane had expanded her creative world, and you never knew where any of it would lead.

There were noises from the kitchen. Phillipa was back from the viewing. At breakfast earlier that morning, she'd been on a high. Apparently a number of people, including Henbane's lead singer, had recognised her. And now there was an invitation to tickle Pip's taste buds. With less than forty eight hours to go before her departure, Florence was determined to send her sister off with a smile firmly in place.

'Nice walk, Flo?'

'Lovely. What was the house like?'

'Needs too much work. Alec would have a coronary. Tea?'

'Thanks. I met Theo at the river. We've been ordered to appear at Cleavers, tomorrow night.'

'For dinner? How marvellous!'

Florence waited for more, and then, 'Theo and Erica were at The Assembly Rooms.'

'Were they?'

'I'd appreciate it if you didn't mention it tomorrow night.'

Phillipa covered the teapot with the knitted cosy. She had no intention of mentioning the event, and neither would Theo. They each had their secrets. Florence may have been skilful at eliciting gossip, but regurgitating it was something else. Sean Nesbitt had no trouble on that score. The over-the-counter tattle was doled out *gratis*. Why hadn't Theo mentioned he was married to one of the most influential and controversial women in British publishing history? He must have known she'd find out. Sheelagh Spicer had been a significant influence, and now they were invited to dinner! 'Thank you for accepting, Flo. I know it isn't your thing.'

'Would I scupper your chance of meeting Theo again?'

'Morning Flo!'

Erica came clattering in and was carrying a canvas laundry bag. 'Oh, sorry for interrupting. I'm Erica Briggs. You must be Dr Darby. Hughie's not stopped talking about you. How do you like Kinsley?'

'Phillipa, please. Your village is adorable, Erica, as are its inhabitants. I've just made tea. Will you join us?'

'Never say no to a brew.' Erica dropped into a chair and made a fuss of Cavell while apologising for the non-appearance of Kiki. Then she looked at Florence, her face beaming. 'Flo, I've been busting to tell you about my night out with Theo. He invited me to see Ellis Eckley, of all people, at the Assembly Rooms!'

Florence and Phillipa exchanged a look. 'So that's why you're flushed, Erica. And here's me thinking it was from lugging the laundry bag across Pignut Meadow.'

'Last night's vibe would have turned even Margery Crisp's face crimson. I don't know where to start.'

Phillipa joined her at the table. 'We're in no hurry, Erica, so why not begin at the beginning.'

'Well, I flip-flopped my way to Cleavers as Theo offered to drive, but I slipped on my heels just before the gate, y'know, to make an entrance. His eyes popped at my frock, or maybe it was the tattoo, but you should have seen his smooth operator outfit. Anyway, when we got to Ludlow, the lobby was heaving with folk buying beer and merchandise. I managed to snaffle a box of cards, painted by Rae – that's the artist who designs the book covers and suchlike – and I bought Hughie a Henbane CD. I'm so glad I did as they were m-e-n-t-a-l,' Erica cackled.

'Theo wouldn't take any money for the ticket. They were given to him by someone who couldn't go, so he bought thirty pounds' worth of raffle tickets, and guess what! He won a prize and gave it to the man who gave him the tickets.'

'That was generous, Erica.'

'It's typical of Theo, Phillipa. Anyway, when the opening song – or was it a hymn? Whatever it was, it gave me the goosebumps. Well, anyway after that, Ellis read – no, she didn't read it as she said it off the cuff – she told the part of the story when Jake dies, and Marcy finds his poetry book. That was when Ebony Farrell, the real poet came on the stage. By the time Henbane played their last number, we were all on our feet, but by then I had ditched the heels for my flip flops, not that anyone would've cared.' Erica gulped her tea. 'Sorry, it's impossible to do it justice. Theo's weren't the only moist eyes in the auditorium. Now there's a man whose not afraid of showing his emotions.'

Phillipa refilled Erica's mug. 'How fascinating. I'll have to join his fan club when I move to Kinsley.'

'Ha! When I told Hughie about Theo's invite, he said that if I insisted on having a crush on someone, why wouldn't it be Theo Coppersmith?'

'Erica, we need your advice. Sheelagh Spicer has invited us to dine at Cleavers. What can we expect?'

'Being a doctor and all that, I should think Sheelagh will give you her full attention while Theo does the fetching and carrying. She's done a lot for Kinsley, and for Hughie and me, so I shouldn't criticize, but …'

'Erica, please don't think we would repeat anything you told us in confidence.'

'No, of course not, and you must speak as you find, Phillipa, but if my Hughie had prostate cancer, I wouldn't dream of sodding off to Australia, leaving strangers to nurse him.'

Florence felt sick. Her deceit was bad enough, but her sister's interrogation had an unpleasant edge to it. At the hair salon earlier that week, Birdy had painstakingly recounted 'Theo's abandonment' and had rattled off Sheelagh's misdemeanours as judge and jury, but unreliable narrators were Florence's speciality, and there was always another side to the story. Right now, though, she was desperate to change the subject. Phillipa was like a dog with a bone once she got started. 'Erica, thank you for bringing the clean laundry. I'll see you on Monday morning, for a walk.'

Erica pushed back her chair and stood. 'Don't you want me to mop the floors, Flo?'

'Why don't you go home and put your feet up? You must be worn out after last night's excitement.'

'That's really good of you. Those slingbacks have left me with blisters. Well then, Phillipa, it's been nice to meet you, and good luck with the house-hunting. If the property needs a makeover, Hughie Briggs is your man.'

Phillipa waited until Erica was out of earshot. 'Did you know Theo was treated for prostate cancer? I wonder if his equipment is in working order. Wouldn't that be a travesty?' She stretched her long arms above her head and yawned. 'Who said village life was uneventful? I can't wait to meet Sheelagh Spicer *in person*. She was *sooo* important to me when I was at college. And as for Ellis Eckley, your cover-up could run and run, Flo.'

Florence fought an instinct to either shout at or shake her sister. Instead, she put the cups in the sink and wiped the worktop. The floors could have done with a mop, but she didn't want Erica to see the rest of the cottage. Apart from making the occasional cup of tea, not only had Pip the expectation to be waited on, but her paraphernalia was everywhere. 'This isn't a game, Phillipa, although it might seem like it to you. I'm beginning to regret this whole bloody thing.'

'But this is what happens when you live your life behind a mask, Florence. Letting the world see you as you are takes courage, and I'm not sure you have that.'

'What d'you mean? I'm the one doing the flippin' legwork, writing the books, trawling the country, spending time away from home.'

'Ardraig's not your home. That shoddy static caravan isn't a home. You've never committed to anything, Flo. When the going gets tough, you're off again. That is your inherent weakness.'

Her sister had touched a nerve, even if it were only half true. But before she could leave Pip to stew in her own toxic juice, there was something that had to be said. 'You may be right about me, but when it comes to our children, I am always honest and upfront. By now, Rae will have told Gabriel about your house hunting project. We thought it best he hear such important news from family. Maybe you should take your own advice and face up to your weaknesses. It takes courage to ask for help, and I'm not sure you've got that.'

Phillipa watched her sister grab her bag and call the dog before taking off in the car. She couldn't recall a time when they had ever faced each other in such a way. Florence was often hard to read but was never touchy. Her behaviour that morning had been odd, to say the least. She had batted off a post-gig debrief using fatigue as an excuse. It must be the hormones. Hadn't Flo commented on her changing body shape? And as for telling Gabriel about the house move, Phillipa wasn't overly concerned. Trying to keep track of who knew what with this constant brain fog was a bloody nuisance, and besides, Alec couldn't keep anything to himself. It was better that her son heard the news from Rae. She would have been on the phone first thing to her mother, seeing as they were *best friends*.

Phillipa roused herself and flew upstairs to select a suitable outfit. Events were speeding along. The dinner invitation prompted mixed feelings. To meet the formidable publisher was beyond thrilling, but her wish to see Theo again had been granted, and that could be awkward. Erica's 'village hero' account had amplified Phillipa's belief that she warranted special favour. Theo clearly knew about the Ellis / Florence connection, but he'd come to the Assembly Rooms especially to see *her*, and their intimate hug confirmed it. Not that Phillipa would ever betray Alec, but even a theoretical fling was an improvement on these terrifying bouts of emptiness and despair. Kinsley was the answer to everything. There were so many benefits to be had, not least a friendship with the Spicers, and that alone merited serious consideration.

19
A tale of two dinner guests

Theo slid the tray of stuffed butternut squash into the oven while at the worktop, Sheelagh uncorked a wine bottle.

'What time are they due?'

'In half an hour, Sheelagh. The dining table is laid, the starter prepared, and I've made up a vase. Shouldn't you be dressed?'

'That won't take long.' She half-filled a balloon glass. 'Join me.'

'I'll wait, thanks.' He sat down beside Tulip and stroked her downy head. 'Are you glad to be back?'

'Now that Viola has resolved my speaker issue, and Margery is in a better frame of mind, yes, I am. It's a pity I have to return to London on Monday for the Guild meeting, but it should quieten down after that, and I can focus on the festival.' Sheelagh popped an olive into her mouth. 'What do you make of Viola's wish to wind up Quirk?'

'I thought she might give it a while longer, but her plan to move into charitable work was her original intention. Viola isn't cut from the same cloth as you, Sheelagh.'

'Nevertheless there have been victories, Harumi Kita being one, and of course, her break up with Gracie.'

'You didn't think much of her.'

'You can't kid a kidder, as they say. It was a challenge to stand back while that noxious woman hoodwinked our daughter. I'm not sure how much longer I could have held my vicious tongue,' she said with a cruel smile. 'I wonder if Viola might benefit from a summer in Kinsley. We'll ask her to stay on after the festival, share family time.'

It's a little late for that. Sheelagh wafted out of the kitchen, leaving Theo to prepare the vegetables She was never predictable, but this had come so far out of the blue, he was at a loss how to respond. Although they were a family of three, they were rarely in the same place at the same time. Historically, holidays for Sheelagh involved a large degree of toil while an obligatory guest or three, who just happened to 'pop in', inevitably stayed on to soak up the fabled Spicer hospitality. Theo, meanwhile, took every opportunity to escape to Northumberland with Viola. When they weren't roaming coasts and castles or nibbling away at Hadrian's eighty-four mile wall, they'd get mucky on Bennett and Miriam's small holding with her cousins, and of course, Kinsley was her second home. The last family holiday, before Viola began her degree, was in Picardy, several years ago. But with every day a step further away from that dreadful illness, and possessed with a tremendous urgency, Theo was eager to make his own arrangements.

Comfortably attired and lightly sprayed, Sheelagh had returned to the living room and was scrolling through Spotify. 'What shall we play for our guests? You said that Florence Hobbes was considerably younger than we predicted. Margery puts her at the forty mark, although

134

these days, who can really tell, and does it really matter? Regardless, it must have come as a shock.'

'We could leave the music off.'

'And sit in embarrassed silence, I think not, Theo. How about the *Buena Vista Social Club* … oh, that must be them, and right on cue. You'll let them in.'

Theo went to the door with the foreboding of entering Sibyl's Cave. If ever there was a time he wanted to be elsewhere, tonight was it.

'That was a wonderful meal, Sheelagh.'

'Can't take credit for that, but the wine was my choice.'

'An excellent one. Florence has never developed a taste for a good grape, have you, Flo?'

Florence stared at her sister. While they hadn't exactly smoothed over their differences, Phillipa had played the history teacher for all it was worth in the intervening hours. She had banged on about Kinsley's bell tower, and how it resembled the Swedish bell houses, and wasn't it impressive to find the timbers dated to 1207! and the royal charter gave Kinsley market and fair rights, and on it went while Florence retreated into her familiar silent space. This had continued during the walk to Cleavers and on, into the meal. After several failed attempts to bring her into the conversation, surely Phillipa was close to throwing in the towel. Five minutes more, and Florence would take off. The likelihood of the best buddies noticing her disappearance was zero, although it was clear who was sitting at whose size nines. Theo looked about as comfortable as a lobster about to be boiled and would, any minute now, escape to his kitchen refuge.

'A glass or two of fine wine makes my day worthwhile, so I must thank you for your generous contribution. Sean is obliging, in that respect. Speaking of which, has he been of any help with your ancestral research?'

'Yes, he has. It's extraordinary to come face to face with the names of those who have an earthly connection to our family. As I uncover the lives of our great greats, each reveal brings me a step closer to Kinsley.'

Sheelagh got up to fetch a box folder. 'This might help: information my mother collected, before she became incapable of doing anything useful. It will be of no surprise to learn that there was a scandal some generations ago, but by today's standards it's incredibly tame. Who knows, Phillipa, we may find ourselves distant cousins.'

'That would be thrilling!' Phillipa rested the folder reverentially on the table beside her. 'Tell me, Sheelagh, how did your festival come about? According to Sean, people travel for miles to attend.'

'When you're born into this business, you never really leave. I'm happy to say that Kinsley is no longer a cultural desert. Our daughter, Viola, has her own literary agency. Her big find is headlining.'

'Viola must be inundated with manuscripts.'

'Despite strict submission guidelines, the majority are unsolicited. She's finding it increasingly difficult to unearth a treasure.'

'Unsolicited or not, I guess they keep the industry's wheels turning. Apparently, we all have a book inside us.'

'No doubt, Phillipa, but I agree with Hitchens when he says that for the most part, that is where it ought to stay'. Sheelagh's tone softened. 'No matter there are numerous gatekeepers that lie between the hopeful writer and their aspiration, still the fantasy of a grateful publisher tending to the needs of her revered author persists. Today's writers have to be infinitely versatile – they have to be prepared to market themselves, to be readily available, to move out of their comfort zones. This can be a challenge, particularly for seasoned authors unused to touting for business.'

'Which is why events such as yours are essential, Sheelagh. Without you, how else would authors find an audience?'

'Well, that's good of you to say, Phillipa. Harumi Kita is an exciting new writer, and a coup for Viola. In fact, when the submission arrived she came immediately to Kinsley, to show it exclusively to us. The agency hadn't been up and running for long, so you can imagine her reaction. Sadly there's been nothing quite like it since, and I fear that the recent press articles have cast a shadow.'

'*A Cloud of Mushrooms* divided opinion. I read it as a critique of our cultural differences, while my husband took it as a political swipe at the West,' said Phillipa.

'Perhaps both. It was clever to situate the Takemoto family in nineteen seventies' Sizewell. The scientist father's decision to rent the village house had repercussions that are relevant today. It is the daughter, Michiko, who is left to clean up, so to speak. Not everyone approves of nuclear power, and less so when it's on the doorstep.'

'Of course, Sheelagh! You were a Greenham peace campaigner. That must have been an incredible ...'

'The name *Michiko* translates as *girl on the right path*. Her unconditional love allows the others, especially the father, to forgive themselves. That's the real heart of the story.'

Three heads spun towards the small voice. No response was immediately forthcoming as the comment required analysing, dissecting, and possibly contradicting, but aware of avoiding a potential embarrassment, Phillipa dived in. 'During her teenage travels, Florence read everything from Cervantes to Voltaire to …'

'Collins, Cookson, le Carré … ' murmured Florence.

'Theo and I were discussing that very subject before your arrival. Viola might enjoy a change of scene, and a family holiday will be just the thing to lift her mood.' Sheelagh bypassed Theo's reproachful stare and refilled Phillipa's glass. 'Do you have children?'

'My son has a temporary job in the north. Kinsley will suit him perfectly.'

St. Mark's gongs suspended talk until the tenth peal faded, after which Phillipa changed the subject. 'Where exactly is your London house, Sheelagh?'

'Farringdon. It belonged to my father. And before you ask, Phillipa, almost everything that has been said of Charles Spicer is true.'

Theo left Sheelagh to reprise the tale of her father's controversial past glories and went into the kitchen to make coffee. He was relieved to see that one of his guests had followed him. 'Florence, may I apologise ...'

'What for? I never acquired the etiquette that higher education bestowed on my siblings. It's me who should apologise.'

'On the contrary, you understood the central message of *A Cloud of Mushrooms* perfectly. Sheelagh may appear to be dismissive, but that's not the whole story.'

'Pip's having a high old time, and that's all that matters. When she and Alec live here, they'll need good people around.'

'Phillipa is serious, then?'

'About as serious as she's ever been. My sister may be respected, Theo, but she doesn't have many friends.'

'And her son?'

Florence didn't reply because she hadn't yet digested Pip's crazy idea. That was why she'd been pumping Theo for details about the cricket team and other village activities. Gabriel was no more likely to live in Kinsley than she was to reunite with Marcus Rafferty.

Theo put the kettle on the stove while Florence set about clearing the kitchen. The living room chatter was the sign of a successful evening, even if only half of the party were enjoying themselves.

'Florence, will you join me in a cup of Moroccan mint?'

'You're not a coffee drinker?'

'One a day, usually at eleven. I take it you know about my illness.'

She nodded.

'When the initial shock faded, I felt a tremendous sense of peace. Somehow I knew it would be alright, that nothing would be the same again in a good way, and that's exactly what happened,' he said with a weary smile. 'Erica's friends donated their therapies and healing skills to aid my recovery. They've helped me to see that while improving the lot of others, I'd lost track of my own needs. My diet, and my way of looking at life has changed considerably ever since.

'And how are you now?'

'So much better, thank you.'

They stood in silence, and after a while Florence said, 'Would you mind if I snuck out the back? Maybe we could meet up during the week, for that garden tour.'

'I'd like that very much. I'll show you where the vetch pops.'

'Sounds fascinating. Will you see Pip back to the cottage? She's about to cross the Rubicon.'

'Of course, although the sofa may be as far as she gets. May I walk you to Bookbinders?'

'No need. Cavell might be old, but he's not lost his bite.' She stood on tiptoe and kissed his warm cheek.

The stars blinked like fairy lights against the inky night. Embedded in the gentle breeze was the hint of imminent heat. Florence and Cavell trod the now familiar path back to the cottage. She had no fear of the dark. In their final year abroad, she and Javier had spent a month in Tissardmine, near the Erg Chebbi sand dunes. The tiny community existed as it always had, and perhaps always would, before the invention of time had cleaved life into past, present, and future. A sandstorm had sequestered the village for days. During the relentless heat, bearable in the early hours only, there were moments when Florence feared that the weight of the empty, endless Saharan desert might crush her, but she would never forget the colours — lapis and lime head scarves set against the infinite ochre sandscape and endless blue horizon.

Observing her sister over dinner, it had struck Florence that if it hadn't have been for their genes, she and Phillipa would never have *chosen* to be friends. They inhabited different worlds. Guilt, and a distorted sense of gratitude had masked the truth. Did they need to be each other's hero? Wanting the other to be different was arrogant at best. But if by a miracle, sometime in the future she and Pip decided to share each other's company, so be it. In the meantime, Gabriel was thriving. If he had battles to fight with his parents, and Phillipa never reconciled with their father, what more could Florence do? Her sister was leaving in the morning, she would return to Ardraig, and Ellis Eckley would fade quietly into retirement.

20
Camelot

How was it that a house could feel so different when one half of its occupants weren't occupying it? Even next door's cat hadn't bothered to come by, despite the handful of treats that Alec had left out on the patio. The 'big night in' with the lads was fun, though. The schoolfriends had cracked up when Gary unwrapped *Rattus Norvegicus* as though the LP were the Magna flippin' Carta. Funnier still was when he challenged everyone to a pogo competition, but that was unanimously voted down.

What wasn't in dispute was Alec's party. He should have known the boys would be one hundred per cent on board. In as much time as it took to do the Macarena, they had put together a music list, a party food menu, and most important of all, beverage requirements. His best mate Jono, The Tuppeny's landlord, was itching to host the party, having dragged his old man's pub into the twenty-first century without sacrificing its East End charm. 'The Room On Top' was now an entertainment space fit for purpose: dedicated bar area, dance floor, and posh loos. Along with the addition of a handful of stylish guest rooms adjacent to the main building, it was perfect for Alec's requirements.

As soon as the details were confirmed, Jono, ever the spokesman, raised the subject of his Herefordshire hop. No one wanted him to go. It was like a game of Jenga, they said, and by pulling away his block the whole thing would topple. Alec felt an acute sense of betrayal. You could have heard a pin drop while they waited for his response. Those boys meant more to him than his own brothers, so he had to be truthful, as much as it hurt. *There are two people who have my heart, the fact of which outweighs everything else. As much as I love you lot, I'd follow Pip and Gabriel to the ends of the earth.*

Phillipa was late. He hadn't heard from her since The Assembly Rooms gig. She had sounded so perky he barely recognised her. Excitement and Dr Darby had never been natural bedfellows, it had to be said. When puberty initiated Alec into the mysterious world of girls, Jason Hobbes's brainiac sister was the one he'd set his sights on. She wasn't classically pretty like Jono's sister. Pip Hobbes was gangly tall, and that manic hair of hers, the colour of his nan's cinnamon sticks, was nothing like he'd ever seen – well, that was when she untied it, which wasn't often. But in his humble opinion, she was beauty personified.

When Jason left for Leeds University, Alec had scrambled around before settling into taxi driving, as a profession. Those three long, hard years to complete what was called 'the knowledge' had soaked up his waking hours, but on Saturday nights, Pip let him take her out, invariably to Aphrodite, one of a handful of affordable restaurants around at that time (his girl was far too sophisticated for Wimpy fries and strawberry milkshakes). Later, when she was at Queen Mary University, nothing gave him more

143

pleasure than picking her up, even though he'd often miss a number of fares to wait for her. And when they set off for Eastgate Road, she'd lean forward, and with those shining shamrock eyes she'd tell him about Héloïse and Abélard, or the works of Chrétien de Troyes, Malory, and suchlike. These spirited accounts provided vital clues to Pip's wish list in a partner. And so, rising to the challenge, Alec secretly pledged to be her knight.

Her grail was to become a medieval scholar, which left little time for extracurricular activities. She had moved into his house during her A levels as it was too noisy at The Barbers, or so she had said. But they regularly returned to the flat for dinners and get togethers because for him, at any rate, The Barbers was a proper home from home. When it came to their son, neither were particularly confident parents, but with Lally, Neville, and Flo on hand, they genuinely believed that Gabriel's balanced diet of East End heritage and intellectual debate would hold him in good stead. Neither of them saw it coming.

When Gabriel quit his philosophy degree after that first year, it wasn't so much of an issue for Alec as it was for his wife. To this day she couldn't understand why he had scuppered his lifetime chances for a campsite job, but as far as Alec were concerned, his boy could pick up his studies later on, if that's what he wanted. To begin with Pip had raised no objection to Gabriel spending half of his summer holidays with Neville and Florence, at Ardraig. They were family, and besides, it suited both their work schedules, and they'd got used to his being away, even if they didn't go themselves. But at the end of that third summer, when Gabriel said he wasn't coming home, (*no,*

Dad, it's not a joke, and please don't try to change my mind as it'll only make things worse) Alec had felt his chest cave in. It was the same crushing abandonment that had almost done for him when his own mother had left home, the day after his tenth birthday. If it hadn't have been for Neville's inter-library chess tournaments, and Jason's insistence that he come to The Barbers for his tea, Alec didn't dare think of where he might have finished up.

The phone buzzed.

ETA 4pm. Lots to tell you. Doc xx

Alec pulled the cork from the wine bottle. The table was set for a salad, the only meal to have on a sultry evening. Earlier that morning he'd picked a handful of rocket which had a nice peppery taste to it and would go well with Claudio's leek and gruyère tart. With nothing left to do, Alec took the small glass of Rioja onto the patio and settled himself down in the shade.

Everyone had a survival mode. Alec's was to work hard, and to do his best. On the rare occasions he lost his rag, it was mostly about football or politics, but according to Lally, his heart was in the right place. And yet, it was impossible to shake off an impending sense of doom. The thought had crossed Alec's mind that Pip might have been having an affair. When he picked her up after the Pentacle dinner, she had looked every bit the confident, intelligent woman of earlier days. But if Caleb Hegarty had made a pass at his wife, as long as the line wasn't crossed, Alec didn't give a monkey's. Pip's vows were as binding as the eighteen carat band on her finger – he'd bet his life on it. Whatever was going on, he was confident of finding out tonight.

'So you reckon Kinsley's our Camelot.'

Phillipa folded her hands under her chin in a way that indicated satisfaction. Alec hadn't seen her eyes sparkle like that in ages.

'I'm sure of it. The village setting is adorable, and its inhabitants are *sooo* friendly. We'll all be happy there, Alec. And I can't tell you what it was like to meet a woman with Sheelagh Spicer's pedigree: famous publisher, women's rights champion, and for her to welcome us to Kinsley because *this village is in desperate need of people like you* is thrilling, don't you think? By the way, Sheelagh is nothing at all like her father, not that she was particularly critical or indiscrete during supper.'

'I picked up Charles Spicer in the cab once. He gave me a twenty quid tip, which was a lot of money back then.'

'I'm not suggesting he wasn't generous, Alec. Charles Spicer had the nous to sign an ex-convict when no one else would go within five yards of someone with Micky Nash's reputation. Their collaboration kick-started Spicer Publishing, and those detective stories are still best sellers, even though Nash has been dead for decades.'

Alec knew all about the Nash family. He'd had the misfortune to pick up the youngest brother one blustery November afternoon in Bermondsey. By the time the self-obsessed git got out at Highgate, he hadn't drawn breath, but he had been generous with his tip.

'It's generally believed that Sheelagh was handed the business on a plate, but she had to start at the bottom, just as Charles had done. I had no idea she'd only recently stepped back, but when I asked her about retirement, she

146

laughed. *I'm not yet seventy my dear, and while I've breath in this body, I shall continue to fight the good fight.'*

Alec waited for Phillipa to run out of puff. If he didn't know her so well, he'd say she was on speed. 'Not sure I'd be comfortable supping at her table.'

'Don't be so silly, Alec. Sheelagh couldn't have been friendlier, and she has no need to impress me.'

'So, tell me about the viewings. Your message didn't give much away.'

'The houses needed too much work or had too much acreage. How much space does a small family actually need?'

They looked at each other. So, this was her crazy plan. Gabriel leaving Ardraig for Kinsley? That was about as likely as Alec switching football teams. Flo was barely mentioned. He prayed they hadn't fallen out. She was the only family member giving Pip air time.

'Sheelagh is confident we'll find a suitable property and has promised to keep her nose to the ground. Oh, and the really fabulous news is that we've been invited to the annual book festival … and before you say no, Alec, I've already made your excuses. Sheelagh has generously invited me to stay,' she beamed, 'so naturally I invited her to dinner. No dates as yet, but she'll let me know. We may meet for lunch in the meantime. And Alec when she comes, please go easy on the *cor blimey, guvnor* routine. Florence might not have said much at Cleavers, but she delighted in dropping her aitches. I'm sure she did it to annoy me.'

'That's not her style. Besides, what's wrong in speaking in the vernacular. It doesn't usually bother you, Phillipa.' Her arched eyebrow warned him off. 'Is there a husband?'

'Theo Coppersmith, of Coppersmith Press, you know, the people who stock my publications. He rarely comes to London, but you'll like him. He's the literary 'everyman'.'

'Kids?'

'One daughter, Viola. She lives with Sheelagh in Farringdon, practically neighbours! Unsurprisingly, Viola has her own literary agency which she runs from the basement flat. Quirk were ones who landed that undisclosed signing fee for Harumi Kita, do you remember?' Phillipa sat up. 'Hey, why don't we invite the Spicers to your party? It's the least we can do to repay their hospitality.'

Alec went to the fridge to fetch the *tiramisu*. This was bonkers behaviour. Excluding Dionne, Phillipa had only ever invited two colleagues to the house in all the time she'd been at the university. She was on one of her missions, and he had the feeling he needed to strap himself in. At least she'd come home in a better mood.

He brought the pudding to the table. 'Why don't we wait until you've had your lunch date. There's nothing worse than feeling obliged.'

'Hm, that's a good point.'

'Did you get time to do your research?'

'Not much, although Sheelagh gave me a folder full of useful information. I need to follow up on a couple of things, but it appears that our ancestors actually lived in Bookbinders!' Phillipa leant back in her chair and sighed. 'I must calm down, Alec. There are important decisions to make, and I can't afford to mess this up.'

'*We* can't afford to mess this up, Pip. The boys will have your guts for garters.'

'You told them we're definitely leaving Eastgate Road?'

'Yeah, and they've promised to make my party the party to end all parties. I just hope your new best friends have a strong constitution. '

21
Florence comes clean

Leaving Erica to finish upstairs, Florence put the teapot and mugs on the table before arranging the pastries on the plate. They'd spent a happy hour sprucing up the cottage. With fresh Kinsley air billowing through the windows, and Cavell's bed fleeces drying on the line, it brought back heartfelt memories of cleaning The Barbers, with her mother. Just then, Florence heard the tinkling of bells. *It must be the christening celebrations, over at St. Mark's.*

Phillipa hadn't offered to lend a hand. It was midday before she returned to Bookbinders, exhilarated, and eager to get back to Eastgate Road. Apparently, Sheelagh had insisted she stay the night, and Theo had cooked breakfast, and it would have been rude of her not to accept their hospitality, and besides, they got along *sooo* well, and she didn't want to blow it, or so she had gushed. There wasn't even time for a farewell coffee. Before driving off, Pip gave her the briefest hug. *I'll let you know the results of my research at Alec's party. Thanks, Flo, I had a great time.* And that was that.

For the rest of that day, Florence sank into a pit of gloom. So unaccustomed was she to this state of mind, it was a struggle to know what to do with it. After wandering aimlessly from the living room to the garden and back again, she put Cavell in the car, and drove to a nearby village. Their leaden trek under sombre skies was followed by a cheerless pub lunch during which Cavell had revelled in his chew while Florence did her best to finish the Mulligatawny soup.

When they returned to Bookbinders she lit the fire and spent the rest of the day slumped on the sofa, staring blankly at the television while the contented terrier snored away his exertions. When the rain came, she stripped off her clothes, and stood under the downpour until sufficiently cleansed. Then, she had a shower, made a meal of beans on toast, and by the second cup of tea, Florence resolved that come the following morning, Erica would know her secret.

'All done, Flo. I cleaned up the spillage beside the bed. Could be coffee. I'll pop the rag rug in the machine. The bed linen and towels are changed, and the bathroom's sparkling. Won't be much to do when you leave.'

'Come and sit down, Erica. You've earned a rest. The pastries are from Nan's Place, in Leominster – pistachio, or hazelnut and chocolate cream.'

'What a treat!'

While Erica puzzled over her choices, Florence brought a package from the worktop and set it down beside her.

'Ooh, this hazelnut thingy is seriously delish. Nan's Place, you say? I'll add these to my list.'

'The bells had a nice ring. Was that Margery's grandson being christened?'

'That's next week. I didn't hear any bells – oh, that was me.' She reached into her bag and pulled out a pair of tiny cymbals tied together with a fine cord. 'These are *tingsha* bells. I guess you might call them spiritual air fresheners. They raise the vibration in any space, inside or out. Especially handy when Hughie's mother has been to visit, and at the Leaf and Loaf, but only when Margery's not about. She'd throw us heretics on the pyre before you could say Ash Wednesday.'

Florence passed her friend the package. 'As you know I'm not leaving just yet, but I wanted to give you this today, in case we get side tracked.'

'It's me that should be giving you a leaving present, Flo. Still, when your sister moves here, we'll see you again, won't we?'

'You and Hughie should bring your caravan to Scotland. He says you've not been that far north before, and Ardraig is worth the journey.'

'That's a fabulous idea! Hughie's fed up staying at the same site every year. Kiki and Cavell can fall in love all over again.'

While Erica carefully unwrapped the items, Florence released her ponytail from the hair band, and put on her specs.

'Wow! A signed *Marcy McBride* hardback, *and* a gorgeous tweed bag.'

'My daughter, Rae, made the bag and designed the cover.'

Erica looked up. 'You're Ellis Eckley!'

While Erica recovered her wits, Florence told her the story from her Eastgate Road debut to present day. 'I owe you an apology, Erica. When you and Theo showed up at The Assembly Rooms, I had to confess. I feel awful for misleading you.'

'I think it's brilliant, making your own way like that. There should be more ventures like the Artless Press Collective. How did Inspector Coppersmith work it out?'

'Theo spotted me in Leominster. I'm not sure if Sheelagh knows, though. I'll leave it to you to decide if she'd be interested, but I'd appreciate it if you wait until after I've gone.'

'Theo and me will work it out. Well, now I can boast that I spent three weeks in the company of a first-class writer.'

'How about a friend?'

Erica squeezed her hand. 'Even better.'

'So, you forgive me?'

'Nothing to forgive, Flo. How could you do your research if everyone knew who you were? They'd either be suspicious, tell fibs, or play up to the role, wouldn't they?'

Relieved, and immensely grateful, Florence hugged her friend, and refilled the kettle.

22
Raspberry lemonade

Whether animal, mineral, plant, or human, every entity basked in the first serious heat of the season. In Cleavers' freshly composted herbaceous borders, Cavell and Tulip snuffled and sniffed, pausing occasionally to lift their snouts in the direction of their owners' scent. Theo didn't seem to mind his shrubs receiving the rough treatment. Florence couldn't imagine him as the fretting type. She ambled towards the loungers, at the far end of the garden. Elevenses had started and finished in the kitchen, and now they were to continue for a while longer under the shelter of a huge sycamore. Theo approached with two long green cushions draped over his shoulder, and carrying a tray,

'These will be more comfortable. I have halloumi wraps, and raspberry lemonade, made from last year's harvest.'

Florence settled herself on the cushion before taking the long glass from her attentive host. Zingy liquid exploded into her mouth. 'I gave my granddaughter a personalised straw on her fourth birthday.'

'How old is she now?'

'Briar is six, going on sixteen. She gives everyone the run around, especially my nephew. I wondered if living in

Rae and Levon's house with a toddler might have been too much for Gabriel, but that was the best thing that could have happened.'

'May I ask why?'

'Gabriel and Rae have always been close. She and Levon offered him a place to stay when he left London, and he's still there. Raising Briar is a family affair. It's done us all good.'

'Ardraig must be special, or else there's a magician lurking in a nearby cave, hexing the unsuspecting.'

'You could be onto something. Levon has three children from two previous relationships. If that weren't enough of a blotted copybook, Phillipa has cast him as the Black Knight and Rae as Morgan le Fay, who between them conspired to lure Gabriel away. Needless to say there is friction.'

'I guessed there was a reason why Phillipa was reluctant to talk about Gabriel. She gave the impression he was on his way home.'

'It's called denial, Theo.' Florence was so unused to offloading, but Theo's kindly nature had the effect of unleashing thoughts and emotions that had been firmly battened down. But wasn't that the role of the stranger, the passing ship who carries your troubles effortlessly away? Except that Theo was no longer a shadowy figure, and Florence wasn't sure at what point the veil had dropped. 'I'm so glad Erica knows. This whole disguise thing is weighing me down.'

'You have no greater supporters than Erica and Hughie. They are determined to travel Ardraig next Spring.'

'It'll be lovely to see them again. Maybe it's time you wrote the sequel to *The Road Trip That Almost Was*, Theo.'

He laughed. 'Your recall is admirable, Florence. I wonder you didn't follow in your siblings footsteps. Phillipa mentioned you were home-schooled for some of your teens.'

'I've been blessed and cursed with a photographic memory. At school, I was drawing unwanted attention, and my parents didn't want me to be singled out as special, but it wasn't only that. When Jason left England, they took it badly, so they came up with the idea of home-schooling, to get me through the exams. After that, I went to Spain.'

'But you returned with more than a knowledge of European culture and language.'

'Pip told you.'

'Do you mind?'

Florence waited for the bubble of frustration to evaporate. She wasn't about to let her slack-jawed sister spoil a lovely afternoon, but she was determined he would know the truth, and not Pip's skewed version.

'Javier and I were kicking the dust off of our moccasins in Rabat, thinking about our next move. There were jobs going at a swanky holiday complex in Agadir, so we signed up for a final season. Javier had acquired enough experience to last ten lifetimes and had no further need of a Sancho Panza, and anyway, he'd met Paulo by then. I'd pretty much had my fill, so we decided to make it our last hurrah.

'At that time, Morocco was fast becoming *the* holiday destination. The resort had three swimming pools, a posh health suite, and a dedicated sports and entertainment team. Javier and I used to guess which of the new holidaymakers would be next in line to get it on with the hot team leader. To be fair, we all loved Yass. His wealthy, liberal family suggested he have fun before taking his responsibilities seriously, so he did just that. Anyway, the week before I left, we hooked up.'

'Does Rae know who her father is?'

'How do you tell a three-year-old that her biological father has no knowledge of her existence, and in all likelihood wouldn't want to know? I said he had to work overseas on important business. When she was older, I told her the truth.'

'Did she ask to meet him?'

'No, and neither did she want me to find him. Cultivating a patch of paradise in The Barbers with Rae and my parents was my priority.'

'Like *Candide*.'

'But without the natural disasters, the wicked violence, and a prematurely aged lover waiting for my return.'

Theo threw his head back and laughed. 'And now?'

'Meeting new people and seeing other cultures shines a light on our own relationships and way of life. I can't imagine ever getting tired of that. But according to Dr Phillipa Darby, travelling is my get out clause. And now Rae and my dad want me to settle in Ardraig, the closest I may ever get to an El Dorado, which will mean putting down roots. Maybe they are right.'

Florence's honest self-appraisal impressed and surprised Theo. He had assumed hers was the perfect life, and yet she too was at a pivotal point. 'Children often make great teachers. Viola showed me where the vetch popped.'

'I had no idea vetch 'popped'. At Ardraig, the purple vetch has to wait until sunset to do its thing, but I'm usually in bed by then, so the mystery remains unsolved. So, where is this infamous plant?'

He pointed to the area behind the loungers. 'Viola's grandmother used to bring her out here for adventures. Had Alice lived longer, I feel sure they would have been friends.'

In the conversation interlude, a pastoral refrain of rustling branches, gurgling river, and bird chatter rose and fell, as natural a breathing.

'I've not met many people who are on such familiar terms with *The Acts of King Arthur,*' said Theo, breaking the spell.

'Steinbeck's letters to his editors are as good as any writer's guide. Imagine spending six months in Somerset just to 'absorb' Malory. Susan Fletcher writes of a similar experience, in Glencoe.'

'*Witch Light* is a wonderfully evocative tale.'

Florence smiled to herself. Of course he had read it. 'What I know for sure is that every place sings its own song. Talking of music, Theo, what tunes were you listening to whilst swanning around the cloisters?'

'All sorts, really. The most memorable album of that era was *Avalon*, a musical love token from Eliza Nugent, the first to chart our brief relationship. We fell in love to *More Than This*, and she cast me off to *Oh, Yeah*.'

'Who better to help you drown your sorrows than Bryan Ferry. But on the bright side, if that door hadn't closed, you wouldn't have had Viola.'

'I've never thought of it that way.' Theo refilled her glass. 'It's not easy to stand by while our children struggle, is it. Viola is at a crossroads, but just as Rae and Gabriel have found their way, I'm certain she will be steered by her inner compass. Alas, that was never my disposition. Sheelagh considers me a prize-winning day dreamer, although in my defence, we can't all be a Baret or a Shackleton.'

'One of the joys of writing is to write the ending we want, Theo.' Florence's phone pinged. 'Do you mind?'

'Not at all. I'll check on the dogs.'

Theo wandered into the kitchen to find Tulip and Cavell sprawled across the tiled floor. They certainly epitomised a dog's life. He was surprised to find it was past two o'clock. Meandering from one topic to another with Florence was tremendously enjoyable. Several times he'd been on the verge of telling her about Hughie's caravan offer but had held back. This incredible gesture had set Theo's mind in a whirl. His account contained just enough funds from the sale of his late father's T.E. Lawrence to finance the campervan hire, but now he wouldn't have to go cap in hand to Sheelagh to fund his whim. He could visit his Derbyshire friends; stay with Bennett and Miriam and honour his promise to see his retired Classics professor in Edinburgh.

And Ardraig? Theo's mouth dried at the thought of it. Just a few moments ago, Florence had said that the joy of writing was to write the ending we want, and in a roundabout way, it was an invitation. September was four months hence. With the festival almost upon them, and so many summer commitments to honour, the weeks would dash by. In Ardraig there would be freedom to talk or not talk, to get to know each other, to form a meaningful friendship.

Florence's appearance in the kitchen cut Theo's fantasy short. He was painfully aware that come tomorrow, Kinsley would never be the same again.

'That was Rae. She's priming me before I get back. The *Greenaway Women* launch will require a larger venue. Speculation is rife, but the odds are on London, where it all started. I'm to give it some thought,' she said, wryly. 'My family are a crafty bunch. They actually called a Round Table to discuss it.'

'A round table – how delightful.'

'It's an Ardraigian tradition. When you get the call you have to be there, come hell or high water.'

Theo put down the tea towel and faced his guest. 'Dare I venture an opinion, Florence?'

'Why not.'

'From my limited but no less memorable experience of Ellis Eckley, I sense that she is about to bid her readers farewell. May I suggest you take a while to consider. It's an emotional time, and perhaps not the most conducive for a decision of this magnitude.'

Florence wrapped her arms about him, and there they stood, long enough to leave the other with a hint of something before she and Cavell made their final walk to Bookbinders.

23
Au revoir

Erica had sent a message earlier that morning. Could Theo meet her at Bookbinders, but not to panic as there was nothing wrong. The next lot of holidaymakers weren't due until four o'clock, and it was now eleven thirty.

The friends sat opposite each other at the kitchen table. Between them lay an envelope and a box.

'You open them, Theo. I've already had two lovely presents.'

'But they are addressed to us both. Shall I read the card, and you open the box?'

'Deal.'

Theo slid the postcard from the envelope. It was a beach scene, Ardraig? – too stunning for words. He turned it over.

> To my dear friends, Erica and Theo
>
> I rode into Kinsley's dusty western village a lone-ranger and have been overwhelmed by an oasis of kindness. One day we will reunite on the shores of Ardraig and I will repay your hospitality. Until then, I leave in your care my 'special brew' tea caddy, a reminder of our wonderful kitchen table chats.
>
> With love
>
> Flo x

Erica placed the caddy in the centre of the table. Theo recognised the cerulean and salamander honeycomb prisms – an exquisite example of Mocarabe design – from a long ago trip to the Alhambra. Tied to the lid was a dark cotton sash on a copper ring. It was a beautiful object. He passed Erica his handkerchief, although he too could have done with a good blow. Well, he had asked for a sign and there it was, and as Theo sipped the tea, an extraordinary calm flowed over him. It was like a blessing, and he basked in it until it faded, and the sound of Erica's voice brought with it the present moment.

'Flo has blitzed the place from top to bottom. I've never known it in all the years I've been cleaning. The cottage is ready for the next guests, and I'm a free agent.'

'That was kind. When we've finished here, let's take the dogs over the meadow. We can discuss our reply.'

'You mean, write her a letter?'

'Is it a bad idea?'

'It's a brilliant idea! I asked Flo if she'd like to set up a What's App chat, y'know, send each other photos, but we never got around to it.'

'A letter then, filled with Kinsley's tales.'

Erica gathered the cups together. 'We'll see her again, Theo.'

'Erica, I believe we will.'

24
Summer Solstice

Florence tucked the last item of her meagre haul into the crate, ready to cart it the distance of two hundred yards to her new home. Choosing an ancient festival day on which to move out of the static caravan was important: it signified the beginning of a new phase, both planetary and emotionally, and with luck, would bode well. Her decision to move into the old hay barn was one of a number made during the leisurely drive back to Ardraig, via the Lake District. Sensing the family's well-intentioned net tighten around her had triggered an impulse to snip the strings. Needing each other wouldn't help any of them, in the long run.

Kendal Lodge was still in business. Mr Foley had since passed away, but Hilda Foley kept the quant B&B chugging along. She offered Florence an evening meal, nothing fancy, but the company would be nice, she said. It was refreshing to be at liberty to listen to her landlady's *yatter* of the bygone without having to talk about books. Those three wonderful Cumbrian days had gone some way to re-filling an almost empty tank. Never before had a road trip felt so utterly draining.

In fairness, when Florence returned to the campsite, the

family hadn't made a huge fuss, and even Briar had waited for a cuddle before opening her presents. When they left her alone, what was meant to be a nap became a deep sleep, and by the time the sun rose the following morning, Florence felt as if she had never been away. Kathleen, who until then had kept a healthy distance from the Hobbes' dramas, had taken her aside. *Neville is so pleased that your living conditions are on the up.* What Kathleen meant was that her father was relieved his daughter was staying put.

At the brewhouse later that week, Rae and Gabriel brought her up to speed. Henbane and Ebony Farrell had received a shed load of attention. Inevitably, questions as to the identity of Ellis Eckley had re-surfaced. To her artistic friends' credit, they had steered the curious away from the identity of their mystery benefactor and focused on the benefits of collective creativity. Rae had also found herself in the spotlight. A number of commissions had arrived, one of which was to create the cover for a new magazine featuring independent and sustainable enterprises, such as the Artless Press Collective.

When it came to book sales, *Marcy McBride* units had increased by ten percent while the *Greenaway Girls* reprint had sold three thousand copies and counting. The pre-order list for *Greenaway Women* currently numbered fifteen thousand, (a thousand of these were limited edition hardbacks), the proceeds of which would considerably increase the following year's profits. Florence was no accountant, but this was the opportunity she had wished for. There would be enough in the kitty to give Rae, Gabriel, and her father a lump sum, a sort of redundancy payment, to soften the impact when she put away her pen.

When her commitment to launch *Greenaway Women* had been honoured, Florence would take a sabbatical. Yes, that's what she'd call it, mindful of Theo's advice not to act in haste.

Theo Coppersmith. His tranquil disposition filtered into her mind, filling the spaces between words. At certain moments during the journey, she found herself replaying their conversations. Florence had made a living by writing about wavelengths, and there was no denying that she and Theo were on the same frequency. Being with him was like being in a different time zone – neither felt the need to boost the conversation lull or change the subject – but it was during their companiable afternoon at Cleavers that Florence had an inkling of what she might have been missing. Until then, it hadn't occurred to her to *want* a companion. *But Theo isn't free.* No, he wasn't free in that sense, but the point was that there had been a shift. Florence was, at long last, prepared to consider the possibility of a relationship.

The joint letter was a lovely surprise. Theo and Erica had thanked her for the tea caddy, which was to be shared, rather than to leave it at Bookbinders where Erica fretted it might get pinched. In spite of Margery's flapping, the festival had gone well. The remainder of unsold tickets had shifted on the day, which had pleased the dynamic duo.

Theo: You'll be aware that Phillipa's 'Celtic Wonder-Women' talk attracted quite a number, but what you may not know was that Sheelagh suggested it as a means of introducing your sister to the village. We shall have the pleasure of meeting Alec soon. He and Phillipa are making plans to view Knapweed (you may recall the empty property in Frog Lane, beside the village stores?) now that probate is resolved. Hughie has kindly given it the once over and only a minimal update is required.

Erica: Still missing you, Flo. Kiki has found a new boyfriend, but you might not want to let on to Cavell. Hughie hopes to win 'best in show' for his French beans, but Judge Margery will find a way to deduct points. Congrats on the book sales! Lots of fab online feedback. We're ticking off the months till we see you at Ardraig, but with all that swag, you might have flitted off to Rio!

Theo: This brings me to the end of our Kinsley bulletin. The horticultural show is next on the agenda, followed by the village fête, and if the rain gods are smiling, our fields may re-green by the full blue moon.

With very best wishes,

Erica, Kiki, Theo, and Tulip

*

Feeling frustrated and confused by her sister's unpredictable behaviour, Florence had called a Round Table. With Alec's party on the horizon, it was time to find out what the plan was. To everyone's surprise, her father had undergone a change of heart. If Pip and Alec were on the move, he wanted to say a final goodbye to Eastgate Road, and whilst there, he would attempt a reconciliation. As half the family were travelling south during the campsite's peak season, Kathleen had opted to stay behind to help Dan and Ros. Levon's daughter, Niamh, had joined the team for another summer. Her offer to come to London as Briar's companion to give the adults fun time had raised a cheer. A unanimous vote was taken to stay at The Tuppeny for a single night, despite the mileage involved, seeing as there were enough of them to share the driving.

On the surface, nothing appeared to be out of the ordinary. Florence, however, had noticed a subtle change in her daughter. In an effort to disguise her lack of enthusiasm for the trip, Rae had suggested the one night only stay, *it will relieve the burden for Pip and Alec as they'll be up to their eyes*. It was common knowledge that Pip wasn't one for a party, so under the circumstances it was a sensible idea, but when her sister's mad Kinsley plan came to light, Rae would find it hard to keep her counsel.

Rae and Pip's mutual dislike increased with every passing year. Pip considered her niece a butterfly, always on the lookout for the next new thing, whereas Rae had no sympathy for her hidebound aunt's estrangement from Gabriel and Neville, despite being a mother herself. Florence was tired of being in the middle of it. Determined to pre-empt any potential fireworks before they set off, she arranged to take her daughter out for the day.

*

The journey to Kinlochie cut through vast, pristine rockscapes and infinite skies. Consciousness-expanding, mind-bending, awe-inspiring – it was easy to imagine you were alone on an alien planet, if it weren't for other travellers seeking the same trippy experience. Still, it was a timely reminder to Florence to explore the terrain close to home.

Upon entering the restaurant, Florence and Rae were shown to a table overlooking the loch and were presented with a menu which promised the finest forest, field and sea produce.

Rae surveyed the interior. 'This is nicely understated, Mum. And the food looks good. Is this an attempt to soften me up before unleashing the bad news?'

'This is a 'thank you', Rae. It doesn't scratch the surface, but it's a start. Shall we have a glass of fizz?'

Rae studied the drinks menu. 'Think I'll go for the pressed apple and ginger juice.'

'Oh, okay, but as I'm driving, I thought you might fancy a …'

Their eyes met.

'You're pregnant!' Florence jumped out of her chair to hug her daughter. 'I should have guessed. You've been out of sorts for weeks, but I've been too embroiled in my own pot boiler to notice.' Suddenly aware of onlookers, she sat down. 'I'm so sorry, Rae.'

'What for? We're both travelling on Mother Nature's magical mystery tours, but I've had a baby so I know what to expect, whereas your changes could be seismic. Kathleen woke me up to the magnitude of the menopause and I was shocked,' she said, filling the tumblers with fresh mint water. 'Mum, I'm really sorry to have put you through it at the Assembly Rooms, and already the pressure's building for next year's novel. At the rate the APC is galloping along, you might not have the wherewithal to write *Greenaway Women*.'

While their orders were taken, Florence caught her breath. Rae's uplifting news had instantly downgraded hers. A new baby really was something to celebrate.

'As I was saying Mum, if you're energy is low, we can postpone the book till the following year.'

172

'No need.'

A pause. 'You've bloody written it!'

'And a second collection of short stories, as an insurance policy.' The drinks arrived, in time for a toast. 'Here's to us, Rae, to new adventures. But be warned: the story will knock a few skittles over.'

'Let me guess who's for the chop … Tracy! I'm *sooo* pleased about that. She's such a bitch, shagging Elaine's fella, and passing off his child as her husband's.' Rae's eyes sparkled. 'Oh my giddy goat, the readers will have a fit.'

'You know what they say about bangs and whimpers. It's just as well I'll be taking off afterwards.'

Rae's stomach rolled. She had known this was going to happen but couldn't bring herself to face it. With her hormones raging, just the thought of having this baby without her mother nearby was beginning to freak her out. But before her imagination flipped into overdrive, her mother reached for her hand.

'Rae, I won't be going very far, or for very long, and I'll be here to welcome Briar's competition,' Florence said, reassuringly. 'It was never my intention for Ellis Eckley to continue indefinitely. The pressure to write is no longer there. I've finished what I set out to do, and I knew it for certain, that night at The Assembly Rooms.'

She took an envelope from her bag and passed it to her daughter.

'I stopped off to see Edie Robertson, on my way home from Kinsley. She knows I'm not interested in long-term investments and all that caper, which is why she's the perfect accountant. Think of the money as a bonus. The APC will continue to go from strength to strength with the

Betsy Pugh collection, your artwork, and future book sales. And who knows, Rae, I may not put my pen away forever.'

Rae stared at the figure. 'Thirty grand! Mum, this is too much. Even if I wanted to take it, Levon will never accept it.'

'I thought you might say that. Edie suggested I buy the hay barn. With my healthy deposit, she'll arrange a do-able mortgage. Look, Rae, I can't tell you how to use the money, and if you want to help Levon with the recording studio that's your business, but you might put some aside for Briar, and the new bairn.'

'Spoken like a true local. But if your intention is to do the same for Grandad and Gabriel, don't be surprised if they refuse your hard-earned cash.'

'Dad's only got his state pension to rely on. His savings went towards Kath's van. He and Mum never wanted to buy their flat, and he feels guilty for living off Kathleen, as he puts it. I think he'll accept something, maybe ten thousand at a push, but I'll let you know, ' said Florence, hopefully. 'Gabriel doesn't have a permanent home of his own. He could put the money towards a deposit, although I can't see him buying any dwelling at the moment.' Florence sensed Rae's discomfort. 'I know how much you love having your cousin living with you, but with a new baby coming, this makes sense.'

'I s'pose Gabriel wouldn't have to move out for a while yet, and there are various options.' Rae's frown melted. 'Yes, you're right, Mum. And thank you – for everything. I can't see how anyone would object. Not sure how the family will take the news of your sabbatical, and as for your readers ...'

'Let's wait until Alec's party is over, then we'll make a plan.'

'Okay. I wouldn't want to hit Gabriel with this while he's facing the trip south. He hasn't said much about Phillipa and Alec leaving Eastgate Road, or her crazy Kinsley scheme.'

'I wondered how he might react, but you know him better than anyone, Rae. How is he, really?'

'Something's up. It's been hard to sleep these last few weeks, so I've been going downstairs to make a drink. Gabriel's night light has been on every time. This could be a regular thing. He may be reading, or surfing the net, but he's usually too knackered to stay up past nine o'clock.'

Florence was about to reply when the meal arrived. While out walking the previous week, Gabriel had attributed his tiredness to working alongside Levon. After casually chatting about his mother, at no point had he expressed concern. From time to time, Florence noticed him scribbling in his notebook. Maybe he was using it as a journal, as a way of offloading.

Never one for superficial talk, Gabriel's attentive manner made him a magnet for those in need, and he was often sought out at the fire, or on the beach. As for relationships, there had been the potential of a romance the previous year. Everyone rooted for Tamsin Petrie, a support volunteer from Manchester. Gabriel had organised a programme for the youth group which included a guided walk, a beach clean, and a body boarding session. Florence had seen him talking with Tamsin several times, but nothing had come of it. When they lived at Eastgate Road, she wondered if he and Esha Mehta would get together, but the job in

Stockholm had taken her away, and that was that.

But there was no doubting her nephew's capacity to love, however it manifested itself. Even as a small child, Gabriel expressed joy as the rule, rather than exception. According to Lally, he was an old soul who possessed an extraordinary ability to alleviate the suffering of others. True or not, when her mother died, he had set about taking care of everyone else's needs: making tea, running errands, watering his nan's garden. When Gabriel told her that Lally's spirit had guided him during that time, it had comforted Florence.

'Alec's party will be a test for all of us, but I get the feeling that Gabriel will surprise us all in the not too distant future.'

'You could be right, Mum. Anyway, I haven't asked if you met anyone special in Herefordshire. There must have been more to admire than the fruit trees. What about Theo Coppersmith, the two-full-stops-in-a-paragraph fella?'

Florence smiled. This was usually Rae's first question following a trip. 'Kinsley is delightful, and yes, I met some special people – Erica and Hughie Briggs, and Birdy.'

'They must have been special for you to have left them your Spanish caddy. It's just as well you've got a spare.'

'I can't tell you how many hours we spent chatting in Bookbinders' cosy kitchen. It was an appropriate parting gift. Theo and Sheelagh were gracious hosts. Pip has her eye on both of them, for different reasons.'

'Really? I thought she and Alec were the ultimate end-of-days lovers.'

'There's no harm in looking, Rae. Actually, there was someone super cute. Her name is Tulip.'

'Trust you to fall in love with a dog. Hey, here comes our grub. As Nanny Lally used to say, best we stop yakking and eat.'

25
Theo goes to Farringdon

Theo closed the car boot, walked through the gate and into the kitchen. Having dispatched the last box of empty wine bottles, cardboard hoard, and numerous out-of-date posters, he was ready for a cup of coffee. Then, at long last, he'd attend to his project.

Like most unpleasant habits, Cleavers had reverted to its semi-cantankerous mood. The house had never taken well to guests, and there had been many. Viola had stayed on for a week after the festival, but without a replacement for Garvey, it was incumbent upon her to keep Quirk's pages turning, and so she reluctantly returned to Farringdon. Her presence, even though of short duration, was exactly what he needed. Viola had inherited equal amounts of her mother's fizz and, it had been said, his affability, both of which had come in extremely useful during the hectic weekend.

But far from the anticipated lull, a number of essential village affairs had arisen, leaving him scarcely the time or the energy to dedicate to Project JK, his nod to Jack Kerouac's Beat novel, *On The Road*. Aside from securing the hire of Hughie and Erica's touring caravan for September (he had tentatively asked for two weeks, but Hughie had insisted he factor in a month, in the likely event that he was having fun, and they weren't using it, so why not?), Theo's itinerary was yet to be confirmed. Sheelagh was still unaware of his plan. He didn't need her approval – their relationship wasn't built upon those conditions – but there were considerable matters to resolve: namely, Bookbinders' upcoming holidaymakers, the café, and the house. Just as he was beginning to doubt the wisdom of his adventure, an unexpected missive arrived from Phillipa Darby. It was an invitation, to Alec's sixtieth birthday party.

Assuming he wouldn't want to travel to London, Sheelagh had asked Viola instead. There followed a slightly tetchy conversation during which Theo felt he had to justify his reasons for going, the first of which was that Viola was clearly in need of both her parents' support whilst considering her next step. Second, as Alec would soon be their neighbour, and as Theo hadn't yet met the man, surely it was in order to buy the host a beer. The third, and perhaps the most important (but undeclared) reason was to see Florence again. She hadn't replied to his and Erica's letter, but to send another so soon felt excessive to say the least.

The day after the dinner party, Sheelagh had commented on Bookbinders' unassuming guest who, she was convinced, had been quietly sussing them out. Theo allowed the comment to pass without coming to Florence's defence, although that was the moment when he ought to have come clean about The Assembly Rooms, despite the possibility that Sheelagh already knew. She had met Phillipa for lunch and was subsequently invited to dine at Eastgate Road. Phillipa had discovered a connection between their families and was eager to share the details of her research.

Sheelagh didn't seem in the least bothered by the 'discovery', whereas Theo thought it tremendously exciting. He was familiar with certain aspects of the Parry history as Viola had poked about in the archives years ago. Of the number of portraits previously in the possession of Alice Spicer and now collecting dust in Cleaver's loft, one portrayed a young Emily Parry, the middle daughter of Sir James, and dated to 1875. When Emily fell in love with a local tenant farmer's son, Benjamin Eckley, she left High Court Manor for a life of relative hardship in Bookbinders. Sheelagh had mentioned the bookbinder's name way back when, but he'd forgotten it.

During the period that Theo liked to think of as their 'courtship', Sheelagh produced a book of sonnets, the very collection that Emily had taken to Benjamin to repair. To think that such a commonplace act had precipitated the downfall of the Parry family! A hundred years after Emily's death, the sonnets were found in Bookbinders' workshop and were duly returned to an ecstatic Alice Spicer, to add to her growing collection of family memorabilia. Sheelagh was fully aware of her ancestry, so why encourage Phillipa to delve around, unless it was to cement their connection, thus enticing the Darbys to Kinsley. But like Theo, Viola had been buoyed by the reminder. She couldn't wait for Alec's party, to meet her 'old/new' family.

And so, he was to travel to Farringdon where, at the first convenient juncture, Theo determined to announce his travel plans. In the unlikely event of an objection, Viola's unswerving loyalty was bound to help his cause. Spurred on to write to his potential hosts, his initial enquiries had born fruit. Bennett was delighted to hear of his brother's intended visit. If Theo was feeling energetic, there were harvests to harvest, and new ales to sup. Kevin and Jilly were thrilled that their old friend's long-awaited pilgrimage would soon be underway, and he was welcome to stay indefinitely. With regards Bookbinders and the cafe, Erica had insisted that she and Hughie step in, and he wasn't to fret, but to have a cracking time.

As for the last leg of his journey, Theo had to wait until Alec's party before he could confirm it. Not until he saw Florence again would he know that her invitation to reunite on the shores of Ardraig was genuine. He was under no illusion that she felt anything other than friendship, and even that was yet to be tested. Phillipa had painted her sister as a gregarious loner, happy to be in a crowd, but only for so long before withdrawing into the refuge of her own company, so maybe he was kidding himself.

But there was something about Florence Hobbes that had ignited Theo's imagination. Admittedly, the very nature of being elusive was certain to elicit the desire to want to know more, but it went so much further than that. Their verbal exchanges sparked like flints and were often followed by reflective moments which slowed time to the point where she was unreachable again, but never distant. In many ways he felt as if he knew her, that they had been together somewhere, somehow, in the dim and distant past. Keenly aware of his tendency to romanticize, Theo redirected his attention to practical matters. What wasn't in doubt was his desire for connection, however and whatever form it took.

Regardless of his personal fancy, palpable forces to fuse the Spicer and Eckley families were already at work.

The Darby's relocation would unquestionably influence the village dynamic. Margery was eager to welcome the couple, but Erica was sceptical. Clearly there had been a point during which she had formed a hostile opinion of Phillipa. The last thing Theo needed was to smooth over relations with the newcomers, as much as Erica insisted she would do her best to be friendly, if only for Florence's sake.

Nevertheless, it would be a mistake to plunge headlong into village life before seeing how the land lay. There were sensitive toes in Kinsley. Theo and the villagers had acclimatised to each other incrementally, leaving few surprises when his relocation to Cleavers became permanent. With luck, there might be an opportunity to chat to Alec at his party, and this went some way to easing Theo's unease at what might lie ahead.

26
Duty calls

It had been muggy all day. Everyone, including the dogs, were skulking around. Florence was cloistered on the tiny patio with her mobile phone eyeing her from the nearby table. Try as she might to tune into the joyful sounds rising up from the campsite, her mind leapfrogged to the call she was about to make. Who knew what reception she might get from Pip, particularly as the party was just a week away, and her sister would be feeling the strain.

Their fraught exchange at Bookbinders had been a factor in Florence's decision to give up writing. As much as it had pained her to acknowledge it, the time had come for the world to see her as she was, without Ellis Eckley as a prop. It was also true that until recently, she hadn't wanted or needed a long-term partner, but her commitment to the family was unbreakable, and this had prompted Florence's decision to seek advice about her finances, and perhaps to buy the hay barn. Already there were sighs of relief, even if she had no intention to live in it permanently. She was buoyed by her father's wholehearted approval of her sabbatical (*without contemplative periods, Flo, how can inspiration arise?*), and following his tearful acceptance of her 'thank you for everything' financial gift, Kathleen insisted they celebrate with dinner, just the three of them. Whatever the future of the campsite, or in her personal life, there was always a room at Ardraig.

Gabriel's reaction had been harder to gauge. They were at the cove, watching Briar and Levon splash about. It was one of those perfect summer evenings which would soften the hardest attitude. Before offering him the money, Florence had paved the way with a conversation about acceptance: how the giving of a gift, in itself, contained all the joy required for living a happy life – after all, what was money for if not to move it around, rather than stuffing it in a mattress for the benefit of dust mites. Gabriel had been philosophical about her intended break. He humbly accepted the cheque, and echoed her father's opinion, *if we keep doing the same thing, Flo, how do we ever experience anything new?*

Eastgate Road hadn't come up in conversation that day, although Florence sensed her nephew's apprehension. Didn't she feel the same, the closer it came? As a rule, the Darby/Hobbes clan enjoyed a knees up, but the lack of collective enthusiasm was striking. In a bid to raise the temperature, Levon had ramped up rehearsals for the sing-and-play-off between The Cockney Charmers and The Celtic Pretenders, as he had called them. This had gone some way to elevating the mood. *If we've got to trek thirteen hundred miles, we might as well have a craic.*

It was four o'clock – time to get it over with.

'Hi Pip. How are you?'

'Florence. I was about to leave for my swim session.'

'Oh – right, I'll make it quick, then. The party's coming

184

around fast, so I thought it best to check in. How's it going?'

'Jono and Co were meant to have organised the bulk of it, but they forgot the table cloths, the decorations, and a million other things. So, in answer to your question, the cauldrons are on the boil.'

'I hear the festival was a success.'

'Who told you that?'

'I had a letter from Theo and Erica. Your talk went well.'

A pause. 'Sheelagh insisted I do it. Why you make so much fuss about public speaking is beyond me, Florence. I absolutely loved it, *and* I've been invited back.'

'Congratulations. Theo also mentioned the Frog Lane property. Have you and Alec seen it yet?'

'So, Theo Coppersmith is Kinsley's town crier as well as heartthrob. How disappointing.'

'I was there when you went for those viewings, remember? It's hardly a secret. Anyway, Dad's coming to Alec's party, but not Kathleen. She'll stay behind to help on the campsite. Levon's daughter has offered to keep an eye on Briar for the evening. Dad suggested we book rooms at The Tuppeny, seeing as you'll have your hands full.'

Silence.

'You wanted him to come, Phillipa, so he's coming. Please say if it's not convenient, and we'll change our plans.'

'Of course it's convenient, and besides, Alec will be overjoyed to hear that his father-in-law has changed his mind. May I ask why?'

'Dad wants to see his beloved daughter, and to say a final farewell to Eastgate Road. Now that you're on your way, it's unlikely we'll go back. I think it's a good idea, don't you? We can all move on. Start again.'

'You're the expert at moving on, Florence, so who am I to disagree. Anyway, I doubt there will be time for more than a quick chat. Sheelagh and her family are coming, although if Alec's mates are hell bent on making it a night to remember, the Spicers won't stay long.'

'It'll be good fun, whatever happens. Have you made inroads into our ancestry?'

'Oh – yes. I haven't had time to update you. I'll email a summary.'

'Thanks. Oh, before I go, you might like to know that Rae's pregnant. A Spring baby.'

'That's quite a tally for Levon.'

'Don't be nasty, Phillipa.'

'Look, Flo, you know what I'm like at times like these. I promise to talk to Dad and to congratulate Rae. And no, we haven't seen the Frog Lane house yet. Alec wants to wait until after the party.'

'Okay. We'll see you next week, then.'

Seized by a volcanic fury, Florence walked into her new bedroom and hollered into the pillow. She'd worked herself up to make the call, having chosen to override the gut feeling to do otherwise, but at least now she knew what reception to expect. Predictably, Pip hadn't asked after anyone. She and Gabriel were as distant as ever, and her father's hopes of a reconciliation were, in Florence's view, spectacularly optimistic. On the plus side, the Spicers would be there. From Theo's description of Viola, at least she would enjoy herself, but Sheelagh? Whether she'd choose

186

to spend a precious Saturday night with a boisterous crowd was anyone's guess. Pip hadn't mentioned Theo personally, but he had to be on the guest list. Her sister had made her feelings about him plain, even if it was just a fantasy. But how did *she* feel?

Florence recalled the names on the tombstones: Parry and Eckley. The storyteller in her thrilled at the prospect of this recently revealed umbilical cord. This was good news. A friendship with Theo under these circumstances would be acceptable. Riding a sudden surge of optimism, Florence lifted her fiddle and bow from the stand, and wandered from room to room, playing her way through several tunes in lieu of the weekly fire-circle session. It had become a thing – campers and staff, sharing stories and singalongs – and was always fun.

Happy with her practise, Florence secured the fiddle in its case and prepared a bite to eat.

27
The party to end all parties

Theo paid the taxi driver while Sheelagh and Viola waited at the pub's side entrance. A no-nonsense 'Alec's Do' sign on the door indicated where to go. It was eight o'clock, but from the decibels bellowing through the open sash windows above their heads, the festivities were already full steam ahead.

'Time to gird the loins, folks.'

Theo and Sheelagh followed Viola's Dr. Martens up the stairs, and into a sizeable room awash with streamers and banners, and whose noise levels would have burst Caradoc Crisps' deaf aids. Phillipa must have been on sentry duty. She immediately intercepted them and led the way to the far side of the bar where the new friends could mull, undisturbed, over their wine choices.

Viola grinned mischievously. 'Best you keep a goodly eye on me, Pa. A free bar, a seriously groovy vibe, and what appears to be a sumptuous food table ticks all my squares for a supersonic night.'

Theo ordered a pint of Two Tribes, and a half for Viola. Just as they were about to cheers each other, a hale and hearty young man, sporting a tartan waistcoat sprigged with heather, appeared.

'Hi! I'm Gabriel Darby. Welcome, Cousin Viola. And you must be Theo. So glad you could make it.'

Viola's nerves instantly calmed. Despite outward appearances, she was shy of new people, and the break up with Gracie had dented her confidence further. Always gallant, her father had promised to rescue her if needs be, but maybe not tonight. 'Our reputation proceeds us, Dad. Thanks for the invite, Gabriel. So, which guilty party is the Hardy fan?'

'The birthday boy. According to Dad, the only required reading worth remembering was *Far From The Madding Crowd*. If Mum had got her way, I'd have been lumbered with Galahad or Gawain. Your illustrious name tops mine by a country mile, Viola, but then again, you are descended from gentry.'

Viola laughed out loud at that, and gently elbowed her father. '*Twelfth Night* wasn't it, Pa. Will you find me an Olivia amongst these rowdy revellers, Gabriel?'

'I'll do my very best, milady,' he grinned, and made a low bow. 'Theo, would you mind if I stole your daughter? I'd like to introduce her to some friends.'

Theo watched the youngsters disappear into the crowd. He was amazed at how quickly they gelled, and his daughter wasn't easily won over. It was good to hear her laugh. She'd been subdued, which was unlike her. It was interesting that each had confessed to feeling lonesome and would welcome a new adventure. Theo was on the point of telling her about his upcoming trip but chose to stick to his plan. Even without a signal from Florence, he *had* to get going. If he let this opportunity pass, he may as well put himself out to pasture on Pignut Meadow.

The cask beer tasted grand. Feeling his body unwind, he contemplated the scene. At least a hundred people crowded the room, and all were excellent at lip reading and gesticulating. In his prime, many an evening had been enjoyed in similar circumstances, back when there was nothing to beat being young and high, and the expectation of a golden future was laid out before you, even when you knew it wasn't going to work out like that. Florence must have been in there somewhere, but it was early, so Theo reasoned that if the opportunity to seek her out didn't arise soon, she would find him. Why or how he was so sure was a mystery, but he decided to trust his gut.

Phillipa and Sheelagh may have disappeared from view, but he was far from alone. The first person to materialise was an effusive Alec Darby, whose neck was garlanded in Hawaiian Hulu. Before Theo could answer the cherry-cheeked man's unexpectedly direct question (what was so special about Kinsley that it had got his wife in a right old tizz), he was dragged away. Shortly after, Rae appeared. It was impossible not to stare at the striking young woman whose resemblance to her mother was uncanny, but before the conversation got off the ground, she was accosted by a diminutive version. Rae scooped up her curious daughter, but clearly Briar had no wish to talk to a stranger, and so they too took off.

Alone again, Theo was drawn to the food table. He selected a plate of mouth-watering savouries which he left for Sheelagh on the bar and was about to return for his own when he spotted Florence on the far side of the room. She was in conversation with a group of people (they were in fact all male, but why not?)

'She could be Briar's mother.'

Theo turned to the reedy voice. A painfully thin man with eyes drilled in Florence's direction stood beside him.

'Are you referring to Florence?'

'As lovely as she ever was,' he said, before turning to Theo. 'Briar is our granddaughter – maybe not in biological terms, but as Rae's stepfather, I guess that makes it as official as it can be.'

'Oh – so you and Florence are …'

'Were. Well, if we're being pedantic we never married, or were engaged for that matter, but we were definitely a 'we'. I'm Marcus Rafferty.'

Before Theo could offer his hand, the man returned his gaze to the object of his lament.

'She left me when Rae was a teenager. They went back to her parent's flat. Actually, they never really left The Barbers, and I gave up asking Flo to move in with me. Never could unhook herself from Neville and Lally, which was baffling, bearing in mind she travelled around Europe for years.'

Theo could taste the bitterness clogging the man's throat. 'Can I get you a drink?'

'No, thanks. I'll finish this and take off.' He peered into Theo's face. 'Friend of the family?'

'Florence and Phillipa stayed in our cottage, in Kinsley. They were carrying out ancestral research.'

'That'll be Pip's idea. Flo's not into that kind of thing. I hear she's still weaving her way around the British Isles. The one that got away, that's our Flo.'

'How often do you see Rae?'

He shook his sorry head. 'Levon and I don't get along.

Not everyone's a Rainmaker fan, so why should I lie? Rae hasn't been to London in years. In fact, the last time I saw Briar, she was still in a papoose. Apparently, this is a flying visit. We've barely exchanged pleasantries.'

Theo was shocked to see Marcus wipe his eyes with the back of his shirt sleeve and almost offered the man his handkerchief.

'I never thought she'd last up there in the Highlands, but then again, Florence Hobbes is cut from unpredictable cloth. Pity the fella that falls for a siren like her with those coastal rocks.' He finished his beer. 'There's talk of a play-off tonight. I like to stick around to hear Flo on the fiddle, but the longer I stay, the bigger the odds of a bust-up. Alec's a good sort. He didn't have to invite me, and I wouldn't want to spoil his big night. Anyway, better make myself scarce. Enjoy your evening.'

Theo watched the forlorn man exit before making another attempt at the buffet and was relieved to see it had been replenished. As he munched into a spicy tiger prawn, a familiar body shape caught his attention. Sheelagh was making some very interesting moves with Alec Darby! When was the last time he had seen her dance? Viola had also joined the fray, which was no surprise in such an atmosphere. Even his foot was tapping, although now there were calls to slow down the tempo before getting down to brass tacks, whatever they might be.

Sufficiently fed, Theo popped the paper plate into the bin just as a smartly dressed gentleman strode over. His neat cravat and tartan waistcoat were at odds with his wild white hair.

'Hello, there. You're Theo, aren't you. I'm Neville

Hobbes.' They shook hands. 'I saw Marcus bending your ear and thought you might need first aid. He's nice enough but tends to the melodramatic.'

'That was thoughtful of you, Neville, but I think I've survived the encounter. Is Eastgate Road treating you kindly?'

'You'd have thought we were royalty from the reception. It was humbling, I can tell you. Leaving London wasn't as difficult as people imagine. My Lally's in here,' he said, patting his heart. 'Do you mind if I pick and mix? I'm under strict orders to eat a sandwich as a bare minimum.'

'Go right ahead.'

Neville put several items of food on his plate, chomped on something covered in what looked like jelly, and turned back to Theo. 'Flo enjoyed her stay in Kinsley. If Pip and Alec carry out their threat, from what I've heard they'll be fine with folks like you to settle them in.'

'You're not convinced.'

'Pip's had a bee in her bonnet about Herefordshire ever since her mother died, but I just can't see Alec leaving all this behind.'

A shriek from the dance floor drew their attention. Briar was on another tartan waistcoat's shoulders and almost touched the ceiling.

'Florence speaks highly of you, Neville. Are you still an avid reader?'

'Good old Flo, never a bad word. I'm currently wading through Scottish Highland history. Some of it makes for grim reading, but when has there ever been a time when humans weren't violent? All my kids can spin a yarn. My oldest, Jason, is due to visit this winter. He's in environmental conservation. Flo thinks he might come back to the UK. I just hope Pip sorts herself out before then.'

Theo noted the concern and tactically moved the subject on. 'Is there much in the way of celebrating at Ardraig?'

'Any excuse for a ceilidh. Flo's having fiddle lessons with a friend of Kathleen's. She says it's a good companion to writing – one skill feeds the other. We hope she'll stay put, but you never can tell. D'you know, Theo, Flo once told me that the impulse to keep moving was in many ways a curse. Settling down isn't a phrase in her lexicon.'

'Despite Ardraig's charms?'

Neville smiled at the comment. 'There's a lot to admire. Just recently, an iron age *broch* was excavated. Turned up all manner of fascinating objects. Birdwatching and wildlife enthusiasts are on the increase. I've taken to writing articles for the local magazine to encourage and inform our visitors. Behind the dunes, in what the Gaels call the *machair*, is a fertile grassland. It's not grazed during the summer, so in amongst the wild angelica and Atlantic butterwort are goldfinch and skylarks, and if you're really lucky, a corncrake, although that's only happened once since we've been there.'

'You are fortunate to have landed in such a paradise.'

'I am that.' Neville waved to someone on the far side of the room. 'Well, Theo, if you find yourself our way, take the north coast road to Ardraig and you'll have the holiday of a lifetime.' He took a penny whistle from his breast pocket. 'One of the many things I've learned since moving north. For the first time in our history, my generation has been gifted extra years, and I plan to make the best use of them. But if I pop my clogs on that dance floor tonight, I've had a bloody good run.'

Almost as soon as Neville disappeared, Florence arrived. Theo wondered if this were orchestrated, and then waved the silly notion away. The thrill of her standing beside him was too titanic to take in.

'Now that you've finished chatting up my family, Theo, shall we trip the light fantastic?'

'I thought you'd never ask.' He blushed at his boldness, or was it recklessness? Mindful of Marcus's remarks about sirens and rocks, Theo put his half empty glass on the bar, and followed her iridescent dress through the crowd where they made a space amongst the party goers. 'Without objectifying you in any way, may I say you look wonderful.'

Florence laughed. Alec's friends hadn't been quite so politically correct. 'Thank you. Rae loves to see me in a party frock. The last time was at Briar's naming ceremony, at the cove.'

Theo rested one hand on the sumptuous plum satin of her waist and wrapped his fingers gently around hers. As they swayed, he heard the faint singsong of her voice rise above the noise. Had she asked for *Avalon*, just for him? If so, the song was perfect, and he wallowed in the glorious moment. Even if it were possible to talk, what would he say – that despite all attempts to prevent it, his walks along the Arrow were no longer his; that he had replayed the afternoon at Cleavers countless times; that when she left Kinsley, an ache had plagued him for weeks.

When the song ended, Theo led her away to a quieter corner with the determination to ask his question, but Florence had spotted her nephew.

'Gabriel and Viola have hit it off, ancestral connections or not.'

'That was quite a discovery. Viola could use a good friend right now. From your resume of Gabriel's character, she's in good hands.'

It has to be now. Florence will be waltzed off at any minute.

But then, a miracle.

'Have you thought any more about a road trip, Theo? Ardraig is especially lovely from mid-September.'

'As a matter of fact, Hughie and Erica have offered me the use of their caravan for the entire month.'

'Wow! You'll have tons of fun in the Eriba. Email your dates and I'll book you a prime spot, overlooking the sea.'

Suddenly, Briar flew over and tugged at Florence's dress before being scooped up.

'Briar, I'd like you to meet Theo Coppersmith, Kinsley's Crackerjack'.'

'What's a crackerjack?'

'An exceptionally fine person,' she said, and winked at Theo. 'Pip and I stayed in his cottage.'

'The fairy tale one by the magic meadow, near the whispering willow and the bubbling stream.'

'That's the one! Are we ready to do the Hokey Cokey?' Briar wriggled out of her arms and took flight. Florence turned to Theo, whose grin was as warm as a sunbeam. 'This is her favourite dance. My advice is to get out now or strap yourself in until the wee small hours. It's lovely to see you again, Theo.' She kissed his cheek and was gone.

Theo was elated. He'd got exactly what he came for, and more. Then, a change in mood had everyone form a circle and link arms, just as Sheelagh arrived at his shoulder.

'It's about to get tribal. Shall we leave them to it?'

'Viola?'

In response to his question, they spied her tucked comfortably between Gabriel and Alec, about to put her left arm in.

To a chorus of 'ra, ra, ra,' Theo and Sheelagh followed Phillipa down the stairs where a taxi was waiting by the kerb.

'Thank you so much for taking the trouble to come. I'm sorry there wasn't the opportunity to talk to Alec, but I doubt you'd have heard each other above the din.'

'Alec certainly knows how to enjoy himself. You'll keep an eye on Viola?'. Sheelagh climbed into the taxi. 'We'll talk soon.'

Theo attempted a hug. 'A great party, Phillipa. Please thank Alec on our behalf.'

Phillipa nodded, and as the taxi pulled away from their bewildered host, Theo felt genuinely sorry for her. At no time did he see her do anything other than appear and disappear. She clearly wasn't keen on social gatherings, which may have been why she used alcohol as a prop. And as for Alec, his question had struck Theo as odd. Did he think there was a conspiracy to prize him and Phillipa from London? Obviously there was more to this 'leaving Eastgate Road' affair than met the eye. But putting all that aside, Theo had seen Florence – beautiful, and beguiling. His stomach lurched. There was no turning back now.

28
The Tuppeny courtyard: 12:12 am

After waving Viola off, Gabriel decided to call it a night. It was tempting to go back upstairs to join the hard-core partygoers, but with no idea when the lock-in would end, and only he and Florence still up, it was best to quit while ahead. The trip had gone better than everyone had expected: from the hilarious journey during which they sang songs and shared a picnic, to their arrival at The Tuppeny later that afternoon, when Jono had arranged a meal with his parents.

To an outsider, the reunion might have been typical of any family delighted to meet up again, except that underneath the frivolity rippled a ribbon of tension. Gabriel was shocked by his mother's appearance. Despite looking stylish in a silk trouser suit, there were smudges under her tired eyes and her skin, usually so clear, was a patchwork of reds. His hug was intended to reassure her, but she cut it short, and had mumbled something about feeling hot.

The contrast between his parents was all the greater because his dad was on top form. Losing his mop top to baldness before the age of forty in no way diminished Alec Darby's noble looks. His dark eyes overflowed when they saw each other. Gabriel had to dig deep when wrapped up in his arms, although he needn't have worried. Everyone remarked upon his glowing state of health, that the boy had filled out nicely, and how he was heaps more handsome than Alec had been at that age. Grandad Neville, Rae, and Florence had received similar turbo-charged greetings, while Princess Briar was the star of the show. That was until eleven o'clock, when Niamh carried her exhausted body to the guest bedrooms.

What Gabriel hadn't expected was to have made a new friend in Viola Spicer. How was it that in a nano-second, you could click with someone, as if you've known them for a zillion lifetimes already. Their shared family history added another dimension to the encounter. He had a similar connection with Tamsin Petrie the previous summer, and of course there was Esha, who he would love until his dying breath. Viola had been fascinated by the Artless Press Collective's story, and whilst swapping numbers, he offered to show her around Ardraig sometime.

Just as Gabriel rounded the corner towards the courtyard, the sound of raised voices slowed his pace. Rae and his mother were in a face-off, while Flo hovered nearby like a boxing ring referee. He should have shown himself but was anchored to the pavement.

' … your opinion of me is irrelevant, Phillipa, but to consider yourself a wonderful mother is stretching it. Do you actually know why Gabriel left Eastgate Road?'

'Gabriel gave his word he would come home, but you and Levon brainwashed him into staying put. How convenient that my son is working on your campsite and babysitting your offspring for a pittance when he would have completed his master's degree by now.'

'Your son *had* to leave London or he'd have drowned under your relentless expectations. Instead of trying to understand him, you made this all about you. Oh, the shame of having to tell your colleagues that your brilliant boy was a drop out, a squanderer of talent. There is no worse crime than that, is there, Phillipa?'

'Isn't it typical of you to exaggerate. Gabriel wasn't dragged kicking and screaming into college. He *chose* to study philosophy. In any case, none of this will matter when we move to Kinsley.'

Rae waved away her mother's hand. 'You've definitely lost the plot. Since coming to Ardraig, Gabriel has learned to grow food, to practically build a house, to drive every sort of vehicle, not to mention his fantastic work with the youth groups, and his musical talent. Why on earth would he leave all of that to live in Kinsley? For someone as clever as you, Phillipa, it's staggering that you can't appreciate your son for the truly creative human being he is.'

Before any more home truths could be hurled, Florence led Rae towards the guest rooms. Gabriel's streaming eyes almost blinded him, but as he came towards his mother, she pushed him away and ran towards Eastgate Road.

29

Reluctant revelations over cold toast

Theo put another freshly filled cafetière on the table. Sheelagh, as was her custom, scanned the Sunday newspapers while the slice of buttered toast grew cold. Just as he refilled her cup, Viola sauntered through the door, and dropped a book on the table.

'Morning folks. That was some *crazzee* night.'

Theo reached for another mug. 'What time did you get in?'

'Not quite sure. Midnight, maybe? Alec's cab-driver mate saw me safely home and wouldn't take the fare, good man.' Viola stretched and yawned and plonked herself on a chair. Spying the uneaten toast, she picked it up and bit into it. 'Alec was truly the life and soul of his own party. Was I hallucinating, Mother, or were you and he making serious shapes on the dance floor? I had no idea that you had it in you, or that you even liked The Rolling Stones.'

'There are many things you don't know about me, Viola C. Spicer. Alec has a certain charm – an intelligent rogue, I think.' Sheelagh glanced up from the paper. 'Not sure about the jellied eels, though.'

They laughed, and Viola said, 'The sounds really rocked: Roxy Music, The Clash, Arlo Parks, and Cousin

Gabriel is super sweet. He doesn't miss London *at all*. So, what were you and his mother gassing about for so long?'

'Phillipa ambushed me for practically the entire evening. She assured me that her son would adore living in Kinsley, alongside his ancestors.'

'I doubt it. From Gabriel's description of Ardraig, Shangri-La really does exist.'

'Your father considers Kinsley the land of milk and honey, but even he will admit there are issues.'

'Of course there are, Mum, but regardless of Gabriel's intentions, Hughie Briggs and Alec would definitely gel. Not so sure about Phillipa, though. Her festival lecture was interesting, but she was super-serious the whole time. You'd never guess she and Florence were sisters. Now, *she's* extremely interesting. Dad, did you know she was a novelist?'

Theo laid a plate of fresh marmalade toast on the table, acutely aware that Sheelagh was now paying attention. A certain helplessness fell about him, as if a vase had slipped through his impotent fingers and had smashed into a million fragments.

'Apparently she writes under the name Ellis Eckley. The business operates from Ardraig, and you'll never guess what they're called: The Artless Press Collective. It sounds like a seventies funkster band! The impression I got was of a super-slick operation, and great fun. Apparently they turned over eighty grand last year, but don't quote me on that.'

Sheelagh waited for Theo to look up from his mug of coffee. She had spotted him dancing with Florence, not that this was unusual as he was generally commandeered at parties, but Florence a novelist? 'Phillipa has never mentioned it.'

'She must have assumed you wouldn't be interested in a small-scale self-publishing enterprise like Artless Press.'

'Clearly, Viola, but your father must have known.' Sheelagh turned to Theo. 'Have I been made to look a fool here?'

Theo returned her glower. 'Don't over-react, Sheelagh. Are you interested?'

Sensing a knot of tension between her parents, Viola jumped in. 'Gabriel invited me to Ardraig. Said he'd show me around the campsite, which is by the beach. Hey, Dad, we could go together.'

'As a matter of fact, there is something I want to discuss with you both,' he said, and pulled up a chair. 'I wonder how it would be if I took off in September, for that road trip.'

'Seriously? You're actually committing to a date after all these years of threats?'

'Yes, Viola. I've squared it with Erica and Hughie. He'll deal with Bookbinders' maintenance issues, and she'll cover the meets and greets, as well as being on hand should Margery need her.'

'Exactly how long are you planning to be away?' asked Sheelagh, barely able to hide her shock.

A pause. 'Three, maybe four weeks.'

'Wow! What's your itinerary, Dad?'

'To begin with, I thought of heading to Derbyshire, to see a university friend. Yorkshire would make a good interim en route to Bennett and Miriam's. After that, I plan to drop in on Professor Munslow, in Edinburgh.'

'The camper van hire will be costly.'

'I'm hardly in the habit of raiding the Spicer coffers, Sheelagh,' Theo shot back, his face burning. 'Besides, I still have one or two of my father's books to sell.'

Sheelagh ruffled the pages of her newspaper, but before she could muster up a reply, Theo soldiered valiantly on.

'If you must know, Hughie has offered me his tourer, which considerably reduces the costs. And by the way, Erica and I attended the 'Ellis Eckley and Friends' evening at the Ludlow Assembly Rooms. It was to launch *Marcy McBride*, and to showcase local artists.'

'Gabriel told me about it!' Viola picked up the book. 'It's sold over twenty thousand copies since publication.' She flicked through the pages. 'He couldn't go, but by all accounts it was a humdinger. Wasn't there a poet, and a folk band on the programme? Not at all like the events we're used to.'

'Will you excuse me. Last night's food must have upset my stomach.'

Sheelagh swiftly exited the kitchen, leaving Theo to busy himself with the tidying up. Viola suddenly felt anxious. Her mother wasn't used to being kept in the dark, and obviously had no idea that her father was planning to go away for an entire month, which was in itself, a thunderbolt. But why hadn't he or Phillipa told her who Ellis Eckley was? What was the big deal? Her mother was no longer actively engaged in the publishing business, but little got past her. Even so, this was something else.

Viola had never before heard her parents discuss money. Given the family's heritage and lifestyle, she assumed there was an inexhaustible pot, but this obviously wasn't the case. The Spicer hospitality was a tad too generous in her opinion, but for her father to even contemplate selling his treasured books was awful. It wasn't as if he had a hobby, or went anywhere, or bought anything. And now, he was making plans! Not only had he been granted the loan of the Briggs' tourer, but that the necessary gaps had been plugged proved just how popular he was. Village life suited him much more than her mother which was ironic, given that she was born in Kinsley, and it was her idea to keep Cleavers on. But when he was diagnosed, the villagers had flocked to his side, further evidence of their affection …

Of course! It was the cancer episode that had galvanised him into action. Wasn't that often the case following a trauma, or a near miss? Viola perked up. How could she not have worked it out? That was the event that had precipitated his decision to go on the road trip. Now that he had fully recovered, her dad was finally doing something for himself. She went over to hug him.

'Come with me, Viola.'

'I'd love to Dad, truly I would, but this one's for you. It's been a long time coming, and no one deserves it more.'

'You'll look out for your mother while I'm away?'

'If she'll let me. Just make sure you take the low road home.'

30
Payback

With the last of the birthday cards safely packed away in his 'special occasions' box, Alec dusted down the shelves, and straightened up the ornaments. The boys had nailed it. It *was* the party to end all parties, and they'd be chewing it over for months, especially Levon's sing-and-play off. A steward's enquiry was never on the cards – how could you compare *Knees Up Mother Brown* to *The Wild Goose Shanty*, with the crowd hollering 'Ranzo whey-hey' and linking elbows, barn-dance style? It was as mental as any cup game he'd been to and was worth enduring a fortnight of agony before the swelling on his knee went down.

But what topped it all was the moment Alec laid eyes on his son. Despite his fear of breaking down, he had kept it together. Their hug felt momentous: a fusion of love, and joy and forgiveness. He couldn't have wished for a better reunion. Neville had been mobbed by well-wishers and had looked every bit the laird in his Scottie Dog waistcoat. He blew that old whistle as if he'd been born to it. And Flo, as gorgeous as ever, how the devil she was still footloose was beyond him, although Marcus had made no bones about how he felt, silly sod, gawping at her like a love-sick puppy.

Alec sat on the sofa. He recalled the guest list, mentally ticking each one off, and was satisfied that he had got around to most of them, but with everyone wanting him for something, there hadn't been time to say much more than 'thanks for coming'. Phillipa's whereabouts was a puzzle. One minute she was talking to Sheelagh, and the next, she'd disappeared into thin air. That single slow dance together was a miracle, under the circumstances. Pip had never been one for a smooch, even at their wedding. Alec sighed. Deep down, he knew there'd be payback, but unable to cope with what that might be, he had stuck his head firmly in the sand until events yanked it out.

The morning after the party, he had whizzed over to The Tuppeny, fully expecting the family to be tucking into Jono's famous big brekkie, only to find that they'd shot off early. With no opportunity for a post-party analysis, let alone to say goodbye to his son, Alec felt winded. Oh, the texts were nice enough, and they'd sent several videos during their journey back to Ardraig, but it wasn't the same. Pip had barely responded to his shock announcement. As a matter of fact, she didn't surface until late afternoon, and that was to swallow a couple of pain killers before going back to bed for the rest of the day. She wasn't sick, but he was to leave her be.

Feeling adrift, Alec had lumbered back to the pub. The customary 'morning-after' lunch was ridiculously well attended, bearing in mind that Jono had called time at three am. Hearing everyone's upbeat comments temporarily cheered him, but once home again, the house felt like a mausoleum. He went into Gabriel's bedroom in search of solace, only to find that the toys, photographs, books, and clothes were a painful reminder of happier times. Pip insisted that his room was to remain exactly as it was. She – they had made it into a shrine, as if their boy had died, but he was alive and well, and there was hope.

After crashing out on his son's bed, Alec woke the following morning to find Phillipa sobbing over her muesli. When he attempted to coax it out of her, she had clung to him, and when the wave passed, he put her to bed, where she slept for the best part of twenty-four hours. Despite his alarm, holding her close was just as wonderful as holding his son again, and he had missed it more than anything.

Two weeks had passed since then. Some project or other had kept Phillipa so tied up that he had to drag her out of her office to eat a bite of something. But not tonight. Sheelagh Spicer was finally coming to dinner. Pip had gone off to the hairdresser's after carefully laying out her outfit alongside his best blue polo shirt and chinos. They were to eat early: six-thirty to be precise. Sheelagh was having problems with her digestion, so there was to be no rich pudding, but she might enjoy a cheese board with the St Émilion, the last of the Kinsley wine. Apparently there was important information to be shared. Alice Spicer had collected a trove of photographs and documents which were now on display in the living room, and he wasn't to touch them, but when she gave him the nod, they'd celebrate with frosted flutes of *kir royale*.

Sheelagh Spicer may have inherited a number of pedigree genes through her mother's line, but she didn't strike Alec as a women in dire need of wooing. He wondered at all the fuss. It was as if his wife were preparing for a date, using the best flippin' napkins, the silver cutlery set, and the candelabra (all of which needed a good polish), and in the middle of a flippin' heatwave! Pip had made up the spare bedroom, with flowers, (he didn't advise chocolates in the swelter) but if their venerable guest decided not to stay, he promised to call on a mate to drive her home.

Alec shuffled around the table straightening knives and spoons, buffing up wine glasses, and refolding napkins. He was, unusually, in need of a drink. Evidently, the Frog Lane property was going on the market any day now and Sheelagh wanted them to have first refusal. She was pulling out the stops to get them to Kinsley, the effect of which was pushing him in the opposite direction. If he needed confirmation that Eastgate Road was, and always would be his manor, the party had proved it.

As the prospect of a decision loomed, the age-old fear response tightened Alec's screws. If he told Phillipa his knee operation was imminent, she'd have a fit. But how could he turn it down after waiting so long? Whilst over the allotment that week, Gary had asked why he and Pip would risk viewing a house they weren't in a position to buy, bearing in mind that he'd need, *at least*, a couple of months to recover from the operation, as he wasn't anywhere near as fit as he used to be. Jono had been equally antsy. How could such a monumental decision be made based on genealogy alone? *And do I need to state the bleedin' obvious, mate – you've never even been to Kinsley.* Knowing his friends to be right, Alec decided to tackle it with Pip after the dinner party.

'Thank you for being so accommodating with dinner. Viola insists I have this wretched indigestion investigated, or at the very least, cut out the worst offenders. A Cobb salad was the perfect choice. And these delicious strawberries are …'

'From the allotment, Sheelagh. The soft fruits have done well this year. Pip tells me you've got a veg garden in Kinsley.'

'Theo's the green-fingered one. He sends his regards and looks forward to meeting you in the relative quiet of Cleavers.'

Phillipa scowled at Alec. 'I told you the music was too loud. I could barely hear myself speak.'

'But everyone had fun, particularly Viola, and she appears to have found a good friend in your son. Gabriel has invited her to Ardraig.'

Alec knew his wife so well, he actually felt her body contract. He topped up the glasses to buy her breathing space. 'The family will make her welcome, Sheelagh. We're good at that.'

'Indeed you are, Alec. Florence made a point of saying hello. I scarcely recognised her in the dress and heels. And the little girl, Briar, would I have seen her parents?'

'You can't have missed Levon, with that beard. Rae is our niece: a stunner – long black velvet dress and wearing a head thingy.'

'It's called a circlet, Alec.'

'She's Florence's daughter?'

'The identity of Rae's father remains a riddle, Sheelagh. For those who give a damn, the rumours have ranged from Moroccan prince to swimming pool attendant.'

'Florence is a dark horse. You didn't mention your sister is an author, Phillipa.'

'I didn't think you'd be interested,' she replied, startled by the question.

'Theo said the same thing. I wonder what gives the impression that I'm unable to make up my own mind.'

'Sheelagh, I apologise …'

Sheelagh waved away the remark. 'I understand a launch party for her new novel had taken place in Ludlow during your stay at Bookbinders. Quite an event, by all accounts.' She twirled the stem of her glass. 'I found Eckley's portrayal of non-stereotypical female protagonists refreshing.'

'You've read her novels?'

'Novel. Gabriel gave Viola a copy of *Marcy McBride*. I assume her other books promote female agency and authority, or at least that's what I've gathered from the website. What prompted her to write?'

'I suggested Florence try her hand, but never seriously predicted she'd make a career from it. The books might have a wider readership had she allowed *Greenaway Girls* a comprehensive edit.'

'That's never been Flo's way. She and Rae set up the Artless Press Collective when they moved to Ardraig. It's a real success story,' said Alec, feeling heat bolt into his neck.

'Ellis Eckley's readers are more interested in happy beginnings than stylistic finesse, but there's no doubt that Florence's writing technique has improved over the years.'

'Whatever the publishing route, it takes courage to put one's work in the public arena. Now, Phillipa, I understand you've an update on the family tree.'

'Oh! Yes, let's go into the living room. I've laid it all out.'

Leaving the women to get on with it, Alec loaded the dishwasher. Pip had the perfect opportunity to talk about Gabriel, but she had side-stepped it. If only she could give it up – he was never coming home. And as for her casual dismissal of Flo's talent, well, that had really got his goat. In less than five minutes, she and Sheelagh had shredded those lovely stories. Obviously there were readers who liked to discuss the details, but analytical deconstruction, the likes of which Phillipa and Sheelagh thrived on, was not Flo's bag, *at all*.

He knew it was going to be a wonky night as soon as Sheelagh rang the doorbell. She had none of the light-heartedness of his party. During the meal, Alec got the impression she wanted to be anywhere other than at 96 Eastgate Road. He prided himself in being able to read people: when a fare didn't want to talk, he'd know it within seconds. If Sheelagh Spicer had climbed in the back of his cab in that same mood, he'd have left her to it. But there was something she wanted to get off her chest, and it can't just have been this Ellis Eckley business, although why she didn't know was baffling. He was proud to give a copy of Flo's latest novel to anyone who showed genuine interest. The only good news from the entire evening was that the Frog Lane house hadn't come up in conversation, or not while he was within earshot.

Satisfied that the kitchen was in order, and certain that there would be no *kir royales* required tonight, Alec made his way slowly up the stairs. It was too late for a shower, so he made do with a lick and a promise, as his old man used to call it. With his teeth meticulously cleaned, and face rinsed and moisturised, he hung his shirt and trousers on the wooden hanger, placed his glasses in their case, and climbed heavily into bed. Before drifting into sleep, Alec thought about Gabriel. His son had made that long journey south, just to be at his dad's party. There had been a massive change in him. The boys had noticed it immediately. *You should be chuffed that your lad is making his own way in the world, but he'll never forget his roots.* There was no denying the pain, but it was heartening to hear that.

31
All fall down

While Alec surfed his bitter-sweet dreams, Phillipa sat on the sofa, as rigid as an ironing board. Her trembling hands clung to a large glass of brandy, while scattered around the room were the fruits of her research. With less than an hour of discussion, even less enthusiasm, (and none of that extra special coffee required), Sheelagh had been intent on getting home, where, she said, Viola was expecting her. This was before disclosing the most disturbing information Phillipa had heard since Gabriel abandoned her.

Theo believes himself in love with your sister. I have no idea if Florence reciprocates, but in any case, he is planning to travel to Ardraig to tell her.'

Florence hasn't said anything to me. She's always played her cards close to her chest, Sheelagh, but she's no marriage breaker.

We're not married, Phillipa. I never wanted it. Regardless of that, Theo will leave Cleavers, and in all likelihood, Kinsley.

How could that be? When did that happen? Phillipa rewound the months to April, and forensically examined every scene. Not once could she identify a moment when Florence had shown the slightest interest in the man she had so recently fantasised about. And it was just a fancy

– Phillipa was no Guinevere – but that aside, there was no making sense of it. Her sister may have revelled in her single status, but even if she wanted a relationship, she was far too picky to go the distance. Marcus Rafferty, a perfectly decent man, was still pathetically smitten, and many of Alec's friends couldn't keep from buzzing around her. It must have been the chase, although Florence didn't have a clue how to flirt.

The unopened bottle of champagne on the side table taunted her. Phillipa cringed at the fuss she'd made over the family tree. Admittedly, she scarcely knew Sheelagh, but the woman's unexpected frostiness had failed to thaw, even after being shown what Phillipa believed to be priceless documents. Bookbinders had joined their families, but in the process had torn the Parry family apart.

Shortly after the clandestine marriage between Emily and Benjamin Eckley, the Parry's fortunes began to unravel. In just two generations, High Court Manor had burned to the ground in an unproved arson attack, and the last of the fortune was squandered by Sheelagh's grandfather who never recovered from his wife's death in childbirth. Alice Parry, his only child, had lived in the shadow of her family's downfall until the valiant Charles Spicer, smitten by the fragile beauty's tragic tale, swore to save her. *Cleavers was meant to heal my mother's bitterness at the past, but it had the opposite effect, and quickly alienated my father.*

The women had sat in awkward silence before Sheelagh's suspicions tumbled out. Of course she would be desperate to get home – it must have been a rare occasion to be faced with a situation out of her control – but what Sheelagh couldn't have anticipated was the devastating effects of her disclosure. As the night wore on, Phillipa's mood plummeted. Gabriel and Viola were not simply distant cousins but had, in a blink, become bosom buddies. There had been ample occasion to talk before and during the party, but it was only when Viola went home that her son sought her out. And where was she? Embroiled in a vitriolic encounter with Rae, whose spiteful tirade still sizzled in her veins. What did her niece know of anguish? How could she understand the torture of hearing Gabriel insist that he had to get away from Eastgate Road 'to sort his head out', *but I swear I'll come back.* He had broken his oath. What was anyone worth if they didn't keep their word?

All hope of a fresh start crashed like the Temple of Artemis at Phillipa's feet. The image of Gabriel and Theo playing cricket together while she and Alec joined the spectators on Kinsley's village green faded like a photograph left out in the sun. Festivals, dinner parties, and long river walks now seemed like a pathetic dream. *Theo will leave Cleavers, and in all likelihood, Kinsley.* If Sheelagh's suspicions were correct, how on earth could they move there now? She was rarely there as it was, and without saying as much, Phillipa suspected that Cleavers would be sold to avoid scandal, or embarrassment – there had been too much of that in the Parry family already. Without Theo's *esprit de corps*, the villagers would rejoice in Sheelagh's downturn, and Alec would never forgive her for dragging him from Eastgate Road into a crucible of gossip and spite.

As dark slipped into dawn, misery exploded through her eyes, her nose, her mouth. Come September, Theo would be on the road to Ardraig, to the place that had stolen her son and her father, and with Viola now seduced by the myth, Sheelagh would face the same fate. What was the bloody point? Phillipa could no longer ignore what was glaring at her: Gabriel was never coming home; her father was more interested in Kathleen Dalgety than his own daughter, whose academic excellence was so sought after; and Florence, whose lifelong aversion to commitment was fêted as free-spirited, had once again been lavished with love while she, Dr Phillipa Darby, drowned in bitterness and pain.

*

Alec stepped into the hall, dropped his overnight bag by the stairs, and breathed an exhausted sigh. It was done. Dionne had reassured him that under the circumstances, this was the best solution for Phillipa's wellbeing. He wasn't committing her to an asylum, as he might have made the terrible mistake of doing so in our living history. This was a practical solution, motivated by love. She and her friends would take the very best care of his darling wife for as long as were necessary, and he was to go ahead with the knee operation, confident in the knowledge that there were good people to take care of him.

To Alec's astonishment, Phillipa had agreed to go to Brittany. She'd been pretty much incapacitated after the dinner party and had answered his questions mechanically: she and Sheelagh hadn't fallen out; the Frog Lane house was theirs if they wanted it; and yes, she loved him as much as ever. But this was more than lethargy, or insomnia. Getting her to eat a bowl of cereal was an uphill task, as was taking a bath or even brushing her teeth.

And then, finally, it came cascading out – Theo had fallen in love with Florence! He was going to Ardraig to tell her as much, and would leave Cleavers, or this was Sheelagh's prediction. Viola was also making plans to see their son who, *by the way, is never coming back to Eastgate Road, but has been stringing me along for three bloody years.* Phillipa made him promise not to ask Florence if this business with Theo were true, not that it really mattered because moving to Kinsley was now out of the question.

From the impression Alec had of Sheelagh Spicer, she didn't come across as the warmest of women, but what did he know? Maybe she was unable to show her emotions. If Charles Spicer's reputation were to be believed, living with him must have had an influence. But everyone needed love, no matter what strata of society they were born into, and if Flo and Theo Coppersmith hooked up, Sheelagh was likely to find herself lonely and bitter. Alec considered himself the luckiest man alive to be married to Phillipa: she would never betray him.

There had been only one person to call. Dionne Farleigh overflowed with good sense, and Alec immediately found her to be an ally. Phillipa had no immediate work commitments, so this was a good time to take a break, to be with people who would make no demands or place any expectations on her, and she was free to leave *Le Jardin des hortensias* at any time. Alec fully expected Pip to hit the roof, but instantly she had bucked up. It hadn't occurred to her to let someone outside the family step in, and as Dionne Fairleigh was the only person she trusted, it was agreed. *It's a sensible idea and will benefit everyone.*

Gary had insisted on driving them to Rouen from where Dionne and another friend would take Phillipa on to Morbihan. Her first contract with Pentacle had been honoured, and as there wasn't much else in the pipeline, what else had she to look forward to but another long, cold winter without Gabriel? Although Alec's heart ripped at the thought of her going away, it was for the best. He took Gary's advice and kept the knee op secret. *Why make Pip worry unnecessarily and besides, it'd be a nice surprise when she comes home.*

But what to do about Gabriel? Dionne gently reminded him that their son would want to know his mother was unwell. Why shield him when he was plainly much more mature than he and Phillipa assumed him to be? Despite her perceived injustices, Neville and Florence would be horrified to be kept in the dark. They had never withdrawn from her; they were constants, the bedrock of the family. Dionne was so right about that. During his conversation with Flo, Alec insisted there was no need for anyone to come to Eastgate Road. Gary's wife was a physiotherapist, and the boys would rally round. Their collective concern was overwhelming. If only Pip knew how much she was loved.

32
Shadows on the sundials

The ending of summer brought with it a melancholy unlike anything Florence had ever experienced. Up on the headland, she and her father were in their usual spot with their lenses trained on the sea. It occurred to her that whenever they needed perspective, there was no better place than on the split rock to get it. Late afternoon sunrays spilled over the still water, conjuring up every shade of blue. Two wet-suited paddle boarders synchronized across the bay, while on the beach a solitary dog walker threw a ball for her long-legged hound. Within the hour, the beach would be populated with returning campers, not that it was a bother, but if solitude were needed, Florence was party to several secret spots from where she could bask in the scenery alone.

For weeks now, a listlessness had settled over her. Alec's wonderful party had been tarnished by that final disturbing scene between Rae and Pip. If that weren't enough, his tearful phone call had cut her to pieces. Her sister had gone to Brittany, to stay with Dionne Fairleigh, and Alec was about to have an operation, and would she tell everyone (meaning Gabriel) what the situation was, and if anyone (meaning Gabriel) wanted to call, he'd be more than pleased to hear from them. Immediately afterwards, Florence had called a Round Table. If decisions had to be made, they wouldn't be hers alone. When Rae confessed to the altercation there was no blame, only a unanimous wish to do the right thing. Gabriel admitted to witnessing the exchange. His mother's time out was the best thing all round, and as both his parents were in good hands, and they weren't needed at Eastgate Road, there was nothing more to be done.

It was a relief to know that Pip had accepted help, yet still the agitation persisted. The dispute with Rae alone couldn't have tipped her sister over the edge. Unpleasant as the exchange had been, Florence was a great believer in saying what needed to be said. At least Pip and Rae were aware of the other's opinion, even if they didn't like it. But this meltdown had been building for a long while, and the family's hasty departure from The Tuppeny had been a mistake. It was cowardly, and they had all needlessly suffered as a result. But during her conversation with Alec, Florence sensed he was holding something back. It was only when she reminded him of their loving and honest relationship that he told her of Sheelagh's suspicions.

'If Theo does feel this way about you, Flo, it doesn't exactly warrant a red card. Let's face it, you've been on Jono's wish list since we were at school, and he's not the only one.'

'I appreciate your attempts to make me feel better Alec, but Theo's theoretical feelings aren't the issue. Your relocation to Kinsley is now in jeopardy, and Pip was banking on it working out. There's so much you don't know about the village dynamic. Sheelagh isn't remotely as popular as Theo. You don't need me to spell out the consequences when you move there.'

'Flo, I never intended to leave Eastgate Road. It's shameful to admit that I've been humouring Pip, to keep her buoyed up through this rocky time with Gabriel. Look, I know her. This entire episode was her way of putting Lally's ghost to rest. We've been here before, remember? She had to get this Kinsley business out of her system.'

'So in your opinion, it was never a runner?'

'Me and Pip will be carted out of number 96 in a wicker box, just like Lally. And Flo, this business with Theo – my advice is not to share it with the family. Ardraig may be just another stop on his dream road trip, so how will the poor bugger feel when he gets to the campsite and everyone knows he's in love with you, except that a) he might not be, or b) he is, but he hasn't told Sheelagh or Viola, or c), this is purely speculation on Sheelagh's part?'

And so it was with emotions tumbling like clothes in a dryer that Florence and her father climbed up to the split rock. The view was always different, always changing, and like shadows on a sundial, her mood shifted.

Neville put down his binoculars. 'Thank you for calling us together Flo. I still can't get over it. How could Phillipa still believe that Rae and Levon brainwashed us into leaving Eastgate Road, and that I'm only interested in Kathleen?'

'I don't know, Dad. It can't have been easy to see us disappear after Mum died. Don't forget, Pip had to endure that awful time when her colleague was suspended. She wouldn't have taken redundancy without the stress of it. These things mount up. Alec said she'd been staked out in her office all hours, even though the Pentacle contract had been tied up months before. With few friends and even fewer family members to call upon, the real question is why wouldn't she go downhill?'

'Poor Alec. He adores that girl and now she's gone, and he's recovering from surgery on his own.'

Florence put her arms around her tearful father. What could she say that would ease his concern? Whatever way they looked at it, the outcome would have been the same. 'Pip and Alec were invited to come with us to Ardraig. They've never been left out. Dionne will help her to come to terms with that.'

Neville blew his nose. 'I'm sorry, Flo. I just feel so bloody helpless. Rae is blaming herself, and she's got the baby to think of.'

'Rae will be fine. Kathleen has taken her out for the afternoon. But did you notice that the one who ought to have been in pieces was the most chilled.'

'Gabriel's an unusual lad. He looked as though he were mulling things over.'

'That's what I thought, Dad. Anyway, I promised to make dinner and I need an assistant. Are your spud scrubbing skills up to scratch?'

'Kathleen reckons I'm an expert veg peeler.'

'That's a start. Shall we head back?'

They packed up the rucksack and as they set off down the headland, Neville slowed his step. 'Flo, it just occurred to me that this all blew up after your trip to Kinsley. Could this be something to do with this ancestry business?'

'Pip and Alec had the opportunity to buy the perfect house. Sheelagh couldn't have done more to encourage them, but she's a busy woman, and Alec's a tyre-kicker. In addition, Pip's hormones are all over the place, and that definitely won't have helped matters.'

'I s'pose you're right. In any case, if there was a falling out, Theo Coppersmith would have cancelled his booking. He'll be here in ten days. Let's hope we've pulled ourselves together by then.'

Florence held her breath. Should she tell her dad? But how could she when she hardly knew what to make of it herself. What if Sheelagh had got it wrong, and as Alec had said, this was Theo's long-awaited road trip and nothing more? She pushed the vexing thought away.

'I don't know about you, Dad, but I feel better already. No one has died, Alec is finally getting his knee fixed, and Pip's having a much-needed rest. Look, there's Briar, on her body board. Let's cheer her on.'

'She'd like that. Oh, I forgot to mention Briar's new story. We're under orders not to go home after dinner. Apparently the stage is set for a stellar performance.'

'Right now, dragons and princesses will be just the job.'

*

The sea's lament poured through the bedroom window. If Florence needed a metaphor to encapsulate her current state of confusion, there it was. She'd made a good job of convincing her father that all was well, but the plot was taking an alarming turn.

Historically, 'love' was the preserve of her loved ones. Florence's family had provided much of the inspiration to create her most memorable characters. Neville and

Lavender Hobbes' romance had gifted her a beautiful back story for *Greenaway Girls*. Every Friday, on his way home from the docks, Neville would stop at the flower stall to buy his mother a bunch of flowers and would make a point of asking Lally about her day. On Christmas Eve, he asked her to put together an extra special arrangement, *for his sweetheart*. When he presented the bouquet to his flower girl, Lavender Eckley declared that she would love Neville Hobbes till her dying day.

Similarly, a version of Alec's courtship of Pip had found its way into *Our Sunday Best*. He had faithfully and patiently wooed her for five long years until the day after her graduation when, at Tintagel Castle, Pip accepted his trinity knot ring as an enduring love token. And then there was Levon Tyler, the troubled troubadour whose love for Rae ran as deep as the ocean. *When I saw her up there on the split rock, dancing under the blood moon, that's when my life really kicked off.*

These authentic occurrences, and others gathered from her travels were forever immortalised in the Eckley novels, and whilst Florence hadn't experienced a lasting relationship of that intensity, there had been moments – Marcus, for a while at least, and Yass, but he was never meant to be a life-partner. Their passion had gifted her with Rae, the ultimate grail, a precious keepsake who embodied those five exhilarating years. Now, her body and moods were in flux, but unlike Phillipa, the effects of these ungovernable forces rippled rather than raged, and for that Florence was grateful. But if fulfilment came from her family, her road trips, and Ardraig, why was she buffeted about by these deeply troubling sensations?

Florence wasn't naïve. She could recognise a frisson. At this juncture, why not embark on an affair with Theo if he were free, and willing. According to Erica and Birdy, he was no more than Sheelagh's glorified butler, and had found what he needed through his friendships, and it was a tragedy that he hadn't met his equal. True or not, through chimerical, mystical means, Theo's presence had soaked through her pores. There was nothing with which to compare it. And she had known the moment: sitting beside the ancient apple tree, drinking raspberry lemonade. Florence acknowledged the fear that came with such potent feelings. She reminded herself that her father, irrevocably altered by Lally's death, had made a new life with Kathleen. But was that courageous or foolish, knowing that he might have to undergo the pain all over again?

In ten days, Theo would be here. What to do? Florence considered her options. She could disappear. There were legitimate excuses to avoid seeing him, for a few days, at any rate. But she recalled Phillipa's admonishment. *You've never committed to anything, Flo. When the going gets tough, you're off again. That is your inherent weakness.* Pip was right. Florence was ashamed of her cowardliness. Erica and Theo had been extraordinarily kind and besides, hadn't she reminded him, twice, that if he came to Ardraig, she would repay his hospitality?

So she would be here, but clothed in suitable armour, as to do otherwise would be a mistake. But this Florence knew: whatever Theo's feelings were, he would never leave Kinsley. How could Sheelagh face her detractors without him? And with Cleavers, the café, and the cottage to attend to, Theo was the mainstay, the hub around which the wheels turned. Erica and Hughie had said as much.

Florence sat up and swung her legs over the side of the bed. It was time to scrap the dramatic plotline. There were other ways to satisfy her artistic ego rather than catastrophising. Yes, Sheelagh Spicer may have been unpopular in some circles, but the woman was indomitable, and was committed to improving the lives of others. So what if romance novels were an anathema – everyone was entitled to their opinion. In some ways they were alike: strong mothers of equally strong daughters who were forging their way through a persistently patriarchal world using peaceful and creative means. Surely it would take more than a relationship hiccup to capsize Sheelagh Spicer. She and Theo might even fare better apart, which was often the case when the pains of separation eased.

Tired of thinking on such things, Florence pulled on her jacket, laced up her walking shoes, and went in search of the miraculous.

33
Best not act in haste

Theo came into the kitchen carrying an empty washing basket. Sheelagh was still at the table and was working on something or other. She should have left for London an hour ago. He put the basket away before filling the kettle. At this time of day she would have expected a drink, but for weeks now alcohol had been off the menu, probably due to Viola's insistence that her mother take better care of herself. It had been such an odd time. They'd scarcely been in each other's company, except for the annual fête, when Sheelagh had invited guests for the weekend without alerting him until the last minute. Too frayed to be annoyed, Theo had lived up to his duties as affable host by keeping cups and stomachs filled, while she dealt with the intellectual entertainment.

In the run up to his departure, Theo was staggered to discover just how much there was to do, and how many people he had to call upon to deputise for him, although their well-wishing was truly humbling. Hughie was impressed with his handling of 'Dottie' during the caravan's test run over at the industrial estate, and had insisted he call, if in need. But Theo was determined to avoid all contact with Kinsley's affairs. As yet, he hadn't discussed with Sheelagh his intention to remain offline – not that he expected a protest, as she had never insisted on regular messages, but that was before Phillipa's dinner party. Something had happened that night, but with no way of knowing what that might be, he brushed the uneasy sensation aside. Viola had been extremely busy tying up Quirk's loose ends. Aside from her 'happy holiday' message, they hadn't chatted for a while. But Sheelagh was here, and this was his final opportunity to talk to her.

He brought the coffee pot to the table and sat down. 'Thank you for supporting my trip.'

'I'll be in London most of the time anyway. Phillipa and Alec were scheduled to view Frog Lane, but they've stalled. He sent a message, something about an operation. Apparently, she's in France.'

'Is it a working holiday?'

'I've no idea.'

'I thought they were serious about moving to Kinsley.'

'Phillipa has made the right noises, but Alec looked very much at home at his party, and over dinner at Eastgate Road. There is quite a community in De Beauvoir.'

They looked at each other. Never before had there been awkwardness between them, and though there was no avoiding the impasse, Theo wasn't convinced that this was the right moment to break open the crust of their relationship. His agitation was more than a nuisance. It had taken huge reserves of energy to get through the weeks, even with therapeutic intervention, and now he was on the cusp of a momentous trip, how much easier it would be to abandon ship, to carry on as before. And yet, this was a critical moment. Even if this were a fool's errand and nothing came of Theo's yearning to see Florence again, at least he would have finally experienced a road trip. What happened after that was impossible to predict.

'I'm sure Phillipa will be in touch when she returns.' Theo filled the mugs and placed one beside her laptop. 'What time are you setting off?'

'Soon. Before you leave, is there anything I should know?'

'I've put a fruit and veg box in the boot. Viola especially wanted onions and beetroot. My itinerary is pinned on the board. Margery will organise the refuse collection and pick up the post, but you'll let her know when you plan to return.'

'That's looking increasing unlikely with my current schedule. Viola and I may take a short break.'

'Oh! Well, you'll have fun together. She seems brighter these days.'

'Since meeting Gabriel Darby, you mean.'

'That wasn't what I meant, Sheelagh, but if Gabriel is having a beneficial influence on our daughter, that's to be celebrated.'

'You'll find out soon enough.'

He waited for more, but Sheelagh returned her glare to the screen. As there were still several matters to attend to, he stood. 'I'll leave you to it, then ... as a matter of fact, there is something. I've talked it over with Viola. She's agreed to call only if necessary, likewise with Erica and Margery. Being dragged back to Kinsley when it's taken this long to get away would not be conducive to a holiday.'

'Is that what this is, Theo?'

'It's a four week trip, Sheelagh. If you need to call, please call. Who knows, I may have had enough by Tuesday.'

As convincing as Theo wanted this to sound, his words rang hollow. He skulked guiltily away, leaving Sheelagh's sorry figure to her laptop. By the time he came down again she was gone, but there was a note, tucked under the pepper mill.

Best not act in haste. We'll talk when you get back.

Theo sat down, rested his weary head on his hands, and cried.

*

'Theeeooo!' Erica followed Tulip's waddle into the kitchen and deposited a large hessian bag on the table. 'Ah, there you are. You've picked a grand morning for swanning off.' She pulled out the tea caddy. 'Final brew?'

'Perfect timing. How are you, Erica?'

Erica pulled out a chair and flopped down. 'D'you want the polite version or nothing but the truth?'

Theo smiled through his sadness. This was meant to be a joyful moment, but yesterday's despondency had loitered like a shepherd at a hiring fair. Even Viola's farewell gift hadn't lifted his spirits. She had sent him an exquisite notebook with an inscription by Mark Twain on the front cover, *The Secret of Getting Ahead is Getting Started.* Her message served as a gentle prod to record his experiences, as one fine day he might feel an urge to write about them. The notebook was now stowed in the caravan along with a number of books, his father's ancient field glasses, and a radio. Theo was tempted to pack his laptop but had changed his mind, following the gut wrenching final scene with Sheelagh. If he had to attribute one of the causes that had weakened their relationship, it was her inability to unplug.

But now, his messenger of faith and hope was here, and with heroic might he pulled himself together. 'I'd like the honest truth and nothing but, Erica.'

'As much as we want you to go, we don't really want you to go. Even Margery is glum. But don't worry about Tulip. I know how much you want to take her but with her hip so poorly, she'll be better off at ours. Hughie will lavish her with so much love, you'll be yesterday's news.'

'Thank you Erica. But the caddy, I thought we had a deal.'

'We did, Theo, and I've *sooo* enjoyed sharing its contents at Bookbinders, but this will remind you of us. I sent away for a packet of tea from that place that Flo gets it from, so you shouldn't run out.'

'That's extremely thoughtful. And you've brought a punnet of raspberries and some beef tomatoes.'

'And a selection of goodies you don't grow. Salads are an easy option in the caravan. Hughie and I only cook when the weather's rough. There's always a treat to be had along the way – that's one of the joys of caravanning – but you'll find that out soon enough. Oh, and I thought you might appreciate these.'

One by one, Erica lifted a series of books from the bag, and placed them on the table. Theo was stunned. It was the entire Ellis Eckley collection. In the ensuing silence, he was intensely aware of the mantlepiece clock ticking, the long-tailed tits hustling the woodpecker on the feeder, and the drum roll of his heart. Erica's sad eyes rested on his. As they small-talked their way through tea, she made him promise to send the occasional message, to let them know how he was getting along, but nothing more. When they stood, her embrace was fiercely protective as a mother for her disconsolate child.

After waving her and Tulip farewell, he cleared the kitchen, locked the door behind him, and set off tentatively towards the unknown.

34
Twin sets and Tanqueray

Rather than taking her usual route towards London, Sheelagh was on her way to Dorset. It was imperative to have time alone before going back to Farringdon. Viola was bound to ask questions, and she wasn't in the right frame of mind to answer. Ironically, it was after reading *Marcy McBride* that the idea to revisit the county arose. When Sheelagh was seven, Charles Spicer had taken her and her mother to the Seafleet Hotel on the Jurassic coast, for a two-week vacation. This was the closest they had ever come to a traditional family holiday, and though it wasn't the most appropriate setting for a child about to be sent to boarding school, it was the perfect destination for a professional woman of sixty-eight, flying solo.

Sheelagh drove into the hotel car park and pulled up beside the thick laurel hedge. She clambered out of the Volvo and lifted a small suitcase from the boot. As she wheeled it towards the reception, a gust of mild salty wind whipped at her hair. Pausing for a moment to take a breath, a smartly uniformed woman approached and with a smile, took the suitcase from her before disappearing inside. While 'Irene' and the receptionist sorted out something or other, Sheelagh surveyed the interior. Incredibly, the hotel had lost none of its faded gentility. The patterned upholstered chairs and low mahogany tables, thick grey Wilton carpet, buttermilk walls, and huge yucca plants lining the walls might have been the very same. From the headcount partaking of the obligatory afternoon tea in the lobby's seating area, the clientele (retired military personnel, and mature twin-set ladies in knee length skirts with fully grown, dutiful offspring in attendance) confirmed that the only trend here was to reject trends, to pretend that nothing in the world, pre-1945, had changed. With less than zero chance of being recognised, (Sheelagh had checked in as 'Parry') she could kick back, as Viola liked to say.

The bellboy led her to the first floor, and into The Charmouth Suite, which overlooked the bay. Customary small talk over, Sheelagh asked the solicitous young man for a Tanqueray gin and tonic (room temperature, no ice, and one slice of lemon) before tipping him twenty pounds, just as her father had done to the bellboy's counterpart, six decades before. She was astounded to have received the same goofy smile. Then, she slipped off her sandals and jacket, and checked out the bathroom: different colour bath, obviously; the addition of a walk-in shower, and the usual towel and toiletry paraphernalia. Similarly in the living area: a fully stocked mini bar, magazines, fruit bowl and a box of local fudge.

Why Sheelagh should have been nervous to enter the bedroom she had slept in as a child was bizarre, but it was with some trepidation that she pushed open the door. And there it was on the wall in front of her – the ten inch square beach scene. Reverentially, she walked towards it, feeling strangely off kilter. As she peered at the brush strokes, Sheelagh was instantly reacquainted with *Sixpenny Shower*: the athletic father building sand castles with a fair haired boy while his sister (a twin?) stands at the water's edge, her hands held up to the heavens as the shimmering 'coins' rain down on the sea. The mother, glamorous in a wide brim hat and sculpted legs hadn't moved from the lounger, forever lost in the pages of a glossy.

This scene had been endlessly fascinating, and while her parents stayed below for cognac and cocktails, Sheelagh had passed her solitary evenings inventing countless stories of who this family might be, what adventures they shared, and had wished with all her heart that they were hers.

The knock broke her reverie. Yet another member of staff set the tray down, wished her a pleasant stay, and as the door closed, a burst of sunlight flooded the room. Sheelagh took the highball and the dish of pistachios onto the balcony, and from the comfort of the cushioned wicker chair, sipped the long drink. Perfect. Oh yes, it was the right decision to come, and if she wanted to extend her stay, the receptionist confirmed availability. At four hundred quid a night, room only, of course there was. The Ballantyne family were adept at warding off regular takeover attempts to acquire the perfectly situated hotel, thus keeping the old faithful content. The Seafleet's motorsailer, Wayfarer, was apparently still water worthy and available for hire, with or without crew. Ah, yes, that appalling coastline cruise when Sheelagh tried to hide the vomit stain on her dress from her equally sea-sick parents who were doing their utmost to appear jolly.

A squadron of gulls squawked overhead, releasing a flurry of synonyms from Sheelagh's literary synapses: drove; flight; congregation; troupe; skein, convoy; horde; tribe; clan; family … her family, as small as it was, was about to disintegrate. Theo's going away was significant, his first tentative steps away from her. She had been so sure of his presence, so certain of its certainty that she had stopped paying him the attention he deserved. Circumstances alone had prevented her from being in Kinsley during his cancer treatment. The villagers had no idea how reluctant she was to travel to Australia, but Theo had urged her to go. *There's no need to be concerned, Sheelagh. I'm far too busy to die and will be here when you return.* So, she and Viola had flown to Canberra to deal with her stepmother's estate.

As it had turned out, visiting her father's home for the first and last time was unexpectedly eventful. Although Sheelagh was grateful for his financial generosity, Charles Spicer had remained an iceberg to the last. During their twice-yearly, long-distance chats, news of his granddaughter and even his first wife's death were inconsequential compared to the industry's changing fortunes, information he had lapped up like a thirsty mutt. At some point during their fifteen minutes, he would recall her disastrous decision to cut loose from Spicer Kennedy, conveniently sidestepping the fact that he had done exactly the same.

His death was related to her via the seriously embarrassed family lawyer who mumbled the details of the cremation, scheduled for that same week. Sheelagh had no intention of flying thousands of miles to pretend to grieve, neither did she attend his childless second wife's memorial service a year later, but when advised that she was the sole beneficiary of the substantial remainder of the Spicer estate, there was no choice but to go.

As soon as they arrived at the ghastly mock-Tudor sprawl, Viola immediately rolled up her sleeves and headed upstairs to empty the stranger's vast walk-in wardrobes, leaving Sheelagh to do the boring bit. When Charles' office keys were finally located, she heaved open the door and came face to face with an impressive glass cabinet. In the centre was a framed photograph of her graduation, a newspaper cutting capturing the moment she received an MBE, and a black and white image of father and daughter, windswept and laughing, at Durdle Door. Alongside these startling items was the signed first edition of *The Memoirs of Sherlock Holmes*, her gift to celebrate his fiftieth birthday. The unnerving effect of this discovery still ricocheted, and had been shared with no one, not even Viola. These were the only objects Sheelagh brought home and were now on a shelf in her bedroom, along with Emily Parry's book of sonnets.

A revelation of this magnitude might have made the arduous journey worthwhile, except that when Sheelagh returned to Kinsley, a mood had settled over the village, no matter that Theo's recovery was underway. Even her friendship with Margery had cooled, and it had taken every sinew to regain whatever fragile trust she'd been given to begin with. Her father had consistently warned her not to confuse friendship with business, the results of which had left Sheelagh pretty much denuded of people on whom she could genuinely count on, and this made Margery, second only to Theo and Viola a person of vital importance. With Quirk coming to an end, who knew what her daughter's next step might be, but her budding friendship with Gabriel Darby, far from boding well, had increased Sheelagh's discomfort. What if Viola relocated to Ardraig, as Phillipa's son had done? Would she feel the same sense of abandonment?

Overcome with an alien and terrifying anguish, Sheelagh knocked back the drink. If Theo were to embark on a new life with Florence Hobbes, it would be impossible to remain in a hostile village with so few friends. Sheelagh hadn't exaggerated when she told Phillipa that Cleavers would have to be sold. That final connection to her mother and her ancestors would be severed. Sheelagh placed the empty glass on the table as tears, like heavy rain, fell onto her blouse.

35
Watershed

'I'm so glad the operation went well, Dad'.

Gabriel was sitting at his tiny bedroom desk, overlooking the low stone-walled garden, where a herd of wrens darted on and off the grass in what looked like a game of tag. 'Wendy will have you up and about in no time.'

'I've known Gary since we were knee high to a grasshopper, so you'd think he might have warned me his missus was a secret squaddie. Wendy won't let me get away with a thing.'

'Just as it should be. You'll let me know if I can help, won't you?'

''Course I will, son. The boys are doing a blinding job. They're taking bets on how long it'll be before I'm back in the seven-a-side.'

'I'll stick a pony on six weeks,' said Gabriel, and was overjoyed to hear his father chuckle. 'Have you heard from Dionne?'

'Your mum's eating well, and her sleep is better. It's only been a fortnight, but it feels like ten years. Still, there's not much opportunity to wallow. It's like Piccadilly soddin' Circus in here.'

'Send Mum my love and ask her when I should call. No rush, though. She's safe, and you're on the road to recovery. When Uncle Jason comes home, that'll give us another reason to celebrate.'

'Can't wait ... hold up, Sergeant Wendy's arrived. Thanks for ringing, Gabriel. Love you, son.'

'Love you too, Dad.'

In the bathroom, Gabriel splashed his face with cold water. His dad was obviously in pieces. Two weeks without his sweetheart and with no definite return date was crushing for a couple who had never really been apart. As for him, the urgency to finish his project had increased exponentially. There hadn't been an opportunity to discuss it with Florence. She was either busy planning ahead with Rae, or was out of sight, possibly organising another trip. Only his aunt could shed light on Viola's recently voiced concerns. Apparently, Sheelagh seemed to think that when Theo returned from his travels, their lives wouldn't be the same, but hadn't said why or how.

Whilst acknowledging Viola's anxiety, Gabriel was circumspect. Road trips were meant to be transformative. What would be the point in leaving everything behind in the first place to return the same as you were? Entire libraries of ground breaking books had been written about the very subject, but Viola had been too disturbed to acknowledge this. Not only had her mother's south coast flight rang alarm bells, but the possibility of Cleavers being sold had freaked her out. Viola assumed that as soon as Theo had ticked off the items on his bucket list, he'd hop, skip and jump to Kinsley, and they'd pick up as before.

Gabriel reminded her that most couples went through periods of recalibration, and if there were anything of note to share when Theo arrived, he would do so.

Back in his bedroom, Gabriel pulled on a fresh T-shirt. Reviewing his friendship with Viola, the 'cousins six times removed' revelation had reinforced their mutual protectiveness, as had their single child status, age, and shared sense of purpose. Nevertheless, he had kept quiet about his secret project. His feelings had always been a reliable guide, and in this matter the reading was strong.

Far from winding down at the season's end, it was all go. Flo had suggested the APC kick-start the following year's project well in advance of the baby's arrival. The *Greenaway Women* draft manuscript had been given universal approval, and the London event was confirmed. As this was Ellis Eckley's last novel, everyone agreed she should go out in style. Gabriel had no fears for the future of the Collective. He was totally supportive of Flo's decision, knowing that there were more than enough projects in the pipeline to keep the wheels turning. Momentum was building in the right way, and at the right speed. It was natural to feel anxious at what he was about to unleash. Nevertheless, Gabriel was eager to get on with it.

At the sound of the dinner gong, he tidied his notes, closed the laptop and headed downstairs. Rae's positive reaction to his project was a boost. She'd guessed he was up to something, and now they were doing what they loved best – collaborating on his magical realism adventure story which, when made real, Gabriel was confident his wish would be granted.

36
So far, so very good

Relentless rain harried the caravan from every direction, yet incredibly the panoramic windows were clear of condensation. With a supper of soup, bread and cheese, and a glass of beer acclimatising beside Viola's notebook, Theo wondered if he had ever been so content. Acorn Vale, an independent campsite situated near the Forest of Bowland, had been his home for this, his second week. Walking the breath-taking peaks and mooching the fine historic market towns of Settle and Harrogate had boosted his reserves, but he was powerless to slow the passing of time. Already eight days had vanished. Come tomorrow, Stage 3, he'd be back on the motorway, heading for Northumberland, and his brother.

Theo reached for his notebook. For the purposes of practicality, he had divided his road trip into seven stages:

Stage 1, Derbyshire; Stage 2, North Yorkshire;
Stage 3, Northumberland, Stage 4, Edinburgh; Stage 5, Cairngorm;
Stage 6, Ardraig; Stage 7, Kinsley

Theo flipped back the pages to that first afternoon. For as long as he lived, he would never forget the elation of reaching the Derbyshire campsite, without incident. All thoughts of Kinsley had vaporised upon entering Rockrose Farm, where the amenable owner directed him safely onto the designated hardstanding pitch and after being assured that the rookie could take it from there, she sprinted off to welcome the next arrival. Slowly and methodically, Theo unhitched the car, unwound the steadies, hooked up the electric cable, fixed the aqua roll, and slid the exterior table into its slot. Then he climbed inside. The three-birth tourer was the ultimate in practical design and comfort. When the pop-up roof was raised and the canvas panels unzipped, it was just as Hughie had promised – ample space in which to stretch his long limbs.

Dottie's interior fell roughly into three sections: a large, fixed-in-position bed at the far end; a hob, fridge, and airplane-sized bathroom in the centre, and a dinette at the front end. With the abundance of perimeter lockers and under seat storage, he could, in another life, stay on the road for months. As soon as the power supply was tested, Theo sent Hughie a 'lift-off' text message, after which he celebrated with a pot of Florence's tea. His generous benefactor had warned him not to fall under Dottie's spell, but it was too late: the love affair was well and truly underway.

Later that same afternoon, Theo had followed the urge to explore his surroundings. Adjacent to the campsite lay a nature reserve, Rockrose Wood. The land had been given to the local wildlife trust decades before, the results of which were a hundred acres of mixed broadleaf and watery wonderland. Wide barked paths lined with thick blackberry brambles were laden with busy bees and butterflies, while a host of boisterous birds chattered in noisy abandon. If proof were needed that given the right conditions wildlife would thrive, Rockrose Wood was it. Back at the campsite, Theo sat on the fold up chair with a glass of ale and absorbed the ebb and flow. Fellow travellers, mostly with dogs, stopped to chat, and a friendly walking group invited him for a drink later that evening, but he politely declined. Nothing could have induced him to miss his long-awaited rendezvous with Ellis Eckley.

Fresh from a hot shower in the spotlessly clean facilities block, and with the sun setting splendidly over Derbyshire's regal skies, Theo had settled himself down to read *Greenaway Girls*. But it was not to be. At ten o'clock the following morning the campsite lawn mower roused him. Theo soaked up the soundscape from the comfort of the sizeable bed until hunger urged him up and, in no time at all, he had demolished a breakfast of fruit, toast, and coffee before setting off to see his friends.

If Kevin and Jilly Greening's hearty Buxton welcome were an indicator of what lay in store, Theo basked in fortune's smile. After walking the Monsal Trail, the graduates relived their college days over dusky red wine and wild rice tagine while Jilly, ever the gentle inquisitor, probed Theo's reasons for finally taking to the road. Kevin was affectionately envious and thought it a terrific idea – shouldn't everyone have a sabbatical at some point in their lives? When the visit ended, promises to reunite were made, and this time they would be kept.

And now Theo was in the north of Yorkshire, his eighth day on the road. As the miles steadily clocked up, he was becoming better acquainted with Dottie and was therefore less anxious. Never one to wing it, he'd taken Florence's excellent advice to resist the temptation to see and do too much. *Without a pause here and there, my senses would blow a fuse. It's so important to listen, feel, smell, and taste the surroundings – to experience the 'in-ness,' just as Steinbeck described it.* How right she was, and how much more fascinating she was becoming to him.

With supper finished and his diary written up, Theo undressed for bed. Tonight was the turn of *The Ghost Pond,* novel number five. Anticipation fizzed through him. The ritual of returning from a day out to climb into bed with Ellis Eckley was too intoxicating for words. Maybe he was deluded, but having devoured those first four books, Theo believed he was getting to know the real Florence Hobbes. Her cross-genre stories were set in contemporary British Isles and were seasoned with European scenes, a number of which were familiar.

In *Empty Silhouette,* the Alhambra's dusty mullions and fountains recalled the setting that had marked his and Sheelagh's first official holiday as a couple. Theo had accompanied her to a 'Courtyards and Queens' gala in the Generalife gardens. It was an indication of the sort of life he might expect if they stayed together. That same garden had been used as a backdrop to a passionate encounter between the main protagonists in Eckley's novel. Theo was convinced that a clue to the identity of Rae's father lay in this particular chapter.

Only someone who had experienced the sudden death of a loved one as he had could have written *The Allium*

Graveyard with such sensitivity. The catharsis engendered through these short stories must have helped Florence as she journeyed through her bereavement. They would have been extremely useful to Theo when his father died. Were the garden motifs employed as an attempt to sever the cord between parent and child, or were they simply a loving tribute? This, along with other questions, Theo planned to ask Florence.

Now it was the turn of *The Ghost Pond*. What would these two hundred and ninety four pages have in store? Along with the previous novels, this one was inscribed to another family member, her free-spirited aunt, the first to leave London,

Maxine, la que abrió la puerta

and for a moment, Theo wondered if one day his name might appear on her dedication page in gratitude for opening a door. Embarrassed by the thought, he switched on the reading light before turning expectantly to Chapter One.

*

'I know I've said this once or twice, Theo, but we really will be sad to see you go.'

'Four times, Miriam, not that I'm counting. And steady with that second helping. My not-so-little brother is spoilt enough.' Bennett watched with a kindly eye as his wife filled Theo's dish with another generous wodge of summer fruit pudding. It had been a wonderful week, more especially as Theo had defied all expectations by arranging the trip, and not everyone in Kinsley would have been happy about it.

'This was meant to be a holiday, but once again you've had Theo working in the garden all day.'

'And bloody useful he is too, Miriam,' Bennett said, grinning. 'The timing couldn't have been better. Out of humour the seasons may well be, but the apples have been abundant. I'm seriously impressed by your pickling skills, brother.'

'I've Mum to thank for that. You may not know this, Miriam, but while she and I were chopping for chutney, Bennett and his buddies were out scrumping the shires.'

'And you can guess who was sent to bed early without their tea.'

Theo was warmed by Bennett's recollections. Despite the long gaps between visits, their bond remained strong, and was encouraged by Miriam whose priority was to keep a harmonious hearth and home. When Theo pulled onto the drive the previous week, the entire Coppersmith family had turned out to greet him. Miriam had gathered her brood together for the weekend which was exhilarating and tiring in equal measure. Harvesting garden produce was, by comparison, leisurely. In between, he and Bennett revisited a number of sights, one of which was Bamburgh Castle, the mythical home of Lancelot, and had rekindled happier memories of times spent with their father. Theo was surprised to discover that Bennett's slower pace was due to a recent heart scare. This had culminated in a reduced working week alongside a sizeable change of perspective.

Observing them together, it was impossible to tell where Bennett ended and Miriam began. Was it any wonder they were the heart and soul of the family, and it had happened by chance – a one in a million, as they say. A week before his brother was due to take the bar exam, he was thrown from his bicycle. It was Miriam's final shift at the A&E, as she had accepted a job in her home town of Hexham. By the time she finished treating Bennett's cuts and bruises, he'd fallen *irretrievably and irrevocably in love.*

Theo raised his glass. 'A toast, to your continued blossoming. How can I thank you for making me so welcome?'

'You've more than repaid us, pet. I only hope you've enough energy to complete your journey. We've only ever got as far as Mull, haven't we Bennett. Ardraig's a long way up. Whoever lured you from Kinsley must be special.'

Theo scraped at his empty bowl. How could Miriam know? Erica and Jilly had arrived at similar conclusions. There was no need for Sheelagh to drag it out of him: 'guilty' must have been scrawled, in bold, across his forehead. But if he needed to unburden himself, there were no more honest and loving people than Bennett and Miriam. So, Theo finished his wine and told them everything, from his first meeting with Florence at Bookbinders, to Alec's party, when she said that Ardraig was especially lovely from mid-September.

Bennett broke the ensuing silence. 'Have you and Sheelagh agreed to separate?'

'We haven't discussed it, *per se*, but I'm sure she's aware that we are heading in that direction. We've been living separate lives for so long, I doubt Sheelagh would notice my absence. Look, I may be the biggest fool ever to have walked the earth, and I've no idea if Florence wants anything other than friendship, but I have to go to Ardraig.'

'Of course you must go, Theo. You've been through so much, and in my opinion no one deserves to be loved more than you. And it's not because Sheelagh and I don't get along – she's a good mother and does good things, but when something like this happens …'

'You took my advice and had your name added to Cleavers' title deeds, didn't you Theo?'

Theo's cheeks were beetroot.

'I *knew* you wouldn't bloody do it. Money may be a low priority for you, but with no private means and a state pension years off, surely you must have …' He caught Miriam's warning glance and sighed heavily.

'Bennett, you are right to admonish me. My head has always tended skyward rather than in financial reality, much like our father, but I can assure you that whatever opinion you have of Sheelagh, her generosity isn't in question.'

'This is nothing to do with generosity. It's to do with your legal rights as a common-law husband and business partner. Sheelagh may have bought the café and the cottage, but you have been – are – an unsalaried manager. Economic abuse is a form of coercive behaviour, Theo. It is a crime.'

'I appreciate your concern, and if I have necessity of the law, you shall be my champion. Regardless of what might happen with Florence, my actions have consequences, and I will deal with them, but I have to see this through. I hope you understand.'

Bennett pulled his brother into a bear hug. 'We've four empty bedrooms, and an enormous shed crying out for a revamp. You'll always have a home here, Theo, even though you are better at chess and you make a tastier chutney.'

Theo returned to the caravan, which had been parked on the drive for the duration. Although welcome to sleep in the house, he cited the experience of bunking down with Dottie far too enticing to pass up, which had tickled his brother's funny bone. The following morning, with the tearful farewells over, he drove away from the soft sandstone house, and set off for Edinburgh.

37
Shifting gear – again

At the brewhouse, Rae unpacked the last box of art supplies and came back to the desk, in readiness for the most important task of the day. She took two folders from the drawer just as her mother whooshed in.

'Am I late?'

'Not at all, Mum. Thanks for having Briar this afternoon.'

'I left her with Kathleen, making coleslaw. Dad says the spinach patties are outselling the fish.'

'A sign of the times. When are you leaving for Inverness?'

'Tomorrow morning. I'll be back on Saturday, via Ullapool.' She pulled out her phone. 'I had an interesting text message from Jamie.'

Proofs are ready. Post or collect?

Rae sighed. The game was up, even if Gabriel believed otherwise. With a collective like the Artless Press, everyone knew what everyone else were doing, and it wasn't necessarily a good thing. 'Let's have a brew and I'll tell you what's brewing.'

'With wordplay like that Rae, it can't be too bad. Do you want herbal tea?'

'I'll have a mug of builders and a slice of Briar's marble cake. Have you tasted it yet? She wanted to make the one with chocolate curlicues.'

'Her vocabulary never fails to amaze. I'm not sure I even know what a curlicue is.'

While her mother busied herself in the kitchenette, Rae looked at the folders: *Greenaway Women,* and *The 108.* Once again, their lives were about to be upended, but this time she wasn't nervous. Maybe being pregnant put everything in perspective. Gabriel's book had come together like lightning although it had been three years in the pondering – in fact, Rae could date it from his first holiday at Ardraig. If there were no reconciliation after this, his parents didn't deserve a son like him. As yet, publishing details and sales potential hadn't been discussed, but Rae was optimistic. *The 108* had made her laugh and cry, and every character, if not likeable, was memorable, *and* she'd read it in a single sitting. Her cousin had inherited the Hobbes storytelling gene, no question.

'Here you are – tea and curly cake.' Florence passed her daughter a plate and a mug and sat opposite.

'Thanks. Levon says I'm much more picky this time around. When I was pregnant with Briar, the only thing I couldn't eat was chilli. By the way, did you speak to Alec?'

'He's up and about and reckons he'll be back in the cab before long. Pip will be home in a few days.'

'D'you think she'll have changed?'

'It's hard to say. She'll certainly feel calmer, and might be more accepting of things, although habits by their nature are hard wired. In any case, Dionne will have had a positive influence. Pip is fortunate to have the support and finances to take a long break. Most women going through the Change can only dream about getting away, let alone to have the likes of Dionne Farleigh and her friends to step in,' she said, and felt incredibly sad at the thought. 'On an upbeat note, I saw Gabriel at the beach this morning. He and Cavell were cavorting like Spring lambs.'

'Yeah, he's erm … he's been offloading.'

'Is that what the proof copy is about?'

'*Miss Marple* strikes again! How'd you guess?'

'Gabriel works for an independent publishing business with his novelist aunt and children's author/artist cousin; his mother is a published academic and broadcaster; his grandfather is a former librarian whose obsession with books shows no sign of slowing down. Gabriel is also going through a challenging time, so what better way to clarify his thinking than to write about it. And the arrival of a proof copy from Ullaprint, my dear daughter, proves that someone in the APC has written a book, and it ain't me, babe.' Florence took the draft manuscript from Rae and turned to the dedication page.

For Mum and Dad,
with boundless love

Beneath it was a quote, from *The Allium Graveyard*,

'Death is just the beginning of the adventure, Sandy.
That's when the fun starts.'

Florence swallowed hard. 'Does Gabriel intend to publish?'

'He hasn't got that far. The purpose of the book is to heal the family wounds. He wants you to read it. What happens next hinges on your response, but my guess is this: if you like it, and you will, he'll send it to the rest of the clan. When it gets the go-ahead, which it definitely will,

Gabriel intends to call a Round Table, assuming Phillipa and Alec can come. After that, who knows?'

'Hm. What do you think of the story?'

'Heart-breakingly beautiful, insightful, funny – shall I go on?'

'Give it to me in less than two hundred.'

Rae laughed. It was a game they had played since forever, and a brilliant way of distilling an idea without losing its essence.

'Okay – Noah Knightley is on a downward slide. After bailing out of university, he drifts between zero-contract jobs, weighed down with every kind of guilt and anxiety. His school inspector mother gives him six months to turn things around, while his train driver dad is as useful as a hole in a bucket. Cue best friend, Neev. She convinces Noah to meet her blind, unconventional great aunt Mari and Uncle Amir who live in a ramshackle suburban 12 acres called The 108.

'Thrice weekly, a large group meet there to swap skills, an hour each, and finish every session with lunch. Noah's skills increase exponentially. In a pivotal scene, he swaps his 'eyes' for Mari's 'ears' – he describes the wild flowers, and she hears his heartbreak. This prompts him to tell Neev how he feels about her. When Noah's swaps reach a hundred and eight, there's a huge celebration. A week later Mari dies. The way in which her life is celebrated yet again changes Noah's perspective, and finally he reconciles with his parents. By the end of the summer, he re-joins the cricket team, walks his neighbour's dog, and begins a carpentry apprenticeship.' Rae grinned. 'How did I do?'

'One hundred and ninety five word count. Not bad. So, *The 108* is inspired by Ardraig, and Mari is based on …'

'Nanny Lally. We're all in there, Mum. It's a simple, brilliant tale. When Noah says he's got nothing worth swapping, Neev rattles off his skills; a listening ear; a painterly eye; telling jokes; explaining fractions; spin bowling, playing the harmonica, and on it goes. Anyway, there's so much more, but you'll find out when you read it.'

Florence leaned back in her chair, fighting an alarming wave of tearful exhaustion. The Artless Press Collective was shifting gear again, but this time it felt unsettling. 'What's in the other folder?'

'Just a few ideas for next year's event. We can discuss it another time. You look tired, Mum. Why don't you go home and rest.'

'I'm okay, Rae. Let's deal with it now.'

'If you're sure.' She took out the summary notes. 'Okay, first off, we wanted to find out if a London launch was feasible, so we put the feelers out. There is a venue but we'll have to get cracking to secure it. As popular as you are Mum, it's not the O2, so don't freak out.'

'Where is it?'

'The Royal Festival Hall. There are two options: the Queen Elizabeth Hall seats nine hundred and sixteen: the auditorium, two and a half thousand. Ticket requests currently stand at two thousand. There's interest from readers in Tokyo, the US and Canada. Word's got out that this is your final act.'

'Have you spoken to Ebony?'

'Yep, and Henbane, Chickweed, Gwennie Lyons, and Regan amongst others. They're all super excited to support you. With that crew on stage, you'll be scratching around for something to do. Ebony wondered if we might celebrate each novel sequentially with a performance by its featured artist while you read an excerpt. We could backdrop the stage with images, a potted history of your work. It'll make for an easy-peasy programme.'

Florence visualised the evening, and immediately saw how it would pan out. Rae was right. There would be practically no input required from her. Suddenly the image of a beautiful garden appeared: Lavender's Garden. 'I know exactly what we'll do with the proceeds, Rae – a memorial garden in Eastgate Park, where Mum used to volunteer. What d'you think?'

'Grandad will be chuffed to bits.'

'And Phillipa will have somewhere to go to remember the good times. We'll commission a bench, with a plaque.' Florence sat up. 'Okay, let's do it. Choose a date to suit you, Rae, bearing in mind you'll have a babe-in-arms.'

'Kathleen will be on hand. There's no way I'm missing this one. The Ullaprint staff want to come, and so will the Ardraigians. Alec will be mob handed with the Eastgate Road Brigade.'

'I've been thinking about Alec. Must be tough, with Pip away. He's not as strong as he makes out, but then again, don't most of us hide behind a mask of some sort.'

Rae scrutinised her mother's face. She had expected a lukewarm response to the London event, but this unquestioning agreement was unnerving. It was as if she couldn't wait for it to be over. This was more than a dose of the blues. Rae rose from the desk and sat beside her. 'Mum, are you alright?'

'I've invited Theo to Ardraig.'

'So what's new? We're always inviting people ...'

Rae had seen her mother cry on just two occasions: at Nanny Lally's funeral, and when Briar was born. Not knowing whether to feel afraid or jubilant, Rae wrapped her arms tightly around her. People didn't *choose* to fall in love, and neither did love discriminate. Ellis Eckley had written about it from all angles – unlikely, unexpected, and unrequited – yet beneath those convincing sentences lay a distance between the writer and her characters, a subtle detachment. And now, it was happening to Florence Hobbes, in real time, and there was nothing to be done.

38
Prince of peonies

Arcadia Avenue might have been situated anywhere in the country. When Theo pulled up outside number 20, it took a moment to absorb the fact that the illustrious professor was living out his days in an unremarkable suburban street. Cedric Munslow had changed address twice since leaving Oxford. The death of his partner had led him from the Georgian grandeur of Edinburgh's New Town to his current post code. Theo had seen his professor only a handful of times in thirty years, but they had maintained a lively correspondence throughout the intervening period, and always with the intention to meet again.

Theo walked up the path to the white frost-glazed door. Before his hand reached the bell, a trim, smartly dressed man with silver cropped hair stepped from behind it.

'Theo! How good to see you. And right on time, too.' He extended a slender hand. 'Come on in.'

The professor's strength of grip was heartening. Theo followed his spry footsteps along the hallway and into a cheerfully painted kitchen where the kettle began to whistle. On the tray beside the oven were two mugs, a milk jug, teapot, and a plate of what looked like nut slices.

'I hope you can tolerate these delightful treats. Vanessa made the pecan slices just yesterday, for my very special guest. She and Malcolm are my neighbours', he indicated to his right, 'and on this side lives Omar. Lost his wife last year – dreadful business – so we're rallying round.' He suddenly stopped. 'Forgive my manners, Theo, I haven't asked after you.'

'I'm well, Professor Munslow and not, I'm relieved to say, either diabetic or allergic.'

'Cedric, please. Let's sit outside. It promises to be a fine day, sent for our benefit from the goddess Antheia herself.'

They settled comfortably on padded loungers laid out under a floral parasol, and from here, Cedric shared his sorrowful tale. Retirement was mapped out. He was all set to accompany his opera singer husband on tour, having earmarked several places of interest to visit along the way. But Franz's untimely death had left him flailing, until a fortuitous meeting with Vanessa Lomas at the Edinburgh Botanical Gardens changed his fate. Friendship blossomed and had culminated in Cedric's suburban relocation – without his academic library, research papers, and memorabilia. He had no wish to be dragged backwards. 'The only way to get out of bed every morning, Theo, was to learn to embrace the new.'

Another 'new' was his carefully curated cottage garden. After a splendid tour, Theo was treated to an equally splendid lunch, the appearance of which resembled a Floris van Dyck still life: gourmet cheese and pâté with rounds of crusty bread, set out on an oakwood board amongst olives, figs, grapes, walnuts, and pomegranate seeds, and accompanied by a glass of Côtes de Bordeaux.

The denouement of aromatic coffee and white chocolate truffles would have brought down the plushest house curtain. Theo was surprised to find it was three o'clock. 'I can't thank you enough for today, Cedric. My voyage is two thirds complete, but each visit eclipses the one before.'

'That's very kind of you to say, Theo, but the enjoyment has been much greater on my part. Forgive my cheek, but I wonder if you are suffering those same groaning pains that afflicted my fifth decade.'

'I've never liked the expression 'mid-life crisis', but perhaps the half century mark has led me to take stock, particularly after surviving cancer.'

'And it is marvellous to see you so fit and well.' Cedric raised his glass in confirmation. 'I recall feeling professionally and personally numb at your age. While it might have been reasonable to mistake my expertise in the ancient gods to mean I actually believed in miracles, it took a night at the opera to prove otherwise. A friend bullied me. It was at the Barbican, and it would cheer me up, he said. Modern opera has never been a favourite, but then, *un coup de foudre.* Thirty blissful years with Franz when I least expected it – wouldn't you say that was miraculous, Theo?'

'But no less deserved, Cedric. And your love affair with Oxford?'

'Invitations and lecture requests continue to drop on the mat, but I haven't the faintest wish to relive past glories. However, if melancholy descends, there's always *Morse.*' They laughed. 'Like Professor Tolkien, whose humble beginnings mirrored my own, it is useful to remember that we are the scribes of our heroic adventures. To have had the privilege of witnessing the great man recite *Beauwolf* was equal to finding the Grail, something I dreamt of as a boy.' His bright eyes twinkled in remembrance. 'J.R.R lived out his days quite happily in Bournemouth, you know.'

'And here you are in Bonny Scotland, prince of peonies, king of crossword competitions …'

'And lover of lochs.' Cedric chuckled. 'I'm never lonely, Theo. My sister's family visit with the children, and I have Vanessa and Malcom. You can imagine my delight when they asked me to join them on holiday. We've travelled the length and breadth of the Highlands and Islands and stay in the most delightful dwellings. I'm quite content to remain loch side with sketch pad while they climb the Munros, the magic of which you are about to discover.'

'And I shall write to you immediately upon my return, but now I really must head back to the campsite. Early start tomorrow.'

When they reached the front door, on impulse Theo embraced the old man. In many ways Cedric Munslow was like his father, but in the professor's case there was no mistaking a profound contentment. Before driving away Cedric said, 'I hope you find what you're looking for, my dear,' and had remained on the pavement until Theo turned the corner.

*

The coastal road to Ardraig was as close to a white-knuckle ride as Theo had ever experienced. Even with the passing places, only the initiated could navigate these roads with any degree of confidence. Despite this, his intention to arrive at Ardraig by mid-afternoon was on target.

Cedric Munslow's hints at the splendour of the Cairngorms were nothing to the experience itself. Corries and crags, forests and juniper bushes, burns and lochs – the numinous landscape smashed open Theo's senses and forever altered his view of nature's elemental power. Armed with a copy of *The Living Mountain*, bought from the campsite as a recommended and trusted guide, Theo soaked up as much as he could possibly absorb in an all too brief stay. But he determined it to be the first of many more.

One of the benefits of an uncluttered itinerary was having time to reflect on his current situation. Bennett and Miriam's views may have differed, but they were very much on his side. There was no doubting his brother's valid concerns for his financial vulnerability, but Theo knew Sheelagh of old. She would have already considered the options, and wouldn't leave him wanting, but this was as far as he dared go. It was all so matter of fact – a twenty-five-year relationship reduced to pounds, shillings and pence. Surely they were mature enough to remain friends, and after all, there would be occasions when they came together, for Viola's sake.

Assuming Florence reciprocated his feelings, her domestic situation wasn't exactly run of the mill. Theo's eminently practical sister-in-law had been surprisingly vocal on this point. Miriam had willed for his star to collide, but lovers needed somewhere to live. An itinerant lifestyle was fine and dandy when young but in later years, a secure roof and warmth were essential. She had a point.

From nowhere, an enormous twin axle motorcaravan

hurtled around the bend. Theo pulled into the nearest passing place with suspended breath. And there it was, the campsite sign. Reflecting on his relationship status would have to wait. Safe arrival was now uppermost on his mind.

*

'Theo! It's great to see you again.'

From the campsite office Gabriel had watched the tourer wobble down the drive before coming out to greet the ashen-faced driver.

Theo wound down the window. 'Hello Gabriel. It's just as well I didn't know about the access road in advance, although having prevailed, there is no denying the sense of victory.'

'You're not the first to say that but give it a day or two and you'll think nothing of it. I'll show you 'home' for the duration, and when you've set up, we'll have a site tour. By the way, Neville and Kathleen have invited you to dinner, unless you'd prefer a quiet night.'

'Well, that is generous. I'd like that very much. I can't imagine it'll take long to find my feet. Dottie and I are now on extremely good terms.'

'She's a head-turner, that's for sure. Am I right in saying this is your first road trip?'

'Yes, but it won't be the last. I guess you could say I'm hooked, but you must hear that a lot. I'm only sorry Viola couldn't come. She insisted I do this alone.'

'Good for her. Now, let's get you pitched up.'

Theo followed Gabriel's slow walk to the far side of the campsite where, in an elevated spot lined with flower boxes, he reversed Dottie onto the grass pitch. But before setting about the now familiar routine, Theo's attention was drawn by the extraordinary view. There was nothing between him and the Isles of Lewis and Harris but an expanse of glittering turquoise water and sky. A flutter filled Theo's chest. He had made it.

*

The breeze whipped against the fabric pop up roof, skiffling a merry tune. Underneath it, for the trained ear at any rate, murmured the tranquilising sounds of the sea. Theo curled under the downy duvet, his eyes heavy. Another place, another set of experiences, but these ones were potentially life changing.

If the evening at Kathleen's dinner table was anything to go by, he had a first glimpse of Ardraig's powerful call. Even without Florence's presence, being entertained by her family came a close second. The opportunity to orient himself, to catch his turbulent breath before seeing her again was, Theo reasoned, a stroke of luck. Briar's attentiveness was charming, and Rae's offer of a tour of the business was given without asking. The forthcoming fireside get-together had all the ingredients for a super-charged evening. After years in the wilderness, Levon's former band, Rainmaker, were reforming. The remaining members had come to Ardraig to persuade him to reconsider. To be reminded of those crazy drug-fuelled days which had culminated in two broken relationships and a spell in rehab was the last thing Levon wanted. *Still, it was nice to be asked, and the lads deserve a good send off.*

When the wonderful meal ended, Neville, Gabriel, and Levon invited Theo to walk up to the split rock. The weather had been stubbornly overcast that day, but there was a sunset. While Levon filled the paper cups with single malt whisky in honour of the occasion, Neville announced with some pride, that for a rookie roadster to have crossed ten counties without incident, it was worth a toast.

Settled on the rocks, he gave a spine tingling account of local hero, the Reverend Norman Macleod, who had set sail from that very spot for New Zealand, via Nova Scotia, in what came to be known as the first peacetime migration. The reverend's family, like so many others in that period, had eked out a cattle-rearing living in the area after forced resettlement. Disillusioned with the iniquities of the clearances and lax ministerial behaviour, in 1817, the radical philosophy graduate was to rattle more than a few cages before leaving his homeland forever. Information and relics dedicated to Macleod's memory were preserved in a croft nearby, and if Theo were interested, Neville offered to take him there.

With the whisky warming nicely, Theo recreated the farewell scene in which the hopeful crew and passengers sailed away from the bay for the last time. They must have felt trepidation and excitement, essential ingredients for any adventure – his adventure. As the sky darkened, the new friends headed back down to the campsite, laughing at Neville's 'lady with the van' tale, and before parting for the evening, Gabriel had said, *Flo will be back tomorrow. She's looking forward to seeing you.* This was Theo's last waking thought before yielding to Ardraig's entrancing embrace.

39
The revenant

She came upon him, sitting on the bench overlooking the sea. He was in shirtsleeves and jeans and was peering through an old pair of field glasses at a marvellous (and for him an unfamiliar) sight. The porpoise was a regular around the bay. Theo might have been any one of a number of tourists, except that Florence would have recognised his profile anywhere. His exclamation, full of wonder and delight, brought a smile to her nervous lips. Unwilling to disturb the magical moment, she waited until Theo lowered his glasses before sitting beside him.

'We call him Ambrose.'

Before Theo had time to acknowledge her arrival, Florence trained her binoculars towards the marine mammal. 'He hasn't been here for a while, but now that the water boarders have gone, he'll come out to play.' Relieved to feel her heart beat regulate, she turned to him. 'Hello Theo. It's good to see you. Shall we walk down to the shore? I believe I promised you a greeting.'

'There is nothing I would like more.'

He stood and shook the stiffness from his legs, and once on the beach, they ambled along the shoreline, Florence with her flip flops in her hand. She paused to watch a black-throated diver waddle into the water. 'Gabriel said you just about made it along the coast road. Not for the fainthearted, is it?'

'I must admit to feeling like an apprentice daredevil, but he's assured me it'll get easier.'

'The road wasn't designed for the constant stream of traffic: horses, classic car groups, motorbikes, caravans, and everything in between. The locals aren't too happy, but it brings in money. The trick is knowing when to drive it.' She paused. 'Have you made plans for tomorrow?'

'Rae and Gabriel have promised a tour of the brewhouse sometime, and Neville mentioned an iron age *broch*, but nothing is confirmed.'

'The forecast for the morning is promising. I'll drive you to the lighthouse if you like. There's a café on the way. Not quite the Leaf and Loaf, but we're guaranteed a friendly smile, and I can pick up some pots of homemade chilli jam.'

'I'm in your capable hands, Florence.'

They stood for a while, each with their own thoughts until a familiar voice boomeranged across the beach. Cavell scampered towards them with Gabriel in pursuit. Theo bent down to stroke the cheerful dog.

'Flo, you're back! How did it go?'

'Fine, thanks. I've left a package for you, in the office.'

'Oh! Did Rae tell you?'

Florence put her hand on Gabriel's arm. 'We'll have a chat when you're ready.' Aware of Theo, she said, 'We spotted Ambrose at the bay.'

'Fab! The boy's back in town.'

'I'm taking Theo to Stromer tomorrow.'

271

'You'll need a head for heights, Theo. I promised Viola we'd take special care of you.'

'I shall report back that after twenty-four hours, you're doing a royal job. With regards tomorrow's festivities, do I need to bring along anything in particular?'

Florence looked enquiringly at Gabriel, and then remembered that Rainmaker were camping out. A rowdy session was the last thing she needed. The short break in Inverness hadn't provided her with much respite, but to let Levon down would be unthinkable. Besides, she only had to stay long enough to play a couple of songs before making herself scarce. Word had got around that the newly re-formed band were staying on site, and as most of the campers had lived through that era, it promised to be quite a night. 'A pair of ear buds might be useful. Vaughan Williams it won't be.'

'I'm becoming accustomed to the Hobbes way of doing things. If you recall, I attended the Ludlow event, and Alec's party.'

'Oh, yeah, you were at the Assembly Rooms,' said Gabriel. 'Flo was patchy with the feedback, so I look forward to hearing an authentic spectator's account. By the way, Kath's Van will start serving in the next hour. I'd recommend you get there before the crowd.'

'I had the pleasure of tasting Kathleen's cooking last night, so I wouldn't want to miss those famous chickpea patties.'

As they made their way back to the campsite, Florence felt the tension around her neck soften. Her family had made a welcoming fuss of Theo, and he looked very much at home. Her step lightened. The waiting was over.

40
The perils of lifting anchor

Aherd of Highland cattle had staked their claim on the road and were munching leisurely on the luscious grassy verge. Florence parked the car on a strip of tarmac nearby. Zipped and booted, she took the rucksack from the back seat and waited for Theo to join her. It was humid, heavy, but above, optimistic patches of blue were patiently waiting for the ocean liner clouds to move along.

'I thought we might circumnavigate the lighthouse, and after that take a walk to the Old Man of Stoer.'

Theo looked towards the imposing white structure's precarious position at the edge of a cliff. 'Is it still manned?'

'It's been automated since 1978, when the last family left. They were self-sufficient, but still, it must have been a hard life. Nowadays the building is available as a holiday let.'

As they approached the lighthouse, Theo turned to Florence. 'Would you mind if I waited for you by the gate?'

'And here's me thinking you'd driven six hundred miles for new experiences'. She passed him her binoculars and rucksack. 'Track the water with these. You might catch sight of a Bottlenose, or a Minke whale. There's a flask and cake if you need sustenance. I won't be long.'

Theo did exactly that, and twenty minutes later, and with no definitive sightings, he finished his tea just as Florence returned. At the sight of her eyes shining against her flushed cheeks, he caught his breath. She sat beside him on the grass, so close their shoulders almost touched, and took the cup from him.

'Did you see the seals?'

'I saw quite a bit of movement, but in my ignorance I couldn't be sure what the creatures were.'

'It's reassuring to know they are there, even when you haven't been formerly introduced.' Florence finished the tea and packed the flask away. 'We'll head for the Old Man before stopping for lunch.'

'Will I have to redeem my cowardly self and climb?'

'Only if you like abseiling, Theo. It's a sixty metre sea stack. I'll be keeping my feet firmly on the ground.'

Under the exposed beamed roof of the intimate stone barn, they lunched on Scotch broth and malted bread. The foursome on the adjacent table were staying at Drumbeg, the last leg of their whistlestop tour. Theo was fascinated to hear Florence's friendly chat segue seamlessly from the superficial into an enchanting history of her adopted home. One of the party scribbled down these go-to places, and before they left, were already plotting an extended return. With no apparent need to be anywhere else, Florence nipped back to the main building. She returned with coffee, walnut cake, and two forks.

'Thank you for bringing me here today, Florence. Your head for heights is remarkable. I must admit to holding my breath when you disappeared behind the lighthouse.'

'What you can't see is the field that surrounds it, so you'd have been as safe as houses. I'm an expert at disguise, remember?'

'How could I forget. I've no doubt those holidaymakers will return after hearing your glittering account.'

'I hope so. So much more is revealed when we stick around.'

Theo sipped his coffee. 'This has occurred to me more than once, during my journey north. The novelty of being on the road was quickly superseded by a state I've never experienced before. It's impossible to articulate it in my travel journal.'

'On paper, your itinerary is all about friends and family, but as you've continued to travel northward, Mother Nature takes centre stage, and is impossible to ignore. Could that be a reason for the internal shift?'

'Yes! It's exactly that. I was so glad to have taken your advice and have avoided the temptation to overcrowd my schedule. When walking in the more isolated spaces, I was intensely aware of the terrain, the direction and sound of the wind, the cloud formations. It felt as if nature was reclaiming me.'

He understands. 'And being alone – how has that worked out?'

'Well, that's been very interesting. Once or twice I was overcome with feelings of utter desolation, of complete insignificance, and confess to taking refuge in Dottie's comforting hearth. Are you familiar with this state of mind?'

Florence nodded. 'It's one of the perils when lifting anchor. Witnessing the content of our consciousness can be alarming.'

'Kerouac wrote about a similar experience. He stayed in a remote fire lookout in a place called Desolation Peak for sixty two days in the hope of encountering God, but instead, he came face to face with himself.'

'Without substances to lean on, that must have been a challenge. It takes courage and commitment to sit with whatever comes up.'

They made inroads into the cake, and then, 'How was your visit with your brother?'

'Oh, that was wonderful. Bennett and I talked about Dad, and how his blind commitment to the family business had a devastating impact on us, and of course, our mother. Incredibly, my brother still feels guilty for leaving Oxford, but back then I convinced him I would stop the Coppersmith Press wreck from sinking. But it was Bennett who came to Mum's financial aid after our father's death, whereas I, cast adrift and riddled with remorse, allowed Sheelagh to rescue me.' He stopped talking, suddenly aware of saying too much, but Florence's attention encouraged him. 'When Viola came along, I reasoned that while I hadn't been able to salvage my parents' situation, I could, at the very least keep my daughter safe. Unwittingly, my behaviour has made her vulnerable. She is struggling to break away.'

'But didn't Viola want you to take this trip on your own?'

At that moment, another group of walkers arrived. Florence rose to let them have the table. Outside, a dull grey mizzle had settled over the terrain. The friends drove back to the campsite, saying little but thinking much. Theo had discovered that without his anchors, and in spite of an increasing confidence, other more painful areas of his life had come up for review. Viola had been right not to join him – he needed to be alone. Fresh perspectives were unlikely to arise in familiar settings, and in a place such as Ardraig, there was nowhere to hide. To his intense relief, Florence was exactly the same. There were no outstretched arms, no cries of joy at their reunion. A welcome such as that would have alarmed him, but the nature of their conversation was exactly what Theo had hoped for. Perhaps soon they might move it around to the personal, as only then would he know it wasn't simply wishful thinking on his part.

Meanwhile, Florence's thoughts had taken a different tack. A road trip like this could go one of two ways. If Theo were casting about for a safe haven, she might appear an easy option. Hadn't he just confessed to jumping from Coppersmith's sinking ship into Sheelagh Spicer's convenient life raft? If he intended to leave Kinsley, Florence wasn't prepared to throw him a rope. But if Theo had come all this way to build a friendship, only by getting to know each other would they discover if it were worthwhile, and that she was willing to do. Anything else was at this stage, fiction.

*

They came together again at the fire. A large crowd had assembled, cheery with beer and fresh Ardraig air. Florence had stood to the side, while Theo sat alongside Gabriel and her father, chatting and laughing. It occurred to her that he was the missing generation. They exchanged a wave and for the next hour, the visitors were treated to a selection from the Scots/Irish songbook. Before leaving them to it, Florence played *The Skye Boat Song*. She avoided looking in Theo's direction until that final bow stroke which faded into the night. Then, with firelight burning in his eyes he came to her, and invited her for dinner at Dottie's, the following evening.

41
Stories are living things

Theo zigzagged the headland, dipping into various bays along the way to shelter from the wind. He had slept fitfully, his mind a mirror of the topsy turvy sea, but come the morning, both had calmed.

Into his burgeoning collection of memorabilia went another unforgettable evening. The exuberant crowd were entertained with a number of evocative tunes with titles such as *Swallowtail* and *The Burning of the Piper's Hut*, songs that conveyed all the history, adventure and romance required to show Levon's musician friends why he was staying put. Florence had led a rendition of *The Skye Boat Song*, the effect of which had misted many eyes, including his. Just as she was leaving, he managed to get through the crowd to invite her for dinner before the evening really caught alight. Rainmaker had temporarily reunited with Levon to play a much loved Lindisfarne song, *Clear White Light*. Gabriel gave him a tambourine, and for one night only, Theo was a member of the band.

At one point during his unsettled sleep, he sat up in alarm. What if Florence thought he'd come to Ardraig in need of rescuing? She'd guessed correctly that Viola was in the process of untying his apron strings, but it was liberation that pulsed through him, not fear. Theo was eager for his daughter to come into her own. He felt sure she was on the cusp of a breakthrough. Sheelagh would suffer much more, bearing in mind that she and Viola had scarcely been apart. But he couldn't think about them right now. For once in his life, Theo had to consider *his* needs, *his* wants, *his* heart – and it had found a home. Whether Florence felt it too, he had to find out.

*

Dottie needed no embellishment. Hers was a snug interior, enhanced by Erica's creative curtain and cushion flourishes, and would uplift the dullest outdoor palette. A combination of muted side lights, a bottle of cold Sancerre, and a gently simmering herby risotto made for a salubrious atmosphere. Theo had envisaged an evening like this where, without distraction, he and Florence could speak freely. Now it was a reality, and his heart backflipped, mindful of Cecil Munslow's parting wish that Theo find what he was looking for. Then, a heavenly voice floated in.

'Hello Theo.'

'Florence! Good evening.'

He pulled back the mesh screen to let his first and most important guest stepped inside. She sat at the dinette, and from a string bag, took out a jar filled with heather which she placed on the shelf, along with a round of brie.

'Something smells good.'

'Chestnut and squash risotto. The herb salad is from the campsite's supply, and the wine from Lochinvar. May I pour you a glass?'

'Yes please. One of the best things about caravanning is how little paraphernalia is needed.'

Theo passed her the wine. 'Here's to roads less travelled.' They clinked the recycled beakers. 'I didn't think it possible to travel so light yet in such comfort. Dottie's design is extremely efficient. I'm not sure tenting would tempt me in the same way.'

'Campers are spoilt for choice these days. I've stayed in everything from a bell tent to a camping wagon and would choose an Eriba every time. Have you had a good day?'

'A strange day.' He brought the risotto to the table and spooned it onto the plates. 'I was up at the split rock before the wind blew me down to the bay. Too much space to think. And you?'

'An office day. Rae and I sorted through paperwork, caught up with orders, that sort of thing.'

'Rae and Gabriel will take me around on Wednesday. Tomorrow I'm to accompany Neville and Kathleen to Ullapool, where I'm told there are an abundance of trees.'

'Do you miss them?'

'Not yet. The sea's proximity is bewitching. I can appreciate how a place such as this gets under the skin, ' he said, with a sigh. 'If only time wouldn't slip so helplessly through my fingers.'

'Then let it slip, Theo.'

They ate the rice, making easy conversation, after which Theo cleared the table, and put out fresh plates.

'Is there a board for the cheese?'

'In the cupboard above your head.'

Before Theo could reach for it on her behalf, Florence had popped the nearest cupboard open. Inside were the

Ellis Eckley collection, next to her tea caddy. With his face aflame, Theo quickly closed the door and took down the cheeseboard from the adjacent cupboard. 'Another confession.'

'I hope it's not a habit.'

Theo grinned. 'Before I left Kinsley, Erica lent me your entire collection. She was concerned I might need entertaining, and of course, she wanted me to enjoy a quality cup of tea.'

'And are you entertained?'

'In so many ways, and I have questions, but I understand if you'd rather not talk shop.'

'I don't mind, now I know the books were Erica's idea. But before we start, let's have a cuppa.'

While Florence arranged the cheese and crackers, Theo filled the kettle. 'I was fascinated by the twilight Flamenco scene in *Empty Silhouette*.'

'You've been there?'

'A long time ago, but an atmosphere like that doesn't alter much. Will you tell me about it?'

'Javier, my travelling companion, has family in Granada. That was where the caddy was made. His uncle and aunt live in the apartments above their restaurant. Dolores Moreno is the same age as I am now, but to a seventeen-year-old, she seemed ancient. She taught me the basics of Flamenco. One night, she asked if I would dance for the regulars. She had a dress and shoes, and would make up my face and hair ... I couldn't refuse, despite feeling petrified. That was when I knew the power of disguise.'

'It is a wonderfully evocative chapter. Another is from *The Allium Graveyard*, when Sandy discovers the dead bumble bees clinging to the allium flower heads, during the unseasonal frost. It moved me to tears. I wondered if you used the short stories as a way of exploring the passage of grief.'

'Although I wrote the stories shortly after Mum's death, it wasn't a conscious act to help me get through it. But what I've always known is that stories are living things. They cast light on dark times, they change trajectories, mend broken hearts. Unwittingly, they helped to heal mine.' Florence finished her wine, feeling herself relax. 'Interestingly, most of the letters come from *Graveyard* readers. It may seem naïve to you, Theo, but at the time, I had no idea writing was cathartic.'

'I'm not sure many storytellers know that until they begin to write. Are the environmental themes inspired by your brother?'

'Jason provides the detail, but even if he didn't, how can I pretend that all's well when we're drowning in our own filth? I'm told that the environmental themes are subtle enough to provoke reflection, and sometimes action, but not guilt. In a roundabout way my stories make a difference, even if it's at a micro level.'

They sat for a while in the soft light, drinking tea, chugging along with their own trains of thought. Then, 'I spoke to Alec today. He's back in the cab, but only for a few hours a week to begin with. His recovery is nothing short of remarkable.'

'And Phillipa?'

'She's home now. I haven't spoken to her yet, but Alec is optimistic. Her absence has been hard for him. He's determined to do things differently.'

Theo nodded. Their families, so recently connected through myth and ancestry, were undergoing tectonic shifts, and largely driven by the idea of what constituted home. 'Sheelagh isn't convinced they will move to Kinsley.'

'She's right.'

They looked into each other's eyes, skirting around the nub of it. Neither had mentioned Kinsley, or Bookbinders, or Cleavers until then. Even Erica's name had echoed like that of a distant relative. Theo wondered if Florence wanted or needed to dissect those three weeks, but regardless of that, he knew himself to be changed. His journey had started with the cancer diagnosis and conscious or not, a process of review was well underway. All that was needed was a catalyst, a sign to reveal his purpose, which he had never truly expected, but it *had* arrived, and like Cedric's *coup de foudre*, he was in destiny's arms. With growing courage, Theo was about to do what he had never done before: risk friendship for the slender chance of love.

'Journeys end in lovers meeting. Every wise man's son doth know. Florence, within minutes of our first meeting, we talked about travelling, and you quoted those lines whose provenance I couldn't recall. Earlier today, whilst up on the headland, the origin of the quote appeared, as if from the heavens: *Twelfth Night*. It's not until Viola abandons the Cesario disguise that she is free to express her authentic self. And here we are, unmasked, and at liberty to speak truthfully.' Theo paused just long enough not to lose his nerve. 'Your arrival in Kinsley precipitated a series of events that have brought us to this moment. Maybe I wouldn't have undertaken this trip without that, who knows? But my life with Sheelagh can never be the same.'

Now that he had said what was in his heart, Theo was awash with a profound peace, the same sensation that had coursed through him when he and Erica had read Florence's letter. He searched her devastating eyes for what seemed an eternity before asking the most important question of his life. 'If this were my tale, how would you end it?'

'You're in all my stories, Theo, along with my dad, Alec, Pip, Marcus, Levon. You epitomise the wounded hero archetype: vulnerable, loving, compassionate. Eventually, you find the grail.'

'Well, that's a relief.' They laughed, and he knew it would be alright. 'Do you recall our afternoon at Cleavers? You said I must write my own ending.'

'And how does it pan out?'

'As yet I've no clear picture, but the opening chapter is as familiar to me as *Arthur's* noble tale.'

42
Sight-seeing

Florence found herself a passenger in the back of Kathleen's four wheel drive. They were on the way to Ullapool and her fingers were surreptitiously entwined with Theo's. Her father didn't exactly need to twist her arm to join the day trippers, particularly as they had been gifted a glorious morning, which wasn't so unusual, but following a spell of what every Scot knows as *gloaming*, it was greeted with saucer-sized grins. They passed glittering lochs, towering hills and tumbling valleys, and on the approach to the tree-lined town, the harbour waters shimmered like limpid silver under the autumn sun.

After a restorative frothy coffee and shortbread rounds, Kathleen and Neville had several tasks to complete. The fledgling lovers were left to browse like regular tourists, except that Florence was aware of the novelty value of her situation. At the bookshop, while Theo delved into the generously stocked shelves, she found a wooden jigsaw, for Briar. Then, at the harbour gallery, she helped him to choose for Viola a tiny seascape, made from shells and beach flotsam, before heading outside for French vanilla ice cream cones eaten whilst perched on the harbour wall. There, Theo gave her the collection of Scottish poetry he'd just bought. Neither mentioned the previous night, but much earlier that morning, when Florence returned to the hay barn with the sun on the rise, she had a glimpse of that which her loved ones had been blessed with.

The quartet reunited for a quayside lunch. Of the countless occasions in which Florence had sat at a dinner table with her father and Kathleen, this was extraordinary because of its ordinariness, and it was with considerable reluctance she left the restaurant, homeward bound. Confident that Theo would be entertained by her father's potted history of the area, Florence closed her eyes and was lulled into a delicious, semi-drowsy state. Inevitably, his proximity prompted a replay of the previous night.

As a rule, she avoided writing in any detail about sex. The risks of getting it wrong had ruined many a good story – far better to leave that particular intimacy to her readers' imaginations. Florence smiled to herself. Under no circumstances would she attempt to recreate last night's tryst on the page. She and Theo had revelled in each other's desire for hours, and as the sun climbed, he watched her dress, and then in all seriousness he said, *May I have coffee with my full Scottish.* This had set them off in a fit of giggles. After throwing him a banana, (which was impressively caught) she kissed his merry mouth and left the caravan with fingers crossed for another night together before he left.

Theo had been invited to dinner with Rae and Levon, an early meal, it being term time. Florence had made her excuses. She really needed a good long sleep. When they met again, she had to be clear-headed. An idea was taking shape and was almost ready to share. Although they hadn't talked about a future, when Theo had said that his life with Sheelagh could never be the same, Florence's initial fear of being his safety net evaporated. She was no expert, but she trusted her gut: this *felt* right. A life of shared daily routine wasn't as remotely interesting as travelling together, perhaps even to Europe – now, *that* had real potential.

With these thoughts Catherine-wheeling, Florence climbed out of the car, thanked her hosts for a wonderful day, wished Theo a pleasant evening, and returned to the barn. The manilla envelope, propped up on the hallway table, went unnoticed in her quest to get to bed.

Sometime later, she awoke with a start. It took a while to work out what county she was in, which was often the case, but soon familiar sounds drifted into her ears, plotting her position under the stars. It was half past ten. She went into the bathroom to freshen up. In the mirror, a soft-eyed stranger smiled back at her: Theo.

As she crossed the hallway, the envelope drew her over. It was Gabriel's handwriting:

Flo, I'd appreciate your thoughts. G x

Florence never locked her door, so he must have dropped it in earlier. She made a pot of tea and a sandwich and with her feet on the sofa, she took out the proof copy of *The 108* from the envelope. Three hours later, she dried her sodden face, brushed her teeth, and went back to bed.

43
A heart to heart

Gabriel pulled out a chair for the visitor. 'Take the weight off, Theo. You've had a busy day. Can I get you a beer?'

'Thank you. I'm honoured to be offered a seat at the famous table. Is it true that important decisions are made around it?'

'They sure are.' Gabriel fetched two bottles of beer from the fridge and poured one of them skilfully into a glass, which he gave to Theo. 'We only call an RT if there's something to share, or we need advice. Whoever calls it has to facilitate, and everyone has the opportunity to speak without interruption. We've worked our way through every type of scenario, from publishing matters, to deciding who is hosting the Solstice celebrations.' Gabriel raised his bottle. 'Anyway, cheers! Rae was sorry she had to shoot off. She and Levon have gone for an ultrasound scan.'

'Exciting times. I hope Levon's friends weren't disappointed.'

'They had an inkling. Even if Rae weren't expecting, there's no way he'd go back to Newcastle. He's committed to her and Briar. The good news is that when his studio gets built, Rainmaker have promised to record here.'

'Ardraig has the right atmosphere for it. From what you've told me about the campsite and the APC, the business is in fine fettle.'

'Danny and Ros own the campsite. Levon came to work for them to begin with, but there was nowhere else he wanted to be, so he sank his last penny into buying the adjacent croft. It was pretty run down, and there are still outbuildings to renovate, but this way Levon and Dan have autonomy.'

'A sensible decision. So, how will Rae's maternity leave affect the day-to-day affairs?'

'Not exactly sure. We're well ahead of schedule with *Greenaway Women*, and the launch event has been finalised. The next *Betsy Pugh* book will go out before Christmas, but that's not a huge run – maybe a couple of thousand copies.'

'Every sale counts, Gabriel. What's your turnaround for an Ellis Eckley book?'

'From final draft to print, two to three weeks.'

'Whew – that's impressive.'

'Ullaprint are a top notch company, and we've plenty of hands available. Ros and Danny's kids usually spend the holidays here, and Niamh has asked Levon if she can stick around. Rae and me will show her the ropes. But now that Flo's taking a time out, it's hard to gauge exactly what the impact will be, although next year's publication will keep us occupied and the campsite, on and off season, is always busy.'

Gabriel paused. Should he mention the money? Then he remembered Viola's advice to use her father as a sounding board. 'Flo has given me what she called a redundancy payment – twenty grand! I didn't want to take it, but she's a hard person to say no to.'

Theo casually sipped his beer while absorbing the startling information that Florence had made a decision after all. As she hadn't raised the subject while they were together, he assumed she'd continue as before. Was she thinking of leaving Ardraig? How would that fit into their embryonic relationship? They'd been too immersed in the physicality of each other to talk of anything concrete, but Theo was determined to discuss the next move before he left. There was still so much to say, and so little time in which to say it. If there were a weakness in his character, it was his inability to take decisive action *for himself*. Little wonder Sheelagh had derided his theoretical travels, but he *had* achieved his road trip dream. 'How does Florence feel about such a prestigious venue for the *Greenway Women* launch?'

'Knowing Flo, she won't think about it until the last minute. She's definitely a seat-of-the-pants person. It's both brilliant and scary to be around her. You never know what's coming. I still can't believe it'll be her last book – her tenth novel, in ten years.'

'Where will that leave you, Gabriel?'

Gabriel was moved by Theo's concern. He wasn't so intimately connected to the family to be biased, but already he had a rough idea of the dynamic. What was still unknown was whether *The 108* would have the intended effect. Rae had raved about it, but she was always on his side. Flo had been out all day, so he'd left a copy in the barn. She wouldn't keep him waiting, although every minute felt like an eternity. The proofs were ready to be posted to his parents, but as his mother had only just returned home, the last thing Gabriel wanted was to rock her unsteady boat, and everyone else would need a few days before sending their feedback. But still, his priority was to mend the relationship with his folks, so an objective opinion would be really useful. 'Theo, has my mum or Florence told you my reasons for coming here?'

'Not in any great detail. Your mother believes you're here temporarily. She told Sheelagh and I as much over dinner. She said you'd get on very well in Kinsley.'

'It's not a new idea. Look, Theo, this may sound arrogant, but I had to move away, for all our sakes. I was hoping that after all this time my mum would back off, that she'd understand my motives, but now she's had a sort of breakdown, and my dad is recovering from an operation without her. I had to get the book finished – it's the only way I have of making her understand. The longer it goes on, Mum won't be able to get past it.'

'When did the difficulties begin?'

'Around the time my nan died. It was turmoil at The Barbers – people showing up all hours, my grandad shut away in his bedroom, Flo wandering around in a daze. Over at my house, Mum was planning some crazy great escape while my dad disappeared in his cab. So, I made myself useful. It was easier to cope if I did stuff. Shortly after that, one of the boys from the cricket team died. Cody wasn't a friend. His repartee was as fast as his bowling arm, and often aimed at me. One time at school I gave a talk on Plato's 'theory of souls', so you can imagine the flack I got. Hanging out at his house was not on my wish list, but my friend Ryan asked me to go, so I went, but just the once.

'Cody had this super-cool garden den, choc-a-bloc with the latest gear and gadgets. He passed around the marijuana like a kingpin while complaining at how shit the world was, bearing in mind that one of the boys took care of his disabled brother and Ryan's mum worked three jobs. So, I brought up the subject of happiness. In retrospect it was naïve, egotistic even, and needless to say it killed the atmosphere, although Ryan said that after I left, a half-decent conversation was had.

'Anyway, a week later, Cody was kicked off the cricket team. It all blew up, including my dad. He must have smelt cannabis on my clothes and without any discussion, grounded me, but it was a breakthrough of sorts because finally he was expressing his emotions. A week later Cody came over. He apologised – said he was jealous because my outlook was different, that I didn't follow the crowd, and he should've been following me. When I suggested we hang out, his smile was so sad, it broke me up. That was the last time I saw him.'

'That must have been tough, Gabriel.'

'His funeral was a turning point. I thought that by studying philosophy, I'd discover the secret to a meaningful life because I wasn't seeing that happening around me. Cody's parents gave him everything but their attention, much like mine, although it was much worse for him. Mum's career was hitting the skids, Dad was blaming everyone in authority, and they wanted me to join those same institutions! But in Ardraig, I realised that the only person who could create a meaningful life was me.' Gabriel paused to let his agitation subside.

'Every generation faces a different set of challenges, and

I don't pretend to have the answers, but it's different here. It opened my eyes. I live amongst inspirational people of all ages who pull together, and for the most part they're doing what they love, not taking more than they need, and not blaming anyone else for the state of the world.' Gabriel felt his heart burst with relief for saying it out loud, but Theo had simply listened, just as Viola said he would.

'My mum is convinced the Ardragians are preppers, that me and Grandad were ambushed, and when I come to my senses, I'll gallop back to Eastgate Road, or Kinsley, in a suit of shining armour. Dad doesn't believe it, but he'll never challenge her. He so scared of losing her that it seriously affects his judgement. But despite being blinded by Mum's incredible intellect, deep in her heart she knows that an individual's destiny cannot be plotted by someone else.'

Despite Gabriel's modesty, it occurred to Theo that he possessed a wisdom way beyond his years. He saw the dichotomised life of those around him – the contradictions, the fear – and was finding his way through the maze. His words seemed to be drawn from an ancient wisdom or source. It was uncanny as it was extraordinary. 'And this is why you wrote the book.'

'I invented Noah Knightley as a way of getting clarity and also in the hope that my mum would understand me. But when I began writing, it was amazing, like the words were coming from somewhere else. It felt as if I was empty and was being filled from some strange source. Sentences became paragraphs which became pages which became chapters, and before I knew it, a sixty-five thousand word story was born.'

'That's remarkable, Gabriel.'

He shrugged. 'I wondered if you might take a look.'

'Viola doesn't know?'

'You can understand why I've held back, Theo. Your daughter is a literary agent, and her mother is a Spicer. I didn't want them to think I was after a leg up.'

'Viola would never think that, but I understand your reasons for not telling her. If you think I can be of help, I'd be honoured to read it.'

'You are the perfect person to help. You're not quite an outsider, but already I know I can trust you. To have come all this way to see us takes courage. Viola is so proud of how you dealt with the cancer, and how everyone in Kinsley admires your honesty and integrity. She said that you and Sheelagh are rock-solid parents, and she owes you everything. That's quite a compliment.'

Theo's blood froze. How on earth could he help this vulnerable young man when he was here under false pretences? What would Gabriel think of him when he discovered that Viola's 'rock solid' father spent an unforgettable night and two wonderfully intimate days with his inspirational aunt, under his very nose, and had practically abandoned Sheelagh in the process?

While Theo wrestled with this paralysing realisation, Gabriel walked over to the desk and took out his book.

'Florence has a copy. If you want to discuss it with her before talking to me, I'm cool with that. As a matter of fact, Theo, I'd prefer it. Her opinion is the most important of all. Without her, I wouldn't have a clue how to write a single sentence, let alone a novel, even if it is self-pitying rubbish.'

'I'm sure that isn't the case, Gabriel. Just the act of writing will have clarified your thinking,' said Theo, paddling furiously under his calm exterior.

'Well, it has definitely done that.'

Gabriel's hug contained all the lightness of an unburdened soul. If only Theo could say the same.

44
Crossed wires

If confirmation were needed that the written word had the ability to change hearts and minds, Gabriel's book was it. In the age of instant, the reverberations of a powerful, uplifting story had the potential to reach far and wide. As soon as Theo returned to the caravan, he read *The 108* from cover to cover. When not drowning in his own self-induced guilt trip, he thought of Viola. This was exactly the sort of novel Quirk was looking for, and yet, he was quite sure that Gabriel had no idea of its potential.

Clutching a bag containing the book and a bottle of wine, Theo scuttled to the hay barn. Florence would be as eager as he to discuss it. After all, Gabriel was as good as a son to her. It was unfortunate that the next stage of their adventure would have to be adjourned as an urgency to return to Kinsley had overtaken him. But somewhere within this spectacular muddle existed a life with Florence, and he was convinced that by the end of the evening, she will have helped him to unravel it.

As soon as Florence saw Theo's woeful expression, her breezy welcome dried on her lips. He followed her into the living room and sat heron-spined on the edge of the sofa, while she hovered by the door. The contents of his bag had fallen open, revealing a bottle of wine, and Gabriel's book. His intention to stay for dinner dampened her flutter of anxiety. 'How was your tour?'

'Fascinating, inspiring. Rae's creative talent is enviable, and Gabriel, well, for a young man to possess such rare qualities ...'

'You read his book.'

'As you know, his continuing estrangement from his parents provided the impetus to write it. He wanted an outsider's opinion, believing mine to be of value.'

Theo suddenly appeared to have sunk in the middle. Alarmed, Florence sat beside him and took his hand. 'I'm so sorry we've dragged you into our saga. Phillipa's axe has been grinding for so long, there can't be much blade left, and Alec is torn between her and Gabriel. *The 108* is meant to mend all that.'

'Yes ...' Theo cleared his throat and turned to her. 'Gabriel said you intend to make *Greenaway Women* your final book.'

Ah, so that's why he hasn't swept me up in his arms. He thinks I'm about to take off. 'After talking it over with you at Kinsley, I concluded that the best way of stepping back without causing too much hardship was to take a sabbatical. It'll give me the opportunity to do something different, something new,' she said self-consciously, but instead of Theo picking up the hint, a curtain of silence fell between them. Not knowing what to do or say, Florence was about to stand when he began to speak. His tone was so grave, it made her shiver.

'*The 108* is clearly inspired by Ardraig and its people.

It may draw unwanted attention to Ellis Eckley, to your family, and to the campsite. I'm afraid that your hopes of a peaceful sabbatical will be shattered, Florence. You are Gabriel's inspiration, and when asked, he will want to share that.'

'You think it'll get to that point?'

'Your nephew has remarkable insight for one so young. The story is deceptively simple yet its message is profound. From the little I know of Phillipa, she can't fail to grasp the significance of her son's journey. He is the Galahad of this epic, the virtuous, spotless son who will transform his family's fortunes.'

A scornful sound flew from Florence's throat. Theo's ridiculously inflated image of her nephew, fuelled by his obsession with Malory forced her up, and her hands clenched inside her apron pockets. 'You're seriously over-dramatizing Gabriel's qualities. Take care not to put him on a pedestal, Theo. It's not what we do here.'

Theo also stood, but with no gentle hand to hold, his arms dangled helplessly. 'Florence, I apologise. I've taken advantage of your hospitality, and mistakenly assumed myself an authority on your family's predicament. But if you will indulge me this once, do you think Gabriel will allow me to take his book to Sheelagh and Viola?'

'I've no idea, Theo. You'll have to ask him.'

They stared at each other as strangers might, and for a terrifying moment, Florence felt an upswelling of tears. She walked to the jilted dining table, set with napkins and flowers, and poured herself a glass of water, all the while willing her hands to stop trembling. Theo came to her side.

'During our conversation earlier, Gabriel said that he and Viola believe me to be worthy of their trust. When they learn of our, of my …'

This was more than a roadblock. Theo was backing off! Florence felt his guilt suck at him like quicksand. 'Subterfuge? Or is betrayal the word you're grasping for, Theo? Why should their opinion change anything? If we didn't follow our hearts for fear of upsetting other people, no one would ever do anything for themselves.' She paced the floor. 'And here's me thinking we were on the cusp of something special. I was about to say that while we might choose not to live under the same roof, we might discover new places together…'

'And there is nothing I would like more, Florence, but your nephew believes me to be beyond reproach. Before you and I go any further, surely it would be best if we saw him together, explained our circumstances …'

'No. Gabriel must face his own future, whatever that happens to be. With a loving family on his side, how could he find himself in harm's way? Your reaction is way over the top.'

To stop herself saying something she might regret, Florence went to the window and looked out at the sea. She had to get him out of her home, to restore some sort of order. 'Theo, go back to the caravan. The situation will look different in the morning.'

'Yes, I'll do that. Thank you, Florence, for being so understanding. I will look out for you tomorrow.'

He put the bottle of wine on the table and hurried out.

45
A journey with two ends

It was the penultimate day before the campsite's closure, and there was a tremendous buzz. To mark Theo's departure the following morning, Kathleen had arranged a farewell meal. To stay away would provoke questions, and as Florence hadn't the wherewithal to answer them, she went. He hadn't looked out for her the day after their 'conversation', nor the day after that. Gabriel had taken him here, there, and everywhere, while she had gone about her business as if nothing untoward had happened, but on the inside her emotions swung impotently from anger to despair.

Dinner was almost over. Theo was clearly a reluctant centre of attention. He acknowledged her just once, when she took away his plate before disappearing into the kitchen, to the safety of soap suds. However unsettled she felt, there was no disguising his angst, although this wasn't so unusual after a spell at Ardraig, and the family were sensitive to it. As she worked her way through the pot and pan mountain, Florence reviewed the situation. Maybe she'd assumed too much. Theo knew how she felt about him, but the reality of a long drive home with the prospect of ending a long relationship must have hit him. And now, Gabriel's book had further muddied the water.

But her opinion hadn't changed. There was no way in the world Florence was about to empty the contents of her private life into her nephew's lap, let alone to ask his permission to embark on a relationship, which effectively was what Theo was suggesting. It was all very well to postpone, but as soon as he returned to Kinsley to dissect Gabriel's novel with Sheelagh and Viola, it would be as if he'd never left. The Spicers would regroup over *The 108* as they had done a thousand times before, with no need to break anyone's heart. If it weren't so bloody pathetic, she'd sob. It was blindingly obvious what was meant to happen next: the feedback would be overwhelmingly in favour of putting the novel out through the APC, if that's what Gabriel wanted. Then, she and Theo would take those first steps towards each other.

The ball was already rattling along. Gabriel had arranged for copies of *The 108* to be couriered to Eastgate Road. Within twenty four hours, Pip and Alec, both of whom she had now spoken to, whole-heartedly agreed that the novel should be published. It was what they had been praying for. Now that they better understood their son's journey through the character of Noah Knightley, they were desperate to see him. So far, so predictable.

Despite feeling low, Florence was intensely relieved to talk to her sister. Decisions were being made. Kinsley was definitely off the menu; Jason and Astrid, his new partner, were planning to return to the UK and would stay at Eastgate Road until they found a home; when a date for a Round Table was fixed, the entire family would reunite at Ardraig. Everyone was upbeat. Everyone except Florence.

With the dishes stacked, she slipped away from Kathleen's house and walked back to the barn. Of course she would be there to wave Theo off in the morning, along with everyone else. How could she not? This was generally the season during which she battened down the hatches to write her next novel, but even if Ellis Eckley weren't about to retire, the energy required to create a new story had deserted her. Oh, the irony! Finally, Florence had opened the doors of her heart to a man whose qualities had drawn her irrevocably to him, only to find that those very qualities had led to his colossal (and in her view, misplaced) sense of betrayal to her nephew, to his daughter, and to Sheelagh Spicer.

Pausing on the path, Florence surveyed the surroundings. Oftentimes it was so still she could feel her mother's blood pumping through her arteries. Tonight was such a night, and she was heartened by it. In season, the 10.30pm lights out rule ensured quiet evenings, but in any case, the barn was far enough away from the campsite to guarantee a silent night, so when the call came, it cut through the air like a sword.

They stood before each other, him in despair, her in resignation. 'Are you all set?'

'Just about. I wanted to see you before I leave.'

'Saying goodbye isn't easy, Theo.'

'I don't know how you do it, Florence. First it was Kevin and Jilly, then Bennett and Miriam, Professor Munslow …'

'It was never a problem for me until now.' She sat on the low wall, and when he joined her, she took his cold hand in hers. His pain was profound, and she felt genuinely sorry, for both of them. 'John Steinbeck wrote that there are two ends to a voyage: you have to leave one place to go to another. It sounds so obvious doesn't it, but in the excitement of starting out on a quest, it's easy to overlook the return journey.' Florence scanned his forlorn face. 'Theo, you're a good man. The anguish won't last forever, and even if it lingers, I have no regrets. The irony is that if I were writing another book, the love story would be authentically mine.'

Theo's tears fell onto their hands. 'If only I could let go of this crushing guilt, Florence.'

'When you get back to Kinsley, you'll work it out.'

Florence walked into the barn, leaving Theo with his misery.

46

Home coming or going?

Sheelagh fiddled with the cutlery. Her signature dish, a spicy haricot something or other simmered on the stove. Theo should have arrived at five, but her watch said six-fifty. The mantlepiece clock had stopped several days ago. She'd been at Cleavers for a week, having left Farringdon on the spur of an angry moment. Viola's comments had rankled, although the conversation started out innocuously enough. Theo's adventures had been transmitted via Gabriel and had wended their way through to her ambivalent ears.

The Ardraigians are giving Dad the holiday of a lifetime. Despite being super busy, Gabriel took him for a limber up at the cricket nets and a tour of the local hostelries. He's also had a good mooch around the coastline and has spotted a dolphin, and a number of seals. I knew Dad would love it.

How did you know?

Oh, come on Mum, he's wanted to do this forever, but it was the cancer that made him realise he had to do it. It's not simply that he puts everyone else before him. Dad's always been far too modest when it comes to meeting his own needs.

You see that as a quality, Viola, whereas in my opinion, a person who is unable to effectively articulate what they want is weak. Your father has always taken the path of least resistance.

Well, if that is the case, Mother, then this road trip is even more of a reason to celebrate.

Sheelagh had been on the point of disclosing to her unworldly daughter the real reason for his going, and had she remained at Farringdon, this was likely to have happened. But here, in the quiet of Cleavers, a number of possibilities had occurred to her, and these she were anxious to discuss with Theo.

The previous afternoon, Sheelagh had gone upstairs to fetch a cardigan, and had paused in the doorway to his bedroom – unfamiliar territory – before entering. In the days when they shared a bed, it was always in her much larger room. Theo's was the smallest of the five bedrooms but it had the best view, overlooking the garden, the fields beyond, and within hearing distance of the river.

Feeling slightly uneasy, Sheelagh opened the wardrobe door and ran her hand down the sleeve of his worn cotton shirt, resting at the familiar frayed cuff. Alongside it hung his corduroy jacket, which usually made an appearance when they had guests. A handful of T-shirts, sweaters and a basket of underwear sat the shelf above. His tuxedo, under wraps in a dark cover, hadn't seen the light of day in years. Theo rarely wanted to go out, even though he never told her directly.

Several photographs lined his desk: her, Viola and Theo, picnicking at the Picardy gite; his parents, in their garden; Bennett and Miriam's brood; a beach scene (Lulworth Cove?) in which a much younger bathing-suited Theo stood alone, looking seaward. The photographer was a mystery, and for a moment, Sheelagh was disturbed to discover that she didn't know who it might be. Inside his father's walnut writing slope was the ink pen she had given him, alongside a pair of cufflinks. The pot of sealing wax, the original 'Coppersmith' seal, Theo had retrieved before leaving the ailing business. A number of ancient hardbacks filled the bookcase – Milton, Chaucer, a Shackleton biography – along with several more recent publications. Sheelagh picked up *Twelfth Night* and opened it at the marker. It was a ticket.

Ludlow Assembly Rooms invites you to spend
an Evening with Ellis Eckley and Friends

Ah, yes, the evening Theo had declined to mention for months, and almost certainly when he had fallen for Florence Hobbes. On the page was a faded asterisk, *Journeys end where lovers meet.* An ancient scene sprung into her mind. They were in Farringdon: she was eight months pregnant and lay with swollen ankles on the sofa, while Theo sat beside her, the play held aloft in one hand, the other resting on her bump. From the get-go he had talked to the baby which, to begin with was annoying, but as the weeks passed, Sheelagh had come to enjoy their closeness, the three of them, beginning a life-long adventure.

She sat on the edge of his bed, feeling bone weary. Theo found it difficult being apart from Tulip for just a few days, so how on earth was he to find the strength to leave his partner of three decades? *Perhaps his trip is a way of letting off steam.* That's what Margery had suggested. It was a novelty, and when the good folk of Kinsley's ticker tape welcome was over, the experience would fade, as all experiences did.

In spite of her friend's reassurance, Sheelagh was gripped by an unfamiliar powerlessness. Ordinarily, their lack of contact wouldn't have bothered her, but this was not business as usual. She thought of calling him several times, but to say what exactly? *Please don't leave. Come home and I'll be the partner you've always wanted.* These unspoken pleas were shocking: Sheelagh Spicer had never needed anyone.

Whatever her overall opinion of the novels, there was no denying Ellis Eckley's piercing observations of the family dynamic. *Marcy McBride* could have been Sheelagh's life-story: the only child of a cold-blooded, absent father and embittered mother; needing to grow up fast at boarding school; ambitious to the point of ruthlessness; a dearth of true friends. She could at least take credit for having a decent relationship with Viola, despite her lack of maternal tactility. Theo took care of that side of things. They would often huddle over books and what not, in a cosy club for two. Sheelagh's shoulders sagged. It hadn't occurred to her that he might need affection *from her.* And now, Theo was in love with Florence Hobbes, and she felt like one of those old diseased trees about to be felled.

The wine did little to soothe her eviscerated nerves. Once again, Sheelagh got up to stir the pot when the sound of a car gave her a start. At the doorway entrance, she watched Theo park the caravan after which he made his way slowly up the path.

'Hello Sheelagh.'

His lips felt cold against her warm cheek.

'I'll unpack later,' he said, and she followed him into the kitchen where he pulled out a chair and sat down heavily.

'Dinner is almost ready. Thought you might be bushed. Drink?'

'A cup of tea would be grand. There was a delay on the M6. I'll collect Tulip tomorrow. Sorry, I meant to call. Didn't expect a meal.'

'No, well, I've been here all week. I had a number of matters to attend to.'

While Sheelagh busied herself at the worktop, Theo leant on his elbows, feeling like an itinerant who had stopped off at a remote American diner before moving on. He was home, and it felt utterly alien.

'Viola will be here for the weekend, but you already know that.'

'We spoke last night, when I was in Moffatt.'

Sheelagh brought the mugs to the table. Under the kitchen light, his haggard appearance was so alarming, she almost wouldn't have known him. 'Would you like a shower?'

'Perhaps a bath later. I haven't had one since I stayed with Bennett and Miriam. That feels like a century ago,' he said, rubbing his temples. 'How are things in Kinsley?'

'Margery was here earlier. She's harvested the fruit and vegetables, and left your post in the study, along with a ream of notes. As I said, I've been catching up with outstanding paperwork, and in between I read a novel or two.'

So, this was the moment. Theo wondered how long Sheelagh would wait before bringing Florence up for discussion in that inimitable way of hers.

'She prods in the most uncomfortable places.'

A lorry passed by; the land line rang, and rang, and was ignored. 'Dorset positively leaps off the page.'

'I take it you mean Florence. She stayed there for several weeks, to carry out research.'

'If the books were professionally edited ...'

Theo shook his head.

Sheelagh's laugh was a touch shrill. 'Like me, Theo, thinks she knows best.' The flicker of a grudge was superseded by a sense of admiration. If Theo were about to leave her, better for it to be a woman such as Florence Hobbes. She refilled her glass. 'Have you any idea what's happening with the Frog Lane property? Phillipa hasn't replied to my messages.'

'That's because she's been in Brittany. She was unwell.'

'Oh! Is it serious?'

'I believe it was some kind of nervous exhaustion. Gabriel confirmed that the house move has been jettisoned.'

'Alec had no intention of leaving London, as much as he waxed lyrical about cider-making and country pub quizzes.'

'I expect they got carried away, Sheelagh. You can be very persuasive.'

'Not every time, Theo.' Silence hung between them like winter smog. 'But we can all expect to be caricatured in Eckley's next novel.'

'I think not. *Greenaway Women* will be her last, and it was written before she came to Kinsley.'

Sheelagh got up to serve the casserole. If Florence were about to give up writing, she must be paving the way for something else: taking flight with Theo, no doubt. She put the steaming dishes on the table, and as they ate, tension rumbled like a volcano until she could hold back no longer. 'Do you intend to tell me what is going on?'

Yes, he intended to tell her, but a wave of fatigue slew him. With Herculean effort, he stood to clear the table.

'Leave that.'

Theo studied the face of the woman who he had known for most of his adult life. Her beautiful eyes glared through ferocious tears, but if he reached out to her, she would push him away.

'Look, Theo, just bloody say it. Didn't we swear to be brutally honest?'

'*Brutal* was your adjective, I think.' Yes he would tell her, but first he needed a drink. He went to the dresser and poured two large whiskeys, one of which he placed in front of her. 'When Florence was here, we talked about my oft-abandoned road trip idea. Before leaving, she said that Erica and I would be given a warm welcome if we ever came as far as Ardraig.'

The ensuing silence was worse than anything Sheelagh had ever known. Worse than, in this very spot, when her father's vicious hand was an inch from her mother's face, and she, the deferential daughter had screamed at him to get out. 'And were you?'

Theo nodded.

'Does Florence love you?'

'I don't know.'

'Has she asked you to move to Ardraig?'

'She talked about travelling, possibly to Europe. It was mostly in the abstract, but … ' He reached for Sheelagh's hand only for it to be snatched away. 'I'm so sorry, Sheelagh. I will move out immediately.'

'That's not necessary.'

He stared at her.

'No doubt Bennett will have had something to say about our lack of robust financial arrangements, but in any case, I have an offer you might wish to consider. There's no reason why we shouldn't carry on as before. I'm scarcely here as it is. I'll set up a separate account and pay you a salary for managing the café, and Bookbinders. The lawyers will draw up the papers.'

'That's incredibly generous of you, but would you mind if we discussed this tomorrow. It's been a hell of a day.'

'Oh – yes, of course. You mentioned a book?'

Theo fished out the copy from his rucksack and passed it to her. 'Gabriel Darby wrote this as a means of reconciling with his parents, but I think you'll find it is much more than that.'

'What do you mean?'

'You'll know when you've read the first chapter. Gabriel has put his trust in me. He and Viola believe me to be the best of men. In fact, she encouraged him to seek my opinion. No doubt that will change when they discover my reasons for going to Ardraig.'

Sheelagh ignored the confession. 'Has Viola a copy?'

'We discussed it last night. Gabriel's family want him to publish through the Artless Press Collective. Although that wasn't his original intention, I've a suspicion he may do so. Sheelagh, I realise it's a lot to ask under the circumstances, but there is no one I trust more. However, I completely understand if you decide otherwise.' He rested his hand on her shoulder before leaving the room.

With Theo's palm print still warm on her trembling body, Sheelagh studied the curious proof volume. There was no blurb to hint at what lay beneath the cover, although the image of the young couple standing by the gate spoke volumes, and overall, the quality was impressive to her trained eye. But whatever the content, it had had the magnitude to derail Theo's attempts to design a future with Florence. Gabriel and Viola's opinions ought to have no bearing on any of their decisions. They were no longer children. It was bloody typical of Theo to shoulder the burden of an imaginary responsibility in addition to his guilt at wanting to leave her.

She got up to make coffee. So, Florence hadn't asked him to stay: she wanted him to make the decision. Hadn't Theo been like this from the very first moment they met? Everything that had happened in their personal and professional relationships had been steered by her while he, in that infuriatingly amicable manner, complied. The only time Theo ever challenged her was when it concerned Viola. What would their daughter think of her duplicitous father now? Would she still sing his praises, or perhaps display a degree of maturity that Sheelagh wasn't convinced she possessed.

Disregarding the doctor's advice to reduce her caffeine intake, Sheelagh poured the strong, black liquid into a large mug and opened her notebook to the page where, the night before, she had listed her options.

1. Keep the status quo. (Turn a blind eye?)
2. Complete break. Sell Cleavers, Bookbinders, Leaf and Loaf. Pay Theo off.
3. Sell Cleavers. Offer Theo Bookbinders as a home, and a salaried position as café manager.

With a thick black pen she struck through the first line. Theo had already made his mind up to leave, even without a definitive offer from Florence. Her second option, to sell Cleavers and cut her ties was the most likely – a complete break. Would she be sorry to sell up? Having spent a week in the draughty house alone, the answer was an emphatic 'no'. It had always been a money-pit. On the assumption that Theo had been happy to deal with the issues, Cleavers was a useful place to house her guests, but to keep it would mean serious investment, and what was the point?

She hadn't intended to broach the subject of his staying so soon after his arrival, but when Theo said he'd move out, she panicked. A sixth sense had sent her over to Margery's house earlier that week. Sheelagh had allowed her friend to fuss, and over dinner, brandy, and confidences, they discussed the theoretical options alongside the future of the festival. It would be expanded and renamed the 'Kinsley Festival of Arts and Music'. Hadn't Margery sufficient connections to various societies, choirs, and galleries to fill multiple programmes? This would ensure continuity while releasing Sheelagh from future commitment, whatever the outcome of her relationship with Theo.

Interestingly, at no point had Margery expressed surprise that he'd met someone else (Sheelagh couldn't bring herself to say who it was), but she had promised unlimited support, and exclusive use of the guest annexe whenever Sheelagh came back to Kinsley. But Margery's loyalty had buoyed her. If Theo were unable or unwilling to retain the status quo, she was confident he'd choose the third option. His guilt at her having to quit Kinsley forever would play in her favour. And so, with Cleavers sold and him installed in Bookbinders, Sheelagh would moot the idea of his managing the café on a regular salary. Obviously he was worth so much more, and she had thought of that. A considerable one-off payment would sever all future financial connections between them, leaving Viola the sole heir to what was left of the Spicer fortune.

As she downed the last of the coffee, Sheelagh felt a sliver of optimism. Theo had sought her opinion: *there is no one I trust more*. This is what they did best: Spicer and Coppersmith. Publishing was in their blood. Now that he was back in Kinsley, in the bosom of the community, perhaps his ardour for Florence might wane, and Option One might seem favourable after all.

47
Old friends reunite

It was one of those overcast mornings that hinted at brighter days ahead. For the first time since returning to Kinsley, Theo paid attention to the world outside his discombobulated mind and was reminded of the considerable comfort which came from familiar surroundings. Tulip led him along the circuitous route to Bookbinders. In a million years he would never have predicted what Sheelagh Spicer was capable of. He had witnessed her every mood, behaviour, and reaction, ranging from ridiculous generosity to unsubtle cruelty, but for the most part, she inhabited a region somewhere in the middle unless pushed to the extreme.

And he had done exactly that by taking off, knowing full well of his intentions, but without the guts to tell her beforehand. Did he really believe she wouldn't have known, simply because she hadn't the capacity to openly express affection? He assumed she was too thick-skinned to be hurt. Erica, Jilly, and Miriam had guessed he was in love, so why hadn't he credited that same sensibility to Sheelagh?

She could have kicked him out or let him fight her in the courts for a legal settlement. She might have dragged the Coppersmith name through the inky dirt of their professional circle, and yet, Sheelagh had done, and would do none of those things. Instead, she was prepared to give him the title deeds to Bookbinders and would draw up a salaried contract to co-manage the Leaf and Loaf Café, with Erica. Then she would leave Kinsley, her ancestral home, passing Cleavers into the grasping hands of Sean Nesbitt, who had made no secret of wanting to buy it, *at the right price*. And if Theo wanted none of it, she would make him a generous settlement, enough to purchase a modest house, and to provide a pension, and they would go their separate ways. Even Bennett had been mute at the proposals – that was before Miriam had nabbed the phone to ask Theo for the unabridged update of his pitiful love life.

Without saying it explicitly, Sheelagh wanted him to stay *with her.* He would have given everything to have heard her express those sentiments even three years ago. But to keep things as they were was untenable, even though the thought of bringing despair to anyone filled him with dread, hence his acquiescence to most situations, inappropriate, unsuitable or otherwise.

As for his love for Florence, epically benighted as Theo now believed it to be, their brief encounter had taken on mythic proportions. There was a distinct possibility that memories alone would have to sustain him through the long days and tortuous nights. Florence may have seen through his tendency to melodrama, but in Theo's opinion, Arthurian chivalry meant sacrifice – not every guy got the girl, and even if he did, like Lancelot, life didn't always run smoothly ever after.

Tulip sauntered down to the stream while Theo waited by the bench, the very spot that had taken on a deeper meaning, just a few months before. The water, swollen from the recent torrential rain, hurtled towards the Wye. He had joined with several villagers to make hasty repairs to the damaged boardwalks, but there wasn't much anyone could do for the sections of the river bank that had been hit the hardest. Knee deep in potentially illegal sewage overflow, this very matter was scheduled for discussion at the next council meeting at which his attendance was expected.

Theo's re-entry to Kinsley had been as rapid as a returning space shuttle. Within twenty-four hours, calls and conversations had come charging his way, although it had to be said, the distractions were welcome. Even if his absence had been lamented solely for his utilitarian skills (Kinsley might have been swept away had it not been for his and Caradoc's gargantuan efforts), it was a relief to feel useful. But there was one person who was sure to have missed him for himself.

Erica had arranged to meet him at Bookbinders that morning as the cottage was currently unoccupied. The timing couldn't have been better. Gabriel's book had galvanised the Spicers into action. When Viola arrived at Cleavers, she had taken him aside, and assured him that whatever happened, she was a grown up and could deal with *any* change of circumstances. Somehow, (Theo didn't ask how) she and Gabriel knew about the short-lived affair, and that given time, everyone involved would adjust. Never in his adult life had he cried out such sorrow – for Viola, for Sheelagh, for Florence, and for himself, but it had the effect of a good storm, after which the sun shone, and there was clarity, perhaps for the first time ever.

For best part of Sunday afternoon, the family of three discussed the merits and potential of the novella. They unanimously agreed that, with Gabriel's permission, *The 108* should be sent to their good friends and independent publishers, Byrd and Byrd, if only for interest's sake. Wary of recent events, it was essential to tread carefully. Byrd's relationship with Harumi Kita had until recently been fruitful, but following a series of incidents which included an online backlash against comments she had made during a supposedly private conversation, and a bullying incident at her son's school, Harumi had flown to Tokyo, to stay with her parents, citing mental health concerns as the primary reason.

That her second novel had yet to materialise was causing a considerable amount of anguish. Although the advance had been returned, Viola was feeling bruised by the whole experience, despite her considerable efforts to protect her client. Understandably, she was concerned for Gabriel. No matter how many precautions were taken, it was generally assumed that as soon as a private individual entered the public arena, they were fair game. Sheelagh strongly advised that it was their duty, as publishers with considerable experience, to attend Gabriel's Round Table, if only to put him in the picture.

Whatever the outcome, Theo was confident that he and Sheelagh would always be connected, in one way or another. Literature fused them as a force for good, and *The 108* was exactly that. It was more than quirky, more than a passing fad. Latterly, it had become commonplace to skirt around controversy, to stew in angry silence or resort to anonymous cyber-attacks rather than openly, and with humility, discuss humanity's challenges. Gabriel had somehow made these predicaments surmountable in what essentially was a love story, but also a practical, resourceful book which didn't shy away from the sore spots. He had continued the Ellis Eckley tradition by incorporating, at the back of the novel, not a 'Grail' but a 'Kitbag' which referenced stoic wartime slogans of packing up one's troubles, but more importantly provided useful pointers in the shape of organisations, suggestions for 'swaps', as well as a list of uplifting songs, poems, and books.

It was at this point that Viola had envisaged a new project, one in which she and Gabriel might set up a charitable organisation to empower adolescents and young adults to help navigate important changes and challenges, rather than feeling alienated and anxious. This was what she'd been waiting for, and with books such as *The 108*, there were creative ways to make a difference. How much better to equip those in need, she had said, with her exquisite violet eyes shining. Sheelagh had also acknowledged the project's potential and was prepared to put resources into supporting Viola's venture, with or without Gabriel Darby on board. Nevertheless, the young man had opened their eyes to possibilities, and that in itself, was to be celebrated.

Theo paused at the gate into Pignut Meadow. It was now a field of stubble like any other, except that within this particular soil lay thousands of glorious wildflower seeds, waiting patiently to bring joy and sustenance to many. He followed Tulip around the perimeter in the direction of the cottage. Whatever his future might be with Florence, he accepted Sheelagh's proposal to move into Bookbinders. It was right that he should leave her, but he wasn't ready to leave Kinsley.

He walked through the back door in what was soon to be his home to find Erica waiting for him, with Florence's tea brewing. Before long, his 'thank you' gifts were spread over the kitchen table.

Erica held the painting of Briar's Cove at arm's length. 'This is gorgeous, Theo. What a time you've had! Hughie will be delighted with his whisky, and to have his Dottie back, and sparkling clean. He's so disappointed not to have been here, but he'll see you at The Sexton tomorrow night.'

'You've both been so generous, Erica, it's the very least I could do. And yes, Ardraig was every bit as wonderful as I imagined it to be. If I said that leaving was the hardest thing I've done, would you understand?'

'Leaving Hughie to nurse my dad in Conwy was hard enough, but that's not the same thing, is it?'

'Perhaps not. How are you, Erica?'

'Busy, and fine, mostly. I couldn't believe my eyes when Sheelagh came into the Leaf and Loaf and asked after Tulip. I persuaded her to stay for lunch – after all, it is her café. She sat in the quiet corner and read one of the novels from the shelf.'

'What wasn't so fine?'

'You not being here and finding Bookbinders in a state after the last lot left. It was some leaving present: a tray of burnt potatoes, dog hair on the duvets and I won't mention the bathroom. Took me hours to clean through.'

'I'm so sorry, Erica. That can't have been pleasant. As a matter of fact, I want to talk to you about the cottage, and erm, well, a number of things.'

'You're not ill, are you, Theo? I must admit you don't look as well as I'd expected.'

'Physically I'm fine, but underneath,' he pointed to his heart, 'that's a different story.'

'Flo?'

He nodded, and as best he could, described the events leading up to the guilt and anguish which had tortured him for six hundred miles and more.

'You wouldn't be human if you didn't feel rotten. You and Sheelagh have been together for a long time, and you've a daughter, but your actions and feelings have nothing to do with Viola and Gabriel. And they are, may I remind you, adults.'

'And Viola has made that plain, as has Florence. Nevertheless, I have to work my way through it.' He put down his mug. 'Erica, before the Kinsley grapevine gets going, I want you to know that Sheelagh is selling Cleavers to Sean Nesbitt. It will happen very soon. The holiday business is being wound up as we speak. Tulip and I will live here, at Bookbinders. Assuming you agree, you and I will manage the Leaf and Loaf Café while Margery is occupied with the new-look arts and music pageant. This revised arrangement should cover the financial shortfall caused by your forced retirement from housekeeping.'

'Hold your horses, Theo. Did you just say that Sheelagh is leaving Kinsley, and you'll be moving in here?'

'Yes. She has asked me to stay on, in a new capacity.'

'Does that mean … how did you leave it with Flo?'

'I'm ashamed to say that I didn't mention anything of value or certainty to Florence,' he said, his face flaming. 'I wasn't in a position to offer her a future, with mine so uncertain. She didn't ask me outright to stay, but at the time I had truly made a mess of things and couldn't think straight. I think she was disappointed.'

'Disappointed? That's the understatement of the flippin' century! I'd have thought she was heartbroken. Theo, you must go back for her.'

'I intend to. You see, Erica, a sort of miracle has occurred, in the shape of her nephew's book. It has reunited the Hobbes and Darby families and already has done so much for mine. A friend of ours would like to talk with Gabriel, so we are travelling to Ardraig at the end of October, and I will speak with Florence – that is, if I haven't chased her away with my ridiculous and cowardly indecisiveness'

Erica jumped up and flung her arms around him. 'It's your caring nature that would have captured her heart in the first place, Theo. The best news is that we won't lose you completely, but don't expect Flo to stay at Bookbinders. She'd never embarrass Sheelagh.'

'But given time, that may change. People move on, don't they, Erica?'

Erica smiled at her darling friend. 'Yes, Theo. People move on.'

48
A mother's pride

Autumn sunlight streamed through the sash window and onto the dining table. Phillipa closed the laptop lid and tuned her ears to the urban operetta. It was gang warfare at the bird feeder. A number of disgruntled blue tits were hassling a huge jackdaw, who was chancing his luck on the fat balls. How could she not have noticed these antics before?

To celebrate her homecoming, Alec and their friends had planted a rowan tree amongst her mother's shrubs and roses, many of them still in bloom. As soon as he took her in his arms, Phillipa realised how much she had missed him. She had listened in amazement to the details of his knee operation, and how everyone had done a superb nursing job, and he was now back in his cab, a new man. Alec's increased mobility and trim waistline were noticeable, and he was just as attentive, but less anxious.

She sighed. Those six weeks in Brittany were life changing. Who would have believed that doing nothing could be so enriching. Her room, one of two guest bedrooms at the Morbihan *chaumière*, was cell-like: ice cap walls, a single dark wooden-framed bed, clothes hooks, table and chair. The utilitarian bathroom was shared, and though there was a bath, the property was without mains water supply, so through a combination of well water, storage tanks and a standpipe, these were more than sufficient for *Le Jardin des hortensias'* four permanent residents, when used carefully. Living costs were covered in various ways: respite breaks, for humans and animals; honey and garden produce sold at market, along with Breton aprons, hand stitched by Agnès, the longest serving resident. The only fixed agenda were the meals. By and by, Philippa began to notice a luminescence flooding in through the doors and windows, and before long, the tranquilising atmosphere positively improved her fretful state.

Most mornings, she was encouraged to help in the kitchen or garden which was, as its name stated, filled with hydrangea. During the hot afternoons she kept within the cool stone walls, reading, or sewing, or talking with Dionne, who suggested they visit some of the places on Phillipa's wish list when she felt up to it. Oh, the thrill of standing beside the awesome forty-one stone megalithic dolmen, *La Roche-aux-Fées*, and wandering the *Forêt de Brocéliande*, where Merlin fell under Vivian's spell, would be forever scorched in her soul. After sharing with Dionne the details of her *Shadow Kin* trilogy, her friend thought it marvellous. There was nothing to eclipse the pleasure of creating for its own sake, and if the inclination to publish arose, surely Dr Phillipa Darby had the means and the connections to do so.

Whilst away, Phillipa reflected on all her relationships. The realisation that she had allowed, even encouraged Alec to idolise her had been a breakthrough. He had continuously kept the decks clear so that she could focus on her 'important work', and this had weakened them. It was time to climb down from her ivory tower without his golden rope. There was no reason why she couldn't help out at the allotment, decorate the house or deal with the finances, and fully intended to do so.

The estrangement with her father was, at long last, at an end. During their emotional conversation, Phillipa was gently reminded that Lally was alive in all his children, and he only need look at their beautiful faces for comfort. No one expected her to befriend Kathleen, only that she be polite, and wouldn't her mother expect that of her? Rae's comments had hurt simply because they were true. At that point, Phillipa hadn't been able to truly appreciate her son's uniqueness. But he'd given up a year of his precious life for university, just for her, and in his desperation to unite, he'd written the novel for her and Alec. Gabriel *had* been true to his word after all: he never abandoned his mother.

As for Sheelagh Spicer, any hope of a deep and meaningful friendship was over before it began. Looking at it dispassionately, Phillipa acknowledged that she'd done all the leg work in a bid to establish more than a familial connection with the Spicers, but as Alec reminded her, Gabriel had made friends with Viola, and so something of value had come out of it.

And now she was home, and a miracle in the form of *The 108* had occurred. Phillipa ran her hand affectionately over Gabriel's book. To discover that he had distilled the essence of *Le Jardin des hortensias* into *The 108* was another wonderful surprise. It must have left a profound impression

326

on him when he visited as a rebellious – no – a curious teenager. Rae, as usual, had designed the perfect cover: two people, standing on one side of an elaborate iron gate, with a golden 108 encircled in the centre, while behind it lay a mysteriously ramshackle house and grounds.

This image encapsulated the spirit of Gabriel's novel, and like Merlin's wand, had sprinkled their lives with magic. When the copies arrived, dedicated *To Mum and Dad, with boundless love*, she and Alec had sat together in the living room and through teary eyes, devoured word for word the transformational, tender, and at times hilarious narrative. Every paragraph had been dissected, every nuance disarticulated, and in the final analysis, she and Alec agreed that the most moving chapter was Noah Knightley's response to Mari's death. Rather than dwelling in unending sorrow, (which is exactly what had happened to Neville and Florence, and had prompted their flight from Eastgate Road), not only was Noah able to let the natural passage of grief pass, but he was enriched by it.

Dionne's riveting explanation of the spiritual significance of the number 108 in the mystical traditions of religion, cosmology, numerology, and astrology had prompted Phillipa into a new line of research. Gabriel's novel melded art, science, music, and spirituality in a potent combination to facilitate change. This was another previously unknown and fascinating dimension to her son.

Immediately after finishing the novel, she called Gabriel. Through laughter and tears came a promise to reunite at Ardraig, at his Round Table. After that, she spoke with Florence, who was delighted to hear she was on the mend. The 'romance' wasn't mentioned. Theo's holiday had come and gone and she was in Ardraig – alone – but was making plans. *Greenaway Women* was to be her final novel. Florence insisted on having enough savings with which to fund her sabbatical, however long that might turn out to be. Phillipa had no concerns for her financial wellbeing, although she was keen to reassure her little sister that there was always a bedroom for her at Eastgate Road.

The key clattered in the lock. Alec was back from a tidy up at the allotment, via Claudio's, where he'd arranged to collect a selection of low calorie treats, an oxymoron if ever there was one. To welcome Philippa home, the generous grocer had sent over a sumptuous hamper, along with a bottle of his best sparkling wine for the 'lady in velvet green', which was his special name for her, ever since he prepared their wedding breakfast.

Alec put the bag on the worktop. 'Sorry I'm late, Pip. The boys send their love. We had a good old chinwag about *The 108* – like a proper book club it was.'

'They're not meant to read it yet.'

'I know, but they swore to keep it under wraps. Gary reckons it'll save people a mint on therapy.'

'That's what happens when our son is a living Galahad, although I must stop saying that out loud.'

Alec pulled her to him. 'Let's keep it between us, then. Jono bawled his eyes out when Mari passed away.'

'So did we, Alec.'

They laughed, and Alec released his wife to unpack the bag, his lips smacking at the contents. 'Gawd – Claudio's put in a key lime pie.'

'So much for our healthy eating regime. I wonder if

he'll trade his culinary skills for your punk rock anecdotes.'

'Funny you should say that. Jono reckons we should get some swaps going, maybe not in exactly the same way as in Gabriel's book, but there's more than enough talent between us to share. Jono's granddaughter is musical but wants to grow spuds; Gary's green-fingered and has always wanted to play the guitar.'

'That's a start. I could make a list of our skills. Even if it doesn't last, some good will come of it, won't it, Alec?'

'That's my girl. The simple things are often the most powerful, but they often get overlooked.'

'That's exactly what Dionne said.' Phillipa led him to her laptop. 'I've been researching into the spiritual significance of the number 108. Listen to this:

From the diameter at Stonehenge to the Fibonacci sequence, 108 is the most auspicious number of all as it represents the unity and wholeness of existence and connects the ancient and modern world.

Alec scanned the page. 'It's like the flippin' *Da Vinci Code*, mysterious strands pulling strings under our very noses. Hang about, Pip, I just had a lightbulb moment. We live at number 96, and your mum's flat was number 12. That's 108! D'you think Gabriel worked it out?'

'I wouldn't be at all surprised. We're the ones who have been wearing blinkers, Alec. Our son has been in love with his best friend forever. How did that slip by unnoticed?'

'Yeah, I'll admit it's shameful to have read about it in his book, but I'll tell you something Gabriel doesn't know: Parminder was at the allotments earlier and we chatted about the kids.' He grinned. 'Esha is due home in December.'

49
Too much chit chat

Gabriel flew through the brewhouse door and pulled off his hat. 'Grandad and Kathleen have just got back from Lochinvar.'

Rae looked up from her sewing pattern. 'Did they get the medicine?'

'Yeah, and some other remedies.'

'What's the diagnosis?'

'A chest infection, and a dose of flu. Flo's agreed to see the doctor again if she's not feeling better by tomorrow'

'Well, we know Kathleen: once a nurse, and all that. Mum's run down. She's not as tough as she looks.'

'No.' Gabriel picked up a piece of heather coloured tweed. 'Cavell will look the business in his winter coat. Can I help?'

'Tea would be nice.'

He went over to the kitchenette and filled the kettle. 'D'you think your mum is ill because of this business with Theo? Viola said that he hadn't been the same since he got back. How could I not have clocked that there was something going on between them?'

'You've had your head and hands full, Gabriel. It took Mum by surprise, but I've no idea how they left it. What else did Viola say?'

'That ever since she can remember, her parents have had an unconventional relationship. They get along, but she's never seen them have a cuddle, or anything like that. Viola is relieved that her dad is staying in Kinsley. She told him not to worry about Sheelagh.'

'That's generous of her, bearing in mind that her dad came to Ardraig for my mum, even if he left empty-handed.'

Gabriel came back to the desk and put down the mugs. 'D'you think there's still a chance they'll get together?'

'I don't know, Gabriel.' Rae stood and wiggled about. The baby was constantly on the move, meaning that she was constantly on the move, and on top of that, her mother's illness was concerning. Word had got around that there was something going on. Yoga Joe had spotted her leaving his caravan early one morning and had mentioned it to Kathleen. After spending the day together at Ullapool, she and Neville were convinced that an announcement of some sort would be made.

Theo was popular. He'd pitched in to help Levon and Danny with the new shower unit as well as helping Gabriel restock the gift shop. Rae had seen the way Theo looked at her mother. Little wonder she was under the weather. 'Why don't you pop over to the barn with the local mag? You haven't had a chance to talk to Mum about your book. It'll cheer her up.'

'D'you think so? I'll make her lunch. Briar collected a big haul of eggs this morning. Shall I mention Bookbinders?'

Rae shook her head. 'There's too much chit chat already. If Theo has got something to say, he won't want you or Viola to steal his thunder.'

With the magazine in one hand and a box of feathery eggs in the other, Gabriel crossed the yard towards the barn. For as long as he'd known Flo, she was always consistent – never moody, or angry, or telling him 'what you ought to do' – and had been his go-to person for so many things. But of late she'd been remote, lost in her own thoughts, so he'd given her space. When the news of her and Theo broke, Gabriel felt torn. It was tough for Viola, but he was over the moon that his beloved aunt had at long last found someone to love, although now it looked as if it had ended before they'd even got going.

Gabriel tapped on the door, kicked off his boots and went into the bedroom. Daylight flooded over the tiny figure swaddled under a huge duvet.

'Hello Gabriel.'

'Is it alright to come in?'

'If you haven't caught it by now, you'll be fine.' Florence propped herself up, while the dog trotted over to the visitor for a pet. 'Briar brought Cavell over this morning. He's missing his special walks and wanted to keep me company. Open the window, will you?'

'Are you sure, Flo? It's blowing for gold out there.'

'It's been musical windows in here. Rae closed them after Kathleen opened them.'

Gabriel opened the window furthest from the bed. Satisfied that the stiff breeze wasn't howling in his aunt's direction, he passed her the magazine. She looked so tiny and vulnerable, and it shocked him. 'Rae thought you might like a bite to eat. Shall I rustle up an omelette?'

'Hot water with honey and lemon would be lovely. I've kept down the toast, and Dad is bringing over a broth later.'

When Gabriel returned from the kitchen, Florence had his book on her lap. At last they could discuss it, and while he knew her initial thoughts, he was anxious to hear more. 'The Round Table is all set for the first of November, the day after the Samhain celebrations. I hope you'll be better by then.'

'I'll be up and about tomorrow. Anyway, enough about me, how do you feel, now that the initial stage is over,'

'Like I'm floating. I spoke to Mum earlier. She and Dad can't wait to bring Uncle Jason and Astrid here. Apparently, they're getting on like a house on fire, and it looks as if Jason's coming home for good.'

'Your grandad will be pleased about that.'

'D'you know, Mum actually asked after Kathleen. I told her that we've started our winter woolly sessions, and I learn more about the folklore and local history than I do about knitting socks.'

'Your mum will accept Kathleen much more quickly if we don't push her, but it sounds promising. I hear there's another secret project in the Darby family.'

'Yeah! Mum's been tinkering with an epic high fantasy story since she was a teenager. Dad said it's amazing, a proper saga. She wants to update us around the fire, y'know, get the right atmosphere and all that. I can't say I'm surprised. Are you?'

'Only that it's taken her this long to tell us about it. Now, if you're not sick of it already, Gabriel, shall we chat about your book.'

Before succumbing to influenza, Florence had read *The 108* a second time, curious to test Theo's claim that her nephew was an Übermensch. Gabriel didn't consider himself special in any way. He was simply recounting his experience as a young man wanting to live peacefully and creatively. *The 108* wasn't a massive deal for the Ardraigians, knowing him as they did. They appreciated it as a page turning adventure story which chimed with many of their own experiences. Theo and Sheelagh's background and conditioning were bound to engender a different outlook and opinion, and it was anyone's guess as to their opinion. But whatever it was, Florence was confident that her nephew would remain grounded.

In the meantime, the powerful Spicer/Coppersmith engine was picking up speed. Although Florence had done her utmost not to think about Theo and what had gone before, his embarrassed text message wasn't exactly a thunderbolt. Why wouldn't he want to join the Round Table?

Gabriel put down the hot drink and sat near the bed.

'Thank you. So, who's coming to the RT?'

'All our family. Viola and Sheelagh have asked if they can bring a friend, someone called Isaac Byrd. What's that all about?'

Florence sipped the sweet liquid. '*The 108* is quirky, and the Spicers know a good thing when they see it. They're not the only ones who want to attend.'

They looked at each other, and to Gabriel's relief, Florence laughed, and then she hacked and coughed. He passed her a glass of water. 'You don't mind, Flo?'

'No, Gabriel. Do you?'

'It'll be great to see Theo again. But I am baffled as to why they'd assume I need a publishing deal when we've got the APC. Viola reckons I ought to keep the door open even if I don't walk through it, as you never know what might be on the other side. She's been itching to come up since we met. Actually, she and I had a good long talk about you … and Theo.'

Florence felt the heat from Gabriel's blush, but he needed to say it, and she hadn't the energy to dissuade him. 'And your conclusions are?'

'That love is for everyone, even if those who have fallen in it happen to be her soft-as-soap father and my supersonic aunt.'

'Hm.'

'She also said that it was a bit weird, but her agency is called Quirk, so why not.' Gabriel wondered if he had overstepped the mark. As close as they were, Flo wasn't about to tell him if Theo had exploded in her heart. Thankfully, she changed the subject.

'What are the arrangements?'

'On the way up, the Spicers will stay at Isaac Byrd's house at Hebden Bridge, They'll go home via Lochinvar...'

'Look, Gabriel, can I just say something. This isn't about me, or Theo, or any of us for that matter. This is about you and your beautiful book.'

'You like it, then?'

Affection swelled in her sore chest. 'Those of us who have read *The 108* are forever changed by it. All I ask is that you postpone your launch, whoever it happens to be with, until Rae's baby is born.'

'Actually, I planned to wait until the *Greenaway Women* event is done and dusted. We'll be super stretched with your swansong.'

'Thank you, my darling. Your Noah Knightly isn't about to sink any time soon, is he?'

'No,' replied Gabriel chuckling, 'but Briar will burst my water wings if I don't take her rock pooling this afternoon.'

50
I thought it was obvious

Florence and Neville left the bonfire for a while, and with torchlight leading the way, they walked up to the split rock. It was chilly; the half-moon was crowned by aureoles, bathing the terrain in mystery and awe. The conditions were perfect for the much-anticipated annual festivities. The Ardraigians had spent the day making wreaths, and playing apple bobbing games, and had celebrated the passing of their loved ones with photographs and shared memories. Florence had written her wish on a piece of paper before giving it to the fire. Letting go of the past had been easy enough before, but she had held on to the idea of Theo, so it was time to release him. This was the season for new adventures.

'The Spicers will be here this time tomorrow, Flo.'

'So they will, Dad. I wonder what their publisher friend will make of Artless.'

'Is that why they're coming, to give the APC the once-over?'

'They're coming to offer Gabriel a contract. I'm not sure if your grandson is fully aware of what he's written. Now that he and Pip have made peace, that boy is on such a high, he'd goat-sit Yoga Joe's pet pygmy if asked.'

'It was good of you to offer to put your sister up, but the barn isn't exactly spacious, and they'll be much better off in Ros and Danny's static.'

'Ros doesn't like to leave it empty when she's in Glasgow during the winter months. At least this way Pip and Alec will have privacy. After the Round Table, the Spicers will spend the night at Lochinvar.'

'And Theo?'

'Theo is a Spicer, Dad.'

Neville was troubled. There were unanswered questions, but he had held back in the hope that Florence would talk to him. And then, (unsurprisingly in Kathleen's view), she became ill and needed an entire week in bed. For years he had prayed that his daughter would meet her match. Seeing her and Theo together in Ullapool had given him reason to believe, but it had fizzled out, and everyone was mystified. Rae thought it had something to do with Gabriel's book, and when the time was right, they'd hook up. If only he had his granddaughter's confidence. 'Have you spoken to each other?'

'Theo sent a text message. Would I object if he accompanies Sheelagh and Viola to Ardraig? I could hardly refuse when it's none of my business. Gabriel must make his own decisions.'

'Flo, I'm going to ask you straight out. What happened between the two of you?'

'I don't know, Dad. I thought we had something going, but when Gabriel involved Theo in *The 108*, he backed off. Said he felt guilty, that our actions were underhand.'

'I can understand that to a certain extent as he's a sensitive chap, but didn't you at least talk about a romance?'

'I said it might be nice to travel together, to see a few places. I thought it was obvious.'

Neville put his arms around his daughter. 'If Theo hasn't worked it out by now, he's a sorry excuse for a lover. So, how are you really feeling, Flo?'

'Confused, and heart-sore, like my characters. I've no one to blame, Dad. When I was in Kinsley, Theo told me that he'd dreamed of going on a road trip, so I said we must write our own adventure stories. I took a risk and it didn't pay off. I'll get over it.'

Florence's sorrowful expression brought tears to his eyes. 'Why don't you disappear before the Spicers arrive? Gabriel will understand.'

'He's been tip-toing around for weeks, waiting for me to bring it up in conversation. When I was in my sickbed, Gabriel said that he and Viola weren't about to judge me if Theo and I had feelings for each other. They're quite a pair.' Florence glanced down to Briar's Bay, where the bonfire threw darts of orange into the darkening sky. 'I could make myself scarce, Dad, but I *have* to be there, for Gabriel's sake. This is important. Anyway, whatever happens, Sheelagh's not about to get on her knees and sing *Jolene*, is she?'

'From what I've heard about Sheelagh Spicer, she's more likely to beg you to take her man.'

Florence laughed out loud at that, and they set off, arm in arm, to rejoin the family around the bonfire.

51
Gabriel calls the tune

The afternoon may have been *dreich*, but the brewhouse fizzed with enough energy to power Stromer Lighthouse for at least a week. Twelve kinetic souls had gathered around the great table, under a circle of silver lustre. Each had a glass of water nearby, and a copy of *The 108*. On Gabriel's immediate right sat Florence, Rae, Levon, and Neville. To his left – Phillipa, Alec, and Jason. Directly opposite, and flanked by Theo were Viola, Sheelagh and Isaac Byrd. Casually dressed the publisher may have been, but the occasion was serious enough to have warranted a personal visit to Ardraig. It had been a whirlwind of a day, and was to end with dinner, courtesy of Kathleen, Niamh, Briar, and Astrid, who were currently in the throes of preparing a feast.

With the guests welcomed, and with not much else to say at that point, Gabriel passed the staff to Isaac.

'On behalf of the Spicers, and Byrd & Byrd, thank you so much for inviting us to Ardraig, and for sharing the Artless Press Collective's formidable story. Maddy, my sister and business partner, is extremely disappointed not to be here, but as she became a first-time grannie this week, you'll forgive her non-appearance. And in true big-sister style, she entrusted me to 'do the right thing', and if not, Sheelagh will report back', he announced, and was encouraged by a rebound of warm smiles.

'Before we talk specifically about *The 108*, you may be interested to hear a little of Byrd's back story. Maddy and I began our careers at Spicer Publishing. Shortly after Charles retired, we presented Sheelagh with a plan to set up on our own, and she has continued to offer her support. The reason you may not have heard of us is because we don't publicise or advertise. Our philosophy is to foster harmonious long-term relationships with niche writers, and this is only possible by limiting our signings.'

Jason raised his hand. Gabriel's call had galvanised him, and now in Ardraig, he and Astrid were basking in a much-needed community spirit. 'These are noble sentiments, Isaac, but how do you make a living?'

'In a similar way to the Artless Press Collective, Jason, just on a bigger scale. Last year we signed two writers, one of which was Harumi Kita, thanks to Viola's talent-spotting, and Sheelagh's introduction.'

'I'm Gabriel's grandfather, Neville Hobbes. May I ask, Isaac, how can you tell if a client will adjust to public scrutiny without blowing a gasket? Take our Flo – she's a successful writer, but no one knows who she is ...' Neville paused at the laughter. 'Sorry, Flo, I didn't mean it like that, but you can go about your business without hassle, whereas Gabriel might not want the attention.'

'Neville, thank you for raising such an important issue. Using an alias as Florence does is one way of keeping out of the spotlight, unless you happen to be Robert Galbraith, that is. There are few secrets in the publishing world. In

Harumi's case, we put together a strategy that suited her. She rarely gives interviews and has a limited social media profile. With the support of a personal assistant, in this instance Maddy's daughter, she chooses who, what, and when.'

Isaac and Sheelagh exchanged a glance. 'Having said that, there have been issues. You may have read in the press that Harumi is currently in Japan. While every precaution is taken to protect our clients, sometimes events overtake us.' He sipped his water before continuing. 'There's a lot more to say about Byrd, and as Kathleen has kindly invited us to stay for dinner, I'll be happy to chat to you then, but as you are all terrifically up to speed,' Isaac turned to Gabriel, 'May I move on to specifics?'

Gabriel Darby's placid manner was disconcerting. He'd said and asked almost nothing since they arrived, making it impossible for Isaac to gauge his thoughts or opinions. During the tour, he had left most of the talking to Rae, but his enthusiasm was indisputable.

Isaac picked up the book and turned it over, as if examining a delicate piece of pottery. 'When Sheelagh sent us *The 108* fully formed, and beautifully wrapped, Maddy and I were lost for words. The artwork and the chapter illustrations caught our eye before we'd even read a line. Maddy spotted the absence of endorsement. It's the same with the Eckley novels. Is this an Artless policy?'

Alec raised his hand, and then dropped it, and then raised it again, feeling like he was back at school, which was never a good place to be. 'The thing is, Isaac, we don't see why a celebrity or industry endorsement is necessary to enjoy a good yarn. Novels are so weighed down with testimonials, awards, and rewards that they can't seem to stand up without them.' Alec acknowledged Phillipa's nod and decided to stop there before he got on his soapbox.

'Dad's right. Awards don't necessarily bring people together,' said Gabriel. 'Who actually chooses to be runner up, or second-best? Comparison is a burden – it crushes creativity. But given the right conditions, our inner light will blaze for a lifetime and more.'

Applause broke out at that and was immediately followed by infectious laughter. Isaac wasn't dealing with everyday people here. To be amongst a group who thought and acted quite differently from those he was accustomed to dealing with was refreshing to say the least. 'That's a very interesting point of view, Gabriel, and I'd love to hear more but I'm aware of time slipping by, and there are important details to discuss.' He opened the book at one of the illustrations. 'Rae, I understand you're responsible for the fantastic artwork, design, and copy editing.'

'Mum gives me free rein, but everyone reads the m/s. When the comments come in and the amends are done, we're pretty much good to go. Gabriel's characters didn't *need* illustrating, but it was intuitive. Thankfully everyone likes them. Believe it or not, Isaac, there have been occasions when my contributions have got the thumbs down.'

'Guilty as charged,' grinned Levon, 'but that's to stop Rae getting too big for her Birkenstocks.'

'Spoken like a true rock star, Levon.' Isaac could scarcely believe his luck to be sitting alongside his all-time musical hero who had, for the past decade, been living under the radar in Ardraig. When introduced earlier that afternoon, words actually failed the self-assured publisher.

As a teenager, Rainmaker were *the* band, and Levon Tyler was the finest rhythm guitarist of his generation. Isaac was desperate to ask about the rumoured reunion, although having met Rae and Briar, and seen the set-up, it was fairly obvious why Levon had declined. 'Rae, your illustrations are reminiscent of a Dickens novel, and in this context have enhanced the narrative. That's quite a talent.'

'I've Mum to thank for setting me on the right road. But what I'd like to know is this: given the APC's efficiency, why would Gabriel need Byrd & Byrd?'

'Two reasons, the first being numbers. You've kindly shared the APC's sales figures for the previous three years, and for a small scale enterprise, they are remarkable. But what would happen if you were facing a bigger demand?'

'How big?'

'A million, at the very least.'

A profound silence fell, and all eyes turned to Gabriel, whose expression was unreadable.

'We Hobbes love a fantasy Isaac, but I gather from your tone that you are serious.'

'Phillipa, when it comes to a work of this calibre, I am deadly serious. Your son has written a once-in-a-decade book, perhaps even sparked a new genre. Both my sons wanted to be here today to meet Gabriel, to ask him for guidance, for inspiration, Kiefer especially. He's eighteen, and desperate for a real super-hero to steer him through this increasingly terrifying world where male disenfranchisement, anxiety, and suicide is at an all-time high.' Isaac paused, not for effect, but for his blood pressure to settle. This wasn't the time to think about his precious sons' welfare.

'This brings me to the second point. *The 108* has the potential to be a world-wide multi-million best seller: film and streaming rights, radio, television, TED talks, serialisations, spin-offs, you name it. Could the Artless Press Collective cope with that? Gabriel would become wealthy and well-known overnight. Could you all handle the resulting clamour for his, and potentially, your family's attention?'

Florence, who until now had been absorbing everyone else's elevated sensory output, was feeling remarkably calm. Even Theo's arrival hadn't disturbed her unduly, partly because she'd kept a low profile while the family greeted the visitors. But right now, the pull on her romantic heartstrings were secondary to Gabriel's well-being, and these eleven people might never come together again. 'May I add my two penn'orth worth, Gabriel?'

'I wish you would, Flo,' he replied, ready for a ladle of his aunt's insight.

'To outsiders, Isaac, we may seem like an odd bunch, so it may help if you knew a bit about us, and I'll keep it brief. Our London flat was filled with books. Dad used to rescue them when the libraries closed. Roget's *Thesaurus* and Chambers *Etymology* were two of our bibles. At random times, Dad would say: *give me ten synonyms for 'whimsical'*, or *five adjectives for 'fearsome'.'*

A chorus of knowing murmurs urged Florence on. 'The word, *contract*, was probably borrowed from Latin; its first appearance was in *The Canterbury Tales*. As a noun, a 'contract' is an agreement enforceable by law; as a verb, 'to contract' means to decrease in size, and also it's something you catch – like an infection, or a virus.'

The entire table exploded, and even Sheelagh had let out a bellow, which sparked another round of laughter. Florence winked at Gabriel, and as she ran her hand over the smooth rosewood, changed her tone.

'This table is more than an example of beautiful marquetry, Isaac; it's more than a symbol for us. As individuals who make up the collective, we know that a single decision impacts the whole. Therefore, when we gather around it, we are confident of making the right one. So, you need have no fear of the APC imploding any time soon.

'To be an influencer or a super-hero wouldn't have occurred to Gabriel. Nevertheless, *The 108* is so much more than a book of ideas. Well written it may be, but this comes directly from the heart. It's a reminder of what the human family − our family − had forgotten. Every character, like a cog in a wheel, is as vital as the next. *The 108* is a blueprint of how the world would function if we each took responsibility. Through Noah's eyes, we see that every once in a while, a helping hand is needed to reveal the grail that exists inside each of us. Neev leads Noah to the house, and his potential erupts the moment he steps through the gate: his first step is his last step.'

Florence rested her gaze on the well-meaning outsider. 'So, Isaac, the only relevant question is how to make the best use of this gift, and Gabriel knows the answer to that.'

Isaac wasn't usually moved to silence, but it was clear that everyone needed time, he needed time to absorb what had been said. He desperately wanted the book, but his concerns had suddenly lost their significance. With a dearth of authentic role models, Gabriel could so easily become a poster boy for those clamouring for answers, just as his sons were, but that now seemed unlikely within this strong, loving unit. Isaac had underestimated how much the recent experience with Harumi Kita had made his team hyper vigilant. He'd been caught out by the APC's *modus operandi*. Ellis Eckley, *aka* Florence Hobbes was now firmly on his antennae.

'Florence, thank you, I think, for the velvet gloved right hook.' Isaac hopped on the coattails of this last burst of humour to finish what he had come to say. 'Gabriel, you've three options: publish through the APC; invite Byrd and Byrd to work with you, or don't publish at all. The third option is the most important. It would be remiss of me if I didn't say this, but once *The 108* is out there, no one can predict the outcome. So, without the pressure of a deadline, or a contract,' he said, winking at Florence, 'take as long as you need to think about it.'

Right on cue, Kathleen popped her head around the door to announce dinner. Excited chatter broke out, tempered by concern for their beloved Gabriel. Everyone hugged him in turn before heading off. Viola was the last to leave.

'Wow, your aunt packs a mighty punch.'

'Yeah, I'm lucky to have Flo as my champion. That was some Round Table.'

'It's a fantastic way to have a meeting – the only way, in fact. And now you know why I couldn't say anything on the phone. *The 108* is so much more than an homage to the Arthurian legend, or a nod to *The Catcher in the Rye*. Whatever you decide, Isaac and Maddy are good people and will help in any way they can. But right now cousin,

I'm ready for a trough. If Kathleen's patties are as good as Dad says they are, you've got yourself a lodger.'

52
Monumental meetings

From the quiet of Kathleen's patio, Florence felt the cold night air sooth her hot face, while inside the living room, chatter bubbled like bath foam. In addition to the turbo-charged meeting, Jason's arrival had boiled the family's pot. He and Astrid had confirmed their intention to move back to the UK, permanently. Before her father's happy tears set off a chain reaction, Florence had escaped outside.

Isaac's announcement was no surprise, and neither was his attitude. It happened all the time: the new idea is launched, and without due care and attention, the unwitting instigator of said idea sinks under the yoke of their genius. When the whole of humanity is suffering, a single person cannot be expected to post the solution on a social media platform. Only by empowering the individual was change possible, and that required patience and commitment.

The 108 was a pointer, nothing more. Florence was firmly of the opinion that a writer's job, like any other artist or craftsperson was to earn a living, and if they really enjoyed it, they were fortunate. While receiving letters from grateful readers was a bonus, at no point had she ever felt beholden to them. The unspoken contract was clear. But every once in a while, the world was graced with a new perspective, as in Gabriel's case, and already there were conflicting opinions. Pip would like nothing more than to see her son's name in lights, but if he chose to put the book aside, she would at least respect his decision; Alec was on the fence, and Jason and her father were cautiously supportive. As for Florence, she knew that if Gabriel chose to go on the road to promote *The 108*, Ardraig would call him back, as it called her back, time and again.

Mindful of Kathleen's urges to keep warm, Florence zipped up her padded coat. She was about to wrap the scarf around her neck when the back door creaked open. Sheelagh stepped out and walked towards her. At the Round Table, her presence was undeniably powerful. Who could have failed to notice the pull it exerted on Isaac Byrd? He had kept her in eyeshot throughout the meeting and during dinner. Florence deliberately sat next to her brother, on the far side of the table. In such a crowd, she was able to avoid direct contact with the Spicers without appearing rude.

When the visitors left, her family would stay up late to discuss the momentous happenings, but not her, not yet. If Sheelagh had something to say, far better to say it now as the chances of meeting again were slim.

'Am I disturbing your solitude, Florence?

'Not at all. It's the first time since my mother's funeral that the entire family have been together, so it's full on.'

'Ah, that explains it. Your brother's an interesting fellow. An inspiration to you, I think. Many good things have come from Ellis Eckley's pen.'

'Gabriel and Viola's friendship, especially.'

'And I am glad of it.' She took a step closer. 'I didn't want to leave without thanking you.'

'Whatever for, Sheelagh?'

'For not making it easy for Theo. Steering others on the right path is his specialty, but not so on the personal front. He'll have to follow his heart, whatever may come of it.'

Florence didn't know what to say, so she said nothing.

'If Gabriel decides to go with Maddy and Isaac, rest assured they will take good care of him, as will Viola and her father.'

'But who will take care of you, Sheelagh?'

'Oh, I'll survive, perhaps even thrive without Theo as a prop. I am my father's daughter, after all. In that, we are alike.' She smiled, and her mesmerising eyes glistened in the moonlight. 'Goodbye, Florence.'

The formidable woman disappeared into the house. All at once Florence was shattered. What she needed more than anything was to go to bed. With her recovery still incomplete, and with the furore of Gabriel's book about to unleash, there was no surplus energy to waste.

*

Through the window, streaks of pink and violet garlanded the morning sky, and cast a docile light over the duvet. Florence sat up. *The worst is over*. Theo had come and gone; Jason was here. Sorrow and joy. She sat with the feeling for a while before climbing out of bed and into her warm clothes. With her teeth quickly brushed, she headed for the beach. The heaviness on her chest had finally lifted, and her breath flowed freely. It was a relief to know that for the immediate future at least, she would stay in Ardraig with her loved ones.

Without realising it, the barn's cosy vibes had ensnared her. It had become a haven during her illness, and like all fledgling romances, they had taken small steps towards a budding relationship. As a housewarming present, Rae had painted her a garden scene, exactly as Florence envisaged the Eastgate Road memorial garden to be. It was the first picture she'd hung on the living room wall. Kathleen had made her a rug and curtains (even if she didn't pull them, they would make the room look homely, she said). Ridiculous to think that at forty-nine years old, Florence actually wanted homely.

The breakers' comforting call drew her towards the rocks at the far end of the beach. Yoga Joe was still here. She would take the opportunity to thank him for making such a nice job of the hay barn, particularly for the extra creative touches. According to Kathleen, he'd taken up with a shepherdess over Drumbeg way, and was quite content. Without prompting, he came towards her, muffled in one of Kathleen's ubiquitous scarf and hat sets. Florence paused. He was too tall to be Yoga Joe. Those gangly arms belonged to only one person.

'Good morning, Florence.'

She caught her breath. If there had to be an ending, wasn't she worthy of a memorable one? Before Florence could ask how, what, and where, he said,

'Rae suggested I stay on in the new static caravan – well, not the new static, but the one intended for the retreaters. I hope you don't mind.'

'Why would I mind? You've made friends here. Is Viola with you?'

'She and Sheelagh are on their way to Hebden Bridge. There will be a lot to talk about in Isaac's car, I should think.'

'That was a turn up for the books.'

'Indeed it was. We knew immediately *The 108* was an important novel. Isaac had to come, if only to meet its gifted writer. Your insightful contribution at the Round Table had a big impact.'

'Hm. It must have been an unusual situation for Isaac and Sheelagh to find themselves in.'

'The Artless Press Collective are unique in that respect. Isaac's sons are eager to be involved. His oldest, Thomson, works at Byrd. Various possibilities, albeit theoretical, are already being muted.'

Theo recalled the youthful energy at the Byrd dinner table just two days ago, when they were welcomed by an ecstatic Maddy. In fact, it had been a surprisingly upbeat trip, all things considered. His concerns at the aftermath of his separation from Sheelagh were largely unfounded. The new arrangement seemed to suit her, and while he wouldn't say she was happy, a sort of peace had settled between them.

Far from missing Cleavers, it had freed Theo up in unexpected ways. His intimate connection to Bookbinders had made the transition so much easier. Both he and Tulip delighted in their new home. If there were any gossip, much of it had been kept out of his earshot, doubtlessly due to Erica and Margery's influence. What was unknown, however, was the kind of reception he might get from Florence. Quite frankly, Theo expected her to write him off. His behaviour was impossible to recall without shame. But her swift and not unfriendly reply to his agonised text message had given him hope, and though she wasn't at the welcoming party, she had smiled at him at the Round Table.

Her obvious frailty was, according to Neville, due to a prolonged bout of influenza. While Theo couldn't claim to know Florence well, she had struck him as being robust and full of life. If he had contributed to her downturn, he was determined to make amends, if she allowed it. 'Viola and Thomson are eager to accompany Gabriel on a tour.'

'These road trips are catching.'

'Whatever the mode of travel, *The 108* will find its way into many hearts and minds.'

'That I don't doubt.'

'Have you any idea what Gabriel will do?'

'No, but we'll be here if he needs rescuing. On the subject of lovely souls, how are Erica, Hughie, and the dogs? '

'Tulip has lots of interesting new scents at Bookbinders, and a cosy spot by the stove. The Briggs' are well. They send their very best to you. We've made tentative travel plans.'

'There will be no stopping you now.'

Their eyes locked, and then, instinctively, Theo took hold of her hand. 'I can't imagine what you must think of me, Florence. All I've done is spread misery in my wake. Fainthearted, that's what I am.'

'How about sensitive? Finely tuned?' They laughed. 'Sheelagh's an incredible woman. It took guts to be here.'

'Wanting the best outcome for Gabriel overrode any personal feelings she might have. I'm certain we will remain friends.'

They walked towards the dunes, her hand still in his. Florence liked the feel of it. 'I don't know about you, Theo, but I could do with a cup of special brew.'

'If you're sure I'm not disturbing. Your family are understandably concerned.'

'It's nothing a good old cuddle couldn't cure.'

Fired by a new courage, Theo drew her to him as gently as his impatience permitted.

Epilogue
Old haunts, new happenings

Everyone said it was an October like no other. During the drive to Dorset, Sheelagh had also been seduced by the colour and the light, but then again, she was so much more attuned to her surroundings these days. Was it really two years since Cleavers had passed into Sean Nesbitt's hands? He hadn't even wanted a survey, so afraid that Sheelagh might change her mind. With Theo installed in Bookbinders, and her permanently in Farringdon, she was relieved to have weathered that particular storm well enough.

Sheelagh had left Viola in Farringdon where, from the basement flat, the new charity, Re-Source, was in full and productive swing. As predicted, *The 108* quickly made waves, but with the diligence of Isaac's tight-knit team coupled with Gabriel's incredible foresight, he was, for the most part, cushioned from unwanted attention. His 'Kitbag' website page overflowed with lifelines, and with Re-Source as an important back up, they were already having an impact.

Gabriel had set out his stall from the get-go: *Project 108* would run for a maximum of two years; he would only talk to those who had read the book (free copies were given to interested schools, and likewise to specific individuals in the media). This was a clever move. Not only did it encourage a young readership, but it also saved time, as only those truly interested in a dialogue were added to the list. Factored into the itinerary were meetings with groups of self-styled swappers who were keen to share their uplifting accounts with the author/instigator before he moved on to other things. The skill-swap phenomenon showed no signs of slowing down. By crossing the age and culture divide, it had morphed into different but no less effective versions of the original, with new ideas and experiences shared via social media.

In Spring of the second year, Gabriel, Violet, and Thomson crossed Europe by rail to honour a number of invitations, the last one scheduled in Bologna. For those countries further afield desperate to meet the gifted young writer, contact was made through the Internet. According to Viola, watching her cousin in action was nothing short of extraordinary. Gabriel's sincerity and humour had disarmed many a critic and there appeared to be unilateral respect for his rejection of publicity for publicity's sake.

Isaac Byrd had quickly grasped that his once-in-a-lifetime signing meant exactly that: when *Project 108* had done its job, his star client would disappear into the sunset with Esha Mehta, or so Viola predicted, although nothing of that nature had happened yet. With no monetary advance required, and the book already nicely produced, unprecedented terms were agreed between Byrd and Byrd and the Artless Press Collective. Never in their careers had Isaac and Maddy encountered such tough negotiators, but

Gabriel Darby was unique, and to ally with him was worth so much more than percentages. Sheelagh had expected as much. The APC were perfectly capable of putting a decent book out and had held all the cards from the start. No matter that *The 108* was supposedly a one-off, the world would see more of this quietly inspirational man in one guise or another, of that Sheelagh was certain.

Phillipa Darby, on the other hand, continued to revel in her public reinvention as epic fantasy writer, and mother of the new kid in town. The first in the *Shadow Kin Trilogy* was in pre-production with Pentacle Film. Caleb Hegarty had also faced tough negotiations with Phillipa who was prepared to take the same publishing route as her son. But at the eleventh hour, an impressive three-book deal was agreed through the American arm of Spicer Kennedy. Her first novel was gaining traction in the US, particularly amongst college educated women interested in this enlightened new genre and was also selling well in the UK.

For a while it seemed that every time Sheelagh opened a newspaper or turned on the radio, her distant cousin was being interviewed by someone or other, but to her credit, Phillipa never mentioned the Spicer/Eckley ancestral connection. But any and all opportunity to celebrate her son's incredible talent wasn't to be sniffed at. If the latest rumour were true, she'd been invited to appear on Desert Island Discs, presumably as the next best thing because, to no one's surprise, Gabriel had declined. He was currently at Ardraig, getting stuck into his next project. To thank Rae and Levon for their 'rescue', he paid for the new recording studio from the proceeds of his first royalty cheque, and who else but Rainmaker were the first to record a reunion album. Ever the gallant knight, Gabriel had arranged for Isaac Byrd to meet his musical heroes on site. And so, the Artless Press Collective continued to thrive.

As was Viola. The inaugural road trip in Gabriel's camper van had been her *best adventure ever*. The threesome had jammed their way around the British Isles (Viola had learned to play the ukelele, and Thomson the harmonica), in between dealing with Gabriel's hectic schedule alongside the serious work of accumulating the necessary requirements to launch Re-Source. On offer were a raft of initiatives and financial support for self-starter swap groups, therapeutic services for young people in need, and a long list of useful organisations. With the essential aid of Sheelagh's address book, Viola had gathered together a fully committed team of volunteers and staff to run the charity, and there was no one more proud than her father.

Sheelagh had been back to Kinsley just once, to celebrate Margery and Caradoc's fiftieth wedding anniversary. It was staggering to think that she hadn't seen Theo for the best part of a year, although they'd kept in contact, mostly via email. He greeted her like the old friend he wanted her to be and had made no comment on her weight loss but was infinitely grateful for her financial settlement. It had paid for his very own Dottie, in which he and Florence travelled in to France. Sheelagh knew this from Viola. Apparently, whilst on their European tour, she, Gabriel and Thomson had met up with Theo and Florence somewhere near Languedoc. Thankfully, Theo was too polite to mention it.

But Florence had stuck to her plan. Ellis Eckley had been put out to graze, and in some style. Curiosity had prompted Sheelagh to obtain a ticket for the Royal Festival Hall event. With a seat at the back of the auditorium and no one to know her, she had to admit it was a marvellous mix of music, poetry, and readings. Eckley had called the entire collective to the stage (perhaps thirty or so) to generous applause and had thanked the public for continuing to support their livelihoods. Sheelagh had spied Theo and Viola through her theatre glasses. They were in the front row, on their feet and clapping wildly – not quite at the heart of this impressive family, but a part of it, nevertheless. That had been the worst moment, when she was seized by a cold shiver of isolation and despair, but it passed soon enough. Sheelagh didn't know it then, but there would be more pressing things to deal with.

With all the kerfuffle around *The 108* and Re-Source, there was barely time to adjust to her new status before an escalation of painful symptoms forced Sheelagh to seek a medical consultation. When subsequent investigations revealed a mass of pre-cancerous cells in her stomach, she endured the terror of facing the end of an (as yet) unfulfilled life, alone. At that time Viola was on the road. The only other person to turn to was Margery Crisp, who immediately answered the call. In Farringdon, the friends implemented a plan: all but the most pressing commitments had to go, along with Sheelagh's reckless attitude towards her health.

And so, with Margery overseeing her from Kinsley, Sheelagh Spicer's proud history of personal neglect came to an end. Morning T'ai chi and evening visualisations (no more late night news) improved her energy and mobility, while the super-food cooking lessons arranged through an acquaintance were more enjoyable than Sheelagh had ever imagined they could be, proof that eating well was more than an industry fad. The irony hadn't escaped her that Theo had done exactly the same after his diagnosis and had benefitted greatly from it.

With the oncologist's good news ringing in her ears, (the gastrointestinal mucosal resection had been a success), she drove to Dorset where, from the comfort of The Charmouth Suite, she began a major life review.

After a last look at the bay, Sheelagh closed the patio doors and gathered up the documents. Although she had no plans to return, it was by no means a sad occasion. The Seafarer Hotel had been instrumental in this exciting new chapter. Dressed in her new apricot linen frock with long tapered sleeves, and the lightest touch of lipstick, Sheelagh was ready to set off to the estate agent.

'Rushes' wasn't quite an impulse buy, as that wasn't her style, but it had *felt* right. As soon as she walked into the old thatched house, Sheelagh was engulfed by a sense of hopefulness, like nothing she'd felt before. Maybe it had something to do with Viola's suggestion – *don't you sometimes wish for a totally new experience, Mum? Surely, deep down in your being there's a hidden quest, an unexplored expedition yet to be undertaken.* It transpired that there was an expedition waiting in the wings, and it had come about unbidden.

It was the day after the 'all clear', a blustery, blindingly bright morning when, to celebrate, Sheelagh had taken herself off to Lyme Regis for a day of treats. Whilst browsing in an art gallery, she saw it – a vivid seascape, ten inches square, in exactly the same style as the *Sixpenny Shower*. According to gallery owner Jeanne Newey, the deceased artist was her father, the landscape painter Solomon Newey. The other child in the painting was the famed portrait artist, Luis Newey, her twin brother.

When Sheelagh mentioned *Sixpenny Shower*, and how it was hanging in The Charmouth Suite, Jeanne's expression changed. It was one of Solomon's finest early works, and until that very moment, its whereabouts were unknown. Sheelagh was so enthused by this unassuming woman's enthusiasm that when Jeanne asked to see it, she insisted the twins come to the hotel, and to join her for lunch after the viewing.

Jeanne Newey was instantly likeable: a ceramicist, of a similar age, whose wry sense of humour was a good match. When Sheelagh mentioned her suite at The Seafarer Hotel, Jeanne's raised eyebrow triggered a mutual fit of giggles. (*No, Jeanne, it's not my 'type' of hotel, but they make a very nice G&T*). Luis was every bit as engaging, and as handsome, as his sister. The twins had continued in their father's footsteps and had founded an artistic community in a nearby hamlet. Neither had married or had children – their coldly neurotic mother had put paid to that – but there had been (and were?) many love affairs, and lots and lots of fun.

During lunch, the Newey's benevolent attention prompted Sheelagh to confess to the challenges of being alone and unwell. With little reason to return to Farringdon, and with her new friends' encouragement, she spent the best part of the summer in their company. It was through the community's artistic eyes that Sheelagh began to appreciate the beauty of the natural world. When Jeanne insisted she try the potter's wheel, together they crafted what would be forever known as 'the wonky pot'.

And then, something quite unexpected occurred. The heir-less printmaker and owner of Rushes died, leaving its fate in the hands of her artist friends. Feeling strongly that Sheelagh would make a fine addition to their group, the twins suggested she buy it.

Luis Newey. How would she explain him to Viola? When he asked to paint her portrait, Sheelagh was uncustomarily stumped. *It would be a crime not to capture such an exquisite face on the canvas, Sheelagh. You'll make a not-so-old artist ecstatically happy.* Despite her many misgivings, she agreed, and it was during the excruciatingly marvellous sessions inside the studio and out on the cliffs that Sheelagh confessed to thoughts and feelings she didn't even know existed. Without being aware of it, Luis Newey had brush stroked his way into her affections. Like Jeanne, he made her laugh from the belly, but in a rare serious moment he said, *this beautiful life is fleeting; to honour it is to savour it, moment by moment.*

When Luis presented her with the portrait in the quiet of his studio, just the two of them, Sheelagh was overcome. He had captured her true spirit, which was more alive than she'd ever imagined it could be. And over a celebratory dinner, when he confessed to wanting, *very much*, to savour the fleeting moments with her, she could think of no earthly reason why not.

Before leaving the hotel, Sheelagh checked her appearance in the long mirror. An unfamiliar reflection smiled back. What was that quote in *Twelfth Night?*

'Journeys end in lovers meeting'

Silently thanking Shakespeare, she picked up her bag, and with the securely wrapped *Sixpenny Shower* under her arm, she skipped down the stairs.

The Grail

Songs

Lindisfarne, *January Song*; *Clear White Light*; *Lady Eleanor*

Oysterband, *Bright Morning Star (Resound, A Musical Tribute, 2017)*

Books

Rachel Carson, *Silent Spring*

Susan Fletcher, *Witch Light*

Thomas Hardy, *Far from the Madding Crowd*

Shakespeare, *Twelfth Night*

Nan Shephard, *The Living Mountain*

John Steinbeck, *The Acts of King Arthur and his Noble Knights*
  (includes the letters to editors Chase Horton, and Elizabeth Otis)

T.H.White, *The Once and Future King* (The Wart is young Arthur's
  pet name)

Nature poets

John Clare; Mary Oliver; Emily Dickinson

Kitbag Essentials

Breaking bread with loved ones; time alone; planting and growing;
dogs; road trips; tea; books; music; sitting under a tree (if it doesn't
mind); silence

By the same author

Quietwater Bridge, mid-morning

Marianne Bly

Hawkweed Cove

The Sandglass

The Roundhouse

The Smallest of Dreams

A Journey of Two Ends is Deborah Rowland's seventh novel.
She lives in Shropshire with her husband.

Acknowledgements

To the collective: Sue Keen, Jane Gregory, Louise Wilkinson, Mal Neate, Sue Warrington, Sally Stephenson, Sandra Waller and Sally St Ledger – a massive thanks! To Linda Storey, thank you for another fine work of art. Richard Vincent: immense gratitude for the inspiring mythical chats. And to John Rowland: *one in a million*.

Printed in Great Britain
by Amazon